INTIMATE DESIRE

"You want to play, huh?" Hunter asked, pleasantly surprised by Martha's behavior.

"No," she wailed, trying to scramble away.

"Oh, no you don't. You aren't going to start something, then try to get away without paying a price!" He grabbed her ankle and dragged her back, flipping her onto his lap.

Martha was stunned—and angry. "Let me go! The wagons are almost here. What will everyone think?"

"I'm surprised it should matter to you what that bunch of vicious tongues say about you." He hated to let her go, but couldn't dismiss her panicked entreaty. "Okay, quit fighting and I'll help you up." He held her shoulders and, when their eyes met, pulled her to him and pressed his lips to hers, savoring her soft, textured warmth.

She managed to break away, but felt even more confused by his sudden kiss. She ran her fingers over her mouth while her eyes trailed the curves of Hunter's full lips. She had never been kissed like that before, and she had never expected to share anything as intimate as a kiss with the arrogant, willful wagon-train captain. If she wasn't careful, why, anything could happen, and somehow, she'd have to make sure that nothing did. . . .

ZEBRA'S GOT THE ROMANCE
TO SET YOUR HEART AFIRE!

RAGING DESIRE   (2242, $3.75)
by Colleen Faulkner
A wealthy gentleman and officer in General Washington's army,
Devon Marsh wasn't meant for the likes of Cassie O'Flynn, an im-
migrant bond servant. But from the moment their lips first met,
Cassie knew she could love no other . . . even if it meant marching
into the flames of war to make him hers!

TEXAS TWILIGHT   (2241, $3.75)
by Vivian Vaughan
When handsome Trace Garrett stepped onto the porch of the Santa
Clara ranch, he wove a rapturous spell around Clara Ehler's heart.
Though Clara planned to sell the spread and move back East,
Trace was determined to keep her on the wild Western frontier
where she belonged — to share with him the glory and the splendor
of the passion-filled TEXAS TWILIGHT.

RENEGADE HEART   (2244, $3.75)
by Marjorie Price
Strong-willed Hannah Hatch resented her imprisonment by Captain Jake Farnsworth, even after the daring Yankee had rescued her
from bloodthirsty marauders. And though Jake's rock-hard physique made Hannah tremble with desire, the spirited beauty was
nevertheless resolved to exploit her femininity to the fullest and
gain her independence from the virile bluecoat.

LOVING CHALLENGE   (2243, $3.75)
by Carol King
When the notorious Captain Dominic Warbrooke burst into
Laurette Harker's eighteenth birthday ball, the accomplished
beauty challenged the arrogant scoundrel to a duel. But when the
captain named her innocence as his stakes, Laurette was terrified
she'd not only lose the fight, but her heart as well!

*Available wherever paperbacks are sold, or order direct from the
Publisher. Send cover price plus 50¢ per copy for mailing and handling to Zebra Books, Dept. 2640, 475 Park Avenue South, New
York, N.Y. 10016. Residents of New York, New Jersey and Pennsylvania must include sales tax. DO NOT SEND CASH.*

PASSIONATE POSSESSION

GWEN CLEARY

ZEBRA BOOKS
KENSINGTON PUBLISHING CORP.

ZEBRA BOOKS

are published by

Kensington Publishing Corp.
475 Park Avenue South
New York, NY 10016

First printing: April, 1989

Printed in the United States of America

To my husband, Don;
you believed.
And to Samantha,
the greatest joy of my life.

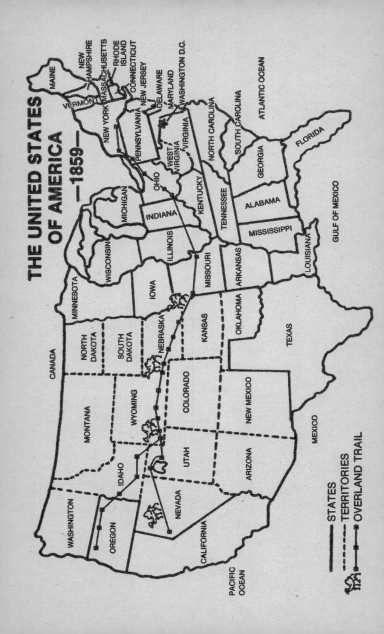

Part One

"Troubles"

Our days begin with trouble here,
Our life is but a span,
And cruel death is always near,
So frail a thing is man.
    —*The New England Primer*

Chapter One

Her nerves reeling, Martha smoothed the blue-striped skirt on her redingote dress, and tucked errant brown locks of hair back into the strands gathered at the nape of her neck. Prepared for the worst, she stiffened her spine against the straight-back chair in the tiny living room of her mother's white, plank cottage. Outside, the gate crashed with a loud thud causing her to wince. That harsh sound sealed the end of one chapter in her life, but it also meant the beginning of another.

"I'm sorry you don't approve of my decision, Mother." Martha raised her chin in an attempt to demonstrate her firm resolve to stand up against what she knew was coming due to the displeased frown on her mother's wizened face.

"Your decision, indeed. Such foolishness to turn down an opportunity to wed a successful banker, and for some sudden whim." The aging woman shifted her generous girth and wrung her hands as she glanced out the window at the retreating stocky figure of the sandy-haired young man she had desperately hoped to call son.

"It's not foolishness, Mother. And this isn't a sudden whim. It's a shame that more Americans do not want to see their own country instead of going off to Europe. I've dreamed of going West ever since I overheard Mr. Farley speak, nearly a year ago to the men of our church, about the great opportunities which exist out in the wild, untamed territories. It's our destiny to spread from sea to sea, the great adventure of American growth, and I intend to be a part of it."

From the look on her mother's face, Martha was certain the older woman was about to deliver another one of her chastising lectures.

"You will never be able to travel across this country alone without trouble and tribulation breaking your spirit and heart," Lavinia Collins stated flatly. "It is just too dangerous!" Then she softened a bit. "My dear, it is simply unheard of for a young woman to travel by herself—unmarried—even if she is a twenty-year-old, plain-looking spinster."

Lavinia's words stabbed at Martha. She knew she wasn't pretty and her mother considered her somewhat of a handful, but she was secretly glad she had the spunk to live her own life and not be like her sop of a brother, who had always been the model child. "I'm sorry if I'm a disappointment to you, but this is something I must do. You'll have George and his family nearby. But I've dreamed of seeing Oregon, and since the Donation Act passed in Congress more and more families are leaving the states every day to claim their six hundred forty acres. And if families are going, they'll need teachers for their children. Please try not to be too upset."

"But Clinton—"

Martha sighed, remembering Clinton's utter shock at her refusal of his proposal. Then in an effort to account for the reasons behind her actions and Clinton's stormy departure, she said, "I tried to tell Clinton that there was no room for marriage in my life right now. It's a pity he became so enraged when I tried to explain, although I understand the fierceness of his anger. It won't be easy for him to face people after boasting to everyone in town that we would be married in June. But he should have spoken with me first." Martha paused and leaned forward; her eyes entreating her mother to understand. "Oh, don't you see, Mother, this will be such a great adventure—the opportunity of a lifetime, and I have the chance to be a part of it."

Lavinia felt her heart split as she looked into the beseeching green eyes of her daughter. A part of the older woman wanted her to marry and settle down, like her faithful son, George, had done; another part remembered the glorious freedom and undaunted confidence of youth. And Lavinia loved her daughter too much to let her leave with a dampened spirit, especially now when Martha seemed to glow as she spoke such nonsense. Conceding defeat, Lavinia said, "I am afraid I see all too clearly." She let out a long sigh. "There is nothing I can say to make you change your mind, is there?"

"Oh, Mother"—Martha jumped from her chair and threw her arms around the older woman's neck—"thank you for not fighting me. I love you so, and I shall miss you. But I'll write every day, I promise."

"I suppose you will have the first half-naked savage you encounter deliver your letters."

Tears of joy slid down Martha's cheeks at the ease with which her mother had accepted her desire to traverse their great country. "Mother, I know the trip won't prove to be an easy venture, but I shall be worthy of it. I'll even take the time to write in a journal along the way, so someday when you visit you'll be able to read all about my adventures."

"Yes, dear," Lavinia said sadly, knowing she'd never see her daughter again once Martha left, "when I visit I'll have the chance to read this journal in which you intend to record your adventurous undertaking."

Martha gave her mother another squeeze, then headed toward her room to record her first victory in the journal she had purchased to serve as a log on her trip. . . .

My Diary Across The Miles Monday, February 21, 1859— Elmira, New York. I can no longer deny my dream, for I want so desperately to be a part of history in the making. The urge I feel is overwhelming. I still experience difficulty believing the ease of Mother's acceptance of my desire to traverse this great country. I do not expect this enterprise to prove an easy venture, but, God willing, I shall be worthy of this enormous undertaking. . . .
—Martha Rockford Collins

Although the snow was piled thick on the ground, Martha barely noticed as she scurried about town making arrangements for the trip. She had a hundred things to do before spring when the muddy roads began to harden and the wagon trains set off on the long trek across the continent.

Martha took a deep breath before she entered Elmira's largest bank. She was not looking forward to the task facing her. Clinton Marks, the man she had just spurned, was bent over his desk, poring over a stack of papers. With measured steps she walked to the open door and cleared her throat to draw his attention.

Cinton looked up, annoyance twisting on his lips. "Miss Collins." He rose, straight and stiff, his angry face almost too pretty to be considered masculine if it weren't for the immaculately trimmed shadow of a beard bordering his chin. "Is there something more which needs to be said, and does that bring you here?" He looked past her at the local busybodies intently staring at them.

"I have a financial matter to discuss." Her gaze followed his cold amber eyes. If only she had been able to save more from the meager salary she had earned as a teacher she would not be forced to put him in this difficult position. And of all times, she had chosen to talk to him just when the gossipy old Carter sisters were hunched over the teller's cage, berating poor scrawny Mr. Simmons.

"Then by all means do come in and sit down." His tone was clipped and most businesslike.

After Martha had carefully laid out the details of her plan to travel to Oregon and continue teaching, she presented her request for two hundred and fifty dollars—a loan, to be paid back without delay once she secured a position in her new home.

"I am certain you have only the best of intentions, but you must realize I do have to consider the interests of the bank first. I am sure you can appreciate my position." Clinton picked up the quill pen on his desk and began to twirl it between his fingers. That annoying habit reminded Martha of how he had often fingered his pen in the past in an irritating show of superiority. She had no regrets. She only wondered how she could ever have allowed him to court her. Even if she weren't about to embark on a journey of such magnitude, she now knew she would have turned down the pompous banker.

"Yes, of course," she said woodenly.

"Then you could not have seriously believed, even for a minute, that I would grant such a loan since you are about to engage in a dubious undertaking at best."

Unable to remain seated and listen to the man's pretentious statements, Martha abruptly rose. "I'm sorry you do not feel I'm a good risk. Good day to you, sir," she said, without displaying the slightest hint of the disappointment curdling the contents of her stomach.

"Martha, do not be so foolish," he called out to her retreating back in spite of the Carter sisters' raised eyebrows which denoted their enjoyment of this latest bit of gossip. "A loan, huh? You may be pleasantly attractive to the male eye—and the most intelligent woman in town—Martha Rockford Collins, but there are a few lessons you have yet to learn," Clinton mumbled bitterly to himself. Then he slammed the frosted glass door behind him.

Discouraged but not defeated, Martha drew on one of her last options and walked up the icy hill to the three-story Wakefield estate. She took a deep breath and knocked on the heavily carved door.

A delicate hand pulled back the sheer curtains at the window to the left of the porch. For an instant Martha wished she had not decided to speak to Barton Wakefield. "Martha?" The frown spread from Jannet Wakefield's lips to her eyes when she'd opened the door, but the attractive young woman, a year younger than Martha, quickly recovered herself. "How nice of you to stop by. Do come in."

Martha felt a twinge of guilt; she knew Jannet had few callers. Ordinarily she would have taken tea with her, but now was not the time for idle chatter.

"Thank you. Actually I came to see your father. . . ."

After a most unusual, hour-long interview with the eccentric Mr. Wakefield, Martha left the big gabled house with five shining twenty-dollar gold pieces. The paunchy man's words, spoken as he raked his full brush of whiskers, echoed in her ears while she covered the distance home. . . .

"Jannet has told me at length about your plans, and I am more than pleased to loan you the money." Barton Wakefield seemed to ponder a moment. Then a peculiar light flickered in his eyes, and he added, "There is one stipulation, of course."

"A stipulation?" Martha was uncertain of whether she wanted to hear what he was about to say.

"Yes." He looked wistfully around the vast library, filled to capacity with heavy furniture and books. "You may have the money if you allow Jannet and me to meet you in Independence and travel West on the same train—without informing anyone before you leave, or letting those on the train become aware that you know us."

Martha was astounded by the strange request. "But why?"

He wrinkled his forehead and shrugged. "For Jannet."

Martha tried to figure out why Barton Wakefield would want to go West for his daughter's sake. It did not make sense. Then again, few things the man did made sense.

There were times in one's life, Wakefield said, when pride dictated that one struggle on alone, but there were also times when letting pride get in the way was self-defeating. Hesitantly Martha agreed to his terms without further question. And Martha was not going to be defeated! She knew she would repay the money as soon as she could. She thought of Jannet Wakefield, and of how her father had repeatedly expressed his appreciation that Martha had made it a point to befriend his daughter when, years ago, the other children had refused to include the self-centered, mean little girl in their games. Except for Nancy Cooke and Martha, Jannet did not have any friends. Perhaps Barton Wakefield thought that by going West with his daughter, he would give her a chance to make a new start. Martha pondered the strange request a moment longer, decided it would be rather nice not to be totally alone in a new land, and let the matter drop.

Her spirits buoyed by her success, Martha went about humming to herself as she packed her trunk and put the rest of her affairs in order. She still needed one hundred and fifty dollars, but she did not doubt that she would get the money somehow, even if she had to sell some of the treasured pieces of jewelry she'd inherited from her grandmother.

But shortly before she had to leave for Independence, Missouri, in order to purchase passage on one of the wagon trains, she received a most unusual missive in the mail. To her surprise the envelope contained the sum of two hundred dollars and a brief note, left unsigned. Certainly this was more than she could accept, wasn't it?

"Never look a gift horse in the mouth," Lavinia Collins crooned in response to her daughter's bewilderment.

"Yes, I know, St. Jerome from *On The Epistle to the Ephesians*."

"Quit showing off that fine education of yours and wise up," Lavinia said shortly, exasperated with her daughter.

"Mother, you didn't withdraw your savings, did you?" Concern softened the lines of determination drawn around Martha's lips.

"I wish I could tell you that it was I, but it was not."

"Do you have any idea who would send such an amount and why?" Martha was troubled, and suspicious of the ease with which her mother seemed to accept the offering. If Lavinia had sent it, she would find out from George, who never could keep a secret, and she'd make sure that the money was repaid. She did not want to cause her mother any undue hardship. The lovable, cantankerous Lavinia had worked too hard at sewing for the ladies in the town to keep the family together and to educate her children after Martha's father had died ten years ago.

"How would I be any more privy than you to the generosity of someone who obviously wishes to remain anonymous. But let me see the note. I may recognize the handwriting." Lavinia had always prided herself on knowing much about the townspeople. If anyone could recognize who had written the note, she was certain she could. She took the letter and read it out loud.

My Dear Miss Collins:
    You have rendered me a service for which I shall be hard pressed ever to repay you in full. Therefore, I hope

17

you will accept the enclosed funds, a small token of my desire to contribute toward your adventurous undertaking.

An Interested Party

"The writing seems most unusual." Lavinia frowned. There was something familiar about the way the *p's* were looped with such a flourish, yet their creator eluded her. "It appears to have been penned by a literate hand," observed the older woman. After all, Martha was well liked. It could even be from a group of well-wishers who knew she would never accept charity. Dismissing the note, Lavinia tucked it into her apron pocket.

"This is an awful lot of money, Mother. Are you certain I shouldn't attempt to return it?" Martha fanned the newly minted bills, wondering why anyone would send her such a large sum. Wouldn't the sender wish to be reimbursed?

"My dear child, the money is your ticket to your precious West. And besides, who would you return it to?"

But what service have I rendered to warrant such a sum? Martha silently asked herself.

After a moment's thought, her lips spread into a wide smile. Her mother was right. She would be foolish not to accept the offering. Her dream was actually becoming a reality. With joy swelling her heart, she let her questions about the funds' source slip into the back of her mind. She hugged Lavinia, then swung around to hurry out and buy a ticket on the next Thursday's stage.

An early spring snow flurry was gently falling when her tall, pole of a brother drove the family carriage to the station to see her off.

Dressed in her best quilted skirt, Martha stood fidgeting in front of the stage-line office. All the past weeks of planning and getting ready for the trip had been like a fantasy, as if she were reaching for that elusive quest, which no matter how hard you strive always remains just out of your grasp. Now here, a few feet from the stage, was reality. She had actually taken hold of her own life. It gave her a heady feeling, like sipping too much wine. Yet, as she watched the swirl of snowflakes, she hoped the late snow wasn't an omen of what to expect during the trip. She would miss her friends and family. They had given her a farewell social at the church hall the night before, and by the end of the evening, there hadn't been a dry eye to be found. It was comforting to know so many people cared about her, but in spite of her questioning, no one had known the name of her benefactor. It had to be her mother.

Tears flowed down Lavinia's heavily lined cheeks as she cradled her daughter in her arms for what she was sure was the last time. She knew she had to let go; she had to let Martha find her own way in life. Why was it that sometimes one's children were only a temporary gift from God? *Oh Lord, I prayed Martha would marry and settle nearby.* She swallowed a sob and continued her silent prayer. *Please walk with my little girl through life, and hold her hand should she fall.* Still clinging to her only daughter, Lavinia smoothed Martha's hair. "Just because your are going so far away, do not forget you have a family."

"Mother, you know I'll never forget all you've done for me." Close to tears herself, Martha gave the older woman another hug, then turned to George and his very round wife, and hugged them both. "And you two know I'll miss you and those four darling little nieces of mine." She rose up on her toes to give George a kiss, and whispered in his ear. "Tell Mother I'll repay the money."

George looked somewhat befuddled, but nodded compliantly.

"Here, take this basket." Lavinia sniffled and thrust a large wicker basket into Martha's hands just as the stage driver called out for the passengers who were traveling to Cleveland and points west to board. "It's full of your favorite foods, and I put the latest copy of the newspaper in for you to read. I just do not know what this town is coming to. The number of thefts are increasing every day. Why only three days ago there was the most awful robbery. I do not understand how anyone with a conscience could have taken such a large sum of money—"

Martha broke in. "Mother, I really must leave." She embraced Lavinia one last time, then hurriedly gathered up her skirt and climbed up into the stage.

She set the basket down near her feet. Not giving it another thought, she leaned out the window, waving good-bye as the coach lurched forward. Snowflakes settled atop Martha's bonnet as she watched her family fade into the gentle flutter of white. Then her spirits took flight at the thought that she was finally on her way; she was going to Oregon to teach. Despite all the horror stories she had heard since announcing her intention and despite her mother's warnings, Martha was certain the trip would be a glorious adventure—one she would always remember.

Chapter Two

Friday, April 15, 1859—Independence, Missouri. I arrived without incident. I am hopeful of booking passage on the first available wagon train. I am experiencing firsthand the enormity of such a venture. The number of emigrants traveling West is beyond my imagination. The wonder that I could have undertaken such an expedition still amazes me. Yet I am filled with high spirits and have not the slightest regret. . . .

Independence swarmed with activity as hundreds of wagons filled the town, jammed the roads, and camped on the outskirts amid herds of cattle and sheep. Women and children crowded the wagons which rumbled through the streets, while Indians, trappers, and gold miners shouldered along the dusty thoroughfares lined with overcrowded hotels and shops bursting with provisions.

Martha slipped into her favorite blue and white morning dress, and wrapped a shawl around her shoulders. With a sigh born of frustration, she walked to the tiny window and peered out of her second-story room in the Overland Hotel. She had been in Independence for nearly two weeks and had not been able to convince one of the fifteen wagon-train captains with whom she'd spoken to accept her. Always it was the same story: no lone women. Had she been born male, she would have been on her way West already. But her gender was not going to stop her! Below her, the town was a beehive of activity, and

Martha was determined to be part of it. Knowing she wasn't going to get anywhere by remaining at the hotel, she picked up her bonnet and left the room.

Outside the blacksmith's shop, loud, angry voices were drawing a crowd of spectators.

"Now look, you old polecat, don't go getting so hot under the collar," Hunter Brody, a landmark of a man, clad in plaid shirt and denims, a gun slung low over his hip, said calmly to a grubby man with a slight build.

"I'm dadblamed sick 'n tired of bein' camped next t' ya and those stinkin' creatures, ya pigheaded sonofabitch. If ya don't get them hump-backed monsters away from the wagons 'n stock, there's a group of us who's gonna up 'n shoot 'em."

Martha joined the crowd to watch the exchange, completely mesmerized. It was her first encounter with the roughness and crudeness of the West, yet instead of being frightened or finding the language offensive, she was fascinated. And the fact that she was the only woman in a group of rowdy-tongued men did not unduly concern her either. It was all too exciting and new, this way of life, to worry about proper decorum. Her eyes fixed on the younger of the two men causing all the ruckus. How masculinely handsome he was compared to Clinton. She stared at his ruggedly cut face, deeply tanned, and at the waves of blond hair curling about the nape of his powerful neck. He couldn't be much over thirty, she guessed. Whereas, the other man had to be at least half a century old.

"I wouldn't even think about it, if I were you, Finis," the powerfully built fellow growled in response to the older man's threat.

"It's Crutcher—Mr. Crutcher—t' ya, Brody." The man spit out a wad of tobacco and swung around, intending to put an abrupt end to the argument. But a muscular arm reached out and furiously jerked Finis Crutcher back.

"You'd best listen if you know what's good for your health, Crutcher. I don't take kindly to threats. Those hump-backed monsters you were referring to are called camels, and they belong to me. If you or your people harm even one hair on their backs, I'll come looking for you, personally. You understand?" The big man's teeth were clenched, and he tightened his stranglehold on the front of Finis Crutcher's shirt, and drew him in closer until they were nearly nose to nose. "I asked if you understand?"

Finis Crutcher choked out, "Sure . . . sure, I get the message."

"And if you try asking in a more sociable way, you may find people a mite bit more neighborly."

Finis glared at Hunter Brody. The older man knew of Brody's reputation. Rumor had it that he had once lived among the Indians, and from that arrowhead hanging from the leather thong around his neck, Finis had no doubt all he'd heard was true. Though Hunter Brody had always been deemed a fair and honest sort, civilized people considered him little more than a savage. But the one thing that stood out in Finis Crutcher's mind was that Brody was not known to make idle threats. The older man swallowed hard, as if forcing himself to gulp down his bruised pride. "All right. I'm askin' if ya'd be so kind as t' move your *camels* so as not t' frighten the rest of the stock camped nearby ya, I'd be obliged . . . please."

"Now, that's all you had to say in the first place." The big man shoved Finis Crutcher back, his eyes softening from hard hazel slits. "Since we at last understand each other, I'll be happy to move my camels. Now I suggest you go back to your people and tell them you found me agreeable."

Finis pushed through the crowd, his face redder than summer cherries, as Martha stepped up to speak to him.

"Mr. Crutcher, may I please have another word with you?"

"Look, lady, I already told ya I wasn't takin' no single female on. 'N I don't know no other respectable train that'll take ya on either," he snarled, still reeling from the crushing defeat he had just suffered.

"But if you will only listen to what I have to say—"

"There's nothin' ya can say that'd change my mind." Crutcher had a scowl chiseled on his face, and Martha felt her spirits shrivel. He was not even going to give her a chance. Then, for some reason she could not fathom, the man's lips broke into a smile. "Tell ya what. Ya really want t' go West?"

"More than anything."

"Then ya might try askin' Brody over there." Finis thumbed

in Hunter's direction. "I understand he's tryin' t' put a company together 'n needs the money." He'd barely finished his sentence before he broke out into a hardy belly laugh, and then left Martha standing alone in the street, looking after him. She glanced at Hunter Brody, who had engaged the blacksmith in what appeared to be a cordial conversation, set her chin resolutely. Although the idea of seeing a real camel up close pricked her curiosity, since she had read about the Arabian desert creatures, that dreadful man's train would have to be the last one on earth before she would even consider asking to join it.

Hunter pulled out his money clip and slowly counted the bills. A frown darkened his already bronzed face. "We've known each other a long time, Hank. Doesn't friendship count for nothing?"

The big-shouldered blacksmith grinned. "This ain't friendship; it's business, clear and simple. As it is, I'm already givin' you a break over what I charge them sodbusters and gold panners." His face sobered. "I just can't shoe those horses of yours for less. I already got more work than I can handle. Bustin' my ass dawn to dusk. Sorry."

Hunter crammed the money back into his pocket. "Can't blame you. I know you've got a family to support. But I've got to get those camels to Nevada by fall or I'll lose my ranch."

"You always did come up with some of the damnedest crazy schemes. Have to admit though, you always come out a winner. Still can't figure how you manage it." The blacksmith just shook his head. "But camels. Hell, why and how did you bring those crazy animals to this country?"

"That's my business," Hunter said coolly, ending any further discussion on the topic. "Say hello to the missus for me. I'll be back as soon as I get the rest of the cash." Without waiting for a reply, Hunter mounted his horse and rode back toward his encampment just outside of town.

"I don't know why we must cross the river so early, unless

it's due to those disgusting animals we're forced to endure. Why, it's barely dawn." Harriet Belshaw's coffee-colored eyes, blazed. She directed her most disapproving frown at Hunter, then headed her amply porportioned body, clad in a loose-fitting tan calico dress, back toward the wagon.

"Mrs. Belshaw," Hunter boomed, stopping the galling woman flat in her tracks, "you and your husband may have a couple of years on me but you are not leading this train. You and the other sixteen people paid me to see you safely across this country. That I intend to do—my way." He noticed heads bob in his direction. "If you or any of the rest do not feel you can follow my commands, then I suggest you find another outfit to take you on." Hunter knew he sounded heartless, but with the bickering and hardheaded ignorance this group had already displayed, there was no other way to deal with them if he intended to avoid a needless disaster.

"Well, I never!" Harriet huffed.

William Belshaw took the large woman's hand in his puny one and patted it gently. "Honey, I know you had a hard time leaving the store back in Iowa, but as soon as we get to California, we'll be able to get another one and I'll buy you a big house right in the center of town. No more living in the back of a store for us. You'll see, this time we'll make it big. There's lots of opportunities out West for people like us." His bloodshot eyes pleaded with her. "Mr. Brody is just trying to do his job." Belshaw scratched his head, mussing thinning strands of silver-shot light hair. "Now come on, let's see to the children."

After the Belshaws returned to the wagon in which their three children were stirring noisily, Hunter shook his head in disgust. He turned to scan the rest of the motley group of greenhorns he had saddled himself with for the next six months. If only he hadn't needed the money . . .

Cecilia Stewart was sitting in the shade of her wagon, a wilting Southern belle, who looked as if she were going to a ball in her fancy ruffles. Her doting bridegroom was fanning her. Poor young fools should have stayed in Virginia, Hunter thought as he passed the handsome couple. When it came Cecilia's turn to cook for the company, Hunter had the feeling they'd all suffer. Still she'd have to pull her weight. He remembered how hopeful, and determined to strike it rich, he had been at twenty-two when he'd set out with his own bride. Derek Stewart was green, all right, but Hunter had to give the young man credit for determination.

Hunter's eyes fell on the old Nelson couple. Why had he agreed to take on a couple in their fifties with four children? No one else would take them, and those two already looked as worn out as the farm in Ohio they'd told him they'd left. But Hunter was certain the older woman would provide them with some good grub when it was her turn to fix the meals. And that tall fancy-dressed dandy, Cornelius Potter, talking to the older couple, was always fiddling with that black box. He was sure to be a royal pain in the backside the way he kept setting up the thing and asking people to hold still a minute. Unlike the rest of the men, who shared responsibility for repairs and hunting, Potter was to drive the spring wagon. Hunter questioned whether the man was even capable of handling a team of horses as he looked at those soft hands of his.

But the most curious pair to join the train stood quietly at the tongue of the Stewarts' wagon. That honeymoon couple must have needed the money pretty bad to share their wagon with those two women, especially the gorgeous mahogany-tressed one dressed as if she were about to receive guests in a parlor instead of travel in a dust-covered wagon. It was hard to figure why such a beautiful young woman would be going West with such a sour maiden aunt—who was probably uglier than mud because she always wore a big floppy hat and a veil over her face. A young woman with Jannet Wakefield's looks must have had her pick of rich, eligible suitors back in New York. Hunter shrugged. Other than making sure the pair held up their end of the chores, it wasn't his job to get involved in their lives. He was paid to get them across the country in one piece, that was all.

Then he noticed the Collins woman standing off by herself. His frown deepened. He'd charged her double what he'd charged the others and when he'd discovered she'd tricked him, he'd added the chore of washing his clothes in addition to taking a turn with the cooking; still, the woman had accepted

26

his terms.

"Well, what are all of you waiting for?" Hunter blasted out with unrelenting authority when he noticed not one person had lifted a foot to get started. "Finish packing up so we can get moving." With that he swung about on his heel to see that the camels boarded the barges without incident.

"He don't seem to mince no words," observed Winnie Nelson, as she stuffed escaping strands of gray hair back into her old rumpled bonnet. "But then I think it's goin' to take a man with a good mite of strength to manage this group; us gettin' a late start on the trail and all."

"Why I declare"—Cecilia Stewart's big china-blue eyes got rounder, and she toyed with a red ringlet hanging at her neck—"you can't possibly excuse such ill-mannered behavior, now can you? Back home in Virginia, Daddy would have had him horsewhipped for talking in such an ungentlemanly manner."

"I think the man's got his hands full," Winnie responded. "Don't go forgettin' he was the only one of them wagon train captains who'd take any of us on."

Cecilia was not convinced. "Only after he took our money and forced us to agree to perform any chores he set forth," Cecilia complained, glancing down at her manicured nails.

"I'm sure he had his reasons for the terms he set out. If we listen to him it'll be a more pleasurable trip," Winnie advised, smoothing her rumpled gray cotton dress down over her sparse frame.

"You're right, Mrs. Nelson," Derek Steward agreed, snaking a protective arm around his delicate, young bride whose crisp blue dress matched her eyes.

"I'm just plain old Winnie to everybody."

"That's downright nice of you, Winnie. Cecilia and I appreciate it, don't we honey?" Derek's dark eyes fell on his wife.

"Sure enough." Cecilia pouted, then raised herself up on tiptoe and ran a hand through his black hair. "I daresay I'll never understand why we just could not have stayed at Shadow Glen with Daddy. If we were home, you wouldn't be forced to wear plain old work clothes like our overseer wears."

"We'll talk about it later," her husband said indulgently.

27

"Now we must pack our belongings so we don't hold up the rest of the group." He led the fragile, petite redhead away.

"Well, I for one don't think Mr. Brody had the right to speak to Mrs. Belshaw so roughly." Jannet Wakefield was indignant. When no one responded to her statement, she tucked her hand under her lame aunt's arm. "Come along Aunt Velina, we don't want him yelling at us, too." Her thick mahogany mane bounced freely as she helped the veiled, stocky woman into the wagon they shared with the newlyweds.

Martha had been surprised when Jannet had appeared with her aunt the day before the company was to leave. She had expected Barton Wakefield to accompany his daughter. But true to her promise to the old man, she had remained silent, although questions plagued her.

Having listened to the crusty Mrs. Nelson, Martha couldn't help but consider that exchange. There were too many dominant personalities in this company to expect a peaceful trip. No doubt, the crossing was not going to be dull. She seemed to be the only woman willingly traveling West. From what she had observed the others had been forced to follow their men. At least she had the advantage of wanting to be on this train, even if she'd had to deceive the big wagon-train captain by sending him that note signed with the name Mat, the nickname her father had bestowed on her in her childhood. Hunter Brody had been livid. After accepting the money for her passage from Finis Crutcher, he'd come face to face with a woman when he'd expected a man. No doubt that was why he had demanded she launder his clothes in addition to doing the cooking chores required of all the women.

She hadn't wanted to deceive Hunter Brody, but she had been turned down by all the other captains due to her gender and the fact that she was traveling alone. She had been correct in assuming that Brody would prove to be no different. But being born a female was not going to stop her!

"You look as if you are deep in thought," said Cornelius Potter as he came up behind her.

Startled out of her reverie, Martha glanced up, straight into the camera set up by the tall scholarly man dressed impeccably in Eastern wear. "Hold that pose." The shutter clicked and held a moment. "It appears that the crossing will not prove to be a bore."

"Why did you take my picture, mister . . . mister?" Martha was annoyed by such boldness.

"Cornelius Potter. Please, do forgive me if I upset you. It is simply that you have a most interesting face. Not everyone is blessed with high cheekbones and a chin which shows strength of character. I think you will make an excellent subject for the picture book I am working on. Missus . . ."

"It is *Miss*." She corrected him, hoping she did not sound too defensive since it was becoming all too clear unmarried ladies traveling alone were not considered acceptable. "Miss Martha Collins." When the stranger seemed unaffected, she asked, "A picture book?"

Cornelius smiled. "Yes, it is to be a photograph album of frontier history. I hope to capture the character of the American migration West using photographs of daily life on a wagon train. Will you consent to be one of my primary models, or victims if you prefer?" He hopefully grinned.

"Mr. Potter, I don't know what to say. You've taken me by surprise." Martha couldn't help but smile back at the nice-looking man with the dark hair and the neatly trimmed mustache. But why would he want to use her as a model when someone as beautiful as Jannet Wakefield was about? Martha wasn't sure she wanted to be photographed anyway.

"Well, I know what to say," Hunter barked as he returned from the riverbank. Why did seeing the Collins woman in the company of that dandy rake his nerves and hone his tongue? "Quit wasting time and get yourselves down to the barge before I decide to leave you two here."

He stared at Martha for a minute longer than necessary, making her ill at ease under the intensity of his gaze before calling the wagons to move out.

"I shall consider your offer, Mr. Potter. Now if you'll excuse me, I must hurry," she said, trying to mask the hurt and uncertainty Hunter Brody had aroused in her. "Mr. Brody," she hesitantly called out.

He heaved a weary sigh. "What now, Miss Collins?"

"Did you notice those two Indians across the river? They

seemed to be staring quite intently in this direction." Her apprehension was evident.

Hunter glanced across the wide expanse of water. There wasn't an Indian in sight. More gruffly than he intended, he replied, "Look lady, you might as well get used to the idea of seeing Indians. We're heading into their territory. But if you're worried about hanging on to your scalp, it isn't too late to turn back."

Martha's fingers wound around an errant strand of hair as she looked across the river and noticed the Indians were gone. Maybe she had become too impressionable after listening to so many horrid stories about Indians. Still, he didn't have to be so rude. "Mr. Brody, I have no intention of turning back," she said firmly.

"Well then, you'd best get yourself down to the river with the rest of the group before you're left behind." Silently, he upbraided himself for his curtness. Something about the woman brought out the worst in him. He wasn't usually this ill-bred around ladies. As a matter of fact, most women considered his company desirable.

Martha seethed as she hurriedly boarded the barge with the rest of the company, and perched on a large packing crate off in a corner. She watched the boatmen manipulate the ropes, pulling the barge slowly across the wide, muddy river.

The churning sounds of water and the nearby voices faded as she decided that Hunter Brody was not going to convince her to change her mind about being a member of the train. She looked over at him. He was openly staring at her, his expression unreadable. For a moment their eyes held. Then, self-conscious, she flushed and dropped her eyes. Why was he so often staring at her? And worse, why did she so often find herself staring back? She could never be interested in anyone so different from herself, she thought, trying to negate that threatening flash of attraction.

Once the three prairie schooners and the light spring wagon were brought across the river and everyone was in position, the trek West really got under way. Martha regretted it was her lot to travel with the Belshaws. Mrs. Belshaw was overbearing and shouted orders at everyone, while six-year-old Fuller Belshaw cowered in the corner, sucking his thumb. He was a frail youngster who had his father's ruddy complexion and light, earth-colored hair. The little boy appeared to Martha to be trying to blend into the baggage so as to stay out of his mother's way.

Clara Belshaw, a ten-year-old miniature of her mother, had lined up her dolls and was shaking her pudgy finger at them, scolding like an overstuffed parrot. Martha said nothing, but reflected that the young Belshaw girl would likely grow into quite a shrew if she wasn't taken in hand before long.

Little Gertrude Belshaw toddled over to Martha and held up her chubby arms. "Up. Up." She begged.

Martha picked up the gentle eighteen-month-old, caressed her deep chestnut curls, and then rocked the tot on her lap. The toddler cooed as Martha gazed out the rear of the wagon, taking in the awe-inspiring, rolling prairie.

Petty differences seemed insignificant when compared to the vastness of the adventure she had just begun. Martha knew she was a part of something much bigger than just one wagon train. Although her world would revolve around the small cluster of people she traveled with for the next six months, no one, not even Hunter Brody, could trample her spirit. Not when she could look out the wagon and see the land that lay before her in all its glory. She envisioned herself inside a warm, cozy house nestled amid rolling prairie thick with grasses and flowers, but near a riverbank lined with wide belts of timber.

Martha was still hugging little Gertrude to her when Hunter rode up. "Seems you've got some strong mothering instincts," he said without a smile.

The man's words were kind. Martha hoped he was softening toward her. It would make the trip so much more pleasant if they could get along. With that in mind, she gave him one of her brightest smiles. "I've always loved children. Someday I hope to have a houseful."

"Then why didn't you stay in New York, marry some dandy like Potter, and have that houseful of kids instead of trying to take on the responsibility of a man on a wagon train?"

Chapter Three

Thursday, June 9, 1859—Approximately five miles east of Fort Kearney. I have been experiencing firsthand the adventure of travel and must comment on the strained relationships among the women, and, of course, with the leader of our company. But I continue to hold my head high despite the inner turmoil I encounter. If one thing can build character and test the will of God, it is my traveling companions. Still I remain undaunted and refuse to give in to lesser feelings. . . .

For two weeks Martha had silently tried to ignore the unkind comments Mrs. Belshaw generously tossed in her direction. Of course, the woman's perpetual disapproval was not cast directly upon Martha, but she made sure her target was always within earshot. And Cecilia and Jannet, by the look of them finding the hardships of the journey difficult to endure, seemed to be willing listeners.

"No respectable woman would leave her home willingly, let alone ever think of traveling alone without the protection of family," Harriet Belshaw told the two younger women before climbing into the wagon so they might move out at dawn.

That afternoon, as the sun beat down on the canvas cover of the wagon and tempers were short, Martha could remain silent no longer and confronted a stunned Harriet Belshaw. When the company made camp for the night amid a few sparse shrubs near a stream, the overbearing Harriet wasted no time in going directly to Hunter Brody and demanding that a change be made in wagon assignments.

"Mr. Brody, this trip is difficult enough for the decent women on this train as it is without being forced to associate with undesirables."

"Yeah, well, what's the problem, Mrs. Belshaw?" Hunter wasn't eager to hear yet another of her complaints.

Harriet's eyes flashed as she noted his apparent indifference. "My family can no longer tolerate Miss Collins's continued presence in our wagon. My husband and I don't want our innocent daughter, Clara, subjected to that type of woman."

Hunter cocked an eyebrow. The Belshaw woman was a pain in the backside. And he resented her inference that Martha Collins was undesirable. At least the Collins woman didn't gripe about everything from the weather to the whiskers on his chin. "And just what type of woman is Miss Collins?"

"You know perfectly well what she is." Crossing her big arms in front of her, Harriet Belshaw sneered.

"No, I don't. But I have a feeling you're going to enlighten me."

She put her hand over her heart and drew in a deep breath. "She's . . . she's single. And unmanageable."

He contemplated the large woman's statement for only a fraction of a second before answering. "I can't say you're incorrect in your observations. Miss Collins is an unmarried woman, and I'm sure you've had nothing but trouble trying to control her." As he spoke, he laughed to himself. It must really stick in the woman's craw that she couldn't bend Martha Collins to her will like she'd done with the members of her family.

"Why I've never tried to control anyone!" Harriet Belshaw protested, and her face contorted as she tried to curb her rage. "Just get that woman out of my wagon!" Her beige-checked skirts swished against her legs as she swung around and stalked off.

"You needn't worry yourself any longer, Mrs. Belshaw," Hunter called out to her broad back. "Not even Miss Collins deserves to be part of your wagon. What a shrew," he muttered to himself as he began looking about at the other wagons in order to settle yet another problem. He looked at the camels contentedly grazing at the edge of camp, away from the rest of the stock. At least he'd finally managed to get his camels into this country, and was on his way to Nevada. If only he hadn't been forced to finance the journey West by forming a wagon train and dragging along this disagreeable group of misfits that no one else would take on . . .

"Mr. Stewart," Hunter called to the black-haired, young man bent over the tongue of his wagon, "trouble with your wagon?"

"No." Derek looked up and straightened his suspenders. "Just making sure everything's in good shape."

Hunter nodded his approval of the young man's efforts. At least one man on the train wasn't proving to be helpless. "Have you seen Miss Collins?"

Cecilia Stewart stuck her head out the flap of the wagon, a knowing smile on her delicate lips. "Why, I saw Miss Collins head toward the stream a little while ago, Mr. Brody."

"Thanks." Hunter tipped his hat, ignoring the young bride's tone, and started off toward the stream.

"Oh, Mr. Brody, sir." Cecilia practically sang the words in her sweet Southern drawl. "Mr. Potter was with her."

Women! Why should he care who was with the Collins woman? When Hunter reached the stream, Cornelius Potter was standing over a big square box, a black cloth covering his head. Martha was kneeling over the edge of the stream, her brown curls hanging freely about her red calico dress as she dipped a frilly undergarment into the clear running water.

For some reason Hunter could not put his finger on, the sight did not please him at all. And their proximity annoyed him in a different way than it had before. Previously, Martha Collins had simply been another faceless female who had deceived him. Now he wasn't sure what she was to him, and that ate at his insides. "Miss Collins," he said in a commanding voice.

Surprised, Martha sprang to her feet, losing her footing on the loose rocks, and would have toppled headfirst into the icy water had not Hunter rushed forth and grabbed her around the waist. His big hands clung to her as he delved into her startled green eyes.

"That's good. Hold that pose," said Cornelius and promptly exposed the plate in his camera as the surprised pair momentarily remained frozen, their mouths agape.

"Dammit, Potter, I came down here to talk to Miss Collins, not to get my picture taken. If you don't get that infernal contraption out of here right quick, I might just haul off and smash it."

"I shall be more than happy to leave and take my equipment with me if that is what Miss Collins desires." Cornelius looked directly at Martha who squirmed, embarrassed, in Hunter's lingering embrace.

"It's all right, Mr. Potter," she shyly said. Feeling a bit uneasy yet strangely warmed by Hunter Brody's touch, she knelt back down to continue with her washing.

After Cornelius left, Hunter glared at Martha. "What do you think you're doing?"

"Why, my wash, of course," she said calmly, although she felt anything but calm as she gazed up at the big man clad in worn denims.

"So I noticed, you holding those lacy drawers of yours up for Potter to photograph so all the world can see." Angered by her nonchalance, he grabbed the undergarment out of her hand and slung it onto a nearby bush; it promptly dropped into the dirt.

The warmth Martha had felt instantly cooled. She was furious that the work she had done had just come to naught. Now she would have to scrub mud and twigs out of that piece of clothing. "I fail to see that it's any of your concern." She returned his glare, determined not to let him intimidate her.

Momentarily flustered by the quiet strength in her reply, Hunter clenched his fists at his sides. He hadn't come down here to fight with the woman. But he was losing his temper again. "It's bad enough having some unattached female on my train. But when you start showing off your unmentionables to the men in this company, it is my business. Don't let it happen again." He pointed an accusing finger at her. "You understand?"

"I quite understand. And I'll thank you to lower your finger and your voice. Now, what is it you wished to speak with me about?" Martha did not avert her gaze, although maintaining it took all the courage she could muster. She was not about to explain that Mr. Potter had set up his equipment without her knowledge, while she was busy doing her laundry. After all, he had said he was going to take photographs of their daily routine so she couldn't fault him. But why had Hunter Brody, of all people, come along and gotten the wrong impression? Whether he approved or disapproved of her should not matter, but it did.

Having a woman stand up to him the way Martha Collins was doing, was a new experience for Hunter. His voice softened. "I came to tell you that you won't be traveling in the Belshaws' wagon any longer. Mrs. Belshaw seems to think you might be more comfortable in one of the other wagons."

"I am certain she does," Martha returned shortly. She wasn't unhappy about the change. Life wasn't easy for women on the trail. But Harriet Belshaw was a most difficult woman, and the wagon reeked of cheap whiskey for Mr. Belshaw was constantly nipping at the jug he had tucked away, probably so he could endure his wife's incessant harping.

It was obvious to Hunter that Martha saw through his attempt to smooth over his explanation of why she had to leave the Belshaws' wagon. Well, she would just have to adjust. "The Nelsons already have six in their wagon, so you'll have to move in with the Stewarts and the Wakefield woman and her aunt."

"No." Her short response rang with finality. Cecilia Stewart and Jannet Wakefield had been anything but cordial to her after hearing Harriet Belshaw's razor-sharp criticisms. And Jannet's aunt was most strange, though there was something familiar about Velina Wakefield. Martha tried to recall where she'd seen her before. She decided she must have met the tight-lipped woman years ago, as a child, and shifted her attention back to the pressing problem at hand. She would rather sleep out in the open than be subjected to another four and a half months of rude silence and sniping comments.

"What do you mean, no?" Hunter was taken aback by the firmness of her response.

"I refuse to be forced upon people who would rather I did not travel with them."

"Neither Derek Stewart nor his wife ever said one unkind word about you. Nor have the two women—"

"Not in front of you, they haven't. No. I'll ride with Mr. Potter in the spring wagon."

"Like hell you will! I don't care if you want to give those people more ammunition to use against you, but I don't want petty gossip keeping everyone riled up." Hunter was careful not to let on that the idea of Martha riding with Cornelius Potter roiled in his gut.

"Well then, what do you suggest?" Martha rose and faced him squarely. She was over a head shorter than Brody, but she would not be deterred by his height or his crude language. She decided to ignore his swearing. She would not give him the satisfaction of thinking he could rankle her with it. She raised her chin to show her determination.

God she's a proud woman, Hunter thought, staring into those green eyes. Not bad looking either. Not pretty in the usual sense, but not bad at all. And he had to give her credit for her strength. Any normal female would have resorted to tears in an effort to win his favor, but not Martha Collins. That further disturbed him.

He considered his options for a moment before he spoke.

"You've got a choice. You can either force yourself to ride with the Stewarts or I can saddle one of the camels for you and you can ride it during the day. You can sleep in Happy's tent at night. He can move in with me."

"Surely you're jesting." Stunned, Martha looked at the big man with blond hair waving over the edge of his collar.

"I'm dead serious. You've got until we move out in the morning to let me know what you've decided. I'll be back at camp by the time you're ready to give me your decision." Hunter walked off, smiling to himself. There was more than one way to tame a stubborn filly.

Martha stared at his wide retreating back. How could he be so infuriating? She reviewed the options he'd given her. The Stewarts and the Wakefields or the camel. She couldn't blame Cecilia Stewart for her coldness. That young woman had left a comfortable home in Virginia to travel West on her honeymoon, and the trek must be a rude awakening for this coddled daughter of a plantation owner. But how could Jannet Wakefield listen to such slander and believe it? That troubled Martha. Still, she knew one thing for certain, she was going West on this wagon train, and she was not going to ride with the Stewarts and Wakefields!

By the time Martha returned to the wagons, Winnie Nelson had already driven two forked sticks into the ground, had laid a pole across them, and was hanging a heavy kettle over the crackling campfire she had built.

"You go hang your wash from my wagon, then come on over here and talk to me while I finish gettin' supper. You can tell me all about yourself and what you're doin' travelin' West all alone. We got us some time to get acquainted since Mr. Brody rode over to the fort a while ago and ain't due back for a spell."

"Thank you, Mrs. Nelson." Martha wished the wagon train had stopped at the fort, but Mr. Brody had told them that since they had gotten a late start there wouldn't be time. At least he had consented to post her letters home.

"Winnie, I keep tellin' everybody."

"Winnie." Martha smiled. She was thankful Winnie Nelson didn't seem to have paid any attention to Harriet Belshaw's comments. "As soon as I get my things out of the Belshaws' wagon, I'll try to come back."

"Don't you forget now, gal." Winnie turned toward her own wagon and hollered, "Lucy, hurry up with that bacon before I come and lead you here by those long pigtails of yours. You're the slowest child." A look of deep pain came over Winnie, then her gaze fell on Martha. "Lucy ain't talked since she was six. It's been well on two years since she saw her pa wring her pet chicken's neck 'cause we needed it for the pot, us havin' six bellies to fill 'n all. But she knows what's told her." A heavy sadness flickered into the older woman's tired eyes. "Don't reckon she'll ever get over it."

"It must have been a difficult time for all of you," Martha said sympathetically, in an effort to share Winnie's burden before leaving the rumpled woman to her chores.

Winnie Nelson was kind, but she was much too busy with

her own brood to take on any more problems. Martha knew she couldn't unload her troubles on the harried woman.

She finished removing her trunk and the basket her mother had packed for her from the Belshaws' wagon, under the eagle eye of pudgy, little Clara, who'd undoubtedly been sent by her mother to see that their traveling companion took only her own things. Then Martha heard the camels snort. She had not yet gone near the creatures, but since she had a decision to make, there was no time like the present to look them over. With unsure steps, she moved closer to the strange, smelly beasts.

"Missy Collins, you like see camels up close? Come. Come." Happy waved, a proud smile on his deep brown face. As he stood near the corral he had built, Martha inched her way closer to him. She did not want the little man with the unusual-looking white cloth wrapped around his head to think her afraid. "They no bite you if you with me." He pulled on the neck of one of the creatures standing next to him. "Here, you pet, you see. You pet."

Martha forced herself to stroke the animal's nose. It tossed its head, causing her to jump back, but then stretched its neck out and stood eying her with big brown gentle eyes as if waiting for her to resume stroking its nose.

"He like you. You pet." Happy, the camel driver, gave her a white-toothed grin. "Some think camels dumb, not so. They know good people from bad. They know."

"Why, thank you, Happy," Martha said gratefully. At least she had a couple of supporters among the people on the train, even if Hunter Brody wasn't one of them.

"Tell me, Happy, what on earth ever possessed Mr. Brody to bring camels to this country?"

"If you're so interested, why don't you ask me?" Hunter was a formidable sight. Seated atop his big horse, he took in the smirking Happy. "Don't you have enough work to keep you busy?"

"I go. I go." Happy laughed, his gaze switching back and forth, from Martha to Hunter, as if he knew something they did not.

"I apologize. I hadn't meant to pry. I was merely making

conversation while trying to decide how I'd be traveling tomorrow." Martha turned to leave. She wasn't going to give him a chance to provoke her. She had already had enough aggravation that day.

"Then you weren't really interested in knowing why I brought the camels over?" he said congenially.

"I suppose I was, actually," Martha admitted, turning back sheepishly.

"Well then, sit down over here"—he motioned to a flat rock nearby—"and I'll tell you."

Martha settled onto the rock and straightened her red calico dress. Hunter dismounted, tied up the nervous bay at some distance from the camels, then perched on a rock near Martha.

After an awkward moment or two, they began to relax and he poured out his story.

"You know, with a lot of settlers going West there is an enormous need for supplies out there. Camels are accustomed to living in the desert, and can much better endure extremes of weather—cold as well as heat. And they can haul twice as much as any mule, so I mean to use them to carry supplies across the desert from my ranch on the Carson River in Nevada—that's in Utah Territory—to the gold diggings in California—if I get back there in time to pay off the creditors."

Martha stared at the arrowhead hanging at his throat; it was a three-pointed bone, sharp and polished smooth. Then her gaze shifted to the plain gold band around the little finger of his left hand. Why did he always wear these two ornaments? What significance could they have for him? As Hunter continued to talk her thoughts drifted. He had to be desperate for money to be seeing a group of settlers all the way to California and Oregon. She wondered if he was going to send the camels on with Happy while he saw the train through. No wonder he was in a hurry. He had a lot of miles to cover before he could get his business started. She blinked her eyes to draw her attention back from the man himself to what he was saying.

"The way I figure it, there'll be a tidy profit in it. . . ."

Martha sat quietly watching Hunter Brody's hazel eyes come to life as he finished speaking about his planned venture. A boyish excitement showed through the hardened exterior he presented to the world. It seemed to soften his features and to lend him a particularly handsome cast, despite his whiskered chin.

"But how did you ever come up with the idea of using camels?"

"Years ago I read in a newspaper about a Major Crossman, who tried to get the government to appropriate funds to purchase camels for use in the military. He got write-ups in a number of newspapers, which helped to promote the idea, and four years ago Congress finally allotted thirty thousand dollars to buy the beasts."

"Come to think of it, I vaguely remember Jefferson Davis supporting such a measure when he was a senator. At the time a friend offered to lend me a copy of *The Camel Hunt*, but I'm afraid I didn't have the time to read it."

"Well, as I was saying, last year I saw a group of camels while I was at Fort Tejon out in California near Los Angeles. I was so impressed with them, I decided to go into business. Hasn't turned out to be an easy venture though."

"It's been said that anything worthwhile is worth working for," Martha said quickly for she'd noted the troubled tone to his voice. He had obviously put a great deal of time and effort—and money—into this enterprise and it would be a shame for him to get discouraged so soon.

"Yeah, I know. It's just that it cost more than I was planning to spend. I even had to get a special permit from Mohammed Pasha, the bey of Tunis, before I could export the animals. I was going to bring them back myself, but, lucky for me, Happy volunteered to come along when he discovered what I was up to. He has no family and was living on the streets, begging. We met when he tried to pick my pocket." Hunter chuckled at the memory. "Happy had worked the beasts most of his forty-seven years until he lost his job to a younger camel driver, so I thought, What the hell, why not? Then I finally got them to Texas and the ignorant bastards—"

Martha stiffened, although she had told herself she was going to adjust to his liberal use of vulgar words.

"Sorry. The ignorant *men* at Indianola wouldn't let me ashore with them. Said they didn't want any more of the beasts terrorizing their town. I hear tell a special corral of prickly pear cactus was built to contain the first lot. Most animals will stay clear of a fence of thorns, but the camels just ate the whole damn thing, thorns and all." The thought made him smile. "Anyway, since my plan to use the southern route across country, like the soldiers did with the other batch of camels, got fouled up, I managed to bring them up the Mississippi to the Missouri River and then unload them in Independence. You pretty much know the rest."

"But why didn't you take them to California by ship? Wouldn't it have been closer?" She leaned forward. His enthusiasm was catching, and she couldn't help but feel his excitement over such an undertaking.

"Didn't know those Texans would refuse me. By then, it would've taken just as long to go by way of California, and I was running out of money. So here I am, stuck with a bunch of greenhorns who can't manage to get along for even one day without a hassle."

His comment about greenhorns caused her to wince. She was included in that group.

"I'm sorry you don't approve of me, but just because I'm a woman it doesn't mean I don't have hopes and desires. I have a dream, too, one which I intend to fulfill," she said rigidly.

"It's really nothing personal," Hunter conceded before he heard dried twigs being crushed beneath a heavy step.

Breaking into what had been a pleasant conversation, Harriet Belshaw brusquely announced, "It's getting late and we've been waiting on you two for supper." That continual censuring wrinkle settled onto her brow. "Unless, of course, you two would rather I left you alone."

Before Hunter or Martha could discount what Harriet Belshaw had implied, one of the camels broke away from Happy and rushed toward her, snorting and spitting. The big woman let out a blood-curdling yelp and, bundling her calico skirts up into her arms, hustled her huge girth along faster than Martha had imagined someone of her size could move.

Unable to help themselves, Hunter and Martha laughed until tears rolled down their cheeks as Harriet Belshaw ran from them, shrieking like a speared boar, the camel in hot pursuit and Happy rushing after them.

Still laughing, Martha mumbled to herself, "And some people think camels are dumb."

Hunter overheard her, but decided against commenting. Although Harriet Belshaw fully deserved what she got, it wouldn't pay to let Martha Collins think he was taking her side in front of the others. She might get the idea that he was partial to her and approved of the presence of a single woman on the train, which he did not. He abruptly stood up. "We'd best be joining the others."

"Mr. Brody?" Martha called out, somehow hoping to prolong the moment.

"Yeah?"

When their eyes caught, her nerve faltered. Instead of plying him with additional questions in the hope of learning more about him, she swallowed the inquiries and asked, "Was there any mail for me at the fort?"

"No." For an instant Martha thought she noted an inkling of disappointment flicker into his eyes before he hooked his thumbs into his gunbelt and headed toward the wagons without waiting for her.

Long after she had been left alone and everything had returned to normal, Happy having corraled the offending camel, Martha fretted over Hunter Brody's behavior. It must have been her own imagining that he had, even for an instant, wanted to continue their conversation. One minute they had been enjoying an amicable chat; the next, he had walked off without so much as a good-bye. What troubled her most was the awakening realization of how much she had just enjoyed being with him.

No longer trying to figure out Hunter Brody or her feelings, Martha turned her attention to the camels now peacefully grazing in a nearby clearing. Although she could not deny she had delighted in Harriet Belshaw's comeuppance, the animal's disagreeable behavior, seemingly without provocation, worried her. She had a decision to make that night, and the camel's little escapade did not make it any easier.

Chapter Four

Friday, June 19, 1859—Along the Platte River, Nebraska Territory. I pray I am equal to the decision I have been required to make. Each new dawning seems to hold yet another test of my strength. I do not mean to sound at all ungrateful, for that would be quite contrary to the truth. When I have the time to ponder my position, I realize I have been granted more fortitude of spirit than I thought humanly possible for a mortal woman to possess. . . .

Throughout the stormy afternoon Martha continued to cling to her precarious position upon the camel's back; the newly christened Humphrey was at least surefooted and not frightened by the pelting rain or gale-force winds. But no matter how hard she had tried not to judge her fellow man, she began to think that her first assessment of Hunter Brody had been accurate—he was little more than an unfeeling brute.

By the time the storm began to abate, Martha was past caring about the distant hills or the cottonwood trees skirting the banks of the Platte River, which looked even more yellow against the dark gray sky. She was soaked to the bone and numb from the cold. Her sunbonnet, now a sorry, sodden rag, drooped over her left eye. But she was grateful that Winnie had kindly offered to take her pasteboard bonnet into the Nelson wagon before it had started to rain.

"The grass looks pretty good on the left side of the road just up ahead. We'll be making camp there for the night so the stock can get their fill before starting out tomorrow," Hunter stated without emotion as he rode up alongside Martha. The woman was a soggy mess, but he had to give her credit. She wasn't complaining, and had stuck to her decision.

"I'm happy you were able to find an adequate spot for the animals."

Hunter's head snapped up at Martha's sarcastic tone. "What's the matter, Mat, aren't you enjoying the ride? You did have a choice, you know. Or don't you remember?"

Oh, she remembered. How could she forget? And she would continue to ride the dromedary—through snow if necessary—before she would endure the Stewarts and Jannet Wakefield and her aunt. "What did you call me? Mat?" She resented the familiarity he took in cannibalizing her name to suit himself, yet at the same time a shock wave reverberated through her at hearing him call her by the endearment her father had bestowed on her when she was a child.

"I just thought it wouldn't hurt since we're practically living together." He grinned wickedly.

She bristled at the implication. "Mr. Brody, we are not practically living together! Far from it. Furthermore, sir, you have not been given permission to use my given name, which you may now know is Martha. Mat is the name my father teasingly gave me when I was a girl because he considered me a rambunctious tomboy. I no longer fit that description. Furthermore, Mat sounds more like a man's name, and I am not a male."

"No, you're most definitely not." Hunter stared openly at the bit of leg revealed beneath her dripping-wet skirt. "You're just trying to act like one."

Martha's eyes followed his gaze. Then she jerked her leg up underneath her skirt and away from his offensive, heated stare. "Why you . . . you uncouth lecher!"

Furious, she reined in her camel, directing it toward Happy, who was busy erecting a special corral—he had told her it was called a *khan*—to contain the beasts for the night. Happy smiled broadly and grabbed the reins. "You make good camel driver. I watch you today. You good with camel. Good

45

with camel."

"Please, just hold Humphrey still until I dismount." Near tears, Martha was in a hurry to seek the private shelter of the tent which would be her own quarters for the next four and a half months. She was determined to get the canvas set up and to be safely inside before the others came along to laugh at her as Hunter Brody, earlier in the day, had warned they might.

"Hump-prey?" Happy laughed. "Yes. Yes. I like. I like." He rolled the name around on his tongue a few times, but when he saw that Martha was not going to wait for his help, his wide grin turned to dismay, then horror. "No. No. You hang on. I help you. I help you."

The little man with the large nose looked horrified as Martha, ignoring his pleas, whipped off the India-rubber coat Hunter had loaned her and started to slide from the saddle.

The camel seemed to sense it was time to relax, and began to fold its legs beneath it. In her haste to dismount Martha was totally unprepared when the dromedary went down on its knees, sending her careening forward.

"Oh!" she cried, losing her grip and tumbling into a big mud puddle left by the storm.

She came up sputtering, gooey mud running down her cheeks and clinging to her wet hair and making patterns on her muslin dress. She was a sight, and the more she tried to wipe the muck from her face the worse it got.

"Happy, get that camel corraled with the rest. And take care of my horse, too," Hunter ordered. He swung easily down from his saddle and headed toward Martha, fearing she had been hurt.

"Yes. Yes. I do. I do." The small man tried to stifle his amusement behind a brown palm as he led the animals toward the khan, the horse attempting to shy away from the strange beasts.

When Hunter reached the edge of Martha's muddy bath, he let out a relief-filled sigh. She was filthy but apparently unharmed.

"Maybe that'll teach you to listen," he barked. Then he howled with mirth at seeing the miserable mud queen before him, almost forgetting the resentment he had felt at having to take on a single woman who'd tricked him into doing it. All of a sudden his laughter stopped, and he stood over her quietly staring.

In all her misery, Martha had not realized her skirt lay in her lap and the hooks at the top of her bodice had been ripped open.

Although covered with mud, Hunter found her a most bewitching vision with her breasts pushed up and straining over the fabric, and her unstockinged legs no longer hidden from view.

"Please turn your back," she said in anguish, frantically trying to cover herself as she realized the state of her undress.

He smirked. "But I haven't enjoyed the view in these parts so much in years."

"If you were a gentleman I wouldn't have to request that you turn around."

"Lady, if I weren't a gentleman you'd probably still be stuck back in Independence."

Hunter made no attempt to avert his eyes. He couldn't have even if he'd wanted to. Despite all the mud and the hassles her presence on his train caused, she was a most fetching sight. Her legs were long and well turned, like an Indian maiden's, not like the skinny crow legs or the flabby thighs of pampered Eastern women incapable of walking as far as the pump to get themselves a glass of water. God knows, he'd had more than his share of both. But it was Martha's full, rounded breasts which held him mesmerized. He rubbed his fingers together, thinking how soft and velvety their luscious flesh could be to the touch or against his face if he buried it within the valley between them.

Her modesty restored, Martha held out her hand and said hotly, "Even though, as far as I'm concerned, you've proved you're not a gentleman, the least you can do is offer me a hand up."

"My pleasure."

He was so engrossed in his own thoughts that he failed to notice the vengeful gleam in Martha's eyes when he offered his assistance. Instead of meekly accepting his outstretched hand, she took a deep breath to buoy her nerve, then yanked with all her strength. Hunter was thrown off balance and spilled into the puddle right next to her.

It was Martha's turn to laugh as dark muddy brown stains swelled into enormous patches on what had been a white shirt. Hunter wore buckskin pants, so the effect wasn't nearly as dramatic on those, but even the thick, dark blond chest hairs exposed by his open collar were dyed a mud color. Not yet satisfied with her handiwork, Martha scooped up a generous handful of the oozing slime and smeared the sticky glob down Hunter's straight, proud nose.

"You want to play, huh?" he said, feeling pleasantly surprised by her behavior.

"No," she wailed. Realizing too late the consequences of her actions, she tried to scramble away.

"Oh, no you don't." He grinned crookedly. "You aren't going to start something and think you're going to get away with it without paying a price, not with me you're not." He grabbed her ankle and dragged her back, flipping her onto his lap.

Martha was stunned. She had never sat on a man's lap before, except on her father's when she was a little girl. Fear gripped her at the foreign sensations Hunter's hard muscular thighs wrought through her thin muslin dress, and she struggled to free herself. The wagons were almost upon them. What would the rest of the company think? They were sure to get the wrong impression and make the trip even more difficult.

"You must let me up, the wagons are almost here. What will everyone say?"

"I'm surprised it should matter so much what that bunch of vicious tongues say about you. You know it won't make any difference, no matter how hard you try. Those women simply have it in for you."

"Please," Martha pleaded, fear of her own feelings threatening to surface along with her fear of what the others would think of her.

He hated to let her go, but could not dismiss her panicked entreaty. "Quit fighting and I'll help you up." He grabbed her shoulders to shake some sense back into her. But when she ceased her efforts to get away from him and their eyes met and held, Hunter couldn't help himself. He pulled her to him and pressed his lips to hers, savoring their soft textured warmth.

She managed to break away, but felt even more confused by his sudden kiss. Her lips tingled with undefined sensations. She had never been kissed like that before! She had been used to the chaste pecks Clinton had bestowed upon her, and although Hunter Brody's kiss had not been welcome, she could not say it was unpleasant; quite the opposite, if truth be known. Questioningly she ran her fingers over her mouth, while her eyes trailed the curves of Hunter's full lips.

The nicker of a horse broke into her thoughts and she straightened. "Mr. Brody, please."

"I think we know each other well enough to use first names now, don't you, Martha?"

"How could you?" she protested.

"Easy. You want me to show you again?" He grinned devilishly and leaned closer to her.

"No. No!"

"Then will you call me Hunter?" He wasn't quite sure why it was so important that this woman call him by his given name, but after the kiss they had just shared, it was.

"Please, the wagons are almost here. We can't be found in such a compromising position."

"Then Hunter it is?"

"All right, all right . . . Hunter."

His name sounded strangely rich and melodious on her lips, those softly full imploring lips that were so tempting. He wished he hadn't insisted those damned wagons stay so close behind the camels that day, but true to his word, Hunter tempered his inclinations and rose to help Martha to her feet just as the Belshaws' wagon rounded the bend and pulled up a short distance from them.

"You know you really are a sorry sight to behold." Hunter started to chuckle in order to suppress a simmering desire he hadn't felt in years. Oh, he had experienced raw lust—with Pearl at the Trails in Independence, just before the wagon train had pulled out. But not the troubling desire he felt now. And he didn't like it!

"Well I wouldn't laugh so hard if I were you. You don't

exactly look your Sunday best either." Unable to help herself, Martha forgot about the Belshaws and broke out into a most unladylike giggle.

The moment of shared laughter caught in their throats when they looked up to see Harriet Belshaw next to her husband on the wagon seat, her perpetual frown of condemnation settled directly on them.

As they neared the Platte River Forks Martha continued to trouble over the recent events with Hunter Brody. She'd never expected to share laughter with a wagon train captain who had been so adamantly opposed to her presence on the train, let alone anything so intimate as a kiss. Somehow she'd have to make sure it didn't happen again.

For days, Martha kept to herself, except for Cornelius Potter's visits after they'd stopped for the night. Hunter Brody growled at her on several occasions, but except for those few cross words, he did not approach her. Although that bothered Martha, she decided it was just as well he was keeping his distance. Harriet Belshaw had circulated an exaggerated story of Martha's scandalous behavior with Hunter Brody, and except for Winnie Nelson, whose gown looked rumpled as usual, the rest of the women now avoided Martha as if she had leprosy. Even Jannet's aunt had turned from her when she'd tried to inquire after the lame woman's health. But that close-lipped lady constantly kept her bonnet drawn low over her eyes, and rarely spoke to the others anyway.

"You're becoming a pretty good rider," Hunter admitted begrudgingly one afternoon, infringing on his self-imposed distance.

"I manage," she responded coolly. Without encouraging any further discourse, Martha averted her eyes so Hunter rode on.

During the day Martha held her head up atop Humphrey despite her awareness of the guffaws suppressed by the backs of open hands, and of accusing eyes. She concentrated her attention on the scenery and the vegetation. There was hardly a tree in sight except those on the scattered islands in the middle of the Platte River. Attempts by the women to maintain modesty while attending to bodily functions entailed taking turns holding out their skirts to allow a sparse measure of privacy to one woman. Cecilia and Winnie did this for Martha, although Martha knew Winnie had shamed Cecilia into doing it.

Martha pitied the poor women who crossed the prairie only in the company of men. The weather once again had become stiflingly warm during the day, and they had little water for drinking or washing. Tempers flared, children went unattended, and bedraggled appearances became the norm; although the women continued to cling to their white aprons as if those pieces of cloth represented the last vestiges of the civilization they had been forced to leave.

They had been warned not to drink the water from the swift-flowing Platte without first boiling it since it was known to make people ill. Stocky Henry Nelson, a typical mischievous, freckle-faced twelve-year-old paid dearly for testing the wisdom of Hunter's advice. The pug-nosed boy developed a severe case of the runs, and had to be fed nothing but dried peaches and rice for three days.

Worst of all were the mosquitoes.

After helping set up camp and steadying the side rails on the portable khan for Happy while he erected it, Martha left Humphrey grazing on the slim patches of grass. She was about to assemble her tent for the night when a forlorn, little Barsina Nelson, her face smudged and dirty dress torn, appeared with a tin of tallow in her hand.

"My dear, are you all right?" Martha's voice was filled with tenderness for the child. "You look as if you have the measles."

"I itch," the bright-eyed six-year-old whined. "Mama said maybe you'd help me put this"—she held out the can—"on my bumps."

"Of course I will. You just sit down on my blanket and we'll get you fixed up in no time." Lovingly, Martha applied thick dabs of the lard to Barsina's face and arms.

Cornelius Potter watched from a distance as Martha crooned to the little carrot-top child. Cornelius had traveled most of his life after finishing college in Philadelphia, and had photographed the great beauties of Europe. But none of those women had stirred him the way Martha Collins did. She had such strength of character in her face, and an inner beauty radiated through to give her a most appealing countenance. Yes, she had the true spirit of a pioneer. She was a woman who silently endured the misfortunes of life, and was the better for it. Although she had more chores than the other women on the train, she found time to help a small child. She was a woman any man would be proud to call his, in spite of what Harriet Belshaw had been saying. His heart stirred as he snapped another picture.

Chapter Five

Friday, June 17, 1859—Platte River Forks. I am finding this trip so much more than I ever anticipated. It appears I am the recipient of attentions I find most surprising, if not unexplainably pleasant, for one considered plain. I cannot say that I do not find my own feelings disturbing, for they are most foreign to me, as are the sensations which have begun to invade my body. . . .

For the last two nights Cornelius had hovered over Martha more closely than ever. The minute the wagons pulled into camp, he'd jumped down and rushed to her side.

"Did the umbrella help shade you from the sun?" he now asked, looking concerned.

Jed Nelson's bald head bobbed up from unhitching his team of oxen. "I'd say if nothin' else she was a real eye-catchin' sight." The short man, leathered from years of toiling under the sun, grinned over the bib of his overalls. "No offense meant, Miss Martha." He dipped his head cordially.

"None taken."

"Me and Winnie been talkin' it over and if you don't mind the squeeze none we'd be much obliged to have you share our wagon."

"Mr. Nelson—"

"Jed. Like the missus is Winnie. Folks call me Jed."

"Jed, I appreciate your concern, but I've grown rather fond of Humphrey, really," Martha answered, careful not to reveal her feelings. The Nelson family was overly generous considering the pressures they had to deal with. Handling four lively children day in and day out in the confines of a covered wagon, with temperatures well over one hundred degrees, had taken its toll on this older couple who had sold their decrepit farm and were now making an arduous journey in search of a better life. Jed Nelson did not look at all well; his face was pasty, his gray eyes were set in sunken hollows. And Winnie seemed to have aged ten years in the month since they had left Independence; the crevices in her face were carved much deeper, across her forehead and around her eyes.

"If you change your mind, little lady, just give a holler."

"Thank you, I will." Martha's heart warmed as she watched the aging man lead his oxen toward the short clumps of grass. She smiled to herself. He was at least two inches shorter than her five-foot-seven-inch height yet he called her little lady.

"Martha, I think you should accept the Nelsons' kind offer. I do not like to see you forced to ride that beast every day," Cornelius announced quite unexpectedly.

Martha's eyes grew wide at the earnestness with which he expressed this unsought advice. And she was surprised by the take-charge tone in his voice. Up until now, he had refrained from voicing his opinions on decisions that were hers to make. "I appreciate your concern, but I think I'm capable of managing without too much difficulty.

"You cannot be serious?" He cast her a disbelieving look.

"I most certainly am. I appreciate the loan of your umbrella. It's helped against the sun. But just because I accepted it, that doesn't mean I'm in need of male protection."

She could have bitten her tongue. Cornelius suddenly looked crestfallen, almost as wilted as his white ruffled dress shirt. She didn't want to cause a rift in their friendship. He had been spending a great deal of time with her, and she had to admit that she enjoyed the attention. It was most pleasurable to be treated like a lady, especially considering the way Hunter Brody endlessly shouted commands at them all.

"I'm sorry, Cornelius. I don't want you to think I don't appreciate your concern. I guess I'm just tired. We made nearly twenty miles today."

"No need for you ever to apologize. Why not let me escort you down by the river? You can rest there while I pick you an armful of wildflowers." He beamed and offered his arm.

How could Martha resist such a romantic offer? The idea of a fragrant bouquet selected from the canvas of brilliant colors dotting the hills near the river raised her spirits. She couldn't deny how thoughtful and attentive Cornelius had been, not after Hunter Brody had shown just how forward he could be. She slipped her arm through Cornelius's. "Only if you allow me time to bathe."

She had barely gotten the words out of her mouth when she caught sight of Hunter leaning against the Stewarts' wagon, staring intently at her. It was hard to read the man. She wasn't sure whether his face registered disapproval or something too heavily veiled to discern. She flushed. It was none of his business what she did. *Why should I care whether he approves or not?* Martha murmured to herself, yet she glanced back over her shoulder at the handsome man clad in trail-worn denim as Cornelius led her away from camp.

Cornelius left Martha at the edge of the river, promising to pick her a riot of flowers. They were still in sight of the camp, so she started inching her way through the tangle of cottonwood trees to find a spot offering some privacy. Just as she rounded a bend in the river she heard the rustle of brush.

"Who's there?" she called out, her heart starting to race with apprehension. Cautiously, she took three more steps. If Hunter hadn't so sternly lectured her days before about Indians she would have sworn she saw a fleeting glimpse of one. She stood and listened for a few minutes. It must have been her imagination. Feeling self-assured once again, she went a little farther until she came upon a clearing secluded from view by a large crest of giant granite boulders and some gnarled branches.

Wasting little time, she stripped off her shoes, light gingham dress, undergarments, and white stockings. The Platte River was very riley, yet she had found a delightful private pond. Feeling grimy and smelly from the dusty ride atop Humphrey, she languidly stretched her arms over her head and unpinned her thick brown hair, letting it fall gracefully down her back.

Then she tiptoed off the bank. The water was cool and felt refreshing as it splashed over her hot feet. It was pure luxury to bathe nude without concern that someone would come along. She waded out to her waist and dipped into the water.

After Hunter had watched Martha stroll off with that overeducated photographer, he whirled on his heel, his jaw tightening into a hard angle.

"Oh, Mr. Brody," Jannet Wakefield called, as she helped her aunt from the wagon.

When Hunter ignored her, Jannet scowled and turned to her aunt. "Well, what do you think of that? At least he could have helped you down."

Her aunt, who had been closely observing the whole scene, responded with a sour grin. "I think Martha Collins is about to learn a few lessons." The tight-lipped woman turned icy amber eyes on Jannet. "Perhaps you should get to know Mr. Brody better."

Janet frowned petulantly at the stooped woman. "I still don't understand why Papa asked you to accompany me."

"I told you he had some loose ends to tie up at the bank. He would have told you himself except he did not want to cast any suspicion on you when all that money was discovered missing," she said in a raspy voice.

"I can hardly believe Papa told you about that," Jannet scoffed. She was careful not to reveal too much to an aunt she hadn't seen since she was seven years old, indeed, not until a little over a month ago when the strange woman had met her stage. The letter from her father had stated he had been held up and Aunt Velina could be trusted—completely. But why had he written Aunt Velina in quotation marks? Jannet thought about that a moment longer, then turned calculating eyes toward the rapidly retreating wagon-train captain.

After Hunter left the camp he went down by the river to cool off. He was becoming much too aware of Martha's presence, and that gnawed at his gut. He had no time for women other than to satisfy his baser needs, yet she was beginning to monopolize his conscious thoughts.

56

He looked around. The lovely shaded spot at the river's edge brought back haunting memories. He hadn't been back here since forty seven when, as a young trapper, he had first made love to his precious bride, Dancing Wind. Visions of how he had claimed the beautiful Indian maiden in a nearby cove shortly before she'd died of the white man's disease, cholera, threatened to pierce his resolve.

He stood quietly, remembering. She had been carrying his unborn child when he'd left her with her family to sell the furs he had trapped. If only he had taken her with him . . . "Damn you, War Arrow. I should've killed you when you challenged me for wanting your sister," Hunter muttered. "You greedy red bastard. If you hadn't dug up those bodies and taken the clothes back to your village, Dancing Wind and my child would be alive today."

Although Hunter had spoken in little more than a murmur, his words fell on the ears of two Indians concealed nearby.

"Why do you wait?" the girl whispered.

The older Indian held up a hand for silence. "Now is not the time. Have I not told you of my vision? Has it not brought us to Yellow Fire? No. We will continue to watch and wait as the vision has shown me, until the time to act is upon us."

Soundlessly they remained hidden from all eyes . . . watching . . . waiting. . . .

As Hunter walked along the edge of the river, he continued to mull over the past. He had almost gone mad after losing Dancing Wind. Her family had listened to War Arrow's hateful words, and hadn't even let him remain among them long enough to mourn at her grave. So he'd drifted aimlessly for a couple of years, and had finally ended up in Nevada determined never again to come face to face with the pain of losing someone he loved. In his mind the best way to do that was not to love another. Yet lately Martha Collins had been filling his thoughts.

Maybe returning to that cove would help get the woman off his mind. It would serve as a reminder of what he had lost. With a volcano of old emotions bubbling within him, Hunter parted the mat of branches shielding the cove and stepped between them.

"What the hell?" He stiffened and then muttered something guttural when his eyes dropped to the naked white back turned toward him. Almost immediately he recognized that it belonged to Martha Collins. God, she was beautiful. How had she found this place, his special hidden cove? Very few people, other than his Indian brothers, knew of its existence. It was one of the rare spots along the river where an underground spring flowed into the murky waters.

Even from behind, Hunter could see that Martha's body was full and ripe. She was such a lovely creature. Years of hostility melted under the heat of his own body, as desire, wild and hot, spread through him. Damn! He couldn't let this woman so easily break down his hard-won barriers.

"Miss Collins, I'd be more careful where I undress from now on if I were you. Some Indian might come along, take a liking to that tempting hide of yours, and carry you off," Hunter said gruffly, crossing his arms over his chest in a reproving gesture.

At the sound of his voice, Martha's pulse quickened and she swung around, clutching her arms across her breasts. How dare he spy on her! "What are you doing here?" she demanded. Although she remained rigid, she felt as if her knees were about to buckle. Why did such an exasperating brute affect her so?

Hunter's eyes rode down her shoulders and over her smooth, creamy flesh, drinking in every revealing curve. Damn! The woman and water made an overpowering combination.

"I might ask you the same question." He stood motionless, staring.

"Turn your head and hand me my clothing." Martha sank into the water up to her neck.

The hot ache of desire coiled inside Hunter as he forced himself to fight his instincts and toss her the light gingham dress.

Martha caught it and drew it on. Then, her dress wet and clinging, her heart dueling with her mind, she tried to scramble up out of the pool. In her haste she started to slide back down the bank, but Hunter caught her up in his arms and pulled her to him.

"What are you trying to do to me?" he groaned. For the first time in years, he felt controlled by his emotions. He knew he should release her and leave before it was too late. The feelings he was experiencing were madness, utter madness.

"What am I doing to you?" Martha murmured weakly. His body was so hard. She looked over his manly features: the straight proud nose, full curving lips, heated hazel eyes, and thick blond hair. He was awakening feelings she thought existed only in the wrong kind of woman. Her heart began to flutter, and instead of trying to push out of his embrace, she reached up and lightly ran trembling fingers along his lower lip.

He swallowed hard. She smelled of fresh-cut roses on a warm morning. God, how he wanted her. And she seemed to have less control than he did. It would be so easy to take her right here. Hunter's restraint was being stretched beyond endurance. His lips closed over hers and he tasted her submission, her almost eager response. His hands slipped down her back to her waist, pulled her tighter against his hips.

Martha's mind spun in figure eights. What was happening to her? She not only wasn't fighting against him, she was a willing partner in the searing kiss, the sudden seductive intimacy. She no longer cared about anything but the delicious sensations coursing through her and awakening a powerful hunger. She pressed tighter against him, feeling his desire as the passion of his kiss swept over her.

"Martha? Martha?" Cornelius's voice broke in on them.

Hunter tore his arms from around Martha. He stared grimly down at her, and forced himself to say, "You'd best go to him. He's expecting you. And you wouldn't want him to find you here."

Martha stared back at him in disbelief. The heat and the rough feel of his callused fingers still lingered where he'd touched her. How quickly he seemed to change. One moment he was growling at her, then he was kissing her, then he was sending her away. Confusion reigned in her mind, and she did not move.

Without another word Hunter turned her around and gave her a shove back through the tangle of branches. Martha

59

looked back at him. He stood motionless, his arms dangling at his sides, his expression unfathomable. She bit into her lip to keep from crying out, then pinned her hair back and blindly hurried toward the sound of Cornelius's voice.

"I hope I did not rush you." Cornelius smiled warmly at her, taking in Martha's disheveled appearance, but he prudently refrained from mentioning her wet dress. "Hold out your arms."

Martha obediently thrust out her hands, hoping Cornelius did not notice the flush of desire still warming her cheeks.

With alacrity, Cornelius placed the enormous multicolored bouquet in her arms, his soft fingers lingering ever so briefly on her skin. How different were Cornelius's smooth hands from Hunter's big chapped ones.

"Do you like them?" He leaned forward expectantly, his face registering pride in his efforts.

"They're beautiful." Martha sniffed at the sweet, fragrant petals. "You really shouldn't have gone to so much trouble."

Cornelius reached for her arm. "For you I would do much more."

His manner was urgent, yet gentle. His dark blue eyes caressed her tenderly. He looked as if he could devour her, but he held himself in check.

"I don't know quite what to say." Martha was troubled. She admired Cornelius. He was every inch a true gentleman, and that warmed her heart. Yet his touch did not set her afire.

"Do not say anything. Now now. Not yet." He placed a hand on Martha's back and escorted her toward camp.

Hunter watched them from the edge of the river. Martha seemed to accept the flowers eagerly. He decided he was foolish for letting her get to him the way she had, then shook his head. It had to be the hot weather melting his brain and causing him to act like a fool over this damned woman. And she'd not only been dishonest, obviously she was toying with them both. If he ever got so close to Martha Collins again it would be for one thing and one thing only! He never should have let a single woman traveling alone come along on a trip like this.

Two hours later, Hunter found Martha struggling with her tent. "You might try stringing that corner pole first." He pointed to the listing offender.

Martha looked up, annoyed by this riddle of a man. "And you might try giving me a hand instead of merely standing by."

"I might. But I wouldn't think of depriving you of your efforts to wear the pants around here." He stood above her grinning devilishly. "Oh, and speaking of pants"—he pulled his hands from behind his back—"you might try learning to hang on to your own." Hunter tossed her the underwear she had left behind at the cove, and walked off. Once he would have been laughing; now he felt like he had been kicked in the chest.

Martha was livid. He was the most totally exasperating, yet strangely exciting man she had ever met! Then her lips lifted in a smile. "So you think I'm trying to wear the pants, do you? Well, Hunter Brody, we'll just have to see about that."

Chapter Six

Sunday, June 19, 1859—Heading toward Ash Hollow. Crossing the Platte River was most frightening. The river was a quarter-mile wide where we forded it. It was not so very deep, but the current was swift and the bottom pebbled quicksand. I could not help but breathe a long sigh of relief when we all made it across without incident. This is the first Sabbath we have not been forced to travel. I am grateful for the opportunity to rest and attempt to gather my feelings into some meaningful pattern. . . .

Martha fixed herself a breakfast of coffee, bread, pickles, and dried beef. This morning she was determined to join the others at the table set up near the wagons instead of taking her meal alone inside her tent. She had been letting those wagging tongues drive her from the group, but no more. She had paid for her passage. For now, she would continue to ride Humphrey since it gave her a sense of accomplishment—how many women could say they could ride a camel . . . how many men, for that matter?—and it annoyed Hunter Brody.

She picked up her plate and went over to the long board set up as a table at the side of the Nelsons' wagon. The Belshaw and Nelson youngsters were busy devouring their meal, and didn't even look up, except for Clara.

"Mama, look who's here," the shrewish little girl squawked.

"Hush up, Clara, and eat your food," Harriet snapped, but

she directed a hostile frown at Martha.

"Good morning," Martha said as nonchalantly as she could, addressing the group, and sat down at the only place left: a small space between Hunter and Cornelius.

"I'm glad you're here," Hunter said tonelessly, not looking up from his plate, although his jaw tensed.

"You are?" She realized she sounded too hopeful before noticing all eyes were settled on her, and dropped her hands into her lap, feeling subdued by the censuring looks.

"Yes. Now I can announce to all of you that we won't be traveling today."

Martha's jaw dropped. He wasn't pleased to see her. He was just glad he wouldn't be forced to repeat himself. She turned her attention to her plate, trying not to show her disappointment. The man was a bundle of contradictions.

Hunter grabbed a second helping of bread and ate silently, considering Martha and Cornelius out of the corner of his eye.

Martha rose immediately after finishing her meal. She had to busy herself so her thoughts wouldn't keep straying to Hunter Brody.

"Miss Collins," he said stiffly. "I want to see you by the spring wagon in ten minutes."

She resented the sharp edge to his voice. Did he think he could simply announce that he wanted to see her and she would come running? Well, if he wanted to speak with her, he would have to seek her out. She had no intention of meekly complying with his every command, although her heart had thumped at the idea of seeing him alone.

"I'm afraid you'll have to wait," she said tersely. "I plan to worship with the others. Then I have chores to which I must attend. Perhaps later in the day."

The rest of the company looked up as if expecting Hunter Brody to unleash his fury and put Martha in her place. But when he merely grunted and left the table, hushed whispers passed through the group.

Hunter found Martha two hours later at the camel khan feeding dried apples to Humphrey. "So these are the chores you were talking about," he grated out, obviously annoyed by her priorities. "Have you forgotten that the food we have has to last all of us the entire trip." Although his voice was stern, he found himself admiring the kindness she showed, even to the animals.

"You needn't concern yourself." She looked down at the shriveled fruit. She used to like apples, but she'd eaten so many lately she didn't doubt that if she never saw another dried apple for the rest of her life she'd be content. She gave her shoulders a flippant shrug. "If we begin to run short of apples I'll simply do without."

Damn stubborn woman. "We'll see if you sing that same tune when you get hungry." Didn't she realize that a few dried apples could mean the difference between life or death out on the trail?

Why was he constantly trying to provoke her after the way he had kissed her? And why had he kissed her? Had he merely used her to satiate his animal lusts? Martha's pride suddenly felt as shriveled as the dried apple she held, for despite her fears, she found herself longing to feel and taste that full, sensual mouth of his.

She forced herself to ask, "What was it you wanted?"

"Since you're working for part of your passage, I brought my wash. You should have time to get it all done today while we're camped." Hunter dumped the huge bag of smelly laundry at her feet next to her own small bundle. "Pay extra attention to my white shirts, especially the white one with the mud stains."

Martha stood at the khan blankly staring at the bulky sack. He couldn't be serious, could he? Although she'd kept the agreement to wash his clothes and share the cooking chores, this batch looked like a month's worth of laundry—not his usual few items. She had her own clothes to wash, the bread to bake, and the supplies to air out before she would have any time to relax and write to her family or to make entries in her journal as she'd told her mother she would.

"When you're done, just put them with the rest of my things in the spring wagon."

"Is there anything else I can do for you today?" she said sarcastically, smarting from the matter-of-fact way he had just ordered her to do this enormous amount of laundry.

Hunter shrugged. "If I think of something else, I'll let you know."

"You do that."

"Don't worry, I will."

"I am sure you will."

Women! They always had to have the last word. Hunter shook his head and left her to look for Happy, confident he had given her enough to do to keep her busy and away from that damned Potter.

After Hunter was out of sight, she contemplated his behavior for a moment, then turned back to Humphrey. Men! They acted as if women were put on this earth to serve them.

Cornelius photographed Martha as she held out a large chunk of apple to the eager camel. That done, he asked, "Are you all right? I saw Hunter Brody leave. He did not upset you, did he?" Cornelius had seen the dark frown on Brody's face when he'd stalked off. He picked up his equipment and walked over to join her at the khan.

"I'm fine, but I'm afraid I won't have much time to spend with you today. I have Mr. Brody's wash to do as well as my own." Martha fed Humphrey the rest of the apple slices she'd brought, then bent down to retrieve Hunter's bundle.

"If you would like some company, I shall get my wash and join you."

"Your company is always welcome."

When Hunter saw Martha lugging the heavy bundles toward the section of the riverbank where there were enough nearby shrubs on which to spread the clothes out to dry, he quickly retraced his steps and relieved her of the load. Without a word he carried the bags to the water's edge before leaving again. With great effort, as Martha tried to decipher that small act of kindness in light of his previous behavior, she suppressed the temptation to toss Hunter's clothes into the current and watch the river carry them away.

By the time Cornelius joined her, Martha had three bushes

draped with Hunter's shirts.

Cornelius knelt down, rolled up his sleeves, and began scrubbing a shirt. "Oh dear, I seem to have forgotten the soap."

"This river has enough alkali in it to make soap," Martha observed, wiping perspiration from her brow.

"I understand that it has been done."

They both chuckled. Somehow, having someone to share a laugh with made the drudgery seem easier. After she finished scrubbing Hunter's things with a vengeance, Martha washed her own clothing while Cornelius kept her company.

She had just hung a blouse on what seemed to be the last available branch and was wiping her raw hands on her apron when she saw Hunter coming toward her, toting another bag.

Hunter nodded curtly to Cornelius, who was perched on a nearby rock, and looked around. "Good"—his voice thinly disguised traces of gratitude—"you're about done. It looks like you have time to do Happy's wash, too. He's busy tending the camels so I thought you could give him a hand." He looked at Martha's rough red hands.

Cornelius noted the way Hunter's eyes softened. He rubbed his chin. It was one of the few times he had seen the steel-hard wagon-train captain display the slightest feeling for anyone in the company.

"Here," Hunter took a jar of skin balm out of his pocket, "this might help. Put it on your face and arms as well as those hands. You've been getting a lot of sun lately and that little nose of yours is pretty pink."

Martha took the clothes and the balm, and Hunter seemed almost like an awkward schoolboy for a moment. Then a curtain dropped over his face as he took in the fact that Martha and Cornelius were together.

"Thank you." Martha was genuinely pleased to be shown yet another small act of kindness by this man. But she had to wonder about herself. Hunter Brody could make her so mad at one minute she could scream; then he'd do something thoughtful and she'd melt like snow on a hot day. What kind of fool was she, having these thoughts about someone brought up to behave so differently from what she had been taught to expect?

"Just don't waste the whole day down here. Harriet Belshaw told me to remind you that it's your turn to bake the bread." Hunter directed a disgruntled frown at Cornelius and, before Martha could reply, headed back toward camp, secretly wishing Potter hadn't ruined his plan to use Happy's wash as an excuse to spend time with the Collins woman.

"That man makes me furious." Martha stiffened, stung by Hunter's last remark.

Cornelius cocked his brow questioningly. "Yes, so I have noticed."

"I can hardly wait until this trip is over so I won't ever again have to see Hunter Brody."

"No doubt." Cornelius smiled grimly and rose to his feet. "I hope you will not be upset if I do not remain any longer. Since this seems to be one of the few days we may have without traveling I want to get some photographs showing how the rest of the company spends it. You know, children at play, women sewing, men mending broken harnesses, and especially Happy tending the camels. Someday, I have no doubt, the pictures of the camels will become collectors' items."

"Before you go, tell me, how much did you pay for your passage?" Martha could not deny her curiosity any longer. Cornelius did not have to work for his passage, other than driving the spring wagon. It would almost be worth giving Hunter Brody some extra money to unburden herself of some of her heavy load of her duties.

"Seventy-two dollars. Why?"

Martha's eyes saucered at the small amount, but she quickly hid her astonishment. "No particular reason." So Brody had charged her twice as much as the others after he'd found out she was a woman, and he was making her work harder than they did on top of it. Well, she'd see about that!

After Cornelius left her, Martha scrubbed Happy's clothes with stabbing rancor. But when she came to the funny-looking pants the little brown man wore, a purposeful smile curved her lips.

After she had finished with her chores for the day, Martha finally settled down with her journal, determined not to give in

67

to exhaustion until she had written an account of the trip's events.

> *Thursday, June 23, 1859—Continuing toward Ash Hollow. Although I would never presume to say this trip is an easy undertaking, I believe it could be a delightful journey if the company were more agreeable. When I look about me, I cannot help noticing how wild and untamed this country is. So much like my own feelings for a man I know so little about. . . .*

Martha put the cherished ledger down and closed her eyes. A strange sense of peace pervaded her each time she was able to describe her strains and stresses in the journal. Doing that seemed to provide an outlet for her frustrations, to cleanse her emotionally, and to renew and fortify her so she might face whatever lay ahead.

For two days they pushed on through blazing sunlight interspersed with drenching showers that lasted but a short time before the sun blazed hotter than ever. The number of trees dwindled to only the few on distant islands in the river, and as they crossed the wide prairie, Martha concentrated her attention on poppies, China asters, cactus, and the different kinds of straw-colored flowers.

She felt she was a spectacle in the strange outfit she had borrowed from Happy, but after Hunter Brody's remark about her trying to wear the pants, she didn't care. When she had returned Happy's wash, she'd asked him to loan her an outfit. He had laughed and had handed her a shirt, pants, and a turban. She remembered how she had grinned at thinking about what she was going to say to Hunter Brody the next time she saw him. Then, almost as if he had been reading her thoughts, Hunter joined her.

"Well, I see you've finally managed it."

"Wh-what?" she stammered, taken off guard by his pleasant drawl.

"You're wearing the pants." He laughed, but underneath he

would have liked nothing better than to remove them—personally . . . ardently. The thought heated his blood and left him squirming uncomfortably in the saddle. In his mind, he pictured Martha in a field of golden poppies, walking slowly toward him, her arms spread open, her lips slightly parted, inviting. When she reached him, she'd curl her arms around his neck, teasing him by placing those full ripe breasts against his bare chest. And he'd wrap her in his embrace, lifting her face to his and savoring the sweet, honeyed texture of her full sensuous mouth before they joined together on the warm earth. . . .

"Mr. Brody!"

Hunter blinked his eyes to bring himself back to the present. "Did you say something?"

"I said . . . I fully intend to continue wearing pants."

Hunter let his eyes openly glide over Martha's gently rounded curves. A wicked grin tugged at his lips.

At his appraisal, a fissure of heat broke through her resolve. "Just what do you think you're doing?"

"I was thinking that you remind me of something. But for the life of me, I can't think of what."

"Then don't let me detain you." Her outfit had not had the desired effect, and at the moment she wished he would leave before he noticed her reddened cheeks.

"Oh yes, I remember now."

Martha's spirits plummeted.

"You look just like one of those Egyptian mummies I saw in a museum while I was buying camels."

"I do not!" she burst out. "You just like to laugh when I get tangled up in my long skirts."

"Actually, I have to admit I like the new cut of your clothes. I wouldn't dream of suggesting that you go back to those loose, faded dresses the other women wear. And you've given those wagging tongues plenty to talk about for at least another week."

At first Martha wanted to turn her back on him and ride off; he made her so angry. Yet his words seemed to mean one thing, while his eyes said quite another. Martha tugged at the ankle-length pants which had ridden up past the top of her button

69

shoes. A tingling sensation radiated down her spine and her pulse quickened under his gaze.

"Oh, by the way, Mrs. Stewart and Miss Wakefield need some help with the cooking chores tonight. They have to lighten their wagon. I've no doubt they'll spend a lot of time stewing over that."

Of all the nerve! She did not want to seem uncharitable, but those two had been anything but kind. And she had paid more for the trip than the others. She had hoped to have her feet planted firmly on the ground when she had this conversation with him, but he was not going to treat her like a servant!

"I'm afraid they'll just have to manage without me."

Her refusal surprised him. But he had to admire her nerve. That old shrew Harriet Belshaw was right about one thing: Martha Collins certainly wasn't manageable! "Need I remind you that you're working for part of your passage?"

"Not anymore."

"What?"

"I thought I had made myself perfectly clear. I said—"

"I heard what you said. But the agreement included—"

It was Martha's turn to interrupt. "Did it also include that I pay twice as much as the rest of the company?"

"I didn't want you along," he snapped out before thinking.

Martha's expression showed she was hurt. Damn! Well, he hadn't wanted her along. A single woman traveling alone was nothing but trouble. Wasn't she proving that right now? Then he thought about the last month. He had given her a hard time, hoping she would admit she'd made a mistake and he could send her back with a returning train. But she had surprised him. She hadn't constantly complained like the rest of the women. She'd had enough guts to make decisions and stick to them. And she had just confronted him. He knew the others griped about him behind his back—they didn't understand the hardships of the trail, the need to keep moving—but they didn't have the gumption to voice their complaints to his face. Dammit! She was one hell of a woman!

After he thought about it for a minute longer, he realized he had come to expect that she would be there to step in and help out when the others had problems. He found he had been

70

letting himself depend on her, but he wasn't about to let her know it. He hadn't needed or wanted anyone's help since Dancing Wind had died. He wasn't going to start doing it now.

"I'm afraid I'm here. You'll just have to accept that fact. Since I paid more than the others for the passage, you can take my share of the work out of that." Martha's hands shook, and she clamped them into fists to keep them from trembling. Yet she wondered if she were trembling because of this confrontation and rebuff she expected or because of his nearness. Well, she wouldn't back down now. "And starting tomorrow I intend to ride in the wagon with Cornelius."

Hunter scowled at the ease with which she said that bumbling Easterner's first name when she continued to call him Mr. Brody. But no matter how it rankled, he had to look on the practical side. It was her money he'd used to have the horses shod back in Independence. If only he hadn't needed that damn money so badly.

Reluctantly, he accepted her decision.

Chapter Seven

Thursday, June 23, 1859—Heading toward Ash Hollow. I have found my conscience does not carry a heavy burden of guilt or remorse for standing up to our captain. Henceforth, I shall have more time to enjoy the trip and to contemplate my muddled state of mind. . . .

Hunter stared at the two women. He hadn't seen either of them look more worn out. Jannet Wakefield's mahogany tresses hung limply around her dirt-streaked face, and Cecilia Stewart hadn't fared much better. Her eyes were red from crying and her powder blue dress was smudged with dirt. His gaze trailed to the meager pile of pots and pans and bedding. Then he scratched his head in weary understanding. Women out here on the trail had a hard time of it when forced to leave behind their possessions, but it had to be done. He couldn't allow them to think he was soft or they'd manage to keep everything and would put the whole company in jeopardy.

He said firmly, "I suggest you two get busy and toss out some more of your belongings before I'm forced to do it for you."

"I declare, you wouldn't do such a thing, now would you? Those are the only things I have left of home," Cecilia wailed.

"Honey, I'm afraid he must." Derek Stewart straightened his suspenders and smiled sympathetically at his bride. "I know these are your treasures. But we have to think of the oxen and the hills ahead of us." He tried to soothe her as if she were a small child.

But Cecilia bridled. "Why, this is supposed to be my honeymoon and look at me. If only you hadn't been so proud and so determined to show Daddy how capable you are, we could have been sitting on a veranda and drinking a cool glass of lemonade right now, instead of heading to God knows where," she cried and ran into the wagon.

"Don't pay her any mind. She's not used to having to do without," Derek offered lamely. Then he hurried after his wife.

Jannet pouted. "I hope you're happy." She looked up to see her aunt standing near the wagon tongue, and immediately changed her tone to one of compassionate understanding. "But I know you have a difficult job, Mr. Brody."

Hunter ignored her attempts to ply him with feminine wiles. "Yeah, well, I have some more bad news for you, ladies. You'll have to take your turn with the cooking tonight."

Surprise rounded Jannet's eyes. "You mean Martha won't be doing it? Didn't you tell her how busy we are?" She frowned, thinking how much she'd hated Martha Collins ever since they were children.

"She knows." Hunter shrugged.

He started to leave, but Jannet grabbed his arm. "Mr. Brody . . . Hunter," she practically purred, "would you at least be so kind as to help me fetch the water?"

She stood looking up at him, her eyes as provocative as those of the best whores he had known. There was something about Jannet Wakefield and her aunt which bothered Hunter. Neither one fit the picture of an emigrant. Of course, neither did Martha Collins. Oh hell, he just didn't like helpless females; they always wanted to get their hooks into some poor unsuspecting man and drain him dry.

Without giving him a chance to say no, Jannet picked up a bucket and slid her arm through his.

With calculating eyes, Aunt Velina watched them stroll from camp, then she limped off in the opposite direction in search of some privacy. Some distance away, on the far side of a gently rolling knoll, the grouchy aunt bunched up her skirts, ripped off her hat, and sank to the ground.

*　　　*　　　*

"Now don't go workin' yourself into a lather," Winnie advised a pettish Jannet Wakefield.

"I have been calling—"

"Hollerin' your head off would be a bit more like it," the older woman declared.

Jannet glared at her. "As I was trying to say, I have been calling for my aunt. Where could that woman have gone?"

"Why didn't you just try askin' in the first place?" Winnie pointed south. "I saw her headin' over there, by that hill."

Jannet swished off, grumbling to herself. "If I have to do the cooking tonight that old bag can do her share. I will never forgive Papa for sending that unsociable witch in his place. He's going to get an earful as soon as I see him again."

At the top of the hill Jannet's mouth dropped open in shock. Then a strange grin twisted her lips. "Well, what do we have here, Mr. Clinton Marks all dressed up like my Aunt Velina?" She rested an elbow on one palm while rubbing her index finger across her mouth. "No beard. No wonder neither Martha nor I recognized you." How could she have been so easily deceived? Her eyes flashed with an evil spark as she stepped closer. "People back home always did think you were so handsome you were pretty." She looked him up and down. "Now I understand what they meant. Without that bit of pussy-willow fuzz hiding your face, why you'd attract any man. How long have you been dressing up in petticoats, Clinton?"

Clinton had been so deep in thought that he hadn't heard her approach. Startled at first, he gaped at the young woman, then quickly recovered himself and grabbed her ankle. Tumbling her to the ground beside him, he rolled on top of her and clamped a hurtful hand over her mouth.

His cold amber eyes held a threat not to be taken lightly. "I warn you, if you cry out I will squeeze the life out of that beautiful throat of yours, do you understand?"

Taken aback by this new side to the stuffy Clinton Marks, Jannet nodded her agreement. When he removed his hand, she shoved him off her and smoothed her lavender dress. "What are you doing, following Martha Collins?" Her hatred of Martha had blinded her thinking.

He thought fast, letting her acid comments about his

masculinity drop from his mind. Jannet had always been jealous of Martha. Perhaps he could use that to help him find the money he knew Jannet and her father had stolen from his bank. Blast! He'd never planned on having to travel this far dressed as a woman, let alone get away with it this long. Of course, the masquerade had been easy with everyone so busy trying to survive on the trail. But Jannet was more clever than her father. That weakling had confessed to everything but the location of the money right after Clinton had begun interrogating him.

"Do you think I would go to this much trouble if I were merely interested in Martha Collins?" He shrewdly drew Jannet out.

She arched her brow. What he said could be true. Everyone knew his first love was the bank. Still suspicious, she answered, "No."

"Your father told me how you two tricked that stupid teller. Poor old Simmons was so smitten by you that he didn't even miss the key to the bank that evening you had him lapping at your skirts."

"You can't prove a thing," Jannet snapped.

"Who says I'm trying to? I slaved at that bank a long time. Maybe I've decided it's time I get my share."

Jannet studied him. She could expose him, but then she might have to answer questions which could prove to be more damaging than embarrassing. He hadn't tried to arrest her. Maybe he was telling the truth about wanting part of the money. And it would do her heart good to have someone help her pin the blame on Martha Collins. With Clinton's help, Martha would never be able to prove her innocence. Jannet smiled cruelly, and remembered how, at her seventh birthday party, Martha had revealed that Jannet had stolen Nancy Cooke's locket.

"How about sharing some of what you gave scrawny old Simmons?" Clinton leered and groped beneath her skirts. Why shouldn't he enjoy this dumb bitch's favors until he could get her to tell him where she had hidden the money? When Jannet didn't protest, he unbuttoned her bodice and fastened his mouth on a soft, pointed breast.

She heaved a sigh, bored. "Oh, for heaven's sake, wait!" She pushed at his shoulders. "If we are going to have a good time"—she slipped out of her clothing and tugged at his until she was fondling his engorged member—"let's do it right."

Licking her lips, she settled back against the ground and spread her legs. . . .

Despite raised brows, Martha was riding with Cornelius now. She missed the sense of accomplishment she'd gotten from riding Humphrey. But she wasn't totally distressed. Since taking to the wagon, she'd had more time to write in her journal. She scribbled the last sentence and set her pencil down as the wagon dipped into a rut. Tears came to her eyes as she reread her last entry:

Saturday, June 25, 1859—Heading toward Court House Rock. I have been thinking of brother George and his family, safe and cozy back home. While I still do not regret my decision, sometimes I find myself dreaming of anything rather than bread, bacon, dried apples, and peaches. And oh, for a warm bath! But God has granted even the weakest of us perseverance out here. No doubt we shall all be the better for this trip. . . .

Happy had told her Humphrey had been most disagreeable since she'd left him to be tied to the other beasts. Maybe she would ride the camel again. Not every day. Cornelius had bundled his jacket, insisting that she use it as a cushion, and she almost felt guilty over the ease of the trip now. She squinted at a lone formation off to the left of the trail.

"Isn't it unusual?" she said, pointing at the high-rising granite and tapping Cornelius on the shoulder. "That must be Court House Rock."

"Do you suppose Mr. Brody would mind if we stopped so I could photograph it?"

"We paid for our passage. And for what I paid, I don't think he should mind if we rode over to it."

Cornelius looked at her questioningly, but pulled on the

76

reins. They left the road and traveled several miles before coming to the base of the giant rock formation that rose hundreds of feet in the air.

"It's magnificent," Martha breathed out, and she hopped out of the wagon to run her fingers along the jagged texture of the base. "It looks like a building with a dome on top of it."

Cornelius was getting his equipment out of the back of the wagon when he looked over his shoulder to see Martha standing with her hands on her hips, her head stretched back as she gazed up at the formidable landmark.

"Would you mind terribly if I rode back far enough to catch that pose and the top of the formation?"

Martha glanced around them. There was nothing for miles. Still, everything seemed all right, although it was a rather lonely spot and, though she hadn't seen anyone for some time, she'd had the strangest feeling that she was being watched. "No. But don't leave without me." She forced herself to disguise the hint of trepidation she felt.

"I would never do that to you." His eyes were serious; then he smiled. "Remember, hold that pose."

As Martha watched the wagon diminish in size, sand started to whirl about her. She had to hold on to her bonnet or risk losing it while she prayed Cornelius would hurry. By the time he returned, she could barely see five feet in front of her. She could not tell where the trail was, and refrained from asking Cornelius for fear he didn't know either. He urged the horses on at the slowest of paces. It seemed an eternity since they had left the wagon train, and Martha was certain they were lost when a silhouette of a man upon a horse appeared among the whipping sands.

"What the hell do you two think you're doing, Potter? Can't you follow a wagon? What do I have to do, tie a rope from the wagons to the horses?" Hunter's hat was pulled down nearly to the kerchief he wore over his mouth.

After sighing with relief at knowing that they were no longer lost, Martha couldn't help herself—she started to laugh.

"God dammit! What's so all-fired funny? I might not have found you. Or maybe you would have preferred it that way." Hunter was so infuriated his left cheek twitched.

Noting that Cornelius looked daunted, Martha started to laugh all the harder.

"No. No. It isn't that." She giggled. "It's you."

"Me?"

"Yes. You look like a bandit or a raccoon with a droopy hat."

"If I were a bandit, I can guarantee you wouldn't be sitting there laughing right now." No, he thought, you would be lying naked beneath me.

"Sorry." She giggled again.

Hunter was not amused. She could have been hurt. He might not have found her. When Jed Nelson had told him the spring wagon had turned off the road just before the sandstorm had started, Hunter had immediately left the train to search for her. It hadn't been the supplies the wagon train would have had to do without or Cornelius Potter which filled his thoughts. It was Martha. When he'd thought there was even the slightest possibility that he would never see her again, he'd ached inside. Now she was sitting next to that damn Easterner with his fancy suits and ruffled shirts, laughing at him. He would put a stop to that!

"Thanks to you two we've lost an afternoon's travel. The train had to camp near the bluffs about five miles ahead."

Cornelius hesitated under the scorching reprimand, but finally spoke up. "I am sorry. I am afraid it was my fault. Martha would never have dreamed of leaving the train. If there are to be any consequences, I should suffer them."

"Damn! If you had half a brain and could realize what you could've cost the train, I'd beat the hell out of you. But as it is, I think I'll have you ride my horse for a while. Then, if you pull another ignorant stunt like this, it'll only be you who's lost and not the supplies."

Martha sobered. That was the only thing Hunter was concerned about—the provisions. The thought made her boil. "It wasn't Cornelius's fault. I suggested we leave the trail."

"I should've known." Hunter glared at her.

"So, if there are to be consequences I'm the one who should suffer them."

"Martha—" Cornelius tried to shush her but it was already too late.

78

"If you were a man I'd . . . I'd—" Hunter stopped.

"You'd what?" Martha's chin jutted out.

"Nothing." Hunter just shook his head. How could he say he was glad she wasn't a man, that he wanted to take her in his arms and show her exactly what was on his mind?

"Does this mean I'll be riding Humphrey again?" Martha fully expected to be isolated. And maybe she did deserve it this time. She hadn't realized that such an innocent excursion could have such far-reaching repercussions.

"At this moment, no. It means that you're going to ride with me, where I can keep an eye on you." Hunter dismounted and tied his horse to the back of the wagon. He then walked around to Martha's side of it. "Move over and give me those goddamned reins, Potter!"

By the time they reached camp the sandstorm had died down and the sky to the west was a fading orange glow. The children were engaged in a lively game of tag, but the adults were seated around a campfire; the women chatting and doing mending, Mrs. Belshaw holding little Gerturde; the men whittling and smoking. Even Happy was there, sitting cross-legged next to poor puny William Belshaw and his upended jug.

When Jannet caught sight of Hunter she sprang to her feet and hurried to his side. "I'm so happy you're all right. I . . . we"—she paused to lower her lashes—"were worried sick that something could've happened to you."

Jannet completely ignored Martha and Cornelius, which annoyed Martha beyond words.

"Now you just come right over here by the fire and let me pour you a hot cup of coffee." Jannet tugged on Hunter's sleeve and led him over toward the wagons.

Cornelius helped Martha down. "I shall take care of the horses. Why not join the others and get something to take the chill off. It's getting downright cold out here."

"You're very kind. But I think I'll get my tent set up first." She ventured a glance at Jannet and Hunter. Why did seeing them together bother her so?

Martha unloaded the canvas from the spring wagon and carefully avoided the scolding glares directed at her while she struggled with the tent. Though thirst plagued her and even bread and bacon sounded good, she forced herself to wait until Cornelius was through unhitching the team. She did not want to face those accusing eyes alone. She dipped her head. What was she thinking? Was she beginning to depend on Cornelius? Or could it be something more than that? He was kind. And protective. And thoughtful. He was her constant companion. Could a woman expect more? Hunter had aroused emotions she didn't understand—emotions she had been taught no good Christian woman should feel. She shook her head. Somehow she had to force herself to stop thinking about Hunter Brody. She dug a shawl out of her bag and wrapped it around her as Cornelius, now finished with the horses, came to join her.

He held out his hand. "Shall we face them together?"

"Look!" Martha heard Harriet Belshaw exclaim as they approached, and Martha's heart started to pound. That woman was going to see her crucified before the trip was over. But she noticed that Harriet Belshaw was pointing past her. "What kind of birds are those circling over there?"

"They're turkeys," Hunter answered indifferently, and took a sip of coffee.

"They do resemble our turkeys back home," Harriet said with a tinge of confused excitement.

"Except turkeys can't fly like that," Martha mumbled to herself. She wondered if Hunter was up to something.

"I'm so tired of bacon, fresh meat would taste good. Couldn't you shoot one for us? We can stuff it just like at Thanksgiving." Harriet clasped her hands together in mouth-watering anticipation.

"You promise to eat it if I shoot one?" Hunter drawled.

"Of course. What kind of a silly question is that?" Harriet retorted.

"What's that they're flying over?" Williams Belshaw asked, noting the mound beneath the birds.

"A dead carcass of some animal, I reckon. What would you expect turkey buzzards to fly over?"

Everyone started to laugh.

"As God is my witness, you cannot find it in that black heart of yours to be civil to anyone, can you?" Near tears, Harriet stomped back to her wagon.

"Damn! What did I say now? All I did was tell her what she wanted to know. What more does she expect?" Hunter remained so straight-faced that Martha wasn't sure whether he had been leading Harriet on or not. But at least he had drawn attention away from her own transgression.

And it was the second time Harriet Belshaw had received her just due. Maybe someone was looking out for Martha, after all. She looked upward, then suddenly realized that Happy had been responsible for setting the camels upon Harriet weeks ago. She glanced over at the little man. He was sitting quietly. Yet there was a pleased look on his face.

"You didn't have anything to do with what just happened to Mrs. Belshaw, did you?" Martha whispered to the brown-skinned little man.

"Missy, I no control boss man." He grinned impishly and cast a glance in the direction of the camels. "I no control."

"True. But what about when the camels chased her? You do manage them quite well."

"Some say I work magic. Is old Islamic saying: camel's proud ways and nasty temper come from fact that camel alone know hundred names of Allah. Man know only ninety-nine. It true. Camels have own minds, Missy. I give them good push sometimes. Good push."

Martha smiled to herself. She had wondered what had made the camel take off after Harriet Belshaw a couple of weeks ago. Although Happy would never openly admit to his part in it, there was now no doubt in her mind that he had had a hand in the incident. And Hunter had surely just saved her from another of Harriet Belshaw's scalding lectures.

She watched quietly as the children were rounded up to be fed early. Winnie Nelson looked so tired and haggard that Martha left her place around the fire to give the older woman a hand.

"I'm grateful to you, gal. I was hopin' Lucy would be more help. But for all her eight years she moves like a snail. Such a slow child." Winnie sighed. "Like I told you, me and Jed been worryin' that she won't never speak again." She was repeating herself, but Martha listened intently since it seemed to give Winnie a small measure of solace to have someone share her

81

sorrow. "Lucy, get over here," Winnie hollered.

"Even if Lucy is slow, she's a delightful child. I'd be proud to call her my own." Martha noticed Lucy wring her long reddish pigtails as she shuffled toward them, and her heart went out to the girl. To the world, a chicken meant nothing. But to little Lucy, who was locked into a nightmare of tortured silence, that silly hen had to have been a beloved companion.

"Don't go gettin' me wrong. We wouldn't trade the child. We just worry 'bout her." Winnie turned delving eyes on Martha. "But what about you? You're ripe for havin' babes of your own, and I've watched you with the younguns. You'd be a good ma. What you waitin' for? And why the devil are you traveling alone across the country? Weren't there no good men back where you come from?"

Martha blushed right down to her toes. She wanted to marry eventually, to have children of her own and a home. But how could she explain to Winnie that this trip was her dream? "There are plenty of good men back in New York. I was even engaged once," she blurted out before realizing what she had said.

"Then why ain't you married, gal?" Winnie pressed on, not the least bit shy about questioning her.

"It's hard to explain," Martha hedged, hoping for a reprieve. It was not to come.

"Why don't you just spit it out? I ain't goin' to think nothin' bad 'bout you, gal, no matter what your reasonin'." Winnie placed an understanding hand on Martha's shoulder.

All the pent-up feelings began to pour from Martha. It was such a relief to have another woman to talk to that she told Winnie about her dream and about Clinton. She even described her awakening emotions and went so far as to ask if good Christian women had such wanton feelings. But she stopped just short of telling Winnie about Cornelius and Hunter.

Winnie's eyes were sympathetic, and her voice softened. "Look gal, there ain't nothin' unchristian 'bout women gettin' a hankerin' for their menfolk. It's 'bout as natural as expectin' the sun to come up in the mornin'. Women want and enjoy the lovin' as much as their men. And don't you go lettin' no one tell you no different."

Martha was feeling better than she had since Hunter had kissed her and then pushed her away, until she looked up and saw Jannet practically draped over his arm. They were strolling from camp. Jannet was coyly laughing at something Hunter had said; Hunter was grinning. He looked like he'd fallen under Jannet's spell. As far back as Martha could remember, Jannet had taken an interest in anyone who had paid any attention to Martha. And Jannet was an enchantress. She had even developed a sudden interest in Clinton after he'd begun calling on Martha. No matter how hard Martha tried to convince herself that what Hunter Brody did didn't matter to her in the slightest, she felt a stab of envy. She averted her eyes.

"Like I was sayin', gal, it's natural for a woman to get a hankerin' for a man who catches her eye. If I was you I'd keep that in mind. It looks like that pretty Miss Jannet Wakefield knows it well enough. I wouldn't let no one outdo me if there was someone who caught my fancy." Winnie raised a brow pointedly, and let her gaze shift to Hunter and Jannet.

Chapter Eight

*Friday, July 1, 1859—Heading toward Fort Laramie. I
have so much to learn about this magnificent country. It can
be given to such cruel whims as surely as Man. And it is not
always as forgiving. It offers some so much, others so little. I
find that I know less about human nature than I ever realized
before beginning this journey. But my traveling companions
provide many insights into a way of life I know so little
of. . . .*

Since Cornelius had been forced to ride Hunter's horse after
Hunter had angrily come to fetch them from their side
excursion off the trail, Martha sat bone straight next to Hunter
on the spring wagon as it slowly followed the Stewarts'
Conestoga. Jannet smiled and often coyly waved a frilly
handkerchief at Hunter, and every once in a while, Martha
looked around the edge of her pink sunbonnet at him. He had
shaved off the whiskers from his chin. Without them, he
looked downright handsome. His jaw was set in a firm square
line. But he wasn't a mean man, she decided. It was just that he
must have had his share of disappointments in life, and he had
to be tough to survive out here.

"Would you mind if I asked you where you're from, Mr.
Brody?" Martha ventured, attempting to make conversation
and learn about him.

"No." She still refused to call him by his first name. Damn,
it rankled him.

She waited a reasonable length of time for him to answer. But she just couldn't let it drop. She had to know more about him. "Well?"

"If you're really interested, I'm originally from New Hampshire. My parents died when I was six. I was raised by the only family I had: two maiden aunts who saw to it that I was brought up properly in the Catholic Church. I don't know if you can understand what their idea of proper was, but as soon as I reached seventeen, Seth Nelson's age, I lit out of there so fast you'd've thought the sheriff was hot on my tail. I never went back."

Martha was astounded. Remembering what her brother George had been like at seventeen, she found it difficult to imagine Hunter making his own way at that age. "Where did you go? How did you live?"

He cocked a brow at her questions. She obviously had led a sheltered life. "I was a man by then. I headed west and became a trapper. Doesn't take much to learn how to do that, not if you've got good instincts."

"Didn't you ever want to settle down?"

"Are you asking me if I ever wanted to get married?" He gave her a suspicious glance, but she had lowered her eyes.

Martha blushed. She was curious but she didn't want him to think she was prying. "I suppose."

"I was married, but my wife died while she was carrying my unborn child." The loss was still painful for him, Martha noticed; for his jaw tightened.

"I'm sorry. I'm sure the doctor did all he could." She felt a genuine sympathy for his pain.

"She didn't have a doctor. She was Sioux—one of the buffalo people as some call them." He rigidly straightened his back, then, in order to close the subject, added, "Besides, it was a long time ago." If Martha was shocked she didn't show it, which made Hunter stare at her for a long moment. For some reason it hadn't been unbearably painful to share his past with this woman at his side.

She had heard of white men marrying Indians, but had always thought they would be as savage as the savages they'd married. She had so much more to learn about people than

85

she'd ever realized. The arrowhead hanging around his neck caught her eye. She had noticed it was made of bone. Of buffalo bone? Was it a memento from his deceased wife?

"This is my first venture away from family. I lost my father ten years ago. But I suppose I was lucky. My mother and older brother, George, provided a loving home."

"Yeah, well, I guess you were lucky."

Noting the uneasiness in his voice, she dropped her eyes and then turned her attention to the barren hills. But there wasn't much to look at, and the road was marked with holes and rocks the size of Texas. Although Martha tried to refocus her attention, her mind drifted back to thoughts of Hunter. He must have been devastated to lose his wife. And after having had such a difficult upbringing, too. His life had been so different from hers. She and her brother George had known only security and warmth as children. Funny how life had a way of giving so much to some while taking so much from others.

Hunter broke into her thoughts. "See that cloud of dust off in the distance . . . just below that big rock that looks like a pole?"

Martha scanned the landscape until she focused on the rock. "Yes."

"That's a herd of buffalo below Chimney Rock," he pointed out, as if trying to break the silence.

"Do you think we'll get a closer look at them?" Martha was excited, for she had heard stories of the vast numbers of buffalo which populated the plains.

Hunter was disturbed by her proximity. It was doing crazy things to his mind. He couldn't let that happen! "I'd say you will. And since there aren't any trees to be found near here, you can take a bag with you this afternoon, walk alongside the wagon, and pick up buffalo chips for firewood."

She wrinkled her nose. "You can't be serious?"

Three hours later, in spite of an earlier vow not to do any more chores after she'd discovered she'd been overcharged, Martha found herself gathering the dried patties and dropping them into a bag. It wasn't nearly as distasteful as she had imagined. She actually found herself laughing when Henry, Seth, Lucy, and even the six-year-olds, Barsina and Fuller, joined her and they had a grand contest going as to who could gather the most and the largest. The children had asked Clara to join them, but she turned up her little nose at the idea and stayed in the wagon playing with her dolls. When Martha looked up several times, she found Hunter intensely studying her; one time it seemed that he smiled faintly. Somehow she managed to conceal the clamorous feelings his gaze brought forth in her.

After they had set up camp for the night, Martha built a roaring fire with the chips. She was just putting beans in the kettle to cook when gunshots ricocheted through the twilight air and Henry Nelson's squeaky voice called out frantically. "Hurry! Hurry! I got me a skunk cornered. Help me before it gets me!"

Hunter rolled his eyes and grabbed his rifle. The Nelson lad was a nice boy, but at twelve he was still years away from being mature in judgment or appearance.

Jed Nelson and William Belshaw also heard the boy and came running. Jed with a club, William with a pan.

Martha ran after the men, worrying that the boy had been injured or sprayed as the familiar odor assaulted her nostrils. When she rounded a cluster of boulders, the men were practically rolling on the ground laughing at the stocky youth whose face was as red as his tattered shirt.

"This is Henry's skunk," roared Hunter, holding up a black and white lamb. "It must have wandered away from a passing herd. Good thing it's been weaned or it probably would've been dead by now." He smiled as if a thought had just popped into his head. "It'll make a tasty stew tonight."

A different idea came into Martha's mind. "Oh, no it won't." She snatched the lamb from Hunter.

Amazed that she'd simply reached out and grabbed the animal right out of his arms, Hunter made no attempt to reclaim the lamb.

Martha noticed the dead skunk lying half-hidden near the base of one of the boulders. She stepped over to the daunted

Henry and put her free arm around his shoulders. "It's all right. It was an honest mistake. The laugh is on them." She directed a quelling frown at Hunter. "If those grown men had taken a minute to use all the senses God gave them before being so quick to tease you, their noses would have told them you had a reason to be concerned." She pointed at the dead animal. "Now, let's get you back to camp."

Hunter's sharp retort halted their retreat. "And if Miss Collins had kept her nose where it belonged, she'd be home somewhere right now, using it to make sure she didn't burn the lamb stew." He couldn't stand it when anyone got the better of him.

She ignored his last remark, patted Henry's shoulder, and continued toward camp without looking back. She would not give Hunter the satisfaction of seeing that he had managed to rattle her.

Hunter was sorry the minute the words left his mouth. He hadn't meant to make her the brunt of his temper in front of those men. And if truth be known, whether he liked it or not, she was affecting him.

The minute Martha got back to camp, Henry rushed over to Seth to tell his story. So Martha marched right over to the Nelsons' wagon where Lucy was sitting quietly on the ground, wringing her braids and staring off into space. With the lamb still in her arms, Martha knelt down beside the soulful girl. "See what Henry found?" She held out her arms, the lamb struggling in them. "This poor baby lost its mommy and needs someone to take care of it. I know it's a lot to ask, but do you think you could help me with it?"

"Bah. Bah," the woolly critter bleated.

Lucy's hollow eyes slowly began to fill with the stirrings of life. Although no sound fell from her lips, she mouthed the lamb's cries and cuddled it to her breast.

"I have to go help with supper now. Thank you for taking it for me," Martha said quickly before tears exposed the mixture of sorrow and joy she felt at seeing the mute little girl's response. With quickened steps, she left Lucy rocking the lamb, which had settled itself on her lap.

A short distance away Winnie covered her quivering mouth

with both hands, watching the scene. She silently forced herself not to cry at the sight of her little one responding to the animal, and her misted eyes lifted toward the heavens. "Maybe there's hope, Lord," she whispered brokenly behind trembling palms. "Maybe there's hope." A single tear dampened her cheek.

Dark clouds were gathering, but the weather remained crisp and the wind was howling when they pulled out of camp shortly after dawn the next morning. The camels were unusually skittish, and Happy had his hands full trying to calm them.

"Strange." Martha hugged her heavy shawl around her. "The camels haven't acted like that before. You don't think they sense something is wrong, do you? You know, I've heard animals have a sixth sense about danger."

"Which sense do you suppose they're using? Their sense of smell?" Hunter grunted. But even as he did so, the sweet fragrance of lilac soap she had used to wash with captured his senses and sent disturbing heat waves throughout his body.

"You never forget anything, do you?" She sighed, thinking about the skunk incident, and the disgusted frown he had given her when he'd learned they would be eating beans for supper. But she admired him, too. When he'd seen the effect the lamb had had on Lucy, he'd kept his tongue.

How could she be so strong and yet so sensitive at the same time? he thought. "They're just strange beasts," he muttered, and snapped the reins over the backs of the horses. As he bundled his coat around himself, he noticed Martha's teeth were chattering. He leaned down and pulled a blanket out from under the seat. Patting the space next to him, he said, "Move over here, closer to me."

A hazy warmth crept through Martha at the suggestion that she sit so close to Hunter. She hesitated briefly, but the day was cold. Soon, her body trembling, she scooted over until she was no more than two inches from him. Hunter reached out and pulled her up against him.

"You need to be next to me so we can both share the

blanket." He spread the wrap around her and left his arm draped over her shoulders. He had been out here plenty of times when it was colder and hadn't needed a blanket. Was he merely looking for an excuse to have her by his side?

His touch was gentle, yet firm like Hunter Brody himself. As Martha felt the heat of his fingers, she shuddered and when the muscles in his thigh tensed, she held her breath.

Hunter looked over at her. He was sure the blood in his veins had warmed by twenty degrees, and his body was beginning to throb with mushrooming desire. Damn! Why was it that a woman could hide her passion behind a quiet façade, while a man's desire was all too plainly visible? He felt his need to taste all of Martha rising. He wished he could take her right in the back of the wagon. But she wasn't that kind of woman. It made him feel as if he were going crazy. Why could Martha Collins do that to him? Jannet Wakefield had practically thrown herself at him the night before, yet when he could have eased his need, he'd held himself back.

Jannet had pestered him, pleading that she had to stretch her legs and was scared to go outside the confines of the camp alone, until he'd grudgingly agreed to escort her. Then, once they were away from the wagons, she'd turned to face him.

"You really are a handsome, virile man. I feel so safe out here with you," she said. Then she slid creamy white arms around his neck, letting her cape drop to the ground to expose the luscious mounds of her breasts, touches of puckered coral peeking out from the top of her low-stitched, lavender dress. Her head dropped backward until her hungry eyes devoured him. "Did you notice that big old moon up there?" she asked in a sultry voice. "Some people would say that's a lover's moon. Do you think that's true, Hunter?" Jannet seductively rubbed her hips against him and nibbled at his neck.

"Does your aunt know where you are?" Hunter nearly choked at the young woman's brazen efforts to seduce him. She was like a crawfish that had got hold of a hunk of bacon and wouldn't let go, the way she was wrapped around him.

"What difference does it make?" she purred, and let her hand slide down his chest to shamelessly cup his manhood. "The old sourpuss wouldn't care anyway." Why shouldn't she

90

have both men? And it would be such a coup over Martha to have this one. "Your body is telling me that you're affected the same way I am." She giggled wickedly. "I can feel it throbbing against my fingers." She ran her tongue seductively across her lips. "Wouldn't you like me to show you exactly how I feel?"

She was a nice piece of baggage. No one could deny that. Certainly put together well. But she was no more than a common whore, the only difference being she wore the cloak of respectability. She was trying to force herself on him, and the ache in his pants reminded him that he hadn't had a woman since they'd left Independence. He looked down at Jannet. She was just a little too obvious. Was she trying to prove something to Martha, the way she had been so friendly whenever Martha was near him? Whatever it was, he had no intention of being a party to it.

"I'm not in the market. Even if I were, you wouldn't interest me," Hunter said blandly, pushing her away from him.

Jannet looked totally shocked at the implication that she was selling her favors. Why that would make her a . . . a whore. None of the others had ever declined her offers. But she recovered quickly, throwing out her chin. "You poor sonofabitch. You don't know what you're missing. Martha Collins isn't half the woman I am."

"Maybe . . . maybe not. But I'm sure there are a lot of men out there who know plenty about what kind of a woman you are."

She seethed. "Damn you! Damn you to hell!" Whirling about in her dainty slippers, Jannet stomped back to camp.

"Humph. Such a sweet young thing." He shook his head and slowly followed her toward the wagons. . . .

The wagon hit a rock, jarring Hunter back to the present with a sudden jerk. Silently he gave thanks that he hadn't missed the chunk of granite, for it had jolted Martha's body even tighter up against his.

Ill at ease, Martha wriggled away from the heat of Hunter's thigh. Sitting so close to him, his arm around her, was almost more than she could endure. Her mind whirred with uncensored pictures of him taking her into his arms, kissing and caressing her.

"Martha, I'm not going to bite you. It's cold out here, with no other way to keep warm but to share our body heat."

"I suppose you're right." She moved back against him and forced herself to relax.

Hunter had insisted on traveling without a stop for lunch that day, pointing out the darkening sky, and as they neared the river crossing Martha's head began to nod. After seeing the way Jannet had come back into camp the past night followed by Hunter, she hadn't been able to sleep. Now, unable to fight her drowsiness any longer, she cuddled into the warmth of Hunter's shoulder and leaned her head on his chest. She could feel his heartbeat increase its pace against her ear; her heart joined the race with his.

Hunter nuzzled his chin against the top of her head. She was asleep, secure enough to snuggle next to him. The thought generated a protective instinct in him. He raised his arm and let it drape around her again. Damn. It felt so right to have her tucked into the crook of it.

Cornelius rode back from the ferry to the spring wagon. "Mr. Brody, Happy told me to inform you that the ferry man wants ten dollars to cross the camels. What do you want done?" His eyes flashed at seeing Martha wrapped in a blanket next to Hunter, rubbing the sleep from her eyes.

Hunter took out his money clip and thumbed through its contents. He frowned at the few bills, then slid the clasp and cash inside a leather pouch which he slipped back into his belt. "Tell Happy we'll swim them across."

"If I am not being presumptuous, why are we crossing to the south side of the river? The water looks rather treacherous and the wind is chopping it up."

"Yeah, well, you are being presumptuous. Just go give Happy my message."

Martha sat up straight. "Maybe you should listen to Cornelius. It does look as if could begin to storm at any minute," she observed.

"If I wanted your opinion, I'd ask for it," Hunter grumbled, and removed his arm. He wasn't about to let on that his poor financial position forced him to ford the river whether he wanted to or not.

92

Martha's face looked stricken. How could he be so thoughtful one minute and the next act as if she were some bothersome insect? She jumped out of the wagon and said shortly, "While you talk to Happy, I'll go tell the others the wagons need to be unloaded so they can be floated across."

The minute Martha was gone Hunter regretted the way he had snapped at her. He tried to remind himself that she had been dishonest with him. But, after watching her for over a month, he was sure she must have had a reason. No matter how hard he fought against it he was becoming more deeply enmeshed in unmanageable feelings for her.

He forced her from his thoughts. He had a responsibility to fulfill. The road on the north side of the Platte was nearly impassable, with next to no grass for the animals. The bunch of greenhorns he was taking across country would never hold up under such tough conditions. With that thought in mind, he drove the wagon along the riverbank until he found what looked like the best place to cross.

"I'm sick and tired of unloading and reloading the wagon," Harriet Belshaw wailed in response to Martha's news. "The river doesn't look very deep to me. We can make it without going to so much trouble," she asserted.

"I think Mr. Brody will insist that you take everything out of your wagon." Martha tried to reason with the woman. "Everyone I've seen ford a river since we started this journey sent their possessions across on a ferry or floated them over on a lighter wagon."

Harriet Belshaw dropped her fists onto her hips, and set her lips in a rigid line. "Go tend to your own trunk, you hussy."

Stung, Martha backed away from the woman's cruel tongue and went to join the Nelsons who were nearly ready to cross.

She leaned against their wagon and blindly stared at the camels being driven into the water. Was she making a fool of herself over Hunter Brody? Was Harriet Belshaw aware of some flaw Martha feared to acknowledge?

After crossing the camels and the Stewarts' wagon, Hunter and Happy forced the horses to draw the spring wagon loaded with everyone's possessions back and forth across the river several times. Then, to lighten the load in the Belshaw's wagon, he motioned for Harriet Belshaw and the children and Cornelius to get into the spring wagon, and he took them across. Next he took the Nelsons' wagon, carrying the Nelson family and Martha, into the river. But the wheels slipped over the rocks on the bottom and the animals lost their footing, refusing to go any farther until Hunter took a whip to them. Martha swallowed her screams when the wagon suddenly tilted, not wanting the others to see her fear. She grabbed Barsina and held the little girl on her lap in an effort to soothe the frightened child's tears. Hunter was drenched to the bone, and water had spilled over the sides of the wagon, soaking Martha's shoes and the bottom of her skirt by the time they reached the other side.

As Hunter made the final trip back across the river for the Belshaws' wagon, it started to rain. William Belshaw looked more pale than usual as he whipped the oxen into the choppy water. Wind whistled through the wagon's canvas cover, and rain now poured down in blinding sheets. Lightning flashed immediately before a loud rumble of thunder rolled over the sky like cannon fire and spooked the animals. Hunter fought to hold the panicked oxen, but they began pulling in different directions, sending him beneath the swirling surface of the angry river.

Martha screamed and covered her mouth, watching in terror as the wagon rocked and turned to a forty-five degree angle to the bank. Animals and wagon were being drawn backward by the raging current. Hunter came back to the surface sputtering. He lashed out at the water, fighting to reach the crippled Conestoga.

"Oh, my God! Help me, Brody! Help me! I'm going to die!" William Belshaw screamed just before a wave washed over the side of the wagon.

The man was almost hysterical and Hunter made a futile attempt to reach him. "Damn you, Belshaw! Get a hold of yourself and listen to me!" Hunter shouted for all he was worth. "Grab the reins, man! Keep your head!"

The big slug of whiskey William Belshaw had downed just before taking his seat on the wagon had not helped buoy his frayed nerves. He was past listening, and failed to heed

Hunter's instructions. The frantic man lost his balance and clawed at the wagon as he was thrown into the churning water, crying and screaming like a child. Hunter reached out to him, but Belshaw disappeared, going under the surface just inches from Hunter's grasp. Seconds later—they seemed like hours—when William Belshaw bobbed to the surface; a grisly gash ran down the left side of his contorted face.

While the others helplessly watched from the shore, Harriet Belshaw bellowed her agony and tried to jump into the river, but she was held back by Cornelius and Derek. "Hunter Brody," she screeched, "you're murdering my husband! You're murdering him! God will strike you dead for your sin!"

Hunter heard the hysterical woman's wild accusations, but continued to fight to save the drowning man.

Unable to stand helplessly by and watch the horrifying scene, Martha raced toward the camels tied nearby. Humphrey immediately perked up his ears at the sound of her voice. She did not think of the consequences when her fingers frantically tugged the rope free from his neck.

"Down! Down!" she ordered and jumped on the beast's back, straddling the hump the best she could.

The camel seemed to sense the dire urgency of the situation and forged ahead without hesitation.

"No! No! Missy, you stop. You be killed. You stop!" Happy yelled, waving his arms, as Martha sped past the others and drove the animal into the water, ignoring their horror-struck faces.

The camel did not panic. It swam directly toward the frantically struggling man. Martha courageously clung to the reins, fighting to remain atop the beast and reach William Belshaw before it was too late. Although she hadn't the faintest idea how she was going to rescue him when she did reach him, a greater force seemed to be directing her actions and she managed to lean out and grab him by the collar.

Though she couldn't hold on to him, the gesture seemed to bring William Belshaw back to his senses. He clutched desperately at the camel's long neck, and locked his arms around it. Martha tugged the reins in the direction of the bank. But as Humphrey ploughed through the water, she was swept off the camel's back and into the dark churning swirls.

Hunter cursed Martha's foolish heroism. If that idiot Belshaw hadn't panicked they wouldn't be in this mess now. He doggedly sliced through the icy water, determined to overtake her. His heart pumped furiously, sending a surge of strength through him. She couldn't give up and let the river claim her before he got there, she just couldn't! Martha was flailing her arms in an effort to swim toward the bank, but the weight of her long skirt was drawing her under.

Superhuman power seemed to drive Hunter on until he reached her and threw an arm around her waist, attempting to keep her afloat until they could reach the wagon, which was closer to them than the shore.

"Come on, you can make it," he choked out, swallowing some of the angry slapping water.

He managed to scramble onto the seat, pulled Martha up with him, and gained control of the team. She looked like a half-drowned prairie dog as she sat next to him curled into a tight little ball. She appeared to be nearly in shock, her lips were blue from the cold, her body was trembling.

Hunter studied her for a moment. This woman and water, he thought, then sighed to himself, wondering why she always seemed to do something to his insides. She was trying to smooth her dripping dress, fighting for all she was worth to hold back tears. She needed to be turned over his knee for pulling such a dumb stunt. But she was distraught, yet so intent on appearing calm, he made an effort to cheer her instead.

"If you're worried about what you look like, look at old Belshaw." Hunter grinned and pointed in the direction of the shore.

As he fought to drive the team toward dry land, he watched William Belshaw whose arms were clamped around the camel's long neck. The drenched pair were emerging from the water, the camel dragging the man that hung between its legs. Belshaw was a comical sight, soaked to the bone, his lean frame limply dangling from the jaunty beast like a cooked noodle.

Happy and Jed Nelson ran to the sorry duo. Happy held the camel while Jed pried William Belshaw's fingers open so they could get him into the Stewarts' wagon. As they fought to release him, Cornelius calmly finished setting up his camera equipment.

"Hold that pose." He called, and took a picture of a camel that seemed to be posturing for the camera, two very surprised men who stood stiffly and one embarrassed man slumped from exhaustion.

"You can at least be glad you're not on shore or that damned Potter would probably be taking your picture, too," Hunter said in an attempt to take Martha's attention away from their peril.

She couldn't help but smile at Humphrey who was now flanked by the four men. They had managed to free the camel of its clinging burden and were helping an unsteady William Belshaw toward the wagon when the camel suddenly stretched out its head and rolled its lips back into what looked like an impish smile. Then Humphrey gave a snort and bit the drooping Belshaw in the seat of the pants before haughtily sauntering over to join his own kind. Happy was right behind the camel, his tongue rattling off a rapid speech which no one could understand. Martha leaned her face into Hunter's shoulder, and began to laugh and cry simultaneously over the animal's antics.

Hunter had to fight for every inch of ground they gained toward shore, or he would gladly have cradled Martha's soft body against him. Instead he said, "You don't have to be afraid anymore, it's almost all over now. And look, even Lucy and her lamb are standing at the edge of the water waiting for you."

It was only drizzling when Martha looked up, tears cascading down her cheeks. "I'm not afraid. I'm laughing at Humphrey and Happy."

"Women! You could've gotten us both killed and now you sit here next to me laughing."

Martha grew pensive. Sometimes she was sure men had no understanding at all of women's feelings. She wasn't going to say that, but she didn't want him to think she was making light of a life-threatening situation. Somewhat subdued, she said, "If I didn't laugh I would probably start to cry. Hunter?"

"Yeah, well, what?" If anything could have knocked him off

the wagon seat, it was Martha Collins calling him by his first name.

"Thank you for saving my life," she said softly just before the wagon pitched violently to the right.

Martha's sobering words gave Hunter something to think about. She was a woman of many facets, each one more intriguing, if not more incomprehensible, than the next.

Nearly a half-hour later, wet and bedraggled, Hunter brought the wagon to shore almost a mile downriver. The canvas had been torn off and few of Harriet Belshaw's treasured possessions were left inside.

Still panting, he helped Martha down, then turned the wagon over to Jed Nelson, who had led the company along the riverbank as Hunter had fought to save the Belshaws' remaining belongings. "See that Miss Collins gets something hot inside her. And help Happy get the camp set up. We'll stay here tonight."

"You could've murdered my husband!" Harriet Belshaw sprang from her husband's side in the Stewarts' wagon and attacked Hunter, clawing at him. "You and those awful beasts of yours could've been the death of him!" She glanced back over her shoulder at her husband, who was quietly rubbing his backside. A pitiful sob escaped her. "And now we've not only lost our store and home, but thanks to you, all our possessions as well."

She paused in her attack just long enough for Jed and Derek Stewart to drag her off Hunter, who stared in disbelief at the distraught woman. "Lady, you're lucky Martha Collins risked her neck for that damned-fool husband of yours. And if it weren't for one of *those awful beasts,* he undoubtedly would've drowned and you'd be continuing the trip as a widow."

As Harriet Belshaw stood speechless under Hunter's stinging retort, he motioned for Winnie Nelson. "Get Miss Collins wrapped up in a blanket and bring the medicine box or Belshaw's jug." He gave Harriet a disgusted frown. "Mrs. Belshaw needs a good stiff shot of something to set her mind straight." He looked at Martha, but his words were directed at Jed Nelson. "If anything else happens or you need me, I'll be

98

down by the ferry."

Winnie handed the neatly clad Jannet a blanket. "Get your smug behind out of that wagon and put this over Martha's shoulders. Then get her inside where she can get out of those wet clothes."

Jannet glowered and begrudgingly took the blanket, her slitted eyes shifting between Hunter's retreating back and Martha, who was silently watching him. A cunning glint flickered over her face as she loftily strolled over to Martha.

"Hunter Brody's a heartless devil." Jannet wrapped the blanket around Martha, feigning concern. "You don't know how lucky you are to be safe here with us instead of with that man. Why just last night after he politely asked me to accompany him on a short walk away from the wagons, he tried to take the worst kind of liberties. I was only saved because Aunt Velina started to worry and came looking for me, and the poor old soul lame with gout, too. I shudder to imagine what could have happened otherwise." Jannet's russet eyes saucered with childlike innocence as she spoke.

Hunter had kissed Martha twice without her consent, and she had seen the look on Jannet's face last night upon her return to the wagons moments before Hunter reappeared. Had he tried to take advantage of Jannet? Martha had to fight with herself while she listenened to the girl. She knew Jannet had been jealous of her since childhood, although she had never understood why. Surely Jannet wouldn't make something like that up, would she? If only she'd had enough money or had been able to secure a loan, then she wouldn't be on the same train with Jannet, and she wouldn't feel that she must keep her promise of silence to Jannet's father.

Martha fretted silently as Winnie shoved Jannet aside and took charge. "What you doin' standin' out here?" She gave Jannet a knowing scowl. "I told you to get Martha inside the wagon and changed before she catches her death." She trundled the soaked young woman away.

Martha obediently climbed into the wagon before Winnie, and the older woman helped her peel off her wet dress and slip into a blue checked cotton. Winnie then made Martha sit quietly while she rubbed her hair dry with some clean cloths.

"You was mighty lucky Mr. Brody fetched you out of that river."

"Yes, I know. It was a stupid thing to do. But I just couldn't stand by and watch Mr. Belshaw drown without trying to do something."

"Pity that witch Harriet Belshaw don't seem to appreciate it none."

"It must be terribly difficult at her age to be forced to leave your home."

"She let slip she's thirty-seven. Tarnation gal, Jed and me had to leave our wore-out farm in Ohio and make a new start, and we got more than a few years on her. That Harriet Belshaw's just mean as a billy goat and weak as a sucklin' pup."

As Winnie spoke, Martha thought about how she herself had felt toward Harriet Belshaw. But having more thoroughly considered that the woman had been forced to give up her home and way of life to make the difficult journey west—and with a husband given to drink—Martha had decided to attempt to arrive at a tolerant and understanding stance toward the Belshaw woman.

"She may not show it," Martha said of Harriet Belshaw, "but I'm sure there is goodness in her heart."

"Gal, that woman don't got no heart. And as for that pretty little Miss Jannet Wakefield, who keeps herself all gussied up all the time, you just mind my words, that one ain't near as helpless and innocent as she makes out."

"Jannet's just impulsive." Martha defended the girl because she knew Jannet had had a pampered life. After her mother had died when she was only five, her father had brought her north and had doted on the girl, never denying her anything. Maybe growing up without a mother had caused Jannet to act the way she did.

"Impulsive, maybe." Winnie shrugged. She'd had her say; the rest was out of her hands. "You just lay yourself down and rest 'til supper."

"But after what everyone has been through I should be out there helping," Martha protested.

"Nonsense. Try thinkin' of yourself for a change. I'll see that everyone gets set up and fed."

100

Grateful for Winnie's insistence, Martha settled back onto a pillow and almost immediately fell into an exhausted slumber.

The intensity of the storm was beginning to increase again after supper when Martha retired to her own sanctum, Happy's tent. Since the canvas on the Belshaws' wagon was shredded into a few tattered strips, Harriet Belshaw sent her children to sleep in the Nelsons' wagon after rudely declining Martha's offer to take Clara and Gertrude. The older Belshaws huddled inside the Stewarts' wagon, bemoaning their misfortune at being hooked up with the likes of Hunter Brody. A half-hour later Cornelius politely excused himself and withdrew to the tent Hunter was sharing with Happy. Cornelius had been sleeping under the Stewarts' wagon with Derek, but tonight was no time to be out in the weather, and he'd had enough of Harriet Belshaw's reviling of Hunter Brody.

When the wind whipped up and blew the ropes off the side of Martha's tent, she rushed out and tugged the cords down to the stakes, wrapping them securely before returning to her haven. Her dress soaked, Martha stripped for the second time that day and tossed the garment into a heap in the corner. Since she was alone, she decided there would be no harm in discarding her damp undergarments as well. After wrapping her wool shawl around her, she spread out an India-rubber cloth underneath her bedding and placed one over it to help protect her from the moisture, then climbed into bed. The steady beating of the rain soon lulled her to sleep.

Chapter Nine

After Hunter left the wagon train he made his way down to the old shambles of a shack which housed the big unshaven ferry men. Independence Smith and Platte Morgan, named for their places of birth like so many emigrants' children, were seated around a crude table, sharing a jug, when Hunter joined them.

"I heared you done almost lost one of them wagons of yours." With his shirt, Platte wiped the dust from a chipped cup before plunking it down in front of Hunter.

Independence upended the jug over the mug. "We saw a mighty lot of barrels floatin' by us."

Hunter rolled his eyes, remembering the near disaster. "After I got out in the middle of the river I discovered those damned fools hadn't unloaded their wagon. After their stupidity, it would've served them right to lose it. Hell, I barely managed to pull it out in one piece. Then the old bitch attacked me." Hunter lifted the cup and took a big slug of the homemade rotgut.

"Why do you look so glum? You didn't lose no one." Platte sloshed another round into the cups. "It's either gotta be a woman or money."

The three men chuckled, Hunter careful to mask any expression which might have demonstrated just how close to the truth Platte was. The whiskey flowed freely as Hunter led the burly men away from their much-too-astute observations by recalling shared experiences in a friendship that went back nearly ten years.

It was after midnight when Hunter staggered back into camp, an empty jug in one hand, a lantern in the other, wet as a fish. He tossed the jug aside and split open the flaps of his tent, only to be greeted by the grunts of two snoring men. He grumbled under his breath at the lack of space, the whiskey making him hazy about the switch in sleeping arrangements made weeks ago, he slogged through rain-splattered mud to Happy's tent. Once inside, he set the dim, flickering lantern behind him and stripped off his shirt.

Martha opened her eyes as the cold air rushed over her face, and rolled over toward the light. She was still half-asleep when she caught sight of the muscled torso silhouetted before the lantern. She did not have to look twice before she realized it could be the form of only one man: Hunter Brody.

"What are you doing in here?" Her heart started to skip beats as she took in the sight of him half-naked.

Hunter immediately ceased unbuttoning his pants and sobered. Before him, propped up on one elbow, was Martha Collins. Her bare, white shoulder was exposed over the top of a blanket which drooped diagonally across the top of her swelling breasts. Her thick brown hair, plaited in a heavy braid, rested on her shoulder and continued down her back. It was hair a man would delight in freeing so he might lose himself in those long brown waves. He stood and stared, unable to keep from drinking in such an incredibly desirable sight. Maybe it was that he had faced death that day and won, or maybe it was Harriet Belshaw's damning denunciation. But his nerves were raw, and his need for something he could not quite define kept him nailed to the spot.

"Hunter . . . Mr. Brody, I asked what you're doing in here?" Martha said shakily. She pulled the blanket up around her neck after realizing she had not put on a nightgown and was naked beneath the loose covering.

"What are you doing in here?" he said without thinking, and moved to the side so the light danced sensuously across his handsome face.

"If you'll recall, this was your suggestion." Martha swallowed with difficulty as she gazed at his wide shoulders and his chest which narrowed into a slender muscular waist. Even the grove of curly dark blond hair on his bronzed flesh seemed to form an inviting triangular pattern as it dropped from sight below partially unbuttoned pants.

"On a night like this you should be in the wagon with the rest of the women." He frowned.

"Well, I'm not. I'm here." She stiffened her backbone. He was not going to suddenly enter *her* sleeping quarters, in the middle of the night almost naked, and start grilling her. "I don't know what you're doing in here, but I must ask you to leave."

"I'm here because this is the only dry place with any room left, and I need to get some sleep."

"You'll have to find it . . . somewhere else." She tried to sound annoyed, but her voice quivered with emotion.

Without speaking again, he bent over and shucked off his boots and socks. He then slid his soggy denims down well-muscled legs and stepped out of them, tossing the dripping trousers outside the tent.

"What do you think you're doing now?" Martha's eyes widened. He was dressed only in his underclothes, and she could see the shadowy outline of his swelling manhood. She was intrigued and frightened at the same time. That most private spot between the top of her thighs throbbed wildly, and she felt a sudden rush of moisture there.

"I'm getting ready to go to bed so I can get some sleep." She choked. "N-no."

"You don't want to sleep?" He grinned and took a step toward her.

"No! I-I meant you can't stay here." She shrank back.

"I don't intend to argue. I'm too tired. Now move over." He knew what he should do. He should leave and sleep under one of the wagons. But his mind was being ruled by a stronger urge. Martha was more than he could resist. And even if he couldn't touch her, he felt an overpowering impulse to lie next to her and feel the soothing heat of her body. He knelt down and lifted the edge of one of the blankets.

"You can't do this. I won't allow you to treat me like Jannet, and we're not—"

"I wouldn't think of it, and we're not what?" He cocked a brow, his thoughts on Martha, not on what she had said about Jannet Wakefield.

She couldn't bring herself to say that she had seen him and Jannet Wakefield go off together or to tell him what Jannet had said. And, of course, she could never bring up the subject that only married people should find themselves together as they were right then. A man like Hunter Brody didn't live by the same rules as civilized people. Martha jumped up, the blanket haphazardly wrapped around her, and threw open the tent flap with her free hand. Rain and wind blew in in fierce gusts.

"You're going to get us both soaked." Hunter leaped up and grabbed the flap out of Martha's hand.

His sudden move startled her, and with both hands, she reached out for the flap to demand Hunter exit. The instant she let go of the blanket, it fell into a pile around her ankles.

Hunter turned to face her, fully prepared to disregard her protests and climb into bed. But the sight of her luscious curving body was more than any normal, healthy man could ignore. Before Martha could retrieve the blanket, he pulled her against him.

Thunder boomed, causing Martha to flinch closer into Hunter's embrace. The exquisite sensations of bare flesh against bare flesh flamed the entire length of her.

Hunter slowly ran his fingers along her shoulders, up the long column of her neck to cup her face. His penetrating hazel eyes and the heat from his body caused Martha to forget her nakedness, a hypnotic power drawing her to him as she helplessly returned his scorching gaze, and the feel of skin against naked skin electrified her senses. He bent his head and joined their lips.

Fighting to clear her mind, Martha knew she should get away from him. She considered herself strong enough to deal with most situations, but she had never in her life encountered anything like this. What was he doing to her? She was going West to teach, to fulfill her dream, not to become another one of Hunter Brody's willing victims. Her mind and her natural instincts engaged in a fierce battle as Hunter's lips and tongue led her toward a splendor she'd not known before.

And her mind ceased to protest her body's disloyalty as Hunter deepened their kiss. Her arms wound around his neck; her senses reveled in the sweet softness of his mouth, the graininess of his probing tongue which explored every moist crevice. Following his lead, hesitantly at first and then more boldly, Martha slipped her tongue between Hunter's lips in a celebration of sensations. He tasted of whiskey and tobacco, but to Martha his kiss was as intoxicating as the strongest wine she had ever drunk.

Without breaking the kiss, Hunter carried her to the bed and tenderly glided down upon it, his body coming to lie next to hers. When he stopped kissing her, he ran a finger over her lips, and his gaze delved deeply into her silently questioning, half-lidded eyes.

"If you want me to go, I will," he whispered into her ear.

"I should, but I don't," she answered hoarsely, now beyond the confines of social restraint.

"You're so special." He nibbled on her earlobe before slipping his tongue into her ear and gently blowing warm breath into it.

The sensations that aroused felt heavenly, and tiny hot ripples went through Martha's body, igniting a growing flame inside her. Following her natural instincts, she locked her fingers at the back of Hunter's head and pulled him to her.

He outlined her lips with his tongue. Then he kissed her eyes, the tip of her nose, and her chin before moving down to her throat. He savored the salty taste at the base of her neck and traversed her collarbone.

"What an inviting scar you have." He kissed the length of it—it ran along her shoulder, thin and red, and angled out from her collarbone.

"One of the rewards of being a tomboy as a child," she mumbled, enraptured by what he was doing to her.

He had never taken the time to go slowly with any woman before. But for some reason he knew it was important to sip her sweetness, giving as much as he took. Martha was touching him in ways that weren't just physical; she was touching him all the way to his central being. He knew he should stop this lunacy before it was too late, but he also knew it was already too late.

Before he dipped his head lower, their eyes radiated the silent consent which flows silkenly between lovers. They were swept up in a raging storm stronger than the one which howled around them, were caught in an undeniable urge older than time. Hunter cupped her breasts together while he traced a path to the glen between those incredibly soft globes. He nuzzled his face there, feeling deliriously swallowed up within the mounds.

Martha moaned her pleasure as her nipples darkened and peaked in response to his spiraling tongue. Hunger for him heightened her senses, and she stroked his shoulders as his chest hairs toyed with her stomach. His fingertips joined his tongue and twirled around her nipples and he applied equal attention to both breasts before circling them with long strokes and moving lower so he might slip his tongue into her navel.

At that moment Martha wanted nothing more than to offer him the same delights she was experiencing. She longed to run her hands all over him, to take his stiff maleness between her fingers and learn everything there was to know about him, but while her hunger for him grew, she worried that he would think her a wanton.

As if Hunter were aware of her desire to taste him, his remaining clothes seemed to drift from him before he returned his attention to the softly rounded curves of Martha's ripe body. One hand kneaded her breast, the other drew her palm to his lips. He kissed it, suckled each finger in turn, then guided her hand over his chest.

Martha's movements were shaky at first. His skin was not as soft as hers, and he had small scars on his chest and back. Through her fingers, a thousand sharpened nerves sent sensual messages to her brain as she delighted in the rough texture of him. What was happening to her? She was afire in the center of bubbling lava. She was drowning.

He lightly ran a hand over the inside of her thighs, parting them to allow him access to her most intimate feminine core. She gasped and tensed when his probing fingers caressed her most sensitive flesh.

Hunter immediately withdrew his hand. "Martha, I don't

107

want to hurt you. If you want, I'll stop. But you have to tell me before it's too late. Soon, there'll be no turning back." His voice was thick and husky with passion, and his eyes were dilated and heavy-lidded with desire.

Her mind spun. Her upbringing—everything she had been taught and had believed—demanded that she save her virginity for her wedding night. If they didn't stop now, would she be able to face herself again? To hold her head up? Would what Harriet Belshaw had been saying about her be true?

"Martha?" Hunter took her chin in his hand and looked directly into her silent pleading eyes. "Jesus!" He flung himself to the other side of the bed as if he had just been scorched. What had gotten into him? She wasn't his kind of woman. Why hadn't he left when he'd first seen her? Why had he been so persistent about remaining? Had he meant to have her all along? Self-disgust poking at him, he found his underwear and put it on, turning his back to her.

"Hunter?" Confused, she reached out to him.

"Go to sleep," he growled. His voice was gruff, but the reproof was meant for himself.

Shaking with embarrassment, Martha pulled the blanket up around her throat to hide her shame. She shrank into a protective ball, faced the wall of the tent, and quietly sobbed until she finally fell into a troubled sleep.

Hunter blew out the lantern. He took one of the blankets and moved to the other side of the small shelter, listening to the rain which seemed to be loudly beating its disapproval on the canvas. Damn! He'd never experienced the slightest guilt before when he'd been with a woman. Now he felt lower than a vermin-riddled coyote.

Just before dawn, after the storm had passed, he opened the flap and began to grope about for the trousers he had tossed outside the tent hours earlier.

"These what you lookin' for?" Winnie, one hand on her hip, the other holding out Hunter's wet pants, frowned at him.

"Yeah."

"Looks like there might oughta be a weddin' out here soon." She cocked a bushy gray brow. "I do hope you was plannin' to get hitched." She pointed an accusing finger toward the tent.

"That one in there ain't cut from the same cloth as that Wakefield gal. Martha's the kind one marries, not beds, then moves on."

Her candidness disarmed Hunter. "If you're thinking I . . . ah . . . we . . . I mean . . . we didn't . . ." For the first time since he'd run away from home he felt like an awkward little boy caught stealing a jar of preserves from the pantry. "Damn it! There's no reason to marry her," he barked. Ripping his pants out of Winnie's hand, he stormed off in the direction of the camels.

Winnie watched Hunter stalk away, stumbling as he jammed his legs into the soggy trousers. His reactions were real enough to be honest. She was beginning to think she had been too quick to judge him until she stepped inside the tent and caught sight of Martha. The young woman was sitting upright, trying to cover herself, her eyes big and red, her hand covering a trembling chin.

Winnie's lips stretched into a tight line. "Why that no-account—"

"Winnie, it's not what you think." Martha sniffled, determined not to break into tears.

"Now gal, I don't think nothing' 'cept that Mr. Brody is goin' to do right by you. Get yourself dressed. The others will be stirrin' soon and you don't want them to suspect nothing." She pulled the blanket out of Martha's hands, ending any doubts she might have had about the coupling.

Martha was naked, and although she was innocent, words of denial stuck in her throat. How could she tell the woman that Hunter hadn't done anything she hadn't wanted him to do? She had been the one unable to ask him to stop. She might be innocent of sleeping with him as man and wife, but she was as guilty as any of those wanton women who worked in the saloons down by the river back in her hometown.

Winnie rummaged through Martha's bag and pulled out a red calico dress. "You put this one on. It's the Fourth of July and we're goin' to celebrate tonight regardless of the weather and the fact that we're out in the middle of this godforsaken country."

Martha sucked in her breath at Winnie's words. Did the

older woman mean that her actions last night would cause God to forsake them all? Winnie was one of her few friends. Quietly, Martha prayed that this woman wouldn't start to look down on her like the others.

"I'll be gettin' breakfast. Join me when you're dressed. It'll help take your mind off your troubles."

Martha breathed a sigh of relief. Winnie wasn't judging her. Obediently she put the red dress on and went out to the fire to give her a hand. The Stewarts' wagon was quiet; only the Nelson family was up. Martha again breathed a sigh of relief when fifteen minutes later she saw Cornelius and Happy come out of Hunter's tent, obviously just rising. Her reprieve ended when she noticed Hunter, his jaw stiff and rigid, a scowl on his face. He must hate her. She averted her eyes and poured a cup of coffee, so full she had to lean over and take a sip so she could pick up the mug without spilling it.

Hunter spoke to Happy, briefly, and then as the rest of the company was heading toward the fire to get their breakfast of soda biscuits and bacon, he walked over to join them and filled a plate. Martha choked on her coffee when he took a seat next to her, but he sat calmly as Cornelius rushed over and slapped her on the back.

"I have found in the past that a hard pat between the shoulder blades seems to help when I am choking," Cornelius advised, giving her another whack.

Hunter casually looked over. "Seems that's just what she might need. Too bad I couldn't have snapped a picture of it for you."

Cornelius ignored Hunter's sarcasm. "That would have made a good shot." He rubbed his chin, observing the pair's reactions very closely.

Martha flushed at the exchange, which was gratefully mistaken by all except Winnie as the result of her choking spell.

"Appears to me, she needs a gentler hand," Winnie said, looking pointedly at Hunter.

Hunter abruptly stood up. A man couldn't even eat in peace without some woman waiting her chance to start moralizing about something. "Get the camp picked up. We move out in ten minutes," he ordered. "Anyone who isn't ready will be left behind."

From behind the veiled curtain of his big floppy sunbonnet, Clinton complained in an altered voice. "But we have not had breakfast yet." If he hadn't had to keep up the appearance of being Aunt Velina, he'd happily have thrown a punch at that blasted arrogant wagon-train captain.

"If you can't eat and get ready in ten minutes, you'll just have to do without breakfast." There was finality in Hunter's voice, and he didn't wait to give the strange woman further opportunity to bellyache.

Chapter Ten

"He's a monster!" Jannet whined as she helped her aunt back to the Stewarts' wagon.

Cecilia grabbed a handful of leftovers and rushed after Jannet and her aunt. She climbed into the wagon and perched atop Jannet's trunk.

"Get off there! I told you not to sit on my trunk!" Jannet snapped. Then she softened. "It might not support your weight. It isn't that strong."

Shocked by the woman's vicious tone, Cecilia hopped down and opened the receptacle to examine its structure for herself.

Jannet quickly slammed the lid of the trunk shut, nearly smashing Cecilia's fingers. "Just leave my trunk alone! What were you doing following us anyway?"

Cecilia bristled at the young woman's rudeness. "I beg your pardon." Had Jannet forgotten this was her wagon? She stared indignantly at the rude woman for a moment, then decided it was no use arguing with such a disagreeable person. "If you must ask, I followed you to bring you both some breakfast after the cruel way Mr. Brody treated you two." She held out the leftovers.

"Thank you." Clinton deftly interceded and took the offering. He glanced back at Jannet. "My dear niece did not mean anything by her remarks, really. She is just having a rough time adjusting to the trail, aren't you?" Cinton pinched Jannet's arm, but his eyes studied the trunk.

"I am sorry, Cecilia. I don't know what got into me. Please

accept my apologies." Jannet sounded most sincere, but behind her façade, she felt contempt for the weak Southern belle who was not as beautiful as she. No matter how Cecilia tried to present a sparkling appearance in those dainty, frilly dresses, she just wouldn't match Jannet's looks.

Cecilia's anger faded under the repentant glance of the spoiled young Wakefield woman who obviously lacked proper breeding. She shouldn't be angry with her, she decided. She should pity her. After all, not everyone had had the advantage of a Southern upbringing.

Meanwhile, Harriet followed Cecilia's lead and hurriedly wrapped up two biscuits with bacon for her husband, who was surveying the damage to their wagon. She glared at the wreckage of their Conestoga.

"Don't worry honey, we'll get it fixed up as good as new as soon as we get to the fort. Maybe the Stewarts will let you ride with them so the sun doesn't ruin your complexion." William Belshaw forced a smile.

"No. I'll ride in our wagon, as will the children. If we have nothing else, we still have our pride," Harriet announced, determined to salvage something of what had once been a prominent family. Then her chin quivered. "If only you hadn't gotten so involved in that ridiculous argument about slavery or you hadn't started drinking again, maybe our neighbors wouldn't have quit shopping at the store and we wouldn't be here now."

William Belshaw's shoulders slumped. "Honey, please. I thought we made a decision to put all that behind us."

"Mama!" Clara's wail interrupted her parents' argument. "We don't really have to ride in our wagon, do we?" Her pudgy face became pinched at the thought of being in the hot sun all day long. Well, at least she still had her dolls.

"Hold that pose." Cornelius grinned and snapped a photograph of the petulant child.

Harriet shot Cornelius a disgusted glance, then scolded her daughter. "Hush up Clara and get Fuller and Gertrude into the back. We'll not give that demon any more reason to shout at this family."

William had borrowed a plump pillow from Cecilia Stewart

and had gingerly settled onto it, cursing the camel for all he was worth as the wagons began to pull out.

"Give me your hand," Hunter said, and offered to help Martha up into the spring wagon.

She stared at the big, rough hand which only hours before had so tenderly set her senses on fire. The thought of sitting next to him was more than she could endure. But he must already have forgotten all about their fiasco. What could she say to him if he asked what was wrong with her? She couldn't tell him of her shame, of the feelings which still stirred within her when he was near.

"I've decided to ride Humphrey. I've already asked Happy to get him ready for me."

Hunter's eyes hardened. So she didn't want anything to do with him. He looked at Winnie who was watching them. Just what he needed, two women ganging up on him! The sooner he got this train to Nevada the better.

"Have it your own way. But if you think you're going to go riding off on some crazy wild-goose chase again, you're sorely mistaken." He grumpily yelled at Happy, "Bring that damn camel over here for Miss Collins, and tie it to the side of the wagon."

"You can't!" she lamely protested.

"I not only can, I will. You're getting your own way. You're riding the beast. But you'll ride it next to the wagon."

Winnie grinned and settled back against the seat. Martha bit her lip and let Happy help her up onto Humphrey's back. She settled her skirt over her legs, then gripped the reins so hard that her knuckles turned white.

"Are you ready my little lamb?" Hunter asked so sweetly that Martha cringed.

Martha sat picture-still atop Humphrey until the Nelsons' wagon fell in behind the Belshaws'. She noticed Lucy hugging the lamb to her. Was that why Hunter had called her his little lamb? Or was the familiar name a slur because he had wanted to eat the animal and she had stopped him? Hunter snapped the reins and Humphrey threw his head back, resisting; but given no other option the beast trudged alongside the wagon. Every jolt was magnified twenty times by Martha's raw nerves. For

114

the longest time she stared straight ahead at the desolate, overcast landscape, afraid to venture a glance at Hunter.

Being an unwanted single woman crossing the country seemed a miniscule problem after the events of the past night. She had been so sure of her goal. Nothing was going to stand in her way. She had broken her engagement, faced her disapproving mother, managed to obtain the funds needed to make the trip, and had even tricked Hunter Brody into taking her on.

Yet none of those obstacles could compare with what she was facing now. And the worst part of it was that she was ashamed of herself for being so weak as to give in to lust. Yet she had discovered something more troubling, more totally distressing, than all her other problems put together. Deep down in the innermost corner of her heart, she would not hesitate to act the same way if she were wrapped in Hunter Brody's arms again; she was falling in love with that big, insufferable, arrogant . . . gentle, tender oaf of a man.

For over an hour the only sounds which broke the stillness between Martha and Hunter were the clopping of the animals' hooves and the crunching of wagon wheels on the jagged rocks in the road. Martha looked at the clear-cut, clean lines of Hunter's features. She noted the strength in his arms and thighs as he held the reins and worked the foot brake. Studying him, she remembered the look of pain on his face when he'd told her of his wife's death. It had been an expression of such intense, silent suffering that she wondered if he would ever be able to allow himself to have such strong feelings for a woman again.

Through the tears threatening to fill her eyes, she noticed the many graves marking the trail. Had those people died alone without knowing love, or had they been lucky enough to be blessed with life's greatest gift before death claimed them? Was she to be ill-fated? Would she ever experience that special joy, or would she someday lie beneath a simple wooden cross without having known such precious moments? But she refused to allow such thoughts to plague her. With great effort, she forced her attention away from the lonely, lifeless mounds.

On the distant horizon, rising nearly four hundred feet,

115

were the bluffs, looking like churches with spiraling towers or castles or great domed houses. Martha was staring so intently at the sandstone formations that when a rock made one wheel lurch to the left and the wagon bumped into the camel, she lost her balance and tumbled helplessly into the bed of the spring wagon.

Hunter halted the team and jumped over the seat. He chuckled at her tousled appearance. "I thought you could handle that beast." When Martha didn't immediately respond he scooped her up into his arms and worriedly began checking for broken bones.

"I'm fine." She swatted his hand away from her ankle. It was torture to have him touching her; her near mishap was forgotten in the wake of his nearness.

"I'm not trying to seduce you, so just sit still and let me make sure nothing's broken."

"I said I'm fine." Martha yanked down her skirt and jumped to her feet. But the fall had affected her more than she realized and her knees buckled beneath her.

As Hunter caught her in his arms, he noticed Winnie grinning broadly at him from her wagon. Then the older woman pulled shut the canvas flap as dust rose from turning wheels. Soon he would be completely alone with Martha.

But something about Winnie's grin did not set well with him. Had those two women planned this, Martha playing hard to get this morning until now? Hadn't she asked him aways back if he'd ever wanted to settle down? His face darkened. He had been foolish to think she was different. She had tricked him once; she could be trying to do it again. He hadn't bedded her, and he wasn't going to let any woman get away with trying to trap him.

Winnie's words rang nastily in his ears. So Winnie Nelson expected there'd be a wedding, did she? He had seen her go into Martha's tent after he'd left. The cynical side of him took over. He decided those two must have put their heads together and come up with this clever scheme. Anger struck him and fed his suspicions.

This was not the first time some scheming woman had tried to trap him into marriage. He recalled a half-dozen times in the last four years. One time in particular stood out. A flaming redhead with a temper to match had set it up with her sister to have some hellfire-and damnation-preaching minister catch her naked in Hunter's bed one evening in Council Bluffs shortly after he had returned from a local saloon. The preacher had ranted and raved, ordering Hunter to do right by the bitch who had confessed he'd despoiled her. Hunter's lips curled as he recalled how fast that preacher had run when he'd fired his gun into the floor of the shack in which he'd been staying. But the woman had stubbornly remained, refusing to leave his bed and he'd had to heave her out the door, naked, and then shut the bolt. Hunter had left town shortly after that, just in case that preacher had got the idea to return with reinforcements.

Still Martha's startled expression had seemed genuine enough. How could someone with such an open, innocent air about her turn out to be little more than a scheming female, intent on sinking her claws into him? He narrowed his eyes at her. He had almost fallen for her act. She'd probably even set Jannet Wakefield up to that little game the other night, had her try to seduce him just to get him primed.

He opened his mouth to let Martha know he was on to her tricks, having had them tried on him too many times before; then he clamped his lips shut. No. There was a better way to deal with someone like Martha Collins.

The story old Rushes Hayes had told him a few years back came to his mind. The crusty trader had nearly been tricked into marriage by an overeager dance-hall girl who'd taken a liking to him, but the sly, old fox had gotten one of his friends to pose as a preacher and marry them. For two months while he was in town, he'd enjoyed everything the woman had to offer without it costing him a single cent. Then, when he'd been ready to go, he'd just up and left her flat, still a free man.

A knowing smile split Hunter's lips. He'd play Martha Collins's little game, and beat her at it, he thought, silencing an inner voice which warned he was making a dreadful mistake. "Are you sure you're all right?"

His air of genuine concern disarmed Martha. Even if he didn't care for her the way she cared for him, they might be friends. "I felt a little faint, but I think I'm all right now. If I could just lie down for a moment . . ."

"Of course. Can I get you some water?" Hunter spread out a blanket and helped her down.

"Yes. Thank you." Martha smiled to herself as she watched him jump from the wagon and walk around to the right side. His concern touched her and made her feel special.

He ladled a cool, refreshing drink out of the barrel strapped to the side of the wagon. Careful not to spill a drop, he then climbed back and supported her head while she drank.

"This really isn't necessary," she said between sips, all the while reveling in his display of tenderness.

"Oh, but I insist. I intend to take good care of you from now on. You're very special."

Could she be dreaming? Was he actually feeling something more than friendship? "Hunter—"

"Not now, my darling, don't speak now. Just rest. We'll have plenty of time to talk later." He leaned over and gently kissed the drops of moisture from her lips.

His kiss was so tender, so sweet, that Martha failed to consult her better judgment regarding this sudden change in his behavior. She was adrift on her own hopes and desires, and her experience was too limited to consider that he was being anything but aboveboard with her.

"Would you like to rest back here while we catch up with the others, or would you prefer to sit with me?"

"I'll sit with you, if you're sure it's all right?" she asked, afraid she would pinch herself and find his attentiveness only imagined.

Hunter offered his hand. "Let me help you up."

Martha was still in a daze, walking five feet above the ground, when they stopped early for the night in order to celebrate the date of the country's birth. All afternoon Hunter had showered her with every kindness. Behaving like a doting bridegroom, he'd expressed concern over whether she was too hot or the sun bothered her, of if she was thirsty or wanted to stop and rest in the shade of a lone cottonwood down by the riverbank.

Much to the chagrin of some and the surprise of others, Hunter tucked Martha's arm in his after helping her from the wagon. "I have to see to the animals. Why don't you go freshen up for tonight," he crooned before leaving her.

Cornelius was the first to reach her. He placed a hand on her arm. "I hope you know what you are doing," he said somberly, the twinge of disappointment in his voice barely noticeable. "You know, I only want the best for you." His fingers lingered on her elbow for a moment, as if he were watching a dream fade; and his eyes silently filled with the pain of unrequited love.

"Cornelius, you're a dear friend," Martha said kindly, "and I'll always carry our friendship in my heart. But I know exactly what I'm doing." She rose up and kissed him on the cheek.

"Rather sudden, isn't it?" His brow cocked into a skeptical arch. But he had expected this. He had been watching their silent exchanges for weeks.

Martha beamed. "Sometimes the best things in life happen unexpectedly."

"I suppose I cannot argue with that. Remember, if you need me, all you have to do is call." He squeezed her arm and swiftly walked away, not waiting for a reply.

Martha looked admiringly after the tall photographer, as if he were a brother. She was glad to have gained such a true friend.

Chapter Eleven

As they all sat around the makeshift table eating supper and cordially making conversation, Martha looked about her. Since she had become the recipient of the attentions of the wagon-train captain the rest of the company seemed to accept her; they were not only civil but sociable. Even Jannet Wakefield's tight-lipped Aunt Velina had managed to direct a kind word to her.

Winnie stuffed the last spoonful of beans into her mouth, then stood up, stretched, and started ordering the others about like an army captain. "Cecilia, get the younguns into the wagon and get them outfitted. Harriet, it's your turn to wash the dishes. Jannet, you and your aunt can get the benches set up in a ring around the fire."

Martha had to laugh. She almost expected Winnie to be saluted the way she was shouting out orders. Hunter had announced earlier that he would be away for a time this evening, and though Martha wondered what had taken him from camp, she knew he used to trap near here and his wife had been a Sioux. Evidently her people lived not far from the camp. A twinge of jealousy struck her, and she had to remind herself that the Indian woman was dead and the nomadic Sioux had undoubtedly long since moved elsewhere. There was no reason for such a feeling.

As soon as the children were costumed, everyone took a seat and became so engrossed in Seth Nelson's rendition of George Washington crossing the Delaware that no one noticed Jannet and her aunt stroll from camp.

"Are you sure we shouldn't just leave the train with the money and forget about your scheme to blame it on Martha?" Clinton urged. He wanted to get as far away from Martha as possible after seeing the way she'd looked at that blasted wagon-train captain, Hunter Brody.

"I haven't traveled nearly six hundred miles on this filthy train to abandon my plan now." Jannet sneered as she toyed with Clinton's hat and veil.

"Well, I'm sick and tired of sneaking around to find a place to shave, and of wearing women's clothing and pretending to be your Aunt Velina," Clinton snarled. "Why don't we just leave at Fort Laramie?"

Janet slid her hand along his cheek and scoffed, "You have a little stubble on your chin, auntie dear. Remember, you were the one who dressed up as my aunt. And quit worrying about the money; it's in a very safe place. Besides, I'm not through with Martha Collins yet."

She pouted coquettishly, then threw herself into Clinton's arms.

He pushed her away. "Have you forgotten your father's plan to keep a low profile?"

"He loves me. Furthermore, he plans to have Martha Collins take the blame. I merely want to make sure she gets her due. And I want to take Hunter Brody away from her." Her eyes suddenly took on a distant light and she mumbled to herself, "I've had to suffer long enough in your shadow, Martha Collins." Then, as if she'd suddenly caught her mind wandering, she snapped, "I thought you hated her as much as I do. You're not hoping to win her back and steal the money from me, are you?"

He shook her until her head seemed to rattle. "Do not be so stupid." Savagely, his lips ground down on hers, twisting and turning while his hands roamed all over her.

He grabbed breasts barely tucked beneath a lavender ruffle and squeezed until she whimpered into his mouth. Only her pain made him stop and break the kiss.

"You like it rough, don't you?" His lips rolled back like those of a sly predator about to pounce on its prey.

121

"Isn't that one of the things you love about me?" She giggled and dropped to her knees, stripping off her clothing as he discarded the gray sack dress he had been forced to wear.

"Always the greedy bitch, aren't you?" Still standing, he ground his hips against her while her fingers and her hungry little mouth devoured him. "You would take every drop from me if I gave you a chance."

Clinton brutally threw Jannet to the ground and mounted her . . . and she squealed with delight at the combination of pain and pleasure she derived from his passion.

The Independence Day skits over, Jed Nelson took out his fiddle. Seth reached for his guitar and Henry his mouth organ, and within moments a lively round of music echoed off the bluffs. Cornelius convinced Martha to dance with him and even Harriet and William Belshaw danced a polka. The children flung their arms and legs about to the music, and soon all were changing partners and laughing. Even Lucy seemed more alive than ever. Off in a corner with the lamb in her arms, she was silently swaying. Everyone was having such grand time that it didn't take much coaxing to get William Belshaw to unpack his accordion.

"How about a sing-along?" William announced, propping the instrument on his knee.

When he started to play "Old Kentucky Home," the faces of those around him grew reflective. Then voices trailed off into pensive silence and tears flowed freely as the haunting melody of "Home Sweet Home" filled the cool night air.

As William softly pumped the accordion, Martha's thoughts drifted to her mother and brother back in New York. She missed the laughter and closeness they had shared. She sighed. How she wished they could know how happy she was. She recalled her deceased father, and misty tears of sadness came to her eyes. If only he could have lived to watch her grow into a woman . . . As tears trickled down her cheeks, she decided a few moments alone were what she needed. She wouldn't go far, just far enough to allow room for her private thoughts.

Quietly slipping off the end of the bench, she wrapped her

shawl over her shoulders and strolled toward the river. There was something so peaceful about watching water flow by; unlike life, its course was directed from beginning to end.

"Oh!" Martha was startled. She had almost bumped into Jannet Wakefield. "I'm sorry. I didn't realize you were out here. Are you alone?"

Jannet frowned and looked nervously behind her. "No . . . no, my aunt is with me."

Clinton was pulling the bonnet down over his face when he caught sight of Martha through the bushes. He sucked in his cheeks and joined them. "My dear, where is that wagon-train captain of yours, Mr. Brody?"

"He had other commitments tonight, and I thought I would stroll down by the river."

"Jannet and I have been enjoying a pleasant walk. As a matter of fact, she insisted we return before I was ready. If you would not mind, I would be pleased to accompany you. I have so little opportunity to stretch these stiff old legs of mine."

"But—" Jannet scowled and started to protest.

"Now, now, child, I know how you worry about me. But you go on back. You were anxious to get some rest. I will be just fine with Miss Collins."

Jannet's lips tightened, but she nodded curtly and stomped off toward camp.

Martha had wanted to be alone with her thoughts but felt she couldn't refuse Jannet's lame aunt. The woman clinging to her arm, she slowly walked down to the river.

"We were surprised to see you and Mr. Brody together this afternoon. He was most attentive."

"Yes, he was." Martha smiled inwardly at the change in Hunter, and a sudden warmth crept up her cheeks.

"Is he interested in you?" Clinton asked bluntly in his most feminine voice. If he wasn't handled right, that blasted Brody could spoil everything. And Clinton had to admit that it bothered him to see Martha with another man.

As warm thoughts of Hunter's gentleness and concern filled Martha, she smiled. "I do hope so."

They walked a little farther; then she turned to the left, toward a tree. But when Clinton followed her, he didn't notice a low overhanging branch. He struck his head and whipped back, catching the bonnet on a twig.

"Ugh, that blasted limb," he grunted, neglecting to raise his voice an octave.

Martha stopped dead in her tracks. Her breath caught in her throat, and she clamped a trembling palm against her mouth. Moonlight revealed her confusion as she pivoted around. It took her a moment to recognize him without his beard, yet before her stood the very straight-laced Clinton Marks, angrily rubbing his forehead.

"My God, what are you doing here?" she gasped.

"Shut up!"

"But I don't understand. Why would you, of all people, dress up like a woman? And why are you on the train?"

Clinton grabbed her, digging his fingers into her arms. "I said shut up!"

"You're hurting me." She struggled, her chest heaving. He had courted her, her mother had considered him a prime catch; yet she really didn't know the man at all.

"I will do more than that if you will not be still." He gritted his teeth, barely able to control himself.

"Why?" The word barely escaped her trembling lips.

Mulling over this new complication, Clinton squinted at her. The expression on her face told him she really had no idea what he was doing on the wagon train. That could work to his advantage. He immediately dropped his hands.

"I am sorry, Martha. I hope I did not hurt you. I don't know what came over me." He stared into green eyes, hating and yet loving her.

Martha rubbed her arms. She had to get away from him.

"I guess I got a little carried away."

"Yes, you did." She was ruffled now; indignation was replacing fright.

"I beg you," he pleaded, having settled on the course of action he'd take with her, "please keep our secret. Remember your promise to old Mr. Wakefield. Jannet and I love each other and her father just wanted us to be able to make a fresh start."

"But why the masquerade? No one but me knows anything

about either one of you," she protested.

"You know how eccentric Wakefield is. After you turned me down and started making preparations to go West, he got the idea that Jannet and I should go too. Maybe in his twisted mind he thought you would keep an eye on his daughter if something happened to me. And, of course, knowing we had once been engaged, perhaps he was afraid you would have a change of heart on the trail, which would leave Jannet alone. So, to keep the old man happy, I agreed to alter my appearance. That way he felt there would not be any possibility you would try to come between Jannet and me, and he felt she would have the protection of the two of us." He glared at her, watching her reaction to his story.

Something about his plea didn't ring true, but Martha was too troubled by his sudden display of temper to question him further.

"I think we should be getting back now," she said, drawing her shawl protectively around her.

She doubted his explanation. Clinton was sure of it. He grabbed her arm. "If you think you are going to rush right back and tell that precious wagon-train captain of yours what you just saw here, you had better think again."

"I don't know what you mean." Martha took a half-step backward, fear again engulfing her.

"Well then, let me clarify it for you. If you say anything to anybody about Jannet and me, I will tell Brody that Jannet was helping you and me to run away. Think about that. You have a lot more to lose than we do."

"You wouldn't!" Martha was aghast. Her relationship with Hunter was too fragile. What if he didn't believe her? She couldn't risk losing him. Not now. For the first time in her life, she was in love. Frantically, she tried to think. "I suppose there's no harm done, and I did make a promise to Mr. Wakefield, as you so clearly just reminded me," she conceded.

"Just remember that. Now let's join the others and celebrate." Clinton smiled triumphantly as he readjusted his bonnet.

But Martha no longer felt at all like celebrating.

Clinton, again looking like the lame Aunt Velina, and

125

Martha had not been back at the camp more than a few minutes when Hunter seemed to appear out of nowhere to slip a possessive arm around Martha's waist. Jannet looked down her nose and disappeared into her wagon, but Clinton, speaking in a high-pitched voice, wished everyone a happy Fourth of July, then offered excuses for Jannet's behavior before he followed the shrewish young woman into the Conestoga.

"Am I in time for a dance?" Hunter had eyes only for Martha.

Winnie elbowed Jed. "Play somethin' slow and sweet."

Jed obliged, and Hunter enveloped Martha in his warmest embrace. As they swayed to the music, she leaned against his fringed buckskins, relishing his strength. Everything was so right when he was holding her. Yet he looked almost savage dressed as he was now.

Worry suddenly speared her: he could have seen her down by the river with Clinton. She feared he might not believe the truth. "How long have you been back?" she asked in her most nonchalant manner.

"Not very long. Why?" He sounded indifferent.

"I didn't hear you return."

"If you'll remember, I once lived with the Indians."

A shadow seemed to pass over Hunter's face. Had his answer brought back memories of his dead wife and child? His wife probably had never lied to him.

"Yes, of course." The thought was anything but comforting, although he wasn't acting any differently toward her. She took a deep breath. He couldn't have witnessed anything or surely he would have confronted her.

"It's indecent!" Harriet Belshaw howled, raising her brows at Martha and Hunter.

"Oh hush, you old prune," Winnie said harshly. "Weren't you never young and in love?" Wearily, she shook her head and answered her own question, "No, you probably weren't."

Harriet flashed her contemptuous frown and then turned away.

But Cecilia cuddled deeper into Derek's arms and was soon lost to the music. For once she felt that she was actually on a honeymoon.

126

Bliss pleasured through Martha and she tried to jam Clinton and Jannet into the back of her mind. If they were really running away to be together, they deserved the chance to be as happy as she was. But she couldn't quite make herself believe it.

Hunter settled his cheek into the thick nest of brown hair piled on top of Martha's head. The strands were scented with a slight rose fragrance. A fierce yearning engulfed him. She fit into his arms so perfectly, as if she had been made just for him. He had known more than enough women in his life, but not one of them had ever affected him the way this one did. It was sobering to admit that not even Dancing Wind had stirred him so. Damn Martha Collins! He found himself riddled with thoughts of marriage and a home. He needed his head examined! She was a dishonest schemer and God only knew what else. Besides, he had set in motion his plan to beat her at her own game, and though a voice at the back of his mind continued to tell him he was making a big mistake, he intended to proceed with the ruse he had worked out with that old conniving friend of his, Abe Baker.

When Hunter had left camp earlier he'd ridden eight miles up the bluffs to Abe's lodge. The bowlegged runt of a man lived there quite comfortably with his rotund Indian wife, like many other white men who'd settled on the prairies. He'd taught Hunter everything he knew about the wilderness, and he'd given him a few lessons in collusion. Seemingly without conscience, the old scoundrel enjoyed a good conspiracy and always put his all into it.

"What brings you to these parts, me friend?" Abe had boomed and he'd set his ax down by the hefty wood pile upon seeing Hunter hitch his horse at the post outside the lodge.

"Hell, I couldn't pass up a chance to stop and see an old partner."

"You always was good at slingin' the bull. You been through here lots of times without stoppin'." Abe gave Hunter a friendly slap on the back. "Come on in and tell me what you been up to."

Hunter turned to Abe's stoic squaw, who had worn a straw hat since the day he'd met her, and gave her a warm hug before sitting down by the long window in the two-room, unburnt brick building.

"I have a proposition for you," Hunter stated after Abe swung a chair around and directed his wife to fetch them a jug.

"Aha!" Abe slapped his thigh. "I love a good con. Don't waste time, spell it out."

Hunter easily explained his original intention to bring camels to Nevada and establish a camel train, his difficulties with the venture, and how he had gotten saddled with such a bunch of disagreeable greenhorns. Leaving out the personal details, he told Abe of Martha and how she had tricked him into taking her on, and he described her scheme to entrap him.

"Sounds like a mighty long trip. What's it you want me to do for you?" Abe leaned forward, his black eyes carefully assessing his one time protégé. There was a difference in Hunter. His recklessness had mellowed into responsible maturity since the last time the ruddy old man had seen him, and a strange warm light flickered in his eyes when he spoke of the woman. Yet those hazel eyes still retained the glint of loneliness they'd borne since his wife died.

"You remember Rushes Hayes, don't you?"

"Yup." Abe looked suspicious. "I never done liked the way that mangy bastard with the fruit mark—"

"How many times have I told you that raised, red birthmark on his right cheek is a strawberry mark," Hunter dryly put in.

Abe frowned. "Yup, I know. The mark of the devil like you told me it was called back in the old days by folks that didn't know no better. So anyway, as I was sayin', I never done liked the way that devil-marked Hayes handled his dealin's. I might be thought a scoundrel at heart, but I always played me cons on only the most deservin' rascals."

Hunter ignored his grumblings. "Well, I aim to beat that scheming Collins woman at her own game."

"Oh, and how's that?" Abe inquiringly rubbed his stubbled chin.

"The same way Rushes fooled that dance-hall gal back in Saint Joe."

"You sure this Martha Collins is the scheming woman you think she is?" Abe's lips twisted skeptically. "From everything you been sayin', she sounds more like a gutsy lady." The yellow flecks in Hunter's eyes flared, putting an end to Abe's questioning. "So, lay it out. What role am I to play in this here plan of yours?"

"I want you to show up tomorrow night dressed like a preacher, and perform a wedding ceremony. . . ."

The song ended, abruptly bringing Hunter back from his musings, and Martha slipped from his embrace. But Jed was accommodating. Before their mood shifted, he struck up another song and Hunter again gathered Martha into his arms.

Chapter Twelve

The moon was a glowing slice of soft tangerine high in a black satin sky when Jed Nelson put his fiddle down, yawned, and announced to Martha and Hunter his intention to join the rest of the company, which had gone to bed at least an hour before. Fiddle in hand, he left them alone by the embers of the dying fire.

Hunter wrapped Martha's shawl snugly around her shoulders, then stood gazing deep into her eyes. "Do you want to turn in, or would you like to walk down by the water?"

The river looked like a wavy thread silver against black velvet from where they stood. Martha slipped her hand through Hunter's arm, giving him her silent answer. She leaned her head against his shoulder as they strolled from the wagons.

"Every time I come through these parts I can't help but marvel at the beauty of this land," he said, feeling strangely at peace with himself for the first time in too many years to tally.

"Yes, the bluffs add a certain grandeur to the prairie. Their name sounds as if it was bestowed on them by some passing emigrant."

"They take their name from a man named Scott, who died under them. Seems he and three others were robbed by some Indians. He got sick after being left with no food, and since there was no way to carry him, the others left him at the bluffs. The next spring they found his bones."

"You know a lot about the West, don't you?"

"I've been out here a long time." It seemed easy and natural to talk about these things with her, and he drew her closer to him.

Thinking that the chirping of the crickets and the cries of the coyotes blended well with this wild country and with the untamed man at her side, Martha felt a prick of guilt as they neared the spot where she had discovered Jannet's aunt was really Clinton Marks. When her soul should be full of rejoicing because Hunter seemed to be returning her love, she felt only the hollowness of deceit. She had always believed in honesty, and knew she couldn't base her life on deception. She had to tell him and take her chances that he would believe her.

At the river's edge, Martha's stomach tightened, and she stopped and faced him squarely. "Hunter, there's something I must tell you."

She looked so beautiful in the moonlight—her lips were so ready to be kissed—that Hunter did not listen to her words but bent his head and kissed her. As his arms went around her, he savored the willing surrender of her body.

Her arms slipping around him, Martha ran her hands up and down his taut muscular back, delighting in his firmness. His kiss was a powerful opiate, dulling her mind to what she had, only seconds before, determined to confess. The warmth and power straining against her was overwhelming.

"Oh, my God," he growled, against her lips. She was driving him beyond reason. He had intended to coolly seduce her, but the rounded feel of her was more than even some shy, spineless lizard of a man could bear. And Hunter had never been considered shy or spineless by women. Lifting Martha high in his arms, while continuing to nibble at her lips and neck, he strode purposefully back toward her tent, unaware of the two concealed Indians who quietly watched from nearby brush.

Martha's hands went around his neck, and her heart thudded so loudly it drowned out the gurgling of the river. She did not become aware of her surroundings until they were already inside her tent and Hunter was settling her against a soft pile of blankets.

He kissed her eyelids. "Tonight, my sweet Mat, I'm not going to let you get away from me so easily."

131

Martha wistfully smiled when he called her Mat. "That was my father's nickname for me." The memory caused a sad, reflective line to curve her lips before she again focused on the present. "I'm sorry I had to use it to get you to take me on. Now I'm glad I did." She reached up and ran her fingers through his thick blond hair.

"Right now I'm glad you did, too." He'd felt a twinge of guilt at her cursory concession of the truth, but the morning he had left her tent, he'd seen her and Winnie with their heads together; and he had seen for himself what Martha really was capable of doing.

"You have such a beautiful neck." He lightly stroked her long, white throat. If she were a man he'd like nothing better than to wring it. As it was, he'd had something much better in mind until he had touched her and she'd sent his senses reeling. He kissed the pulse on her neck. It was racing as fast as lightning streaks across a stormy sky.

"God, woman, what you make me do," he mused. His hands gently unfastened the buttons at the front of her dress. He kissed the smooth velvety skin now exposed to her waist. "You're so beautiful," he murmured, slipping the dress off one shoulder and then the other.

Dreamily Martha let herself be carried away by the sweet sensations raging in her everywhere his lips had touched. She had denied him last night, and tonight every inch of her cried out for that intimate, ultimate contact. He hadn't said the words which bespoke love, but his every action shouted them for him. She moaned in pleasure, and following his lead, with shaking fingers helped him shrug out of his buckskin shirt.

"There's so much I want to teach you." He slipped off her petticoats and, with them, her last vestiges of modesty. When she was naked, he did not waste any time joining her in the natural state, and settled his body alongside of hers.

"And there's so much I want to learn from you," she whispered, beyond awareness except of what he was doing to her senses. "I've never felt like this before. Is it always supposed to be like this?"

"Like this and better."

Pleasure, exquisite and hot gripped Martha as his hands and

tongue danced wildly over her flesh. She squirmed, and as that most intimate feminine spot at the juncture of her thighs began to throb with need, she strained to meet him when he separated her legs and settled his weight between them.

Hunter's loins were filled with mind-shattering sensations which told him he must make haste. He fought for control as he separated the lips of her warm, moist femininity and lowered himself into her, aware that she seemed tense until he felt himself break through the obstacle of her virginity.

"My God," he mouthed to himself. He was her first lover. The thought both pleased and confused him. Her movements were awkward, but that could be intentional. The way she had gone about getting old Winnie Nelson on her side had made him think of her as damaged goods looking for a buyer. But she couldn't fake what he had just experienced, though that still didn't explain everything. Disturbing thoughts made him hesitate for a moment, then surging need washed away reason. He was a man inside a most desirable woman, and his maleness had an ungovernable mind of its own.

Rapture racked Martha when he began to move within her and friction built between them as they moved in rhythm, slowly at first then faster and faster. Their bodies, drenched now due to their energetic lovemaking, begged for release, and the tension mounted until Hunter groaned. A low animal sound escaped him then, and he stiffened in sublime ecstasy. Martha felt herself burst in wave after glorious wave of pleasure and she cried out. Hunter had to bury her face against his shoulder to keep her from rousing the others.

They lay quietly joined together until their breathing slowed, then he rolled to her side and propped himself up on his elbow. He wound a length of silken hair around his finger and huskily whispered, "There's nothing I like better than to know I've satisfied you, my sweet Mat, but let's just keep it between the two of us tonight." He smiled. "You might have awakened the entire camp with your screams."

If it were possible for Martha's cheeks to get any redder, they did at that moment. "I'm sorry. It's just that I've never felt anything so wonderful . . . so powerful before. I didn't even realize what I was doing."

"Never apologize for honest emotion, sweet Mat." He dropped a chaste kiss on her forehead and cradled her in his arms. Strange. In some ways she really was an innocent.

Martha settled contentedly into his arms, exhausted by their lovemaking, and without bothering to cover her nakedness, she fell into a joy-filled sleep.

Starry slivers of moonlight slipped into the tent, illuminating her softly curved body, and for the longest time Hunter didn't move. He continued to hold her to him while warring thoughts attacked him, then he gently slipped the nightgown that lay nearby over her head, and moved into a far corner of the tent. Away from her enveloping warmth, he was able at last to fall asleep.

The camp was alive with the hustle and bustle of packing and children's laughing voices when Martha awoke well after dawn. She stretched, ran her hand over the plain cotton gown, and smiled to herself. Hunter. He had thoughtfully put it on her last night. She looked about the tent. His long body was spread out beneath a blanket, not more than three feet away.

The dreamy mist of happiness in which she had floated, suddenly dissipated when the tent flap flew back and, like three avenging angels of doom, Cecilia Stewart, Jannet Wakefield, and Harriet Belshaw stood before her.

Chapter Thirteen

Martha knew the horrors of the damned as she stared, frozen, at the three grim faces. Harriet Belshaw stood above her, a triumphant sneer on her face. Jannet Wakefield's lips were lewdly twisted, and Cecilia Stewart looked shocked.

The noise woke Hunter. He surveyed the scene, taking in Martha's thorough devastation, which seemed to leave her speechless. Although he had meant to beat Martha at her own game, it bothered him that these three self-righteous, witches would now unmercifully see to Martha's ruination. It shouldn't make any difference to him, but it did.

"Are you three looking for something special, or do you merely enjoy gawking?" He cocked a brow.

"Why, we came to look in on her." Harriet, the spokesperson for the group, pointed an accusing finger. "Miss Collins is normally one of the first up so we were worried about her. It is now quite obvious we should have known better."

"And we used to wonder why you went to bed so early, Martha," Jannet said silkily, her sharp talons barely hidden.

"No doubt your curiosity has served to occupy you most admirably." Hunter's sarcasm was evident.

"It is not we who have been caught in a most compromising position," Harriet spat out. "We're not the guilty ones."

Martha seemed so vulnerable, almost childlike, as she sat still as a helpless rabbit, her face white as newly laundered bed linen. Hunter had had about enough of pious condemnations.

"I don't see anyone being compromised here, unless it is by

135

you three."

The three women stood rooted in place, their faces puzzled as if they were trying to make up their minds as to whether their assessment of the situation was accurate.

"Well, I have a wagon train to run. Are you *ladies* intending to stand here the whole blessed day, or can you find another poor soul to crucify?"

Harriet recovered first. "We're not leaving until we hear Miss Collins's explanation for such reprehensible behavior."

"Suit yourselves." Near naked, Hunter stood up and casually began to look for his clothes.

"In God's name!" Harriet stared at his admirable male physique clad only in his underclothes.

Jannet leered and tried to maintain a pose of outrage. Cecilia did the only thing she had been brought up to believe socially acceptable: she fainted.

"Hunter, please," Martha beseeched, wishing he had left earlier, "don't make it any worse than it already is." She would never be able to overcome this, not if she lived two hundred years. She would have to leave the wagon train at Fort Laramie and hope she could find another to take her on, one that had not heard of her shame, if that was possible after these three finished wagging their slashing tongues.

"What's all the ruckus 'bout?" Winnie shoved her way past the women and into Martha's tent. She took one look at Martha's misery and Hunter's amused anger, then turned on the others. Cecilia Stewart was just coming to when Winnie boomed, "What you yawpin' at? Harriet, you been married long enough not to need to learn no lessons 'bout the male shape. You, too, Cecilia Stewart. A woman on her honeymoon gapin' at another man. For shame. As for you, Missy Jannet, I reckon you ain't in no need of furtherin' your education here. Now get!"

"How can you defend them after what we've discovered?" Harriet screeched.

"And what did you discover?" There was a warning in Hunter's eyes as he narrowed them at the women.

"Well?" Winnie put fists on her hips. "Out with it."

"Why I declare, they were both in here when we came to

136

check on Miss Collins," Cecilia chirped, holding her hand to her throat.

"So? Was they goin' at it?" Winnie didn't believe in mincing words.

"Why no. Of course not." Cecilia was stunned by such talk.

"Well then, quit lettin' this old crow put nasty ideas into those empty heads of yours." Winnie waved them off. "Now turn tail and get."

After the three women left, appearing more daunted than Martha would have believed possible, Winnie looked Martha and Hunter up and down.

"It looks to me like there might oughta be a weddin' after all." Winnie propped her left hand on her hip.

"But—" Martha tried to protest. She wanted Hunter's love and he seemed to have given it. Yet she knew far too little about him to jump into anything, even if he happened to want to marry her, which she seriously doubted.

"I don't want to hear no excuses this time," Winnie went on. "You two'd best do some hard talkin' before we reach the fort. There should be a preacher there, and a weddin' will end those evil cuttin' tongues and make sleepin' arrangements a mite less complicated, if you know what I'm gettin' at."

Hunter smiled behind the serious curtain of his face. Winnie Nelson was playing her role to the hilt. If he hadn't seen her and Martha putting their heads together, he would almost have believed her. Women were such devious creatures. With men, a disagreement most often ended in a fair fight, whereas women could be sweet to your face yet destroy you at the same time they were smiling at you.

"Winnie"—Martha retreated behind formality—"Mr. Brody might not want to marry me."

"I've always believed if you're goin' to pick the roses you dadblamed better make sure you buy the bush." Winnie's moralizing was tied to her upbringing on a farm in Ohio, but she managed to get her point across.

"You needn't worry, Mrs. Nelson, I aim to do just that— tonight."

"What?" Martha's mouth dropped to her kneecaps.

"I've been thinking it'd be nice to have someone else to help

137

out with the camels, and Martha sits a male beast pretty well"—he grinned wolfishly at her—"among other things."

Martha blushed at the double meaning of his words. Why, the arrogant brute. And to think she'd thought she loved him, had even let him make love to her. While all the time he was looking for some poor woman to warm his bed and work with those smelly creatures.

"What's this about tonight?" Winnie's question broke into Martha's murderous thoughts.

"I talked to a preacher friend who lives in these parts after I left camp last night. He's agreed to perform the ceremony about ten miles from here—tonight."

Winnie clapped her hands. "The saints be praised. There's nothin' I like better than seein' two young people in love tie the knot. I got to go tell the others. That'll put a stop to those waggin' tongues."

Martha wasn't sure whether Hunter should be shot or strung out over a pit of rattlesnakes. She glared into that disgustingly handsome face of his. "Who said I wanted to be married to some camel driver? And specifically you."

His face hardened. He had insulted her in front of the Nelson woman, but Martha was only getting what she deserved. He'd just see if what she had been after was a *camel driver*. He'd give her a chance to call it off. Abe would make the trip for nothing, but Martha and Winnie Nelson would be through trying to trap him into anything.

"Well, you have until tonight to decide whether you really want to be married to a camel driver," he said dryly. He then swung about and left her staring after him.

Martha spent the day in troubled reflection, riding next to a man who hadn't said more than a dozen curt words to her since they'd started out. In just a few short hours she would either be standing before a minister, tying herself to a man who ignited her senses just by touching her, or she'd be huddled in her tent in disgrace, preparing to leave the wagon train at Fort Laramie.

Martha sat quietly in the shade of the spring wagon, writing a letter home during the noon break, until Winnie joined her.

"Ain't you goin' to eat?"

Winnie's sympathetic expression was more than Martha could endure, and her troubles tumbled out. "Oh, Winnie, this is all so sudden. As a child I dreamed of a huge church wedding. I used to envision myself in a white, flowing gown, floating down the aisle toward a man who would love and cherish me. I know this may sound foolish, but I never imagined standing beside an arrogant wagon-train captain on the prairie, surrounded by people who don't accept me."

"It don't matter so much how and where you get hitched. The important thing is the feelin' you and your man got for each other."

"I know you're right." Martha sighed. She couldn't bring herself to share with the older woman her fear that Hunter would never love her as he had his Indian wife. The pain on Hunter's face when he had told her about his wife came back to her. If she did marry him, would she have to fight a ghost?

"Of course, I am. Now you just stop worryin'. Everythin' is goin' to be right as rain. Now, come and get some food. You got to keep your strength up." Winnie gave Martha a mischievous grin.

They stopped for the night near the banks of the Laramie River. Lucy and little Barsina Nelson skipped out of camp and returned a half-hour later with arms full of multicolored wildflowers. Cecilia flitted about humming and busying herself making apple pies out of the dried apples, while Harriet saw to the children's hastily made decorations, and to the placement of the men and boys. In order to maintain appearances even Jannet and Clinton, dressed as Aunt Velina, pretended to engage in preparations for the wedding couple. Cornelius sported a stiff upper lip, although he did not expect to enjoy photographing Martha's wedding to another.

Winnie found Martha in her tent, sitting quietly on the floor with her legs crossed. "What you doin', gal? You should be down by the river gettin' yourself all sweet smellin' before tonight." When Martha didn't raise her head to respond, Winnie continued. "Look what I brought you so you could be all gussied up for your weddin'." Winnie thrust out her hands, a frothy white lace confection suspended in them like a glittering cloud.

Tears threatened to weave their way through Martha's heavy lashes as she took the offering. "It looks like the gown my mother was married in."

"Cecilia felt a mite guilty and offered the use of her dress. 'Course, I think she had a little push in the right direction by that nice man of hers. Nonetheless, it shows the thimblehead has at least one smart bone in her body. Now, you go get yourself down to that river and then come back here so we can get everybody fed and I can help you put this here dress on."

Martha's hands were trembling when she looked down at the gown. "Thank you, Winnie."

"No need." The older woman gave her a hug. "You put that dress down." Winnie reached for soap and a towel, and placed them in Martha's hands. "Here, get yourself movin'," she said, pushing her from the tent.

At the river Martha found a private spot and dipped into the water.

The sun was rapidly fading in the west, and if she didn't speak up soon she would become the wife of the most arrogant, maddening, insufferable, wildly exciting, untamed, and . . . lovable man she had ever known. While she had to admit she did love him in spite of what he had said to Winnie and the way he'd acted, could he ever come to love her? Oh, he found her most desirable; he lusted after her. And being with him was a joy beyond words. The thought of it caused a warming sensation to invade her breasts. But was that enough to sustain them through a lifetime? Could she marry him knowing he didn't love her?

Her skin began to resemble a shriveled peach pit as she soaked in the chilling water, mulling over what seemed to be an endless assortment of problems. What if she did marry Hunter? Would Clinton carry out his threat because he feared she might inadvertently slip and tell Hunter Brody after he'd become her husband? Clinton had been terribly upset when she'd broken their engagement back in New York. Perhaps he would attempt to destroy her happiness just for spite. Would Hunter cast her out if he found out she had been concealing what she knew about Jannet and Clinton?

She lathered her hair so vigorously her scalp began to tingle before she realized what she was doing. She probably would have remained seated, sudsy water floating in white gobs around her if she hadn't heard Happy's jovial voice trilling to the camels he was leading to the water's edge downriver.

"Mama sent me to fetch you." Clara Belshaw suddenly appeared, parroting her mother's disapproving tone. As Martha was slipping back into her dress Clara frowned. "Did you really bed Mr. Brody? I heard Mama tell Papa you did and that's why you're getting hitched up with him."

If Martha hadn't had so much on her mind she would have seriously considered turning the little girl over her knee for such talk. Children were so honest it sometimes hurt. Still, it was a pity the precious forthright truthfulness of childhood had to be bent into the pretense of civility. As it was, Martha already had too much to think about, and wearily shook her head as she followed Clara back to camp.

By the time Martha sat down to supper next to her straight-lipped fiancé she felt like a tightly wound clock ready to spring its coils. It was nearing dark and the preacher hadn't arrived, which only added to her woes as questioning faces fell heavily on her. Hunter barely grunted when forced to be the recipient of bawdy jokes flung at him by the men, but Martha blushed and wondered why she was allowing herself to be subjected to this.

Eight-thirty found everyone anxious and Martha about ready to run away and take her chances with the Indians. She still hadn't reached a final decision. She had tried desperately to talk to Hunter, but after supper the women had bundled her off to her tent to fuss over her, twisting, turning, and poking until she wanted to scream. Finally, when Martha looked in the mirror Cecilia offered her, she was astounded. Looking back at her was a most attractive woman, not the plain sparrow she had always thought herself.

Her flower-bedecked curls shone golden-brown in the

lantern light, and the ivory lace gown made her feel as if she were a princess. But would she be marrying a prince or a scorpion?

"He's here! He's here!" It was Henry Nelson's cracking voice.

My God, this is it and I still haven't made a decision, Martha silently screamed. I can still call it off. What should I do? She squeezed her eyes shut and bit her lip. Dear God, what should I do?

Hunter glowered at the strange man wearing a backward-turned collar and sitting atop a big sorrel. Distrust darkened the hazel eyes that watched the pot-bellied man dismount, then they became mirrors of murderous rage. The preacher stuffed a hand into his saddlebag to pull out a Bible and then greeted the flock which had gathered around him.

"Dear me"—he took out a handkerchief and wiped the dust off his spectacles before replacing them on the end of his bulbous nose—"I do hope I'm not too late. I was delayed by an unexpected christening."

"Who in the hell are you?" Hunter roared, like a condemned man unwilling to go quietly to his appointed fate.

The startled preacher blinked and stepped back. The others, dumbfounded, stopped talking and gaped at Hunter, who stood with his hand on his holster, his left cheek twitching.

The preacher grasped the Bible to his heart as if it were a shield with which to protect himself from an impending blow. "I am Horace Fishback. I was told my services were required at a wagon train camped here tonight. I am supposed to contact a Mr. Brody. If I've intruded on you good folks, I'll—"

"You'll just come over by the fire and get a cup of coffee while the bride finishes readyin' herself." Winnie stepped forward, cast a disgusted look at the silently hanging heads, and slitted her eyes at Hunter. "Mr. Brody's just a tad bit nervous. Don't you pay him no mind."

"Why don't you all go have a cup of coffee and I'll see to the preacher?" Hunter said darkly, his expression warning the others not to interfere.

He grabbed the preacher by the arm and dragged him toward a nearby clump of cottonwoods.

"Are you the groom?" The pudgy little man's eyes bulged as the hand of iron clamped around his arm.

"You'd best tell me what's going on before I forget who you're presumed to be." Hunter's left cheek twitched in double time.

The man pulled nervously at his collar. "Abe Baker took sick. He said to let you know that everything's all right."

Hunter released his hold on the man. "Then you know what you're supposed to do?"

"I can only assure you I know my job very well. Oh . . . Mr. Baker told me to give you this." Horace dug into his pocket and handed Hunter an envelope.

Hunter's stiffly erect stance eased after he read Abe's note, but the twitch in his cheek didn't stop. For some reason he was wary of the whole situation. Abe's comment about Martha seeming to be a gutsy lady returned to him like a warning spirit.

"Mr. Baker said you're not to worry." Fishback fidgeted, aware of this big man's threatening size.

"Yeah, well, I'm sure he did." Hunter felt a little more at ease, yet something in the back of his mind gnawed at him as he led the man toward the fire.

"Get Fishback here a cup." Hunter said to no one in particular; then he turned toward the little brown man seated nearby. "Happy! I want to see you over by the camels . . . now!" Hunter handed the preacher over to Harriet Belshaw, and stalked off into the darkness, Happy practically running to keep up with his long strides.

"I'll go get the bride." Winnie grinned, relieved now that the fearful moments following the preacher's arrival were over.

"If you do not mind, it would be my pleasure to see to Miss Collins." Clinton offered, his voice pitched into the scratchy tone of Aunt Velina. Winnie gave a nod of consent, and the tight-lipped woman Clinton was portraying limped away from the fire.

Martha looked up as footfalls neared her tent, just in time to see Clinton, outfitted in a loose gray calico dress and big floppy bonnet. "Gray always was your color," she said flippantly, but within her she felt tied into a knot.

"What do you think you are doing?" he snarled.

"I don't know what you mean."

"If you think marrying that blasted wagon-train captain will keep him from dumping you if you tell him about Jannet and me, you'd better think again. You would never be able to hold on to him."

Oddly enough, earlier Martha had been thinking that very thing. Thoughtfully she regarded him, and as she did so, his remarks caused her mind to clear. No matter what others thought of her, she had a sense of her own worth. She had almost forgotten that these last few days. She loved Hunter Brody. He'd offered to marry her. Regardless of whether he loved her or not now, in time she would make him love her.

"Thank you, Clinton."

"What are you thanking me for?" His menacing smile faded into puzzlement.

"I hadn't made up my mind before you came in here trying to intimidate me, but thanks to you I now have." She drew herself up to her full height, and pushed past him before he could recover himself.

Just outside the tent she stopped, astounded. Gaily colored wildflowers were strung between the wagons. A long board covered with a quilt was serving as a table. It was bedecked with bowls of flowers, and hastily wrapped packages and three sunken apple pies, one topped with a little doll that belonged to Barsina Nelson, also rested on it. Even Harriet Belshaw had gotten into the spirit of the occasion by donating one of William's jugs.

Tears of immeasurable joy came to Martha's eyes as she took in the sight before her. The trials of the journey had been put aside; everyone had pitched in to make her wedding a special occasion she would never forget. She caught sight of Hunter, looking undeniably handsome in his best buckskin jacket, a crisp white shirt, a string tie, and snug-fitting trousers. He stood proud and tall on the other side of the fire.

Martha glanced around at all the members of the train. They stopped talking and looked up at her, face-splitting smiles

144

adorning their faces. Wearing their Sunday best, they were gathered in small clusters. Winnie and Harriet wore white aprons over blue calico. Cecilia wore a peach cotton gown, and Jannet a fashionable lavender dress. All the men wore jackets. And even the children looked scrubbed clean.

"I see you've made up your mind." Hunter smiled his appreciation of the lovely sight before him. "Those dowdy calico dresses you've been wearing day in and day out haven't done you justice." She looked so young, so innocent, and so desirable that it made him ache. It almost seemed a shame to do what he'd planned, a shame all this wasn't real.

The brush rustled causing all eyes to turn in the direction of the noise as Happy, wrapped in white, emerged from the shadows leading Humphrey and another camel, a wide pleased grin on his brown lips. The camels were sporting sprigs of yellow and blue flowers behind their ears, and sheets had been placed over their saddles.

Martha's tears of joy dried in her eyes, and long-cherished visions of her dream wedding shattered into bits. How could he? Was he trying to make her change her mind at the last moment with such an underhanded act? She narrowed her eyes at Hunter. Well, if he was expecting her to call off the wedding and flee at such a sight, he was about to discover he had made a big mistake!

For a moment Hunter hated himself for what he had done to her. She'd had a stricken look on her face when she'd seen the camels. Then his second thoughts died when he glimpsed the challenge in her eyes. He brazenly stepped over to the animals and held out his hand, the look of a golden devil on his face. "Your chariot awaits you."

Humphrey snorted and pawed the ground.

"I must say, this is highly unusual." Horace Fishback wiped glistening beads of perspiration from his forehead, wondering why he had let Abe Baker talk him into this.

"You just take your place, Reverend," Martha said, flashing a scorching glance at Hunter. "Will you help me up . . . dear?"

Hunter had noted it before Abe's comment, but the old man was right on target: the damn Collins woman certainly was gutsy. Before a stunned and highly amused group of onlookers

Hunter gave Martha a boost up. "You were the one who referred to me as a camel driver, remember?" he whispered with wolfish pleasure.

"Yes, I did . . . didn't I?" Martha smiled through her teeth.

Cornelius's camera flashed, lighting up the camp, and capturing enough priceless expressions to fill an entire picture book. It was such a spectacle that, although Cornelius's heart ached over his own loss, he couldn't help but respond to the joyful spirits of the others. Cecilia Stewart had a bad moment. She bit her lip, forcing herself not to cry, as she watched her beautiful gown being draped over that dreadful-smelling camel, but there was only one truly dour face present. Clinton could not disguise his feelings. Privately he mourned, not wanting to join in the festivities, and he knew underneath Jannet's expression of joy, she was seething.

Chapter Fourteen

The ceremony was brief and studded with awkward moments. The preacher nearly lost his Bible when Humphrey reached out and tried to eat it, but Happy managed to snatch the black book out of the camel's mouth. The big beast spit at the little brown-skinned man, and in the middle of one of the most solemn passages of the marriage rite, Happy rattled off a string of foreign expletives, so loudly that Martha thought she was in the middle of a terrible comic play. But when Hunter took the plain gold band from his finger and placed it on hers, she felt her heart fill with joyous love.

Afterward, Hunter left her to play hostess while he saw the preacher on his way. "Not a bad job for an amateur," he said, patting the man on the back and slipping a dollar into his pocket.

"Under the circumstances I . . . did my best." Thoroughly bewildered by the strange ceremony, Horace Fishback cocked his head back, still clutching the battered Bible to his chest like a shield.

"When you see him, tell Abe it went beautifully." Hunter gave the man a helping hand up onto his sorrel.

"If you say so, Mr. Brody. Ah . . . congratulations. I'm sure you and Mrs. Brody will be very happy." Fishback regarded Hunter strangely and readjusted his spectacles.

"Mrs. Brody." Hunter laughed. "I like that. It will fit her nicely until we reach Nevada country."

Horace Fishback settled uneasily into the saddle, then

tipped his hat and rode off leaving Hunter to return to his bride.

Hunter decided he had been right after all. He had given Martha every opportunity to back out gracefully, but she had still forged ahead—thinking she would marry him. Whatever she'd been up to, it hadn't worked. He'd seen to that! So why didn't he feel elated over his victory?

"Don't you think we should get started on our honeymoon?" Hunter tugged Martha to him, grinning like a bull moose during mating season, his good humor partly due to the rounds of toasts he'd shared.

"But we're out in the middle of the prairie on a wagon train." She should have been pleased. Maybe under different circumstances she would have been. But after Hunter had deliberately made a spectacle of their wedding, she would have much preferred to refuse him entry to her tent tonight in the camp.

"I know it's only overnight, but I've already taken care of everything. Happy," he boomed out loudly in front of the entire company.

"All ready. I pack all you need. Yes, boss. All ready." Happy tugged on the leads of the two camels.

"Your honeymoon transportation awaits you and is fully equipped with everything we'll need to get off by ourselves for one night."

"What about my clothes?" Martha looked dismayed.

"You won't need any."

Winnie gulped down a laugh.

"You'll pay for this," Martha fumed into Hunter's ear as she was boosted up on Humphrey's back for the second time that night.

"Just as soon as we get the tent set up." Hunter mounted up behind her, the lead rope for the pack camel in one hand. "Move over dear, we're one now."

Martha glared into space, ignoring his comment. If they didn't leave soon she was sure she would die of embarrassment.

"Hold that pose." Cornelius snapped another picture. "If these photos come out, they'll be worth hundreds of dollars in blackmail money alone." He chuckled.

148

Martha was sure they'd be the joke of the camp after they left. She tried to tell herself that at least everyone had forgotten their differences, but she would have preferred that hadn't happened at her expense.

About two miles away from the train at the edge of the river they stopped and in stony, sobering silence set up the tent.

Hunter's arms slid around Martha from behind as she stood, arms across her chest, her back toward their camp. "You were so beautiful tonight I could hardly believe my eyes."

"Then why the camels?" Martha fought back tears. She did not want him to see her weakness.

"I wanted to know if you'd have the nerve to go through with the plan you and Winnie cooked up. I have to hand it to you, you've got guts."

"The plan Winnie and I cooked up?" She swung around, disbelief and confusion on her face. "What do you mean?"

"I saw you two with your heads together after I left your tent that first morning and Winnie suggested we should get married."

"I don't know what you think you saw, but Winnie Nelson and I never cooked up any kind of a plan." Her voice became so calm and so low that Hunter was sure he was about to find out exactly how angry Martha could get. Instead she gave him a shove and flung these words back over her shoulder, "I don't know where you're sleeping tonight, but when you're ready to return to camp in the morning, let me know."

She shut the tent flap so forcefully Hunter imagined he heard it slam. She was so outraged he'd have believed she was telling the truth if he hadn't seen for himself that she had been up to something. But had he had any doubts about her and Winnie Nelson, the little scene he'd observed at the river had laid them to rest.

He stalked to the pack and yanked out the jug he had directed Happy to load. With each swallow, his mood darkened, going from annoyance to ire. He was sitting on the cold ground on what was supposed to be his wedding night, even if it wasn't, a fact his blurry mind neglected to recall in his inebriated state. The glow coming from the tent looked too inviting for his hazy mind to ignore. He had rights and he was

149

going to claim them!

He swaggered to the tent and barged inside. "You belong to me. You can't deny me."

Martha lowered her lashes. She'd had time to think and to regain her composure since her dramatic exit. Fighting over some imaginary plan was no way to start married life, and she intended to make her marriage to Hunter a success.

"I don't want to deny you," she breathed softly, and opened her arms to him.

He hesitated only a moment, the glaze draining from his eyes. His mouth hovered briefly over hers, then dove down into its welcoming depths. As she responded to his kiss, Martha knew there would be no turning back. His movements were fluid, his hands gliding over her flesh; sensations, urgent and enflamed, encapsulating her. Her spirit took flight and soared through a jeweled darkness, demanding a joining of their bodies.

His mouth sought her breasts, her inner thighs, her nectared womanhood, spiraling them toward a harmonic intensity. He teased and tormented, tantalized and probed. She opened to his exploration, her body no longer her own but waiting impatiently to become an extension of his. When she could wait no longer, she drew him into her, enfolding him as they moved as one. She peaked and trembled. He stiffened and shuddered.

For hours Martha lay awake as Hunter slept soundly at her side. He hadn't spoken of his feelings during or after their lovemaking, but he had silently taken her past hunger, past desire, past the sublime. Yet as her lids grew heavy and she gave herself up to the peaceful unconsciousness of sleep, she wondered whether she would ever hear those three most precious words.

Chapter Fifteen

Wednesday, July 6, 1859—Fort Laramie. Prejudices die hard among people who have toiled bitterly to foster them. I am encountering one, the strength of which is taking much soul searching to fully understand its birth. While I had deemed myself free of such attitudes, I am finding it is human nature to distrust and fear those who are different from oneself. It is our shame that we do not choose to remember we are all children of God. . . .

Long before dawn Hunter and Martha had returned to the wagon train to rouse the rest of the camp and prepare to ford the river. This time there was no question of the Belshaws refusing to unload their possessions, for their wagon was a mere shell containing few of the treasures Harriet had so stoutly guarded. With the exception of Jannet's cold stare of hatred, not much was said of Martha's wedding. Life on the trail allowed little time for frivolities; the daily struggle to survive on meager rations under a blazing sun required every ounce of energy the emigrants could muster.

Shortly after they had stopped near a sparse patch of grass for the noon meal and to rest the animals, a cluster of half-naked Indians swarmed into camp carrying fresh potatoes, onions, buffalo meat, and fish.

Martha was sitting in the shade of the spring wagon, knees drawn up, a board on her lap, writing a letter to tell her mother of her marriage. She planned to send it off from the fort. She looked up to see Cecilia clutch at her red curls and run into the wagon, two young Indian boys on her heels, waving slices of meat. "My goodness, could Mother have been closer to the truth than she realized?" Martha chuckled to herself while absently twirling the pencil.

"Closer to what truth?" Hunter rounded the corner of the wagon and knelt down beside her.

"One of those Indians wouldn't handle mail delivery, would he?" She sheepishly giggled.

Hunter tossed her a quizzical gaze. "What the devil are you talking about?"

She had to smile. "It's nothing really. Just that those half-naked savages reminded me of a comment my mother made about one of them delivering my letters to her." The reminiscent moment passed, and Martha grew serious. "They aren't dangerous, are they?"

"They're not as friendly as they used to be before the white man started taking their food and land away from them, but I don't think you have to worry about your scalp," he said wearily.

Somewhat daunted by his tone, Martha turned back to her writing.

His eyes fell on the notebook on her lap. He had often noticed her scribbling in it. "What are you writing now?"

"It's a journal of the trip. Would you like to read the last entry?"

"Yeah, well . . . sure." Martha handed him the book. After a quick glance, he returned it to her. "You don't write like you talk. Why don't you just come right out and say what you're thinking in it?"

"The journal's meant to be read by others, so my writing is more formal and refined."

"It does show that you've had a good schooling," he observed.

"Even if I don't seem to know much about Indians?"

Hunter rolled his eyes at the remark that was typical of someone who didn't know the first thing about the frontier. Throwing up his hands, he shook his head. "Even if you know nothing at all about Indians." He left her and headed toward the three Indian braves gathered around the Belshaw woman.

From his behavior Martha knew she had said the wrong thing. He had lived among the Indians, and as she watched him, it seemed to her he had more respect for those savages then he did for his own people. His actions gave her something to think about.

"No. Now I said that shirt is worth three fish." Harriet swatted a red hand away from the plaid cotton shirt. The Indian held up two large fish and shook his head.

"With the size of those fish I think you'd be getting the better bargain, Mrs. Belshaw." Hunter pinched his lips as he glanced at the tattered shirt Harriet Belshaw was holding back for a higher price.

"You think so, Mr. Brody?" Triumph lighting her face, she snatched both fish from the Indian and tossed him the shirt.

"Tight bitch," Hunter muttered under his breath. The others weren't making out nearly as well as Harriet Belshaw, he noted as he strolled past the haggling clusters.

A young girl's voice drew Martha's attention from her writing. She looked up to catch sight of a buffalo robe draped over the arm of a young Indian maiden; Martha guessed she was about Henry Nelson's age. The robe looked like it would make the perfect cover on the cold nights ahead, so Martha decided to try her hand at the bargaining process.

"I give you this apron and bonnet for the hide," Martha said slowly.

The young girl stared intently at Martha, but shook her head.

"I add this dress." Martha laid the much-patched red calico dress on the stack.

Again the young girl studied Martha. Martha returned her gaze, fascinated by the girl's yellowish brown eyes, her refined features, and by the prominent mark, reddish and feathery on her cheek.

The girl shook her head and pointed to the plain gold band adorning Martha's left hand.

"No!" Aghast at the very idea, Martha clamped her palm over the ring.

Disgusted and tired of mediating the bargaining, Hunter had

decided to rejoin Martha. His face took on a most unusual cast when his eyes fell on her and the young girl. "What's going on here?"

"She won't accept all these clothes." Martha wrinkled her forehead at Hunter. "She thinks I would part with my ring."

Hunter took one look at the pathetic pile of clothing Martha was trying to trade and launched into a tirade. "Do you have a brain in that head of yours? Don't you realize what these people have to go through to get just one hide, the hardships they endure because emigrants like you have no respect for the fact that the Indians are a proud folk, who just happen to have a different way of life."

In a fit of anger provoked by years of watching the white man cheat the Indian, Hunter grasped her wrist and ripped off her finger the ring he'd taken off and given her during their wedding ceremony. "This is paltry payment," he snapped, holding the gold band up as an example.

The girl grinned slyly. Then, quick as a fox, she grabbed the ring and stuffed the robe into Martha's arms. Before Hunter could react she was gone.

He yelled something after her in a strange tongue, then took off in pursuit.

Martha was horror-stricken. He had taken her wedding ring from her finger and had practically allowed that savage to snatch it right out from under his nose. She felt devastated. Not caring who heard her, Martha shrieked at Hunter as he returned, empty-handed. "How could you! Would I mean any more to you if I had been running around the country begging for handouts when we met, or if I were a young half-breed?"

He grabbed her shoulders and shook her unmercifully. "If you knew anything at all about Indian customs you would know they're not merely begging. It's a custom with the Indians that when you cross their land you offer them a present. Not so much different from when you and your *civilized* friends take something to someone you plan to visit, is it! We're crossing land that belonged to the Indians long before the first white ever stepped foot on this shore. This is their home. They're not savages and they're not begging! And don't you ever call any Indian a half-breed again!"

"How can you defend them after some of the atrocities they've committed?" she persisted, although she realized she never should have mentioned the half-breed girl to him since his child would have borne the same label.

"What about the atrocities whites have committed since history began? Should a whole race be condemned for the crimes of a few?"

"Of course not!"

"Then don't condemn all red people."

Happy's shrill voice crackled through the air. "Boss. You come. You come. Indian take camel. You come. Quick." He stood by the camels, frantically whipping his arms above his head.

"Jesus Christ! You people are almost more than a man can tolerate." Hunter dropped his arms and stalked off, leaving Martha to rub her aching shoulders.

She huddled back against the spring wagon, her chin trembling. Tears flowed freely down her cheeks as she stroked the finger which, a few short minutes ago, had been adorned with a plain gold wedding band symbolizing her union with Hunter. Snuffling back a heartsick sob, she picked up her pen and forced herself to write of the joy she no longer felt while tears blotched the ink on the page.

Hunter pushed through the Indians excitedly crowding around the camels.

"What's going on?" he wearily asked.

Happy was tugging on one end of the rope attached to Humphrey and two Indians were tugging on the other. "Help. They take camel. Help."

Hunter motioned to the Indians to stop, and spoke to them in their own tongue. After long minutes of unsuccessfully trying to convince them the camel was not the starved ghost spirit of the buffalo forewarning of the demise of the species, Hunter only managed to sway them by riling the beast up enough for it to spit and bare its teeth at their leader. The Indians gave a whoop and nearly fell over each other trying to scramble away from the camel. And the ill-tempered Humphrey, who seemed to delight in his newfound power, hissed at the retreating Indians.

When, once again, only the usual noises assailed the camp, Cecilia poked her head out of the wagon and hesitantly stepped down. "I dare say now that those dreadful savages are gone we can settle down to a peaceful meal without worrying about them stealing our supplies right out from under our very noses."

Martha stared at Cecilia as she helped her prepare the noon meal. The words which had come out of that delicate woman's mouth made her think. Had she herself sounded just as cruel and ignorant? Cecilia had inadvertently caused a rude awakening in Martha.

"Oh, my God. My God! What am I going to do?" Harriet screeched, such horror in her voice as she dropped the plate she had just dished up that the whole camp thought she was dying.

Martha was the first one to reach the hysterical woman who was hugging her legs. "Mrs. Belshaw, what's wrong?" Martha crouched before Harriet and tried to comfort her.

But Harriet would have none of it. "I can't go on. My God, they've stolen them. What am I going to do? They were here this morning." Bawling and bleating almost incoherently, she refused all efforts to quiet her.

"Landsakes! Such carryin' on ain't goin' to get us to the bottom of her caterwaulin'." Winnie seized Harriet, and when the woman's hysterics continued, she hauled back and smacked her across the face.

"I couldn't have done better myself." Hunter smiled faintly as he strode over to see to yet another problem. "Now what's going on?" He let out an exhausted sigh.

Harriet sprang to her feet, her eyes red and wild with fright. Her fingers grasped Hunter's open-collared shirt and she begged, "Mr. Brody, you have to help me. You have to!"

He pried her fingers from his clothing, and put a soothing arm around her quaking shoulders. "Take a couple of deep breaths and then try to tell us what's wrong so we can help you."

Martha stepped into the background and glanced around, looking for the Belshaw youngsters. She had heard stories about Indians abducting children and holding them for ransom, and the way Harriet Belshaw was carrying on Martha was sure that had to be the problem. She did not see the children, but her eyes fell on Hunter. He had easily taken control of the situation, and now he was calming a woman who had given him nothing but trouble from the start.

"They're gone. What am I going to do?"

"Who's gone, Mrs. Belshaw?"

"Those dreadful, thieving Indians must have taken them."

Hunter's brows seemed to darken. "What?"

Harriet looked at him as if he should know what she was talking about. "Why, my false teeth, of course." She sniffled.

Sighs of relief and snickers were heard around camp; then Hunter ordered everyone to pitch in and look for Harriet Belshaw's false teeth.

Fifteen minutes later Henry Nelson impishly emerged from his wagon, the articles sought in his palm. He hesitantly handed them to the big woman and then looked back over his shoulder at his frowning mother before dropping his eyes.

"Weren't Indians which took your choppers." He chewed on his lip and picked at his fingernails. "I guess you dropped 'em this morning out by the fire. I found 'em." He again looked sheepishly back at Winnie who stood ready to give him what for if his story wasn't accepted. "I didn't mean no harm. I didn't know they was yours, Mrs. Belshaw. Honest."

Cornelius got his equipment set up just in time to catch Harriet staring at the stocky twelve-year-old holding out her teeth. Her face contorted into a combination of silent rage and embarrassment before she swished her skirts, and haughtily stomped off, her nose in the air.

"Enough's enough. The excitement's over. Let's get these wagons rolling so we can reach the fort before dark," Hunter barked.

They had been on the road an hour when Martha edged over on the seat until she was right next to Hunter. "I suppose I still have a lot to learn about this country. I never thought about Indians except as savages until you enlightened me today. It's a shame people have to fear those they don't understand."

157

"Yeah, well," he muttered. He kept his eyes on the road, not looking at Martha.

"You're making an apology awfully difficult."

"I'm not trying to." He paused, then proceeded. "Guess if I hadn't taken that ring off your finger the way I did, that girl wouldn't have made off with it. I didn't mean for you to lose it," he admitted, sincere regret in his voice.

"I know." She gently placed a soft, warm hand over his rough one.

He turned to her. The genuine sadness in her face stabbed at his senses. He had been wrong to use the ring as an example, but he never should have given her the ring in the first place. He'd found he was already regretting what he had done. A false wedding ceremony had seemed like a good idea at the time. A wrong was never righted by another wrong, though. Why did that woman make him forget his common sense and cause him to do such stupid things? When he delved into the fire in those brilliant green eyes and felt himself being helplessly drawn into them, he had his answer.

In an effort to make amends, Hunter handed Martha the reins. He reached around his neck and untied the leather thong which held his long-treasured arrowhead. Leaning over, he lifted her braid and tied the leather strip around her neck.

"It's not a ring, but I want you to wear it. It's for luck. As long as you wear it, it'll help keep you safe from harm." Without another word of explanation, Hunter took the reins back and turned his profile to Martha.

She fingered the three-pointed bone polished smooth and sharp. She wondered exactly what meaning it held for him. Prudently she held her silence, happy yet afraid to learn its story.

Amidst strong gusting winds late in the day, they set up camp a mile from the fort on a gentle knoll that provided barely enough grass and prickly pear cactus to feed the animals while repairs were made on the Belshaws' wagon. Hunter grumbled about the delay, but the rest of the company was pleased by the chance to rest.

There was a particularly ugly aura around Jannet as she stepped up to the khan where Martha stood rubbing

Humphrey's nose. "You've always been a fool for animals." Jannet sneered as she fluffed the frilly skirt of her lavender dress.

Martha looked up, a hint of misgiving seeping through her veneer of self-confidence as the icy feel of Jannet's presence touched her. "Maybe. What do you want?" Her voice was guarded and distant.

"Is that any way to treat your best friend?"

"We were never best friends."

"Do you think that husband of yours will still want you when he finds out your old lover is traveling on this wagon train?" Her eyes were shuttered, but her lips twisted viciously.

"Clinton and I were never lovers!"

Jannet touched Martha's shoulder. "No?"

Her fingers felt cold, even through the thin fabric of Martha's dress. "Don't touch me!" Martha wrenched her shoulder out of Jannet's reach as Humphrey hissed, seeming to sense her distress. "If you come near me again with such threats, I swear I'll unleash the camel on you."

"Sweet innocent Martha. Do you really think that filthy beast can save you?" Jannet's smile was calculating as she took a step toward Martha.

Martha moved nearer to Humphrey, her heart thumping faster. Confusion over Jannet's motives beset her.

"When you weren't at camp, I thought I might find you out here." Approaching the two women, Hunter fully took in the scene. "Miss Wakefield, I've never seen you take an interest in the animals before." He looked pointedly at Jannet. "I do believe your aunt has been looking for you."

"Thank you," Jannet said in her most sensual voice. After shooting Martha a silencing frown, she lifted her lavender skirts and strolled back toward camp.

"What do you think she wanted out here?" Hunter asked, hoping to provoke a reaction from Martha.

She shrugged. "I haven't the vaguest idea."

Behind her look of innocence, however, Martha fretted. Jannet was up to something, and like thunderheads gathering before a storm, it didn't feel right to her.

Chapter Sixteen

Thursday, July 7, 1859—Fort Laramie. As I reread these journal entries, I am finding much of the daily alotted space dedicated to a journal of the heart rather than a record of the trip. I fear I have given vent to my emotions and lost sight of my original intention to provide a detailed log for those of my family and friends who may desire to travel vicariously with me on this incredibly exasperating, but fantastic, journey. . . .

Martha had found sleep unattainable. Jannet's threats and Hunter's questions kept her awake, portents of impending doom surrounded her. She had become Hunter's woman. His wife. But she knew so little about him. Her happiness with him was so fragile; yesterday had proved that. And now Jannet was rudely intruding into that happiness. Why was she acting this way?

Hunter had had a strange look on his face at the camel khan the past night. Although his questions seemed natural enough, there had been a different sparkle in his eyes. Remembering it, Martha could not rid herself of the persistent anxiety, the sense of premonition.

Fog had dropped its gray manteau over the dawn by the time Martha slid from bed, dressed in a muslin sack skirt and cloak, and quietly left Hunter still asleep. Her nervous energy was about to explode. She paced the deserted camp until the snorting of the camels led her on tiptoe toward the khan.

Through the damp mist, the beasts looked like eerie apparitions. As quietly as possible, Martha ordered Humphrey down, and saddled him in record time, slipping into position. At a tug on the reins, the large animal unfolded its legs.

No one in camp stirred as she rode out. She was pleased that she even managed to get past Happy, knowing how fiercely the little man guarded his charges. The air was still, the morning silent as she rode over the hilly terrain, and peace settled on her troubled mind.

Suddenly, the loud whinnying of horses jerked her to awareness. Angry, shouting voices burst into her consciousness.

A deep male voice shot through the fog. "Dammit! I can't hold them. Get your butts over here!" As Martha cautiously drew nearer to the sounds, the hazy blue outlines of male forms met her eyes.

"Shit! What is this?" One of the men pulled out his gun and aimed it directly at her.

"Hold your fire, soldier!" commanded a tall, muscular officer. "You!" he shouted at Martha. "Get over here!"

The men's mounts nearly went wild as Martha brought Humphrey to within three feet of the squared-faced man. The usually sedate military animals whinnied, reared, and began to stampede away from the camel. The men snorted and ran after their mounts, leaving only one man staring at her. When Humphrey folded his legs and Martha hesitantly dismounted, the officer looked the pair of them over as if they were creatures from another world.

"Let me be massacred." He chuckled. "What the devil is that? And who the hellfire are you, and what are you doing here?" He scratched his head.

Martha bristled at his crude manner and rapid-fire questions. She guessed him to be in his middle forties by the silvered gray of his hair and the few wrinkles beginning to line his attractive features. A man that age should have learned some manners to display to a lady. "And just who are you?" she tossed back, raising her chin.

He stiffened into attention. "Captain Portland Holbrook, out of Fort Laramie."

"Well, that's more like it, Captain." Martha's brisk tongue surprised her. She softened. "I'm Mrs. Brody, traveling with a wagon train camped about a mile from the fort."

For a moment he eyed her suspiciously; then he relaxed. "We get a lot of emigrants traveling through, but if you'll forgive me, ma'am, never anything like that." He motioned in Humphrey's direction.

"That, Captain, is a camel. My husband imported them for his ranch in Nevada, Utah Territory." The words *husband* and *Nevada* sounded so natural coming from her lips. She stroked the leather thong at her neck and smiled to herself.

Captain Holbrook's mount continued to fight his efforts to hold it until he ordered it led away from that queer beast, the camel. "No offense meant, ma'am, but a young woman like yourself shouldn't be riding out here alone, especially on that." He raised his brows at Humphrey. "God only knows what could happen to you. The Indians are restless at this time of year, so someone who is trigger happy might shoot first and ask questions later. If you don't mind the advice, you'd best get yourself back to the safety of your camp."

"I think that's excellent advice, Captain." As Hunter rode up, eying the man's stripes, Martha noticed that he was wearing buckskins again.

Hunter's big bay shifted back and forth. Still shy of the camel, it danced uneasily at being so close to Humphrey.

"She seems to have a bit of the wanderlust. I'll see that it doesn't happen again." Hunter's eyes narrowed as he glanced at Martha. "My little lamb." He grinned to himself at thinking of the small creature Martha had saved from the stew pot and given to Lucy Nelson as a pet. Lucy and the lamb were now inseparable. And he had to admit the lamb seemed to be making a difference in the child, who was beginning to become more interested in things around her. "We should be getting back before the others begin to worry about you."

His tone warned Martha that it would not prove wise to protest in front of the captain. She nodded to the officer, and took her seat upon Humphrey while the two men exchanged pleasantries.

As Martha and Hunter started back, the captain's voice

halted them. "Mr. Brody, could I have a word with you?"

"You head on back to camp," Hunter said to Martha. "I'll be along in a minute."

"I can just as well wait for you," she offered. Although she had kept her tongue in front of the captain, she'd have a few things to say to Hunter once they were alone. He had treated her like some empty-headed trinket he had picked up along the trail, and despite her fears, she wasn't going to let him get away with that!

"What is it, Captain?" Hunter remained atop his horse as one of the privates returned the captain's mount.

"I knew your name was familiar when I heard it from your wife. We received some paperwork just last Monday concerning some woman who's reported to be traveling on your train. Appears she's wanted for questioning."

Hunter crossed his wrists over the pommel of his saddle and leaned forward. He had a sneaking hunch he was about to hear the name Wakefield. "What's the woman's name?"

"I don't rightly know. But we were told to keep a lookout for you. The general's been twitching real bad to talk to you since those papers came in. No doubt he would appreciate it if you'd accompany me back to the fort." Of course, the captain didn't say that the general had offered a handsome reward to the man who brought Brody to him. It was not standard procedure, but an extra month's pay could come in pretty handy with Miss Lollie's girls.

"What did this woman do?" Hunter furrowed his brows as the captain shifted in the saddle.

"I don't rightly know that either. But if you'll come with me, I'm sure the general will clear up all your questions."

The captain was nervous about something and awfully insistent Hunter accompany him. Since Hunter was never one to follow blindly, he had no intention to do so now. "My wife's waiting for me. Tell the general I'll stop by while I'm at the fort."

A muscle in the captain's neck pulsed. "Why don't I see you safely back to your wagons? Then we can ride in together."

"I think I can manage, but suit yourself." Hunter shrugged. "Shall we, Captain?"

"I'll just turn over maneuvers to the sergeant, then I'll be along."

"I thought I told you not to wait." Hunter frowned at coming upon Martha just over the hill, standing idly next to the camel.

"I know what you told me," she said defiantly.

Her hair hung in tempting curls down her back and brown tresses lay over the swell of breasts hidden behind her high-necked gown. In the gray misty wilderness, her flashing green eyes were most haunting. Hunter vividly remembered the first time he had tangled his fingers in the lush mass of her hair, and the first time he had eased open the front of her dress and caressed those ripe nipples. She had yielded herself up to him, placed her life in his hands. Not even his lost Dancing Wind had ever let him possess her so completely. He felt himself weakening. It would be too easy to want a real marriage. And marriage and settling down were not a part of his plans.

"Then why didn't you obey me?" he snapped with a forcefulness meant to keep her from getting too close.

"Obey you!" She looked incredulous.

"Isn't that what you agreed to do during the wedding ceremony? I seem to recall you fixing your signature to such a document," he parried. "Well, didn't you?" He pushed her a little further.

"Ah . . . yes . . . but—"

"Then get that creature on its feet. I've got a lot of work to do and I don't have time for you right now."

His words sank into her like the fangs of a mountain lion, and her wounded pride sought surcease in a retort. "I certainly do not wish to burden you further, since you are obviously occupied with more important matters."

"Damn it, Martha!" He was off his horse like lightning. He had meant to indifferently fling her onto the camel's back, but when his hands closed around her waist and her fiery body came into contact with his, he reached up to touch her hair, then yanked her head back and brought his lips down on hers.

Fury and rage, hurt and humiliation swept through Martha.

She wanted to claw at him and cut his black heart out. But he held her, his expert tongue forcing her unwilling response. Under his onslaught, her anger dissolved. Everything his body silently communicated—through lips, fingers, and his pressing maleness—cried out his thirst for her. She could not deny him or her own rising desire despite his stinging words.

Tugging his shirt from his trousers, she let her fingers revel in the taut strength of the muscles corded across his back. Then she delighted in twisting the wiry hairs on his chest and in rubbing his nipples until they hardened against her open palms.

Their passionate kiss begged that they find sweet release, but the clopping of horses' hooves put an abrupt end to the moment. Martha looked into intense hazel eyes probing her own. She bore his name and there was no doubt he desired her physically, but in the innermost recesses of her mind she wondered if anyone would ever fully possess his heart.

Captain Holbrook strolled about the camp taking in the scene while Brody excused himself and went to speak with one of the men. Holbrook's eyes scanned the three young women seated at a table near one of the wagons. Which one was it that the general wanted so badly that he had personally posted a reward, and why?

Although Hunter was talking to Jed, he, too, was studying the faces of the women. There was no doubt in his mind as he walked back to Captain Holbrook.

Cecilia Stewart had come directly from her family's loving arms as a bride. Jannet Wakefield and that so-called aunt of hers appeared capable of anything. Martha was up to something and he didn't totally trust her, yet a tiny voice told him it wasn't her. He stared at her lips, noting the way they curved upward; joy of life danced in her green eyes, and inner strength showed in her movements. He felt himself begin to grow hot just looking at her.

"Are you about ready, Mr. Brody?"

Hunter's attention snapped back to the army captain. "Just waiting for the Belshaws."

"Why are we waiting for the Belshaws?"

"Had a little accident with one of the wagons. Say . . . you might be able to recommend someone who can fix it."

The captain was flattered and walked over to assess the damage. "Looks like more than a little accident, but I'll see what I can do." Holbrook studied the wagon, then looked up in time to see he had been photographed. "Is that all the man does?" he asked.

Hunter gestured his indifference. "Sometimes seems that way. Keeps him occupied. He's not good for much else out here."

While Harriet and William positioned themselves on the seat of the damaged Conestoga, Captain Holbrook asked about the camels. Hunter was discussing the beasts when Martha casually strode over and, to his consternation, hopped into the back of the wagon without bothering to consult him.

"Where do you think you're going?" he demanded, exasperated. He didn't want her waltzing around the fort until he found out what was going on.

"To the fort with you," she replied innocently.

"I'm sure you have chores to do."

She glared at him. "They're all done."

"Then you'll be needed to help watch the Belshaws' children."

"Winnie and Cecilia are taking care of them."

The damned woman was splitting his patience in thirds. He grabbed her arm and yanked her out of the wagon. "You're not going with us, and that's final, dear."

He had always known she had guts. But since that damn ceremony she was growing into a regular pain in the backside.

"Then I'll ride in by myself." She wrinkled her nose defiantly.

"If you think you're going to the fort this morning, you'll have to walk." He abruptly turned toward the camel khan and shouted his authority. "Happy! You best keep a close eye on the animals. Mrs. Brody won't be riding again today."

"That's quite a woman you've got there." Portland chuckled and looked Martha up and down.

"Yes, she is, isn't she?" A warm light flickered in Hunter's

166

eyes, and taking one big step, he swept Martha off her feet and planted a smacking kiss on her surprised lips. That would leave no doubt in the captain's mind as to whose woman she was, but his need to demonstrate that Martha was his disturbed Hunter. He swung around and abruptly left.

Martha stood with legs apart, arms akimbo, her eyes shooting arrows at Hunter's back as he mounted and rode off.

"Hold that pose." Cornelius called out. "I think I shall call this one *Honeymoon's End.*" He envied Brody, but thought him foolish. If he had stood before the preacher with that incredible woman, he never would have left her side. However, one look at Martha's stony expression made his smile droop. She looked as if she could be considering murder. "You are contemplating some action which might not be expected of a lady?" he asked.

"Right now I am," she said, then turned back in time to watch the wagon fade into the lifting fog.

Hunter had denied her access to a more comfortable mode of transportation, but she could walk to the fort. Their marriage did not give him the right to dictate where she could or could not go. And the fact that he'd been so adamant in his refusal to allow her to accompany him made her all the more determined. She swung past Cornelius and into her tent, exchanged her high-button shoes for a more comfortable pair, and grabbed the dainty pink parasol, one of the few luxuries she had allowed herself to bring. Until now, she had been saving it for when she'd settled into her new home.

She opened the tent flap to leave, but let it drop from her hand. An upward curve lifted her lips. The delicate pink dress with the ruffled sleeves and wide satin ribbon at the waist would complement the parasol much better than the dowdy, loose dresses she usually wore on the trail. Making a good impression on her husband's acquaintances was the least a wife could do.

By the time Martha started toward the fort, the fog had lifted and the sun reflected its fire across the dry hillsides.

She stumbled over a rock, cursing Hunter for forcing her to walk. Not that seeing the fort this morning was so important; there would be time for that later. It simply had become a matter of principle. He wasn't going to order her around.

She felt as if she had walked much farther than a mile by the time she neared the one-time trading center for trappers and Indians. The walk had allowed her murderous thoughts toward Hunter to cool, but she was not going to give him the satisfaction of seeing how riled she felt.

A most pleasant smile on her lips, Martha opened the parasol and then strolled past the dozen or so Indian tipis outside the fort, not noticing the two Indians who were staring intensely at her—one twirling a plain gold band around on her finger.

Although the outpost, known as Fort John in the days of the American Fur Company, had become a military fort ten years before, the straggling congregation of barracks, officers' quarters, stores, and storehouses continued to serve informally as a supply depot for emigrants following the Overland Trail.

"Ma'am." A young man tipped his hat, and his wife nodded at Martha. It was a delightful change to be the recipient of the cordial greetings offered by other travelers and by soldiers. Martha even managed to turn a few heads in her ruffled dress, her thick loose curls hanging down her back.

The gold coins she had received from Jannet's father jingled in the small bag hanging from her wrist as she strolled through the fort, absorbing the frontier atmosphere. The sound drew her attention. She had been frugal with her money. Surely she could afford to walk over to the sutler's store or out to one of the Indian squaws selling goods outside the fort, and buy Hunter a gift. She might even purchase something for herself. He couldn't possibly be upset with her if she presented him with a token given out of love. And such a gesture might help to soften his recent fit of ill temper.

Chapter Seventeen

Hunter sat across the desk from the stiffly formal man in blue. "General Thornton, now that I've listened to a lot of double-talk, why don't you just tell me straight out what's going on." Hunter recalled that he'd heard that Thornton shaved his head to discourage a fear of being scalped.

The minute they had reached the fort Captain Holbrook had directed them toward a rickety building which housed the wheelwright and wagonmaker, who had said he'd be able to repair the damaged wagon. Then the captain had disappeared and returned almost immediately with General Harvard Thornton.

Hunter had become even more suspicious of the captain after seeing Holbrook pull the wagonmaker into a darkened corner after he'd gotten Hunter involved with the general. He expected a full explanation once he got inside the commander's office, which turned out to be plastered with medals, flags, and maps. But after listening to one of the army's most cunning generals, he knew without a doubt that there was more involved than a few routine questions, as the general had implied.

"You've got a lot of nerve, Brody. I like that about you. You don't waste time with games. The army could use a man like you." The general, a man of about fifty, wove his fingers together. "As I said, the army is merely cooperating in a civilian matter, but we have a few questions to put to one of the women traveling on your train."

Hunter stared at Thornton for a moment, then picked up his hat to leave.

"Where are you going? I'm not finished with you yet."

Hunter's hand was already around the knob, but he cocked his head and glanced back toward the angry, flushed man.

"I order you to come back here," the general roared.

Hunter showed no emotion when he said, "We have nothing further to discuss." With a look of barely concealed contempt, he opened the door.

The flustered officer conceded. "Wait!" Ill will glowed in his violet eyes. "All right, you win. Come back in and shut the door.

"We recently received information that a young woman on your train stole some money from a prominent citizen in the town in which she lived." The general watched closely for any reaction that would signify disbelief of his story as the big wagon captain returned to the chair. He was being forced to give Brody more information than he would have liked to reveal, but he had no intention of exposing the entire affair to some wagon-train captain. "As you may or may not be aware, our more powerful citizens have a way of seeking governmental assistance in their times of need."

Hunter's expression had been thoughtful. Now it held disdain. "General Thornton, as I said before, we have nothing further to discuss."

"Very well, Brody." Thornton sighed. Furiously trying to come up with some story the man would swallow, he cleared his throat as if he were about to divulge more information than he should. "The woman gave this citizen a merry chase until he set her up as his mistress. I was told he was livid when she ran off before they could . . . ah . . . consummate the relationship. He wants her back. Seems his enormous ego, as well as his bankbook, suffered. Since the gentleman in question is a married man with a family, I'm certain you can understand, he could not openly pursue *our lady*. Therefore, he has offered a substantial reward for her return."

There was something wrong with the general's tale, but for now Hunter decided to accept it and see where it led. "What part do I play in this, and why didn't you ride out when you

170

learned my train was close by and just take her off it, if the woman is, indeed, traveling with my train?"

"We didn't know you were in the area until this morning." Thornton settled back in his chair, obviously pleased with his explanation. "And the army prefers to seek the cooperation of civilians, rather than risk jeopardizing the good will of our civilian population. I'm sure you can appreciate our position and the need for the utmost discretion."

"Naturally." The pompous idiot, Hunter thought. He kept his face impassive. "What can I do to help?"

"Are you merely passing through, or will your train be with us for a short while? I understand one of your wagons sustained extensive damage."

Hunter listened closely to the man weighing his words. The general's attitude and Captain Holbrook's earlier behavior gave him the distinct impression that the wagon repairs would be held up. "I'm interested in continuing on as soon as the wagon's ready."

A sly smile quirked Thornton's thin lips. "Shall we drink to prompt repairs?" He took a bottle and two glasses out of a desk drawer, and poured two shots.

Hunter swigged the amber liquid, then set the empty glass down. "Let's not waste any more time—what's the woman's name?"

Thornton shuffled through the stack of papers on his desk, grumbling in sham frustration at not being able to locate them. "The paperwork is here somewhere." He fanned through the pile a little longer. "I'm afraid the filing system is most inadequate. I'm certain you must be aware that I am merely in temporary command of this post until the regular commanding officer arrives to replace Lieutenant-Colonel Munroe."

"It must be difficult for someone educated at West Point and used to life in Washington to be assigned to a fort so far away from civilization. And there are financial gains to be made by those who would profit if the country goes to war. I've no doubt you feel it your duty to oversee the government's scrutiny of such men," Hunter was fully aware of the general's reputation as an opportunist.

Thornton ground his teeth, and continued searching

through the papers. "Of course, as I told you, I am fortunate in that I shall be returning to Washington as soon as a replacement arrives for Lieutenant-Colonel Munroe. I'm not forced by financial circumstance to deal with these ignorant emigrants." The general looked up and directed a knowing, contemptuous grin at Hunter.

"You are fortunate. There aren't any fancy gambling houses out here," Hunter retorted. Abe had told him the general's vices had earned him this stint at Fort Laramie.

"Touché, Brody. It appears we are both well informed on each other's position."

"Let's stop splitting hairs. If you don't have the papers, I've other business to attend to." Hunter stood up, tired of the man's petty games.

"If you wish to see how the repairs are coming, I will get a clerk in here to straighten out this mess. I'll get back to you before you're ready to return to your camp."

The door had barely closed behind Hunter when Thornton knelt before the safe in his office and twisted the dial.

"What do you mean you don't know when you'll be able to get to the wagon?" Harriet's shrill voice filled the building.

"I've already told you three times, lady." The bull-faced man wrung his hands and then turned to William Belshaw. "Maybe you can explain it to your wife, mister."

William cast a beseeching look at the wheelwright as Hunter joined them. "Mr. Brody," he whined, "thank God you're here. This . . . this person says he doesn't know when the wagon will be ready."

"No doubt," Hunter muttered. He walked over to the man, who had returned to his work. "What's the story?"

With his foot, the wheelwright nudged the door behind him shut. "I told them sodbusters the sawmill here is for army use only. They'll have to wait until the next load of lumber arrives before I'll be able to fix those mashed side boards. It's due any day. Maybe you can explain it to them."

Hunter had noticed the man's feeble attempt to hide the generous stack of lumber that had been visible through the open door. The wheelwright obviously wasn't cut out for whatever the army had involved him in. Recent construction of housing accommodations at the fort had resulted in scraps with which to repair the wagon. "Yeah. Well, I'll explain it to them."

True to form, Harriet wasn't at all satisfied with Hunter's explanation. "I don't know why he just can't take the wood off someone else's wagon. Doesn't he realize we need ours?" The whites of her eyes grew as she was struck by a horrifying thought. "After taking our money, you wouldn't dare leave us stranded here, would you?"

What a tempting idea, Hunter thought. "When I make a bargain, I'm not in the habit of breaking it. You all paid me to see you safely across. I'm not going to leave anyone behind unless it's unavoidable."

"At least you have some conscience, despite the way you and that Collins woman have been carrying on."

Hunter's eyes narrowed into mere slits as he gazed at the bedraggled woman, his left cheek twitching. William Belshaw nervously stepped forward.

"Mr. Brody, Harriet doesn't mean anything by it." He ringed his arm through his wife's, and used all his strength to push her out of Hunter's path.

"How are we supposed to get back to camp?" she bleated.

"Try walking," Hunter said dryly.

"Why you thoughtless . . . wagon-train captain."

Hunter wearily shook his head as the big woman huffed off in the direction of camp.

William lamely started to follow after his wife, then stopped and wrung his hands. "The trip's been tough on her. She's really not a very strong woman. And with losing the store and all—"

"Don't worry about it. Now, you'd better hurry if you're going to catch her before she gets back to camp."

After the puny man nodded his thanks and hurried off, Hunter walked into the dusty heat of the sun. If it hadn't been for the suspicious behavior of General Thornton and Captain Holbrook, Hunter would have seen that the train kept moving. Although time wasn't a critical concern yet, his ranch was at stake. It would have been a blessing to be able to give the Belshaws the money to join another wagon train. Then some other poor unsuspecting bastard would have to deal with that damn family. But he hadn't the funds.

As if he didn't have enough on his mind, he looked up to see Martha surrounded by a group of soldiers who were all over her. "Chrissake, I should've known she'd show up here after I told her to stay at camp."

If that incredible mass of brown hair, glinting gold in the sun, hadn't been dangling freely down her back he might not have recognized her in those fancy clothes.

She was like a cactus, a nondescript little plant that suddenly blossomed forth to display some of the most delicately beautiful flowers in existence. But a cactus had thorns which could pierce a man's heart. And she looked much too desirable in that frilly dress.

Jealousy at the ease with which she was smiling at those young men sliced through him. "I should have had my head examined when I came up with that damned plot," he muttered. Still, a mock ceremony had seemed like a good idea at the time.

Hunter's strides lengthened until he pushed through the men to claim Martha's arm. "My dear, what a pleasant surprise. And how sweet of you to keep these kind gentlemen entertained." He drew his lips back into a bored grin to disguise what he was feeling.

"I'm so glad you're pleased." She smiled sarcastically. Underneath, she was disappointed by his apparent disinterest. He looked so rugged and manly next to the smelly soldiers. By the look of them, they probably hadn't had a bath in months.

"I'm sorry gentlemen, but my wife and I must be going now. We must get you out of the sun . . . dear."

"Oh, but I have my parasol so it won't be necessary." She smiled innocently and twirled the bit of pink lace.

"I'm afraid I must insist, *dear*." He clenched his teeth.

"But all these nice gentlemen—"

"Come along, my little lamb." He took her arm and sunk his fingers into it as he led her away from the gaping men.

Martha was somewhat demoralized because he seemed more

annoyed than interested. But at least she had managed to make her point. He wasn't going to keep her from going where she chose!

"That was a stupid stunt," he growled after they were alone. "Did you ever think that half of those men haven't seen such a beautiful woman since they left home. Any one of them could have yanked you into one of those buildings and taken advantage of you."

Martha's face showed a dawning realization only an innocent would have displayed. "I never thought of it that way," she murmured. Then a sparkle lit up her green eyes. "You said I'm beautiful."

"Yeah, well, so what. How did you *think* of it?" He glowered, not giving her reaction to his compliment a thought.

Disarmed, Martha replied. "After the men began gathering around me, I thought you might notice that they found me interesting to talk to and pay more attention to me."

"Talk! That's the last thing they were thinking about. My God, you haven't had any experience with men, have you? You don't know the first thing about a man."

His words pricked her ego and she snapped back, "That is not true. You don't know how much experience I've had." She raised her chin as she pushed past him. That would give him something to think about.

Hunter had hurt her pride. He was just about to catch up with her and let her know he hadn't meant to do it when General Thornton stepped out of his office.

Thornton looked Martha up and down as if she were a glass of water in the middle of a dry desert. "Miss." He tipped his hat.

"This is *Mrs.* Brody," Hunter drawled.

"Forgive me, ma'am, but you're so enchantingly lovely and your presence such a breath of spring in these barren surroundings that I hopefully assumed you were a single lady." Thornton stretched out his hand in greeting, and when Martha slipped her fingers into the general's, Hunter wanted to cut the bastard's palm off at the wrist. Then, to make matters worse, the man proceeded to slobber all over his woman.

Hunter couldn't believe Thornton's gall. Nor was he prepared for Martha's flattered response. She couldn't be that naïve, could she? Didn't she see the man was trying to charm her, and right in front of her husband no less? Maybe she was trying to make him jealous to get back at him for what he'd just said. Women were impossible.

Thornton stared lustfully into Martha's eyes while he addressed Hunter. "I would be truly honored if you and Mrs. Brody would consider joining me in my quarters for dinner tonight."

"Thanks, but another time," Hunter answered. He wasn't about to spend an evening watching that sonofabitch drool all over her.

"Oh, yes. I . . . we would enjoy it." Martha sprang forward, ignoring Hunter.

Thornton shot Hunter an amused, self-satisfied smirk. "Eight o'clock suit you?"

"That would be fine." Martha smiled.

"Oh, before I forget, being stunned by such a vision"—the general turned to Martha—"I have that name for you." He fumbled in his pocket for the slip of paper. "Here. I have written it down so there'll be no mistake."

Hunter read the paper, crumpled it, and put it into his pocket. He pictured Martha, gold-highlighted brown hair spread over her creamy white shoulders, lying beneath some married man, letting him touch her the way he had. He felt a knife had been thrust into his heart. Suddenly a realization hit him. There hadn't been one shred of truth to what the general had told him earlier. Martha had been a virgin. Her movements had been too awkward, too innocent, when he'd first made love to her. He'd suspected that the general's story had been contrived. Now there was no doubt about it. With shock, he recalled that the man had said the relationship hadn't been consummated.

"Thank you, General." He cupped Martha's elbow. "We must be going now . . . my little lamb. We have already spent far too much time at the fort."

He tried to usher Martha away from Thornton as nonchalantly as possible. He knew she had been hiding something and he wanted to get to the bottom of what was going on before Thornton found out who she was.

But Martha had other ideas.

"What name is that, *dear?*" She was suspicious because of the manner in which Hunter crumpled the paper and too quickly tucked it into his pocket.

"Nothing that concerns you, my little lamb."

"We don't keep secrets from each other," she cooed, determined to discover what he was hiding.

"We'll discuss it later." Whoever had written *obey* into the wedding ceremony probably had had a wife like Martha and had sought to remedy the problem for future generations.

"I suppose there's no harm in showing it to her, Mr. Brody. She will find out anyway." Thornton turned to Martha. "It's merely the name of one of the women traveling on your train. The army has a few questions to ask her."

Martha's curiosity peaked and before Hunter could stop her, she blurted out, "Who?"

"Martha Rockford Collins."

Chapter Eighteen

Disbelief and shock appeared on Martha's face. She stood as still as one of the rock formations they'd passed, gaping at the general. Hunter took one look at Martha and knew if they didn't get out of there immediately the general would guess her name.

"I know it must come as a shock to you, dear, since you two are inseparable. But now I must insist we leave." Hunter gave the general an indifferent nod. "You'll excuse us, General Thornton."

"No." Martha's sense of integrity bolted her to the ground. She drew her arm from Hunter's grasp. "I don't understand. I demand to know what this is all about."

Evidently perturbed, General Thornton looked up at Hunter, who was nearly a head taller, then took the typical stiff military stance, clasping his hands behind his back. "Ma'am, this is a matter between Miss Collins and the army. While I'm certain your concern is most genuine, you must agree that she should not hear of it secondhand."

Recovering from the impact of hearing her own name on the general's lips, Martha remembered that Hunter had merely introduced her as Mrs. Brody, not using her given name, and the general did not know she was Martha Rockford Collins Brody. "Do not patronize me, sir. I have every right to hear this."

There was no stopping her, Hunter realized. By the look on Martha's face she had recovered from the initial shock and was going to tell the general who she was. She was a strong woman. She had proved that. Whatever she had done she could manage to handle the situation. And it wasn't as if he were in truth her husband. He could just walk away. But it wasn't that simple. He knew he couldn't leave her in the clutches of a man like General Harvard Thornton, a man who was out to make a name for himself and didn't give a tinker's damn how he did it.

"What right do you claim, ma'am?"

"I happen to be Martha Rockford Collins Brody." She stood proudly before Thornton, almost as tall as the general.

Martha's steady gaze seemed to rankle the man, but his expression became triumphantly serious. In fact, he looked like a rattlesnake about to strike at a roadrunner. Hunter had to smile. Martha would soon prove to the snake that his prey was anything but some poor helpless bird.

"I don't know what you seem to find so amusing, Mr. Brody. I could have you arrested for trying to protect the suspect. But in view of your apparent lack of involvement in this matter, I will let that matter drop." The general had had Hunter thoroughly checked out and knew he could not have had anything to do with the situation in question. He'd only recently returned to the states from Arabia, and had met and evidently married the Collins woman on the way West. Thornton slanted his violet eyes over to Martha. She had to be quite a woman to catch Hunter Brody from everything he had heard of the man. "Your wife is under arrest," he declared, then took a step toward Martha. "I'm afraid you'll have to come with me, Mrs. Brody."

Hunter put himself between Martha and Thornton. "I thought you only had a few questions to ask, General."

"This is no longer any of your concern."

"Since the lady bears my name, I'm afraid it is my concern."

The general looked as if he were going to ignore Hunter until he saw him deliberately place a hand on the gun holstered on his thigh. "It seems we're at a momentary impasse, Mr. Brody."

"Not at all, General. Simply show me the papers you say you received on this woman."

"I can't do that."

179

"Then I'm afraid she's not going anywhere with you until you do."

"You know, I could summon soldiers and just take her."

"You could. It wouldn't be wise though. You'll have to answer a lot more questions if you do, and somehow I get the feeling you'd rather not."

The general paled. He had not planned on this. Hunter Brody was no fool and he obviously hadn't swallowed that story about a man wanting his mistress back. It was going to take some fancy maneuvering to separate this fellow from his wife. "I'll have to check procedures before I can show you the papers. Therefore, I'm placing her in your custody until that time. I trust you know better than to attempt to leave the area until this matter is settled."

"I have no doubt you're fully aware that repairs on one of the wagons in my train are being held up indefinitely, and that we will not be moving on until it's ready." Hunter's knowing expression squelched any denial that the general had held up the work on the wagon.

"As I said before, Brody, you should be working for the army."

"All right, sit down and tell me what this is all about," Hunter demanded as soon as he and Martha were in their tent and away from curious ears.

"I don't know what you're talking about. I haven't done anything." Martha sucked in her cheeks and fumbled with her full skirts, tucking her feet beneath her. She'd done nothing wrong.

"Dammit! If you don't tell me—and soon—you'll end up sitting in a military jail until you talk to General Thornton. And the way that sonofabitch was looking at you, you might just find being at his mercy more than you bargained for."

Hunter expelled a long breath and raked his fingers through his blond hair.

"There is nothing to tell," Martha said quietly.

"Oh? What about Jannet Wakefield's Aunt Velina," he

threw out.

"What do you mean?"

She was visibly shaken. Hunter probed further. "I saw you two down by the river."

Martha remembered Clinton's threat. She swallowed hard. "What do you think you saw?"

Hunter's jaw worked. She wasn't going to volunteer anything. He ought to leave her to General Thornton. Yet his heart and the look of innocence in her big rounded green eyes kept him from walking out on her. "I saw the woman shaking you and you looked scared out of your wits. She's not the girl's aunt, is she." It was a statement not a question. He waited for an answer.

He hadn't seen Clinton's hat stick on the branch. He didn't know. And Clinton's disguise surely had nothing to do with what General Thornton was talking about. Whatever that was, it must be some dreadful mistake.

The pounding of horses' hooves put an end to their conversation. "It sounds as if you'll get your chance to tell it all to Thornton. This time, stay here until I call you," Hunter ordered, concern in his voice.

Then he left her and strode out to meet the soldiers. Martha could make out the general's gruff voice, although what he was saying was unintelligible to her. She saw no use in remaining in the tent. She wasn't guilty of a crime, and had no intention of hiding as if she were. She rose to her feet, squared her shoulders, and went out to face her accusers.

Hunter was reading a legal-looking document, his face emotionless, and the rest of the company was milling about, whispering. From their expressions, Martha knew they'd decided she was guilty.

Hunter had seen similar documents and the ones before him did not appear to be complete, but without knowing what Martha was hiding, it would be difficult, if not impossible, to stop the general from arresting her.

"The papers seem to be in order," he acknowledged tightly.

"Of course they are, *Mr.* Brody. But what brought me out here without delay was this." General Thornton, flanked by

181

ten mounted soldiers, held out his hand. Fitting nicely in his open palm and shining in the sun was the twenty dollar gold piece Martha had exchanged for smaller currency. Beneath it was the new five-dollar bill she had given the sutler to pay for the gift she'd bought Hunter and had totally forgotten about in all the excitement.

Jannet Wakefield spied the shiny new gold piece, then glanced at Clinton and rushed forward. "Yes, that's one of them. I'd know it anywhere. My father never would have let it out of his sight," she wailed, snatching the piece out of the general's hand. Nearly hysterical she turned on Martha. "This proves you're guilty. How could you!" She drew a hand back to slap Martha, but Hunter grabbed her wrist.

"Why did you stop me?" she shrieked at him. "She stole that coin! Stole it and more from my father!" Jannet let out one last scream and then collapsed in Hunter's arms.

In the confusion General Thornton quietly slipped the five-dollar bill back into his pocket. It was a stroke of luck that the Wakefield woman had suddenly rushed forward. Her charges were working to his advantage. If his good fortune held, they would give credence to the tale he had told Brody earlier and would back up the information in the papers he had been forced to tamper with.

Silence descended on the camp as quickly as the lull before a storm. Hunter carried the limp Jannet back to her wagon, Harriet and Clinton, dressed as Aunt Velina, following him. Cornelius ran for his equipment while Winnie tried to comfort the stricken Martha. That unfortunate young woman had listened to Jannet's ranting, a look of horror on her face, then had remained silent.

"Captain"—the general turned to Holbrook—"search Mrs. Brody's tent." To Martha, he said "Mrs. Martha Rockford Collins Brody, in the name of the Government of the United States of America, I place you under arrest for theft. You will be placed in my custody until such time that you can be transferred back to the states to face trial."

"But I don't understand. Mr. Wakefield gave me five of those coins," Martha mumbled as if she were in the middle of

182

some terrible dream.

As Hunter rejoined her and Thornton, Captain Holbrook emerged from Martha's tent, the basket her mother had given her in his hand. "Sir, I think this newspaper is evidence that Mrs. Brody is lying. The headlines speak for themselves."

Totally forgetting to ask the general how he had come by the coin and the bill, Hunter grabbed the newspaper out of the captain's hands. In big bold letters it read:

MONEY DISCOVERED STOLEN

"But I haven't seen that paper," Martha protested as she noted the headline before Hunter quietly stuffed the paper into his belt.

"Mrs. Brody, please don't waste our time by trying to make us believe that you've carried this all the way from New York without looking at its contents." General Thornton took the basket and earnestly began rummaging through jars of preserves and gaily wrapped packages.

Martha turned to Hunter, tears in her eyes. "You don't believe them, do you?"

General Thornton's tale about a man wanting his runaway mistress back came to Hunter's mind, but he did not doubt that something else was going on and Thornton, for some reason, wasn't telling them of it. The papers Thornton had presented were not complete. And it was odd that Jannet hadn't stepped forward earlier to accuse Martha and that Martha hadn't told him she knew Jannet Wakefield. Now why would the general be pawing through that basket? What was he looking for? And why hadn't he simply shown them papers stating a theft had occurred and then arrested Martha at the fort when he'd learned her identity? But for now it would be to Martha's advantage not to let on that he suspected anything.

"I'm sorry, Martha." Hunter looked away. He couldn't stand to see the pain and devastation on her face. "All the evidence seems to point to your guilt."

"Well, I for one don't believe none of it," Winnie interjected with a grunt. "Don't you worry, gal. Some of us"—she shot Hunter a disgusted look that made him hate himself for what he had to do,—"ain't so stupid as to believe such nonsense."

"Captain, gather the rest of Mrs. Brody's things. We'll be returning to the fort without further delay," General Thornton ordered.

"Thornton, you have my word I'll bring her in myself. Though you probably aren't aware of it, we were only recently wed, and I'd like to speak to her alone before I turn her over to you." Hunter was stalling for time, hoping he could finally get Martha to tell him what she had been hiding without letting the general know he hadn't believed him.

"I have nothing further to say to Mr. Brody, General." Martha straightened her shoulders. She was so overwhelmed by Hunter's apparent assumption of her guilt that she'd reverted to using his formal name. She now wanted no part of him, husband or not.

General Thornton seemed to enjoy her rebuff of Hunter.

If Hunter was taken aback, he didn't show it. He merely shrugged and said, "Suit yourself."

"It's just as well since the seriousness of the crime obviously wouldn't allow you such liberty." Thornton commanded one of the soldiers to bring forward the extra horse that had been brought along. Attempting to maintain as much of her dignity as was possible, Martha allowed the general to help her up upon the cavalry mount. She sat proudly tall, staring straight ahead, concealing the emotions churning inside her.

"Mr. Brody, where are you going?" asked General Thornton. He was nettled, as well as surprised, that the big wagon-train captain was walking away before they had left.

"I have animals that need tending," Hunter called back over his shoulder. He went straight to the camel khan and started checking on the beasts, never once allowing himself to look up as the sounds of horses departing filled him with foreboding that the worst was yet to come.

"Boss. You let blue men take missus away. No try to stop?" Happy was puzzled. "I see way you look at missus. Way missus look at you. You two good pair. Good pair." His white-turbaned head bobbed. "I get camels. We get missus back."

Hunter's dark frown deepened and he glowered at the little brown man. "It's none of your business. Just stick to the camels if you want to keep your job."

Even as Hunter snapped out the harsh words, the tension in his gut neared explosive levels. It was as if the general had just taken away part of his life. And Hunter Brody was not a man to let anyone take anything from him without one hell of a fight!

Chapter Nineteen

Friday, July 15, 1859—Fort Laramie. I cannot recall a time in my life when I have felt so lost and forsaken as I find myself feeling now. Although to the outside world I may appear strong and undaunted by all that has happened to me as of late, inside I fear my bleakest thoughts may become reality and carry me into the depths of despair. . . .

For over a week Martha had been under house arrest, confined to one of the rooms in the general's quarters. A guard was posted outside her door, and another one stood outside the one small window in the sparsely furnished room she occupied.

Martha had to laugh to herself. After General Thornton had so rigidly escorted her to what was to become her prison cell, she'd sat down on the first real bed she had seen since May. It was soft, the linens smooth and clean against her weary flesh. Despite what faced her the next morning, she had slept as soundly as a child that first night.

General Thornton had stood in the doorway on the second morning, his arms filled with books. "My dear, I know how difficult this must be for you, so I brought you some reading material to help you pass the time."

"Thank you," Martha had responded solemnly, forcing herself to look up at the vain man. "I appreciate your kindness. If you will just set them on the table."

"Of course," he'd replied. "If there is anything else I can do to make the situation more tolerable, please let me know."

"You could order the return of my personal belongings."

"Consider it done." Thornton had nodded. This woman was going to require a little coaxing to get her into his bed, he'd thought. "My dear, I want you to know I understand how difficult it must be for a lady such as yourself to be confined to such meager accommodations."

"No doubt you do."

"I suppose one might say in a manner of speaking we are both prisoners."

"If you don't mind, I'd like to rest now." Martha had had enough of such banter.

Long after the general had gone, she'd sat near the window, blankly staring out at the distant hills. How could Hunter have so indifferently let the general arrest her? She'd closed her eyes and tried to blink away the image of Hunter turning his back toward her. Then she'd opened them and gazed at the books, but she hadn't had the slightest inclination to delve between the covers of the volumes the general had so graciously supplied.

"Excuse me, ma'am." A private barely a year or two older than Martha had then entered, carrying her worldly possessions. Martha had turned vacant eyes to the man. "Where'll you be wanting these?"

"Just set them anywhere."

"Yes, ma'am." He placed her belongings into a pile by the small chest of drawers, then backed awkwardly out of the room.

Martha had stared at the small trunk, the cloth-knit bag, and the basket her mother had packed for her. Personal articles of clothing and the few treasures she had been unable to part with had been hastily tossed back into their containers, sleeves and bits of cloth hanging limply over ragged edges which had not been visible before. She'd known she should tidy the rumpled mess, but her heart wasn't in it.

The way Jannet had shrieked at her, accusing her of thievery in front of the entire company had almost been more than she could endure. Cold, convicting eyes had settled on a verdict without a trial. But Harriet Belshaw or Cecilia Stewart hadn't

187

destroyed her will. It was Hunter's decision that she could be guilty of such a crime that had left her devastated. Her heart was bleeding from that wound. Yet she longed for him, for the security of his arms, for those few precious moments when she'd learned how sweet love could be.

Those first few days Martha had been so despondent she'd feared she would never rise from the depths to which she had descended. But her spirit refused to remain numb for long. Despite the disappointment she felt, she was Hunter's wife. Slowly she began to garner inner strength. She had done nothing wrong. The general would soon be coming to question her, and this entire misunderstanding would be righted.

Once Mr. Wakefield could be contacted, Martha believed she would be cleared of Jannet's accusations. She couldn't be upset with her for recognizing the gold pieces. Jannet must not have realized her father had voluntarily parted with those gold coins.

After dismissing the guard, Thornton stood outside Martha's door and smoothed his uniform. He had given the woman a week to cool her heels in that room. He had expected her to send for him, to place herself in his hands. She hadn't, but she should be ready to talk to him by now. Particularly since that husband of hers hadn't even bothered to try to see her. Yes, Martha Brody was at his mercy. He removed his hat and ran a hand over the skin on his head, slippery from the film of perspiration brought forth by the heat of the day.

He rapped twice before entering. He could not simply crash through the door and expect a woman such as Martha Brody to capitulate to his wishes. Despite what she had done, everything about her cried out loudly that she was a lady.

He opened the door wide.

"Mrs. Brody?"

"Yes, General." Seated at the small table next to the bed, Martha looked like a graceful figurine made of the finest porcelain. She was wearing a blue morning dress, and her hair was twisted neatly into a bun fixed at the nape of her neck.

Thornton swallowed hard and kept his hat in front of him to hide the sign of his desire to lie with someone of Martha

Brody's cut rather than one of Miss Lollie's puny girls or an occasional passing emigrant with prairie dirt still caked under her fingernails. He eyed Martha speculatively. He should be able to work her sorry situation to his advantage before he turned her over to the proper authorities for return to the states.

"Some pretty serious charges have been leveled against you. But I think I might be able to help you find a path out of the mire in which you seem to find yourself," he said in a husky voice, being careful not to mention the specific charges against her.

"This is all a dreadful mistake," Martha burst out, having taken in his words but not the intonation of his voice.

"Of course it is, my dear," he responded in a soothing tone. "Why don't I show you around the fort while you tell me about it?"

Thornton held out his arm and escorted Martha outside, past rows of buildings teeming with activity and soldiers busily engaged with their duties. Pompously he explained the functions of the military post. She was captivated by its inner workings and animately intent on pointing out the error which had been made in charging her with theft. So much so that seeing Hunter talking to the barrel-chested sutler only made her more determined than ever to prove her innocence.

The general followed Martha's gaze and felt her tense. He drew her arm in tighter against his side, patting her hand. If the woman was trying to make a point with her husband, he'd oblige her. And it might serve to keep Brody off balance; he didn't like what he had heard about the man doggedly pursuing something until he was satisfied.

He turned his attention back to Martha. "Why don't we return to my quarters? I've taken the liberty of having two places set for the noonday meal. I do hope you'll favor me with your presence."

"I wouldn't think of eating anywhere else." Hunter had stepped up behind them to intrude on their conversation. Although he had a slanted grin on his face, he would have liked nothing better than to have wrenched Martha away from the general. But past experience had taught him the direct approach would cause her to do just the opposite of what he wanted. At least she continued to wear his arrowhead. That gave him a small measure of relief.

He had hoped that by the time he'd returned from seeing Abe Baker Martha would have softened toward him and would be ready to tell him what she was hiding. He should have known better. He had dealt her a devastating blow by not clearly demonstrating in front of the rest of the company that he believed in her innocence, and now he was going to have to proceed with that in mind. A little over a month ago, he would have shrugged and left her to her fate. It was a sobering realization. Yet what he had learned from Abe about General Thornton's double dealings was enough to make him want to see this through despite Martha's attitude toward him.

"I'm afraid there's only enough for two, Brody." Thornton made a face.

Unperturbed, Hunter retorted, "Then you won't be joining us? I know you wouldn't think of separating a man from his wife."

"But you are aware Mrs. Brody is under arrest at present."

"Yes, I can see that." Hunter stood his ground.

"Oh . . . very well." Thornton sighed. "Come along. I'll inform the cook there'll be another guest for lunch." It was a small concession, and it might give him an opportunity to find out how deeply Brody was sticking his nose into the case. He'd save his energy for later battles.

Martha glared at Hunter, but she did not intercede. Something about the general's patronizing manner warned her to be wary. The man had a wicked glint in his eyes. At least with Hunter present she would not have to be concerned about her virtue.

"Dear, may I offer you my arm?" Hunter said easily, knowing full well her dampened pride would demand she refuse.

"You may. But I've no intention of accepting it."

Hunter tipped his head with mock politeness. "Whatever you wish."

Martha's chin reached a new height. How dare he suddenly appear and then invite himself to lunch!

Amusement sparked amid the displeasure evident in his

hazel eyes; then Hunter turned his attention to the general. "What are we having to eat? I'm starved."

Like an oasis in the desert, the dining table, covered with white linen and adorned with fine gold-rimmed china, held a virtual feast. Thin-sliced roast beef, mashed potatoes, and fresh green beans—enough for six—filled the air with a hearty aroma. The general held a chair for Martha and then started to take the seat next to her. Using his superior size, Hunter nudged the man out and sat down. Thornton grumbled, but took a chair across the table from the grinning Hunter, who looked like a savage in the buckskins he wore.

Martha listlessly picked at her meal, watching Hunter eat enough for two and easily parry every probing question Thornton threw at him. Even the general's attempts to learn why Hunter had been talking to the sutler earlier in the day backfired. As they finished the meal, the flustered general was explaining what had happened to the five-dollar bill he had shown them at the camp, along with the twenty-dollar gold piece.

"You presented two pieces of evidence, I believe, Thornton." Hunter cut a piece of meat and popped it into his mouth. "What happened to the five-dollar bill?"

"It didn't seem to be of any importance," Thornton offered calmly, raising a wine glass to his lips.

"Oh? It seemed important enough for you to continue questioning the man at the sutler's after confiscating the gold piece." Hunter scooped some potatoes onto a spoon and pressed green beans on top of the mound before lifting the utensil.

Thornton hesitated too long. He knew Brody was not going to blindly accept any construction he put on the matter as simple truth. He looked at Martha. She appeared more bored by their game than interested. He still might be able to pull it off. "It's my duty to fully question everyone involved with a crime, no matter how remote the involvement."

"How heartening to have someone so thorough as yourself taking an interest in such a case," Hunter responded idly. Then he muttered, "So much like your interest in the progress, or lack of progress, with the Belshaws' wagon's repairs."

"General, if you'll excuse me, I don't want to keep Mr.

Brody from his animals any longer than necessary. I know how devoted he is to the beasts." Martha stood up and swished from the room, putting an abrupt end to the twisted word games the men played in her presence. Why were they engaging in such silly male talk anyway? All that was needed was Mr. Wakefield's corroboration of her story.

After she returned to her room and had time to think, she began to wonder more about the strange meal. Could there be something more to the exchange between Hunter and General Thornton?

In her mind the issue of the theft charge could be quite easily settled; it was no more than a matter of time and of legal procedure before that would be done. She sensed that the charge was not the real issue, that there was some deeper trouble between the general and Hunter. Even if Hunter didn't love her, she was his wife. She felt compelled to help him with the general.

She rushed to her trunk without thinking that the general was no fool, pulled out her Sunday-best dress, and held it up. There was more than one way to loosen a man's tongue. All she needed now was a pair of scissors.

Get a Free
Zebra
Historical
Romance

*a $3.95
value*

ZEBRA HOME SUBSCRIPTION SERVICES, INC.

P.O. BOX 5214

120 BRIGHTON ROAD

CLIFTON, NEW JERSEY 07015-5214

B O O K   C E R T I F I C A T E

FREE

ZEBRA HOME SUBSCRIPTION SERVICE, INC.

YES! Please start my subscription to Zebra Historical Romances and send me my free Zebra Novel along with my first month's Romances. I understand that I may preview these four new Zebra Historical Romances Free for 10 days. If I'm not satisfied with them I may return the four books within 10 days and owe nothing. Otherwise I will pay just $3.50 each; a total of $14.00 (a $15.80 value—I save $1.80). Then each month I will receive the 4 newest titles as soon as they come off the press for the same 10 day Free preview and low price. I may return any shipment and I may cancel this arrangement at any time. There is no minimum number of books to buy and there are no shipping, handling or postage charges. Regardless of what I do, the **FREE** book is mine to keep.

Name _____

_____
(Please Print)

Address _____ Apt. # _____

City _____ State _____ Zip _____

Telephone (____) _____

Signature _____
(if under 18, parent or guardian must sign)

*Terms and offer subject to change without notice.

4-89

MAIL IN THE COUPON BELOW TODAY

GET FREE FREE GIFT

To get your Free **ZEBRA HISTORICAL ROMANCE** fill out the coupon below and send it in today. As soon as we receive the coupon, we'll send your first month's books to preview Free for 10 days along with your **FREE NOVEL.**

Chapter Twenty

Sunday, July 17, 1859—Fort Laramie. I have come to believe that time shall provide my salvation from this tangled web of intrigue in which I find myself. Meanwhile, I pray God will forgive me for what I am about to do. Although my actions may stretch adherence to one of His commandments, I must act in order to preserve another. . . .

Martha took a seat next to General Thornton in the last row of the small room serving as a chapel. The shawl draped over her shoulders caused a thin line of perspiration to form on her upper lip. The day was much too warm for a wrap, but her alterations had left the ruffled décolletage on the rose-appliquéd dress too plunging to wear to a worship service.

As she squirmed on the hard bench, she noticed a runt of a man sitting at the end of the row. The old-timer was the same short, bowlegged man she'd seen watching her on at least six separate occasions during the last two days.

The general had offered her free run of the fort upon entering her room after that disastrous meal with Hunter. Though she had then expected him to question her further, he had merely stated that they would talk on Sunday evening after he'd returned from seeing to a pressing matter. Martha had watched Thornton ride from the fort, then had set out to learn as much about the man as possible.

Now, as the service concluded, Martha leaned over and whispered in Thornton's ear. "If you're concerned that I shall attempt to flee and are having me watched, I can only assure you that I have nowhere to go."

"My dear, perhaps some transient found you as delightful as I do and cannot take his eyes from you, for I can clearly state that it is not I who have been having you watched. Now, where is this man you speak of?"

Martha pointed out the short man in the well-worn buckskins who was casually leaning against the two-story wood frame building to the west of the parade grounds. Thornton drew his brows together. That wasn't the man he had ordered to follow her. Perhaps the old fellow was an acquaintance of Brody, although Thornton didn't recall seeing the man at Brody's camp the day he was out there. And General Harvard Thornton prided himself on his uncanny ability to recall faces.

"If you'll excuse me, my dear." He gave her hand a patronizing pat. "I must speak to Captain Holbrook. Why don't you head back and I'll see you later this afternoon? We still must have that little talk about the coin."

"I had hoped that this matter would be cleared up as soon as you received word from New York." Martha was confident, never for a moment suspecting the general's intentions could be anything but honorable.

"I've no doubt it will; but you must realize how tiresome legalities can be, and I've sworn to uphold the law."

"Yes, of course." She nodded and swiftly headed toward the small room across from the general's, which had become her quarters. She could use the additional time to prepare herself and to talk to Thornton's cook. If she was going to find out what the trouble between Hunter and Thornton was, everything had to be perfect.

As she rounded a corner near the two-story building that housed unmarried officers, termed Bedlam because of the sounds that issued from it, Hunter stepped out of the shadows and grabbed her arm. Frightened, she started to cry out, but he clamped a hand over her mouth.

"You haven't so soon forgotten who your husband is, have you?" He was grinning, but he spoke with a quiet seriousness which warned her against making light of what he had said.

Slowly, he removed his hand. "What do you think you've been doing traipsing so freely about the fort the last few days?

194

Have you forgotten there are serious charges against you and Thornton may have additional plans for you—plans which do not include letting you leave until he has become much more intimately acquainted with you than you ever imagined?"

"I do believe you've issued that lecture before." Martha's lips narrowed into a thin line. Since she had continuously been told how plain she was during her childhood, she could not understand why Hunter seemed to think every soldier, including General Thornton, had less than honorable designs on her. And she hadn't merely been *traipsing*. She had spent a day and a half learning about the general's habits and gathering information from the more talkative women at the fort. She intended to use what she'd learned to gain information from the general this evening.

Hunter grabbed her shoulders. "Well then, try paying some attention to it." Trying to make her listen was like trying to hold back the waters of the Mississippi River. "Martha, look, I've done some checking and there's more to your arrest than the general's willing to admit. Something else is going on. I'm trying to get to the bottom of it, and I don't want to have to worry about you getting into trouble with Thornton. So do me a favor and try to stay out of his way until I can find out exactly what he's up to."

"Your sudden belief in my innocence is quite touching." She was still smarting from the doubt in her he'd shown back at camp, and couldn't help letting him know it. "I can only assure you that I have no intention of getting myself into any further trouble."

"Good. But, just for your information, I've always believed you."

"You have?" She was genuinely touched. "You needn't worry," she said, more earnestly now, "I'll be careful."

Hunter should have felt relieved by her declaration, but he did not. Against his better judgment he decided to tell her about Abe. "Just in case there's any trouble and I'm not around, I have a friend keeping an eye on you. If you need help just call out, he'll be close by."

A concerned line swept her brows. "He wouldn't be a short, older man in old buckskins, would he?"

Knowing Martha, Hunter almost dreaded to learn what

she'd have to say about Abe. "Yeah, why?"

"He must be the man I accused the general of ordering to spy on me."

"Good thing Abe can take care of himself," Hunter muttered. "If I've learned anything at all about General Harvard Thornton, Abe's probably been given a free ride from the fort by now."

Well, at least that man wouldn't try to stop her from helping Hunter this evening as she'd planned, Martha decided. Then she became worried. "General Thornton wouldn't harm him, would he?"

"Thornton wouldn't try anything unless there were no witnesses around. Most likely he's sent Abe packing."

Hunter was closer to the truth than he realized. The minute Martha had left the general, Thornton had gone to Captain Holbrook and had told him to charge Abe with vagrancy and dump him nearly ten miles from the fort, with a warning that he'd be arrested if he ever stepped foot near Fort Laramie again.

The general hadn't counted on the old man having so much grit. Abe had been living on the prairie longer than most soldiers had been in long pants. Idle threats from a few men in blue weren't going to stop him from getting back to Hunter. And the sooner the better after what he had overheard.

The rest of the afternoon Martha scurried about the general's dining room, directing his cook regarding the preparation of the evening meal. She supervised every detail right down to the wine and after-dinner drinks.

The day before she had sought out an officer's wife who'd seemed cordial, and the woman had given her sufficient informaton to allow her to prepare a dinner the general would never forget. A pleased grin lifted Martha's lips as she reflected on how she had managed to learn enough to make her plan successful. . . .

She now sat in a rocking chair that belonged to an officer's wife. She held one of the three remaining china teacups the woman had said she'd managed to salvage during her trek to the fort, and her gaze traveled about the sparsely furnished room. Women living on the frontier had to give up so much.

The officer's wife cleared her throat, and Martha's attention returned to the flighty woman who was squirming in her chair. "I know I should not be conversing with you, you accused of some crime and all. But it is so lonely out here. And of course, Morton—he's a lieutenant you know—well, he says there's talk that you are probably innocent. I'm sorry; I shouldn't be going on like this. What is it that I can do for you?" the nervous, plain-looking bird of a woman asked.

"Thank you for agreeing to talk to me. I'm preparing a dinner menu and I wonder if you would help me. I simply want the general to be in a good frame of mind when my husband comes to ask for his assistance." Martha had decided the woman would believe this.

"Well, the only advice I can give you is to be sure not to give General Thornton too much to drink. After only three drinks he begins to babble incessantly just before he passes out. Oh!" She put fidgeting fingers across her quivering mouth. "Please do not repeat what I said; the general could make Morton's life terribly difficult."

"You needn't worry." Martha reassured the shaken woman.

"Since you promise not to say a word, the general does have a fondness for that dreadful whore, Miss Lollie. And the man married and all, too. But now you must tell me everything you can about civilization. I've been out here for such a long time. . . ."

After a short conversation about life in New York, Martha thanked the lieutenant's wife, pitying her for the restrictive life she had to endure. Then, following the woman's directions, she easily located the tent near the laundries, the one in which Thornton allowed Miss Lollie to carry on her business.

"Excuse me, I'm looking for Miss Lollie," Martha said to the heavily painted redhead lounging in front of the portable shelter.

"You looking for a job?" The buxom woman stood up and waved Martha in before she could state her business.

When Martha was seated in the tent decorated with red tassels, Miss Lollie eyed her suspiciously. "You ain't looking for work. You're Brody's woman, ain't you? I heared you was about."

"I'm Martha Brody," she confessed, a lump forming in her throat as she realized that Hunter must have frequented this place. "Do you know my husband?"

The buxom woman's bosom jiggled as she let out a hearty cackle. "Let's say I seen the man about a time or two." Suddenly she frowned. "Why'd you come here?"

Though Martha wondered if Hunter had visited this garish woman, she strangled the desire to ask. Some things were better left in the past. "I need your help. . . ."

Her conversation with the aging whore had given Martha insight into General Thornton's habits. Enough, she was sure, to guarantee the success of her plan to extract information from the general.

Not long before Thornton was due back, Martha requested that a tub be brought to her room. Using her most fragrantly perfumed soap, she sank into the warm water and scrubbed herself until her skin tingled. Then she donned a robe and sat down to apply the kohl and lip rouge she had obtained from Miss Lollie, who had given out the strangest rolling laugh at the mention of General Thornton. The heavily painted redhead had been hesitant at first to discuss the general, and then had seemed to conclude doing so might be amusing.

After a half-hour's toilette, Martha looked at herself in the mirror and reacted with a start. Her eyes were smudged black and looked nearly twice their normal size, her cheeks looked as if she wore an eternal blush, and her lips were as red as a tomato in August. She wondered if Miss Lollie hadn't overstated the importance of makeup to the general. Martha stared at her reflection but a moment longer before deciding that if this was what it took to loosen the man's tongue and help Hunter, then God was just going to have to forgive her.

It wasn't until she slipped the gown she'd altered over her head and laced it up that she realized what a different picture she was about to present to the world. Second thoughts about the sagacity of her enterprise seized her, but the general's knock prohibited any further consideration of abandoning her mission. She had set the plan into motion and would see it through.

Martha dabbed the reeking perfume Miss Lollie had given her behind her ears. She then licked her lips and pinched her already red cheeks before answering the door. Her ample cleavage was revealed by the gown that now barely covered her rosy nipples, which she fought to keep from the general's hungry view as she opened the door.

General Thornton, decked out in dress blues, smiled wickedly and openly assessed Martha as if she were to be his evening meal. There was no longer any doubt about what was on his mind, and Martha hoped what the officer's wife had told her about the general and liquor was true.

"You look most appetizing tonight, my dear." Thornton's eyes gleamed lewdly. That pathetic woman had expertly followed his instructions; Brody's wife was about to learn that she had been outsmarted at her own little game. "I took the liberty of peeking into the dining room despite the cook's warning that you would object, and I must say I was pleased to find that you had taken such special care in overseeing the dinner arrangements."

"Why, General, it's the least I could do for you after your hospitality and your belief in me." Martha took the man's proffered arm and let him lead her into the dining room.

The cook took one look at Martha and the general and rolled his eyes. All week he had been covering bets that the old bloodhound would never get the prim and proper Mrs. Brody into his bed. Although she was accused of theft, the young cook had come to respect this woman for her refusal to allow the general to intimidate her. Now he shook his head. She had looked like such a nice woman, but at the moment he wasn't sure who was about to seduce whom.

"Aperitif, General?" Martha poured two glasses of the rose-colored liquid.

Much to her amazement and chagrin, Thornton slugged down one drink and then another without showing the slightest effect. And during the evening meal her worst fears were realized. Thornton not only guzzled down a bottle of fine

199

wine, he had an additional bottle delivered as well. By the time Martha served the after-dinner drinks, she was trying furiously to come up with a plan to extricate herself from what she no longer doubted was going to be a very difficult situation. That officer's wife had seemed nervous and Miss Lollie had been hesitant, she recalled. Now she knew why; she had been set up!

Thornton, feeling a warm glow, left the dining area and opened the windows in the small living room. He plunked himself down on the worn, flowered settee in front of one window and patted the place next to him. "Why don't you join me . . . my dear?"

He had a distinctly lecherous grin on his lips, so Martha tried to think fast. "You dismissed the cook. If I keep you company, who's going to clean up?" she asked lamely.

"He can take care of that in the morning." In the blinking of an eye, Thornton reached out and jerked Martha onto his lap.

"General Thornton!" Any lingering doubts she'd had about that officer's wife and Miss Lollie dissolved. "You planned this, didn't you?"

"Of course. There's not much that goes on here that I don't know about. I was told you were eager to learn about me so I thought I would provide all the answers you needed. Those fool women were very accommodating. But enough of that. Real soon we're going to know each other very well. Very well indeed. So why don't we dispense with formality . . . Martha." His hand started to grope about her waist. "And I want you to call me Harvard."

"Harvard—please!" She managed to twist herself off his lap. Hoping she could salvage something from her plan, and not wanting him to see the growing alarm in her eyes, she choked out, "I th-thought we had to talk."

"Let's not play games. I know what you are." His mood was beginning to turn ugly and Martha wished she hadn't been so hasty with Hunter, so that he would have stayed nearby. "I don't know where your accomplice is hiding with all that money, but by the time I'm through with you, you'll tell me everything I want to know. Now, come here."

"B-but I thought you believed that I didn't steal those coins."

"Coins?" The general's laugh was high-pitched and vicious.

Martha's fear increased. She was confused by Thornton's comment, and in her panic couldn't remember what Hunter had said about him. All that came to mind was her plan. Somehow she had to help Hunter. "What is it between you and my husband?" she impulsively asked.

Thornton looked at her as if she'd made an unbelievable attempt at diversion. Then his face flushed with desire and his hand slid down to his throbbing sex. "There hasn't been anything *between* Brody and me until now. But in a short while we'll share a common bond—you."

Martha watched in horror as the bulge in the man's trousers strained against the blue fabric. She edged as far away from him on the settee as she could.

"If you touch me, I'll scream and every soldier in the fort will hear me," she warned, fighting to remain calm.

"Be my guest. It won't be the first time the men have heard some woman cry out from these quarters during the throes of passion. I might add that even if the soldiers thought you were in dire need, no one would help you. You see, I am the commanding officer and they know I'd have any man shot for breaking into my quarters. Rank does have its privileges, my dear." The cruel smile on his mouth swelled to obscene proportions.

"You won't get away with this! That man I told you about this morning is Hunter's friend. He's keeping watch over me." Martha desperately grasped at the slightest hope.

"Ha! That old man you so wisely pointed out to me was given a free ride far away from the fort shortly after you left me this morning. Enough of this talk." He opened his arms wide. "Come into my arms. I guarantee I'll be more gentle with you if you don't fight me. You'll even find I'm a much better lover than that husband of yours. I know all the ways to please a woman. Come to me and let me show you."

Martha had only intended to tease him into drinking too much and then to listen while, in a drunken state, he told her what she hoped to learn about him and Hunter. She had never dreamed it would go this far. General Thornton had changed from a civilized army officer into a monster, and she didn't know how she was going to keep him from using his superior strength to bed her.

The general closed his eyes and puckered his lips, his thick tongue sliming over his mouth. Then he began to inch his way toward Martha. "I'm hot for you and I can already taste every inch of your richly luscious body."

He stretched out his neck, his eyes still tightly shut, his mouth cockled in drooling anticipation. In his excited darkness, visions of Martha naked beneath him danced invitingly. But when he pressed his lips against his prey, his eyes flung open. A mortified gasp escaped him as he swiped his sleeve across his mouth and spit out the filthy taste of dirt and sage.

There before his horror-stricken gaze was the totally repugnant face of a camel, which Thornton swore was smiling at him.

The beast had stuck its head through the window and was practically nose to nose with the surprised general. Thornton's utter astonishment was quickly replaced by livid rage, and he grabbed at the creature without giving a thought to its disagreeable temperament. The camel put back its ears and spit at the startled man before heeding a distant whistle and trotting off into the night.

Thornton bellowed for his soldiers, but not one man answered, fearing the general's wrath if they should break in on another of his cozy liaisons.

"Sweet Lord!" a staggering enlisted man breathed out at the sight of a lone, hump-backed creature sauntering past him. "It's the second coming, the ghost of the resurrection." He dropped to his knees and tossed away his bottle, swearing never again to touch another drop.

"Humphrey!" Martha hugged the smelly camel's neck when it rounded the dark corner and reached them. Visions of old Harvard Thornton kissing the beast and of the priceless look on his face when he'd discovered the switch brought tears of relief and laughter to her eyes.

Huddled as far against the corner of the general's settee as possible, Martha had reached behind her, fumbling for any object with which to beat off the general. Then an iron hand had clamped around her wrist and another over her mouth, stifling any thought of crying out. To her relief it had been Hunter. A dark murderous frown on his face, he'd put his index finger over his lips. Too happy to see him to worry about the lecture she knew he'd give her later, Martha had nodded her understanding.

Then Hunter and Abe had quietly lifted her out of the window the general had so conveniently opened earlier, and they'd positioned the camel just before General Thornton pressed his mouth against Humphrey's curled lips.

"What are you waiting for, for the general to come after you? Maybe you'd prefer the feel of his arms," Hunter mockingly ground out.

The force of Hunter's indictment made Abe's head snap up. He hadn't seen the big man show so much emotion since the death of his wife. A self-satisfied gleam sparked in Abe's black eyes.

"Don't," was all Martha could say in response to Hunter's vehemence.

"Then get up on that beast you're so fond of, and let's get the hell out of here before the soldiers realize that wounded boar howling is Thornton and he means business."

Martha gathered her skirt into her arms and scrambled onto Humphrey's back.

"Okay, Abe, get up behind her and let's move."

"I might be old, but I ain't dumb. I got me LizaBelle hitched behind the sutler's. You two head on out and I'll catch up with you at that cave we stayed in the winter of '54, near the base of the bluffs 'bout ten miles from here."

Hunter nodded and mounted his horse. Then he led Humphrey past the corral in order to spook the military mounts so the soldiers would have a hard time catching them and saddling them.

Chapter Twenty-One

It seemed like it took an eternity before they reached the cave and Hunter parted the brush to the entrance. Bone-weary, Martha crawled through the low opening after him. Once inside, he lit a candle he took from the bag he'd brought along, and Martha stood up and stretched. It was a spacious cavern with damp rock walls, stalactites hanging down from the high ceiling, and stalagmites projecting upward at the back of it.

"Just what did you think you were going to accomplish in that dress, smelling of cheap perfume?" Hunter ran his finger over the bustline of Martha's low-cut gown. "From the look of your dress and all that paint on your face, you were begging him to take you to his bed." His wrath began to dissipate in spite of himself at the velvety feel of Martha's skin. "God, you had me so worried," he blurted out.

Martha's breasts tingled under the pressure of Hunter's callused finger, and her nipples peaked inside the bodice. She raised her hand to push him away. He had hurt her terribly this last week, and she had vowed not to let him touch her again. Yet his words of concern had changed all that, and desire warmed that most intimate place at the top of her thighs.

"I was trying to help you," she said in a small voice heavy with growing desire.

"Let me help you now," Hunter murmured against her ear. He toyed with the laces on her bodice.

"Yes," she breathed, nuzzling into his embrace.

"I need to have my head examined for getting involved with

204

such a notorious woman," he murmured, but he bent his head and nibbled at the top of her breasts.

She responded immediately. Her body strained against his and her thighs throbbed at the heated touch of his legs. She molded herself to him, causing his maleness to swell hard against her belly and setting her flesh afire. Only having him inside her could put out the blaze.

"Why don't you lie down and let me take a look at your head?" she suggested in a honeyed voice.

"I'll let you check out more than my head." He winked.

"You do look as if you need more than your head tended." She had spoken without considering the meaning of her words. Now her eyes dropped to his hard shaft.

Hunter quickly spread out a blanket and unfolded his large frame across it. Placing his arms behind his head, he smiled up at Martha, taking in her reddened cheeks; then he looked down at his proudly standing need. "If you don't get down here right now and ease this aching desire I have for you, I may be the one to rip off that dress."

"There's no reason for that." She drew her fingers up to the laces on her bodice and with determined motions pulled the strings away. Without taking her eyes from her man, she then peeled the ruffles off her shoulders and let the gown drift to the floor.

Hunter drew in a quick breath as she slowly stripped away layers of clothing in the flickering candlelight. How could a proper lady become a most desirable wanton? Never had he felt such longing for a woman, in his heart as well as his maleness. In the heat of his passion, he forgot about the trick he had played on her and thought only about what his eyes were feasting upon: those lushly full breasts, the gentle curve of her waist rounding out to the ripe fullness of hips and well-turned thighs, her slender ankles. His gaze wandered back up to the softly curling dark triangle at the top of her legs.

Then, growling like a primeval man about to possess his mate, Hunter pulled Martha down to him and shucked out of his clothes. He covered her with drugging kisses until they became wildly passionate—tasting, touching and reveling in the uninhibited movements made only at the height of fervent desire.

"I need to feel you inside me," Martha moaned.

"There's no place on earth I'd rather be, my sweet Mat." Hunter raised himself up as Martha opened to him.

With one swift motion, he thrust himself into her. Their bodies clung, united, and then moved as one, joined in limitless abandonment. Martha whimpered her joy and threw her head back, straining faster and faster in time with Hunter's loins.

Her face flushed with rapture as his shaft burrowed deeply within her womanhood, enveloping them in mindless, explosive ecstasy until their bodies shuddered and peaked in exquisite unison.

Honeyed bliss surrounded them while Hunter cradled his exhausted love, drenched with the scent of their lovemaking, in his arms. The same fierce protectiveness that a male timber wolf feels for its mate settled over him. And as trusting, darkened green eyes gazed into his, he crushed her to him, not wanting ever to let her go. Until cold reality hit him. The agonizing pain of what he had done forced him to turn away and gather his clothes.

Bewildered, Martha propped herself up on an elbow. "You're not leaving?"

"You'll be all right here," he said without looking at her. "Abe will keep an eye on you. This time there won't be any soldiers around to drag him off. If he hadn't hotfooted it back to camp after he overheard the soldiers laughing and making bets about how long it would take Thornton to bed you tonight, I might not have been there in time to stop him."

"I could've managed General Thornton," Martha said in a weak, unsure voice.

A loud rustle of brush outside the cave drew their attention. "You'd best cover yourself. I've no desire for anyone to see what's mine."

Martha did not have the chance to retort that she gave herself as wife out of love for him, not because she belonged to him like some parcel of property. Quickly, she put her clothes back on, wishing she had something more proper to wear than her altered rose-appliquéd dress. When she emerged from the cave, Hunter and Abe were perched on boulders not more than ten feet from the entrance.

She walked over to the men and held out her hand to Abe. "I don't believe we've been formally introduced, I'm Martha Brody."

Abe's cracked lips split into a hearty smile. "Well, I'll be damned right into the arms of the devil himself if you ain't. And you can call me Abe, like in Abe Baker." He cranked her arm.

Hunter shot the old man a strange look before gaining his feet. "I've got to get that camel back to camp before the general pays us a visit."

"But he'll know you were responsible. Shouldn't you remain here until we can try to find out what's going on?" Martha knew Thornton would direct his wrath toward Hunter, and she didn't want him arrested for trying to help her.

"Don't you worry none, missus. That bald-headed old bloodhound may know Hunter done the deed, but he ain't gonna come right out and accuse no man for doin' little more than protectin' his wife. As long as Hunter watches his backside, he'll be all right."

"Please call me Martha." She forced a brave smile, then rose on tiptoe and hugged Hunter's neck. "Please, do be careful."

Hunter just stood there, stiff as a plank.

"Ain't you gonna kiss your bride? And you only wed a mere twelve days, too," Abe chided.

The fact that the old man knew exactly how long she and Hunter had been married caught her notice. Somehow the knowing ease with which he mentioned the length of time seemed too fantastic. "However do you know exactly how long Hunter and I have been married?"

Abe looked guilty, and Hunter answered quickly, "If you'll recall, I left camp to make arrangements for our wedding. Abe has lived out here on the prairie a long time and he's the one who helped get the preacher. Now, I've got to get back."

She forced herself to accept his explanation, although his voice had sounded odd, definitely not as level as usual. It was probably just the excitement, she decided.

Hunter mounted his bay, then turned back to Martha. "Oh . . . I almost forgot. I brought along that newspaper your

207

mother packed. It'll give you something to occupy your time with. Be sure to read over that story the captain mentioned. When I return we need to get everything out into the open. No more secrets, understand?" He handed her the crumpled pages now yellowed with age.

"Sounds like a good plan to me," Abe chimed in. He looked like a ferret just leaving a prairie dog's burrow.

Martha tucked the paper under her arm and kissed Hunter one last time as he scowled at Abe. Then she jumped up onto a boulder to watch him ride away, leading Humphrey behind him. After he was gone, she climbed down and faced Abe.

"You've known Hunter a long time. Do you think you could tell me about him? I know so little about my husband."

There was a silent plea in Martha's green eyes. Abe stared at her for a long moment before he said, "It'll be mornin' soon. It's been a long night and you look like you need some sleep. Why don't you take yourself back into the cave and get some shuteye first? After you're not feelin' so tuckered out I'll give you a little piece of insight into that big oaf of a man."

"Thank you, Abe." Martha placed a grateful hand on his arm before turning to crawl back into the cavern. She curled up on the blanket, stuffing the newspaper underneath the square of wool to help ward off the dampness of the cool night. The faint scent of their lovemaking lingered on the blanket, and Martha smiled to herself, the memory of their passion still warm in her heart. She closed her eyes and relived every smoldering moment before falling into a dream-filled sleep.

In her dreams, faces without bodies danced around her. Hideous and grotesque likenesses of Clinton, dressed as Aunt Velina, and of Jannet called out their delight at her troubles. Mrs. Belshaw and Cecilia wrinkled huge disapproving noses, and Harvard Thornton licked monstrous lips. She was spinning, strapped to a chair as their voices taunted her for being a fool. Gold coins fell at her feet and newspapers swirled through the air. *Coins! Accomplice. I don't know where your accomplice is hiding with all that money.* Thornton's vicious voice rang in her ears, as did Miss Lollie's rolling laughter.

Helplessly lost to a dream which had become a ravishing, violating nightmare, Martha thrashed about on the blanket, unable to fend off the freakish phantoms intent on destroying the delicately balanced love she had just shared with Hunter. She reached out and clawed at the air, crying and sobbing, unwilling to let them claim victory without a struggle to the death.

"Martha girl, wake up. Wake up!" Abe's gruff voice intruded into her ordeal.

She fought on, but her wrists were held tight and someone was shaking her. Suddenly with a start, she opened her eyes. Abe released her and sat back on his haunches.

"Tarnation girl. The hellfires of Satan himself must of been on your tail the way you was hollerin' and fightin'. Another minute and I might of got me scratched by a sleepin' she-cat."

"You're all right?" Martha looked terribly concerned. "I didn't hurt you?"

"Naw. But it's a good thing you finally woke up. What the devil was you dreamin' 'bout?"

"Everything that has happened to me in the last few weeks." Martha rubbed her aching temples trying to make some sense out of what her dream was trying to tell her.

Chapter Twenty-Two

For the second morning Martha scrabbled, behind Abe, from the cave and made her way to a pristine spring, bubbling with clear, cool water. The sun burned through the branches of a nearby dogwood tree as she washed and adjusted the ruffles on her dress the best she could. Her thoughts drifted to Hunter. He had seemed to share more of himself than his body two nights ago. In her heart there was a small glimmer of hope that she wasn't merely imagining it.

A new bounce to her walk, Martha joined Abe at the campfire and took the cup of coffee he offered.

"It's a good thing I rode me LizaBelle or we'd be goin' beggin' until that man of yours returns."

She sat on a fallen log near him and sipped at the strong brew. They had talked of many things since Hunter had left, but Abe had not offered the smallest bit of information about Hunter. There were a thousand questions she wanted to ask— so many things she didn't know about the man she called husband.

Abe handed Martha a tin plate filled with raw-fried potatoes and bacon. She toyed with the morsels on her plate while he shoveled food into his mouth, slopping globs on the napkin tucked into the top of his shirt.

"Abe, you said you'd tell me about Hunter," she ventured, no longer able to wait for the old man to initiate the topic.

"Yup, I sure did now, didn't I." He wiped the grimy bit of cotton across his unshaven chin. "Life's hard out here and a man's gotta be tough in order to survive. What's it you lookin' to know 'bout the man other than as long as I knowed him he's been a fair and honest fella." He leaned forward, hoping that would satisfy her, but true to his word, he'd answer her questions as he said he would.

"What about his wife, Abe? Did you know her?"

"That one wasn't no everyday Injun squaw. Dancin' Wind was young and wild. I remember when Rushes Hayes and me introduced them two. She took one look at Hunter and gived old Rushes the air. Sure stuck a burr in his craw. I think he had her staked out for himself. But he got over it right fast enough. Dancin' Wind knew her own mind, and nothin' stopped her from goin' after what she wanted—not even that crazy brother of hers, War Arrow. She wanted Hunter." Abe shook his head. "He never knowed what hit him. They moved around a lot on account of him bein' white and her Injun, until she got too big with child. She was havin' a time of it, her gettin' in a motherly way so soon after they was hitched and all. So Hunter took her back to her people so he could go sell them furs he'd trapped in a hurry. You see, that brother of hers thought their marriage weren't no good because Hunter didn't live with the family for a year and prove his skill at huntin' like a proper brave. Anyways, when Hunter got back and found out that she had up and died, War Arrow kept the three horses Hunter'd paid for Dancin' Wind and talked the tribe into somehow thinkin' it was Hunter's fault. Hunter had to leave right quick without even bein' able to stop at the grave. Nearly destroyed him, yup it did. He didn't come back this way until '54 when we stayed at this here cave."

"I thought Hunter had been accepted by the Indians," Martha said, fascinated yet saddened by the old man's story.

"There's been bad feelings brewin' between whites and Injuns for years. Like in '54. One of them Sioux braves killed a old cow that was laggin' behind a train. The chief, Bear That Scatters, he tried to pay back the owner. But the man was as mad as a wet hen and demanded more money. Then that unthinkin' young Lieutenant Grattan marched thirty men into the Sioux camp to arrest the cow killer. Durin' the parley the soldiers shot the chief so the Sioux killed the whole bunch of

211

them army men. That started killin' on both sides. Then this Brigadier General—William Harney—he marched out of Kansas and demanded the heads of the five Injuns which killed three men on a mail wagon. Well, the five gived themselves up for the good of the Sioux and strolled, just as big as you please, into the fort all dressed up, expectin' to be hung. You know, that's the worst kind of death for a Injun. It shuts him out forever from a warrior's hereafter.

"Hunter tried to help out, but War Arrow seemed more bitter than ever 'bout what he thought Hunter done to his sister and would have none of him."

"Were the Indians hung?"

"Naw. They keeped them in prison for show, then a few months later the president—Pierce, I think it was"—he rubbed his chin—"yup, it was. Anyways, he pardoned them Injuns. Things cooled off a mite again after that. But as I was sayin' 'bout Hunter and Dancin' Wind 'fore I got sidetracked, them two, their love was young and reckless. Not like what you and Hunter got."

Martha faintly smiled. "And what's that, Abe?"

"What do you think it is?" He answered her question with a question.

What she and Hunter seemed to have was one argument and misunderstanding after another. The physical side of their relationship was incredibly wild and wonderful, but love was more than that: it was small acts of kindness, a warm contented feeling that the world was right when that special person was by your side; an assurance that no matter how cold and heartless life could prove that one special person was there, ready and willing to pick up the pieces and share the good with the bad.

"Sometimes I'm not sure," she answered, unable to put her thoughts into words. "Do you think that's strange?"

"Naw."

"Then what do we have?"

"I can't give you them answers. But it's got to be special."

"Why's that?"

"Hunter up and gived you that arrowhead. I ain't knowed him to take it off since Dancin' Wind gived it to him."

She sighed her frustration. "But I still don't know what we have."

"You got to find them answers in your own heart."

"Oh, Abe, there's so much more I need to learn about Hunter, so we can build a strong marriage."

"Ask away."

Martha slid across the log and hugged the runt of a man. "You old dear. How is it you're so wise? Hunter could learn a few lessons from you."

"What is it I could learn from Abe?" Hunter had come upon them without their knowledge and he now stood with his hands on his hips at the head of the clearing.

He looked handsome with the sun shining rich gold through his blond hair, his buckskin shirt open at the neck revealing curling bullion-colored hairs. A pistol hung with authority at his slender waist, pointing toward heavily booted feet. Martha almost had to sigh at thinking about how her friends would virtually swoon over each other to meet such a man, and he was hers.

"Abe and I were just talking about life, that's all."

"And I could learn about life from this old scalawag?" Hunter looked skeptical, but didn't question them further.

He tossed Martha the bundle he had been holding.

The package was soft. "Clothing! Thank you. I was beginning to fear I would be forever forced to wear this dress."

"As a reminder of your escapade?" he asked.

She shot him a tart frown and unwrapped the parcel. Then her face fell markedly. "Isn't this one of Jannet Wakefield's favorite lavender cottons?"

"I wouldn't think of taking anything but the best for you, my little lamb. Since all your clothes are still at the fort what would you have me do? Break into the general's quarters with the explanation that the prisoner who escaped didn't have anything to wear and was in dire need of one of her dresses? I'm not too sure the old bloodhound would be so understanding."

The smirking humor in his eyes did not appease Martha. She forced herself to accept his offering, and retired to the cave to slip into the gown, only to emerge a few minutes later surprised

213

that she had managed to squeeze into the small dress without the aid of a shoe horn. She had a fuller figure than Jannet and could feel the fabric straining at the seams.

In response to Hunter's silent amusement, she said sharply, "Next time you decide to steal something for me, at least pick your victims according to size."

Grinning, Abe turned and left them alone.

Hunter looked quite satisfied with his acquisition. "I like the way the dress fits. It's just fine."

He cleared his throat as if signaling the end of one topic and the beginning of another. "Did you read the newspaper I left?"

"The newspaper?" She searched her memory. "I put it under the blanket to help ward off the dampness in the cave."

"Well, let's go take a look at it. We can't afford to waste any more time. General Thornton paid me a little visit yesterday, looking grizzled and mad as a badger that's been spooked. Seems he has an entire platoon scouring the area. He didn't comment, though, on the seductive powers of a camel."

Martha smothered a giggle and dropped onto her hands and knees. Once inside the cave, she gathered up the newspaper sheets, and Hunter settled onto the blanket next to her.

"What are you staring at?" she asked pertly.

"I was just thinking about how gorgeous you looked in the candlelight the last time I was lying on this blanket." There was a seductive sparkle in his eyes. "Why don't we find out if this blanket is as good a second time?"

"I thought you said we couldn't afford to waste time?" she teased.

He expelled a heavy groan. She was right; he had said time was important and it was true. "Making love to you would never be a waste of time. But you were right to remind me. You'd best start reading while I go take a cold dip."

"A cold dip?"

"Yes, my little lamb. It has a way of restoring certain things to proper order." He smirked.

Martha noticed his rising desire. "Don't you think we could *restore order* in a more pleasant way?"

"I've no doubt of it. And if you don't quit looking at me that way, I just might weaken and let you take advantage of me. So get busy and start reading while I go cool off."

Disappointment fell across Martha's face at this demonstration of his extraordinary ability to control himself. Then she remembered Abe had said a man had to be tough to survive out here. She crossed her legs, settled the paper onto her lap, and began reading.

As she read her expression changed from boredom to horrified fascination, and a frightening comprehension trickled into her pores, causing her to break out into a cold perspiration. Money had been stolen from the bank in Elmira. Dark foreboding settled on her as she read further.

"Oh, my precious Lord!" she gasped, slapping her hand against her mouth. How could she have been so gullible? She had been worse than foolish to think the charges against her concerned the coins. Why hadn't she realized the importance of the newspaper when it was discovered in her basket? Her romanticism had clouded her thinking. She had convinced herself that she had remained silent about Jannet and Clinton in the name of love, but she'd really feared she might lose the happiness she had found with Hunter if she exposed Clinton. General Thornton had been right after all. It looked as if she were an accomplice. An unknowing accomplice to a much greater crime.

She was staring blankly at the printed page when Hunter returned. "You look like you've just seen a ghost. Could it be something you read?"

"Ah . . . no. No!" She turned the page of the paper. "I was just reading." She sneaked a peek at another story on the lower right hand corner. "About Nancy Cooke. She was a childhood friend back home who"—sadness hit her and she mumbled—"was recently killed in a dreadful accident."

"Is that so?"

She had merely meant to use the story as a diversion, yet the news of her friend's death caused goosebumps to rise on her arms. She read further. "Strange . . ."

"What is?"

"For Nancy to be thrown from a horse."

"It has been known to happen to even the best riders."

"But Nancy used to be scared to death of horses."

"Maybe she was trying to overcome her fear. I'm sorry about your friend's accident," he said sincerely. "But we have to think about you right now. Isn't there anything else in that paper that can shed some light on what's going on?"

"I don't understand what's going on?" Martha replied, bemused.

He didn't look as though he believed a word she was saying. She couldn't blame him. She herself could hardly believe what she'd just learned. But until she confronted Clinton and Jannet and heard their explanation she wasn't about to tell anyone! It was too incredible that Clinton could be the one who'd stolen twenty-five thousand dollars from the bank just before she'd left her home. Becoming president of the bank had been his life's dream. And if Clinton and Jannet had done it, why would they be traveling on the same wagon train? But no one knew Clinton was on the train. Could that be what the general had been alluding to when he'd made a comment about all that money?

"Martha, are you telling me there's nothing in that newspaper that means anything to you except the story about that friend of yours?" His voice was stern; he expected an honest reply.

"No. I'm not telling you that," she hedged, unable to come up with another lie.

"Then what is it you're telling me?" He knew she was concealing something; they had talked before about that. Now he wanted to shake it out of her. Put an end to all this. He made no move. He, too, was engaged in a deception. He would wait until she was ready to confide in him. At least he owed her that much.

"I have to go back to the train," Martha stated calmly. She had to confront Jannet and Clinton. She was no longer going to let them ensure her silence with threats.

He noticed her eyes held a purposeful light. If she went back to the train, the general would pounce on her.

Maybe not . . .

Hunter swung on his heel to leave the cave.

"Where are you going?"

"I have something to take care of before you leave here. Just promise me you won't go anywhere until I come to take you back myself."

Martha lowered her eyes.

In two strides he was standing above her, leaning over and pulling her to him.

"Promise me!" He urgently grasped her arms, more from concern than anger.

Martha mistook his actions. She felt he was furious with her for not confiding in him, and asked herself if he'd ever be able to forgive her for what she must do. She took a deep breath and crossed her fingers behind her back.

"I promise."

For a moment he searched her eyes. Then, as if a sudden wave of emotion washed over him, he kissed her long and hard with an urgency and hunger that had never gripped him before. It was a breathless kiss. Then he was gone.

She returned her attention to the newspaper and reread the article, her hands trembling. Regardless of how she tried to defend Clinton's actions, the answer kept coming out the same. It made sense out of her dream.

She set the paper aside and paced the cavern. Abe was sure to be outside. Hunter had undoubtedly warned him to watch her, but she couldn't wait until her husband returned. She had to confront Jannet and Clinton.

Knowing better than to trust the resourceful Martha, Hunter had told Abe to be on the lookout for any attempts to trick him so she could get back to the wagon train.

He drove his big bay until the animal was lathered and strained to obey its master's command. It was late afternoon by the time Hunter entered the fort and handed the horse over to an army private, instructing him to see it was cooled down.

"General Thornton." Hunter burst into the stunned man's office.

"What are you doing here, Brody?" Thornton snarled from behind his desk.

"You're going to give me the whole story about Martha and the charges." Hunter took a threatening step towards the general.

"I don't know what you mean." Thornton uneasily adjusted the buttons at his collar.

Hunter was in no mood to play word games with the man. With the ease of a predator, he reached over the desk and grabbed the bald-headed officer by his blue coat, hauling him onto his back across the desk, his legs dangling helplessly.

"Is your memory coming back to you yet?" Hunter tightened his grasp. "Maybe you need some help?"

"No," Thornton spat out. He had seen that deadly glint in men's eyes before, and knew better than to argue when in such a precarious position. "Let me up and I'll tell you everything you want to know."

Hunter uprighted the sniveling man none too gently. Thornton glared at Hunter, who had comfortably seated himself on the edge of the desk, and then took some papers from his safe and threw them in Hunter's lap.

"They contain the whole damn story about that wife of yours. Just remember, if you recover the money, it couldn't have been without my help and we're partners. Agreed?"

"I've no intention of agreeing to anything," Hunter said with disgust.

Thornton seethed as he straightened himself and settled back into his chair. He had been counting on that reward money to help settle his gambling debts before he returned to Washington. There had to be something he could do. Some way to beat that big sonofabitch out of it.

A tense silence filled the air as Hunter began to pore through the neatly penned pages—ten of them, three of which had been missing when he'd first been shown the papers.

Hunter's lips settled into a calculating line. Everything was beginning to make sense. The events of the last six weeks were taking on new meaning, a third dimension. Even his vague recollection of the way his wagon train had taken shape suddenly started to assume a new clarity. But when he read the section describing how the money was stolen and the command to watch for a young woman, his eyes flared.

"Jesus!" Hunter suddenly bounded to his feet and headed out the door. The truth hit him like needles from a choya cactus, flinging vicious thorns into his gut.

He yanked his horse's reins from a bewildered soldier and leaped onto the bay's back. Digging his booted heels into the animal's soft flanks, Hunter rode from the fort at the speed a grass fire fanned by high winds crosses a dry prairie.

"Saddle me a horse," Thornton roared at the curious Captain Holbrook, who was watching Hunter disappear in a massive cloud of dust.

Chapter Twenty-Three

Stars cluttered a black sky with their silvery glitter by the time Hunter reached the cave at the base of the bluffs. Abe sat nodding by a warming campfire, his rifle balanced across his lap. At the crackling of the surrounding brush, he became alert.

Leaping up on his bowlegs, Abe eased back the hammer on the rifle. "Come out of there and show yourself before I blow your head off."

"Relax." Hunter emerged from the sage.

"I didn't expect you tonight."

"Where's Martha?" There was an urgency in Hunter's voice.

Abe shrugged. "She's in the cave, asleep."

Hunter strode to the entrance and ducked inside. In an instant he was back at Abe's side.

"She's gone. When did you see her last?"

"She said she was all tuckered out and went inside right after supper."

"How long ago?" Hunter was barely able to contain himself.

Abe's mouth sucked into a worried line. "'Bout six hours ago."

"Jesus! She's probably there already."

Abe didn't have to ask where. He immediately kicked dirt on the fire and rushed to saddle LizaBelle. Although Hunter hadn't explained the details, Abe could feel the tension in him.

Hunter didn't wait for the old man. Visions of Martha in

desperate straits hounded him as he mounted his horse and turned it toward the wagon train.

Martha hadn't been able to come up with a successful plan to slip away from the old man's watchful eye before supper. Every time she had left the cave Abe was right there like a shadow in the sunlight. It wasn't until after supper with a full belly and a bottle at his side that Abe's attention to her activities seemed to wane. She took full advantage of his belief that she was truly exhausted when she yawned and said she was going to turn in early. She crawled into the cave, then turned around to lie on her belly and watch him light a cheroot and lean back against a tree stump, contentedly blowing smoke rings and sipping from a full bottle.

Impatiently she waited until it was nearly dark before slithering from her vantage point. Once she thought Abe was going to catch her when she snagged her skirt on a bush. He craned his neck at the noise, but settled down again.

The withering daylight still on her side, Martha got to her feet a short distance from the cave and picked her way through heavy undergrowth until the brush thinned. Uncertain of the location of the wagon train, but knowing the fort was to the east, she turned her back to the fading pink sky in the west.

Had she known the exact location of the train it might not have taken her nearly eight hours to reach it. But night engulfed her, and she walked over hills made slippery by drying grasses, her heart lurching at the shrill sounds and the howls that pervaded the darkness. It seemed like an eternity before the warm yellow lights of the fort shot out, like welcoming hands through the blackness.

Her face was smudged, and strands of brown hair had escaped the coil at the back of her neck by the time she managed to locate the wagon train. She crouched behind a half-dozen huge boulders and listened to voices. . . .

"At least the weather has permitted us to sleep under the wagon instead of being packed together." Derek drew Cecilia closer to him.

"I don't know why we didn't think of taking over that

thieving woman's tent before the Belshaws did," Cecilia whispered petulantly. "We've had no privacy at all with the Wakefield girl and that strange aunt of hers sharing our wagon. We never should've agreed to take them in. Daddy offered you plenty of money."

"You know I couldn't take your father's money. And what they paid us will help us start our ranch. I'm going to show your daddy that I'm worthy of his daughter—without his help. No more talk. Put those hot little fingers around me and squeeze it like I showed you."

Their voices trailed off into muffled giggles and excited moans.

Martha listened for a while longer. The camp was still except for the snores of men. Just as she started for the wagon sheltering Clinton and Jannet, she saw them emerge from the back of it and stroll toward her. Fearing they would spy her before she was ready to confront them, she skittered underneath the nearest shrub.

"Why did we have to come out here?" Jannet obviously was straining to keep her voice low.

"Because those blasted newlyweds are sleeping under the wagon. You wouldn't want them to overhear us, would you?" Clinton expelled an exasperated growl.

"Where did you hide the money? We've got to take it and leave this train." he declared impatiently.

"I told you not to worry so much over the money. It's in a safe place." Jannet smiled triumphantly.

Clinton dug hurting fingers into her sides and almost attacked her mouth. Martha gasped at the violence of their kiss. Clinton never had been anything but dignified and proper in her presence.

As Martha moved slightly, a branch rustled.

"What was that?" Clinton broke the embrace and looked around.

Martha tried to slink further under the bush, but her movements disclosed her presence.

Jannet pointed. "Quick, over there!"

In a flash Clinton locked a hand around Martha's arm and dragged her out into the open, his floppy bonnet falling from his head.

"How convenient. Now we won't have to worry about you anymore," Jannet snarled.

"What are you doing here?" Clinton prodded.

Jannet raised her brows into a furious arch at seeing that Martha was wearing her favorite lavender dress, now covered with dirt and twigs. Like a cat, she bared her claws and reached out to rip Martha's gown. She tore open the bodice and split the seam of the skirt, leaving Martha little more than her thin chemise for cover. Since her hands were clamped tightly together by Clinton, Martha tried to protect herself with her feet.

"What has gotten into you?" Clinton hissed at Jannet. To put an end to the ruckus before they roused the camp, he threw Martha to the ground and bound her hands and feet with shreds he tore from the lavender dress.

Martha trembled, feeing her life was suspended from a frayed cotton thread, and silently made peace with her maker.

"That is my dress she is wearing! That bastard Brody must have stolen it for her."

Clinton looked down at the frazzled pile of rags on the ground. Moments before it had been a mighty handsome gown. "*Was* is right, you little hellcat."

Satisfied that Martha was no longer dressed in her gown, Jannet glared threateningly at her. "He asked you what you're doing here," she said. "And if you're thinking of screaming, I wouldn't if I were you. The slightest peep out of you and it'll be your last."

Martha, who had never seen Jannet behave in such a totally crazed fashion, sat on the cold ground as if in a trance. She had known this woman was jealous of her, but she'd never dreamed her capable of acting like a rabid dog. Jannet took a menacing step toward her.

"I . . . I came to talk to Clinton," Martha stammered. Although she realized her options had narrowed down to next to nothing, she couldn't keep herself from staring at Clinton's feminine attire. "You know," she said to him, "everyone in town always did think you were too handsome to be a man."

Clinton scowled at the implication.

"Listen to her. Why wait?" Jannet spun on him. "Why don't we just kill her now and drag her body out on the prairie? The wolves will dispose of it."

"No," he replied nervously. "I want to hear what she has to say." Clinton hadn't counted on this. Beginning to sweat, he added, "If you want to save that precious neck of yours, Martha, you'd better make it good."

Martha's eyes became rounder after she heard Jannet's intentions. "I finally read that newspaper Mother had packed for me. I don't understand why I was accused of stealing money from Jannet's father." She stopped to catch her breath, then continued. "There was an enormous amount reported missing from the bank in Elmira. Your bank, Clinton. Although I turned down your offer of marriage, you always seemed so dignified and level-headed. If you had stayed at the bank you might have been president someday."

Jannet took another menacing step toward her, and Martha raised her chin defiantly, determined no longer to fear the hand of death should it strike. Her prayers would provide comfort and strength, she told herself. Then she swallowed hard, waiting for that inner fortification to calm her raw nerves.

"Are you just going to stand there until she says it out loud? Why don't we get rid of her now?" Jannet cried.

"Until I say what?" Martha's gaze swung back and forth between her two captors, then settled on Clinton. "It was you who stole or embezzled the money, wasn't it, Clinton?"

"Stop her! Stop her Clinton," Jannet pleaded.

Martha knew she had nothing to lose, not knowing what they intended for her, and since she no longer doubted that she had guessed the truth, she pressed on. "Why did you take the money? For Jannet? Because her father wouldn't accept a penniless banker more than ten years older than his sweet young daughter as good enough for her?"

Clinton grew desperate as Jannet scratched at his shoulder, trying to force him to shut Martha up.

"Think about it, Clinton. Was Jannet a sweet, innocent young girl when you met her?"

"No," he said, half to himself, the hard and ugly awareness

224

that he was going to be forced into action dawning on him.

Jannet was nearly hysterical now. "Don't let her fill your head with lies! Don't believe her!"

"Was taking the money from the bank your idea or Jannet's?"

Clinton started to shake uncontrollably, and Jannet lunged at Martha, a crazed fire in her eyes.

"No!" Clinton pulled her back. "No. Not yet."

Martha held her breath as she watched Clinton fight for control. He seemed to be trying to come to a decision. Martha was sure her fate hung on the outcome.

"You are pretty smart, Martha Rockford Collins Brody," Clinton said with a strange deadly calm. "But I did not steal the money."

Martha turned disbelieving eyes to Jannet. "You took it?"

"Papa and I," Jannet said proudly.

Martha slumped back, drained, and said no more.

"What's the matter? Don't you have anything else to say? You might as well speak out now, you know. You've managed to seal your future, or lack of it, with that tongue of yours." Jannet's eyes were cold." Still, I wouldn't want to see you go to your grave without knowing the whole story. You've guessed most of it already, but let me fill in the few details you left out." Jannet was gloating now. "Papa helped me. I kept scrawny old Simmons busy one evening while Papa used his key to the bank. It was so easy."

The vicious light in Jannet's eyes had a maniacal flicker. "You've always gotten everyting, even after your father died. Everyone thought you were so smart, and the boys I was interested in used to sit in awe of you, even though I was prettier."

"I don't understand."

"You knew I was jealous of you. Don't deny it!"

"Yes . . . but—"

"But you never knew how much, did you? Think about that scar on your shoulder." Jannet grinned scornfully.

Martha subconsciously ran her fingers along the thin red line angling out from her collarbone. "That was an accident."

"Was it? If I hadn't placed that wire a little too low, it would have caught you at the throat that day when you, Nancy, and I were running down the hill near Papa's berry patch." Jannet's lips curled in an evil sneer.

"Nancy? Nancy Cooke?" Martha barely got out the name.

"Yes. That little bitch whose locket I took. And you told on me. Do you remember? I've hated you both for that, for Papa throwing it in my face that I should have been more like you two. He even threatened to send me away after that, but I talked him out of it."

"Nancy was killed recently," Martha said, dread enveloping her.

"She was, wasn't she?" Jannet clicked her tongue. "Such a messy death, too."

"You killed her?" Horror struck Martha at the realization.

"You should have been there." Jannet smiled. "Poor Nancy was simply terrified of horses." She laughed. It was a sinister sound.

"Why?" Martha barely whispered the word. She was astounded by the ease with which Jannet had confessed to murder.

"I merely repaid her for her part in causing trouble between Papa and me."

"Your father had a hand in that, too?"

"Of course not. He just wanted enough money so we could go away and make a fresh start."

"But why with me?" Martha desperately tried to give some semblance of meaning to the incredible story.

"It was so handy, perfect timing you might say. When we heard you were planning to go West, I convinced Papa that going with you would have a good effect on me. And you made everything so much easier by coming to Papa for a loan. He thought you could turn me around," Jannet said spitefully. "Of course, I showed him how you could be blamed for the theft in case anyone figured it out. That's why he made you promise not to tell anyone you knew us. I even sent you the rest of the money you needed."

"You were my benefactor? The money I received was stolen?"

"Where would you expect to get newly minted bills from?"

"What made you think people would believe I took the money?"

Jannet shrugged her shoulders. "You needed the money. You had jilted poor Clinton here." She stroked his back sympathetically before continuing. "And you were leaving town. It would look like you were guilty, and as you spent those new bills on your way across country you would leave a trail a mile wide for the law to follow. Besides, after promising not to tell anyone you knew about Papa and I, how could you make anyone believe you were innocent once you were discovered with the money." Jannet frowned. "Of course, I never thought you'd save nearly every last cent of it until we got this far."

"So the service I rendered my mysterious benefactor was to be blamed for the theft," Martha mumbled, recalling the words in the note accompanying the money she'd recieved so mysteriously. "But why would you want to travel on the same wagon train? I would think you'd want to get as far away from me as was humanly possible. Why not Europe?"

"Europe? That's exactly where everyone would think I'd run off to if something went wrong. And I was careful to provide clues so they would come to that conclusion. But is there a safer place than a wagon train? Oh yes, I even put on a brown wig and purchased a ticket to England in your name. So you can see anyone would think this ghastly trip was just a clever but unsuccessful ruse to throw them off. As far as being on the same wagon train, I still have to finish paying you back for all the trouble you caused me while we were growing up."

"Jannet, you're not well," Martha said earnestly.

"I'll be well enough after I dispose of you. I wanted to take Hunter Brody away from you to hurt you, but you ruined that plan. Now I have Clinton to help me, don't I, Clinton?"

"You do, my greedy little bitch. Just tell me where you hid the money, and I'll go get it. Then we shall see to Martha and be on our way." Clinton drew Jannet to him, and carelessly nipped at the tip of her nose.

"Clinton, you're not a murderer," Martha pleaded.

"You've always known I only wanted one thing," he said nervously.

Jannet practically purred as she rubbed seductively against

him. She knew she had won. Clinton was the only one who had ever satisfied her sexual appetites, and now she would have him and all the money she'd ever desire. And Martha wouldn't be around to haunt her.

"I'm sorry, my dear Martha, but I fear your turn to pay has come. Don't worry, you're lucky; you won't feel the pain Nancy Cooke did. A small tap on the head and you'll never know when the wolves take care of our dirty work for us. It will seem that you died on the prairie, and no one will be any wiser," Jannet said.

"Go get the money while I take care of Martha," Clinton ordered.

Jannet pouted. "I want to do it."

"No! Now get the money," he practically shouted.

As Jannet defied him and bent down to take hold of Martha's arm, Hunter stepped from behind a jagged boulder.

"Thanks for filling me in on all the sordid details, Miss Wakefield. Clinton old man, I think I liked you better when you were a woman, and even then I didn't like you much." Hunter laughed at the man now standing before him in a loose-fitting gown. "I must say, though, in that dress you're a vision of loveliness. But why don't you take it off and give it to Martha. I think she has more need of it than you do."

Jannet looked at Hunter's pistol, gleaming in the light of the moon which clearly outlined their figures, and froze.

Hunter glanced at Martha, shivering on the ground. "I was wondering what you were hiding. You have a strange idea of loyalty . . . my little lamb." He then frowned at Clinton. "Hurry up with that dress."

"If you will just let me explain." Clinton's eyes shot barbs at Hunter, but he slowly stepped from the loose-fitting sack dress to be left only in rolled-up trousers. He tossed the gown at Martha.

"Don't say another word," Hunter warned. He pointed the gun at Jannet. "Bend down real nice and slow and untie my lady."

Jannet's lips curled in an evil smile as she undid the bonds. She glanced sideways at Hunter before helping Martha to her feet, and as Martha was slipping on the dress Jannet suddenly pulled a knife from her skirt pocket and yanked Martha in front of her.

"Toss that little old gun over here, Hunter dear, or I swear I'll slit her neck wide open."

Martha dared not breathe, the knife was held so tightly against her throat. She could feel the tension, the utter hatred in Jannet, and she was sure that her next heartbeat would be her last. By the light of the moon, she could see Hunter's left cheek twitch.

Hunter noticed that Jannet seemed to have a smirk on her face, as if she were waiting to draw first blood and didn't care whose it was.

"What are you waiting for, Hunter dear?" Jannet's voice was calm, calculating.

Hunter watched Jannet like a hawk about to swoop on a hapless squirrel. He stood post-still . . . waiting.

"Get his gun, Clinton. Do it!" Jannet urged, annoyed that he hadn't moved.

"Shut up, bitch!" Clinton snarled so viciously that Hunter suspected he was wishing it were Jannet's throat on the sharp edge of the knife.

"Are you going to force me to make you a widower?" Jannet shrieked at Hunter, her control shattered.

If it had been anyone else but Martha she held, Hunter would have called her bluff. A spark of the crazed coward showed in Jannet's eyes even as she spoke, and Hunter never doubted she was capable of carrying out her threat to kill Martha. But pulling a trigger, and shoving a blade into skin and bone were quite different. He doubted the spoiled young woman could rip through flesh after the first squirt of life-giving blood gushed onto her manicured fingers.

"Calm down. No one is going to force you to do anything," Hunter said in his most soothing voice. "Just let Martha go and I'll drop the gun."

"What do you take me for, a fool?" Jannet tightened her grasp on Martha.

As the knife's sharp, icy blade pressed harder against Martha's skin, tears came to her eyes, and when a twig snapped her whole life flashed before her. Her breath released involuntarily and sounded like a low whistle.

"All right, Jannet. All right. You win. I'm throwing down my gun." Hunter tossed the weapon into the bushes, angering Jannet.

"What did you do that for?" she protested shrilly. She had hoped to exchange the knife for a weapon she could more easily manage.

Clinton immediately fell to his knees and began searching for the gun.

"Hurry up and find it so we can be done with this!"

In the confusion, Jannet did not hear the snorting coming from the camel khan not far from them. Nor did she pay any attention to the padding of split-toed feet or the crunching of dried leaves. Martha did. That skirling sound she had made when Jannet pressed the knife against her throat must have summoned Humphrey. It was the sound Hunter had used to call him when he'd rescued her from the general.

As if Humphrey sensed Martha was in trouble, he hissed, lowered his head, and emerged through the brush. Looking like a stampeding buffalo, he charged toward Jannet and butted her squarely on the derriere. Then, using the great strength in his neck, the animal threw the dazed woman to the ground before placing himself between Martha and the woman who would harm her.

The impact knocked the knife from Jannet's hand, and the weapon flew into the dust. But she spied the gun, not more than three feet from her, and plunged toward it.

Hunter pounced on Clinton, who drew his hands up protectively, wanting no part of a struggle, but Martha froze when she caught sight of Jannet out of the corner of her eyes. Despite Humphrey's presence, Jannet Wakefield had found the gun and was pulling the hammer back. If Martha didn't do something fast, Hunter would be shot.

Fear for him superseding her own fear, Martha scrambled over to Jannet and grabbed her leg. As Jannet kicked at her, Martha furiously sought a way to stop her. Having only one weapon available, she sank her teeth into Jannet's calf. Jannet screamed and dropped the gun. Then, rolling on the ground, the two women clawed, scratched, and ripped at each other.

230

Hunter left Clinton sitting meekly on the ground and stood up. A grin curved his lips as he brushed himself off. He grabbed Humphrey's rope and leaned back against a boulder to catch his breath while the women continued to struggle.

Jannet closed her hands around Martha's neck and squeezed viciously. Although she was slender, she fought like a crazed cat. Martha could not throw her off, so she gave up trying to wrest the woman's hands from her throat. Instead she thrust her open palm against the soft underside of Jannet's chin. Jannet gasped for breath and reached for the intensely painful area. Any thought she might have had about resuming the struggle departed, when Humphrey, who had wrested himself free, stood over her, looking her directly in the eye.

"Bravo!" Hunter clapped.

When Martha picked up the gun and pointed it at Jannet's heartless chest, he stepped over and took the pistol out of her shaking hand. "You and Humphrey make quite a team. I knew you had it in you."

"S-sure," Martha puffed, quite out of breath. She walked three steps and slid to the ground.

"Now is no time to rest. You need to go wake up the camp and get some rope."

"If you don't mind"—she was panting, the full impact of what had just taken place, having just hit her—"I'm not just resting. I think I may faint," she added with a flip of dry humor.

Hunter laughed at the wonderful, courageous woman sitting limply on the ground before him. He knelt down at her side. "Here." He handed her the gun. "Keep it aimed at Jannet. If she moves, blow her crazy head off."

Martha nodded and Hunter rushed off in the direction of camp to seek assistance.

As he did so, Jannet saw her chance and scrambled toward the brush.

"Stop or I'll shoot," Martha called out.

"Then shoot because I'm not waiting around," Jannet yelled over her shoulder, and kept going.

Martha was shaking so badly it was more of an automatic reflex than a deliberate move when she pulled the trigger.

Jannet fell into the thick brush.

Clinton, who remained frozen on the ground, his hands held high, said, "I am not going to move."

Hunter was back in a flash. "Are you all right?"

Martha trembled. "Yes but . . . but I'm afraid Jannet got away."

"She won't get far." Hunter bundled Martha into his arms and held her tight, his heart swelling within him. He lifted his eyes skywards. God, who wouldn't care for such a woman.

Chapter Twenty-Four

Happy appeared barefoot, hopping over sharp rocks and winding a turban about his head. "I hear shot. I come. I come fast." His eyes bulged at the sight before him; then he rattled something off in a foreign language and reached for Humphrey who was quietly standing by.

Less than five minutes later Jed, Seth, Cornelius, and William came running. Derek was not far behind, still buttoning his pants.

"Help Aunt Velina up, Jed," Hunter directed sarcastically.

"Derek, you and Belshaw go search the brush over there"— he pointed—"for Jannet Wakefield. And be careful, she's pretty desperate."

Jed gave Clinton a strange look, but he nodded his agreement as the other two men left to look for Jannet.

"I've been traveling on behalf of the bank," Clinton quickly put in, and pulled his credentials from his pocket.

"Oh, my goodness!" Cornelius covered his mouth, startled. "Aunt Velina is a male!"

"And quite a surprising one at that," Hunter replied, after reading Clinton's documents.

"I should say, I do hope I have time to get my equipment set up." Cornelius turned and fled back toward camp, hoping some of the pictures he'd been taking at night on long exposure times would turn out.

"Why didn't you tell me the truth, Marks?" Hunter growled.

"Sorry, but I wasn't sure who I could trust."

Hunter clenched his fists. "I ought to *trust* you right in the mouth for nearly getting Martha killed."

"I don't understand?" Martha put in.

There was a contrite expression on Clinton's face. "Martha, I am sorry." He took a step toward her, but the warning in Hunter's eyes stopped him. "I tried to give you a hint when I told you I had not changed. The only goal I have ever had, besides wanting you, of course, is to be president of the bank. After the money was stolen, I questioned old Simmons and learned of his liaison with Jannet Wakefield. Someone had used a key to get into the bank, and it didn't take much to figure out how that had happened. After all, what would someone like Jannet see in Simmons? The authorities managed to stop Barton Wakefield just as he was preparing to leave to meet Jannet, and he broke down and told us he had sent her to join you. He tried to implicate you to save his daughter, but I forced him to write Jannet a note telling her he had sent her aunt in his place. Wakefield put the aunt's name in quotation marks to warn Jannet, but luckily she didn't take the hint. I donned my disguise and thought I would catch Jannet before she reached Independence. Unfortunately, as I am certain you are aware, she was a pretty clever woman and had the money well hidden. I convinced her I was her aunt, and later, when she discovered the truth, I made her believe I wanted a share of her money. I never imagined I would have to travel so far to locate it.

"I couldn't tell you the truth when you discovered who I was that night down by the river, Martha. I couldn't take the chance of Jannet becoming suspicious. I never realized, though, that she hated you and poor Nancy enough to kill you both. Her hatred must have driven her insane."

"Yes," Martha said sadly, remembering how she and Nancy had often wished they were as beautiful as Jannet. Poor, dear Nancy. Martha silently grieved for her good friend who had fallen victim to Jannet's madness. But she had learned a lesson on the trail: life must move forward. She turned her attention to Clinton. "But why didn't you trust Hunter?"

"He passed some of the bills to a blacksmith back in Independence. I wasn't sure whether he was involved or not."

"That must have been the money I used to pay for my passage."

Hunter was about to speak up when General Thornton boldly strode onto the scene, with Abe right behind him.

"Good work, Brody." Thornton cleared his throat authoritatively.

Hunter glared at the puffed-up, bald-headed man in blue.

"Sorry, Hunter," Abe said. "He showed up just as I was leavin'. The sonofabitch stuck to LizaBelle's backside like flies on—" Abe looked sheepishly at the ladies present. "Well, you know what I mean."

"Don't worry about it." Hunter turned on Thornton. "What the hell were you doing following me?"

"A matter of deduction. I knew you would lead me to the guilty parties." He motioned to Clinton and Martha, smiling as if he had just won first prize in a turkey shoot. "And the reward money."

"You've made a big mistake. They're not guilty. But I'll give you your reward," Hunter stated with deadly calm, his eyes mere slivers. He swung out and punched the pompous sonofabitch in the nose.

Thornton felt a sharp crack and fell backward in the dirt, clutching at his pain-ridden, bleeding nose. He glanced up through an agonizing haze just in time to see Captain Holbrook join their swelling numbers.

The captain was a career soldier, and despite his personal feelings, his commanding officer lay prone on the ground. Holbrook put his hand on the gun at his side. "What's going on here?"

"I was merely giving the general his reward," Hunter said, straight-faced. "Isn't that right, General?"

Thornton grunted and regained his feet, still holding his displaced nose. He stood to lose if Brody decided to press the issue with his superiors, so he sagely remained mute despite his intense pain.

Hunter furrowed his brows. "What are you doing here, Captain?"

"I followed General Thornton. Seemed a little strange when the general ordered me to get him a horse right after you lit out of the fort like a spooked antelope."

"You've got keen senses." Hunter laughed while the general scowled behind his cupped palm.

"Thank you, sir."

"For you information, Thornton, the guilty party was Jannet Wakefield," Hunter explained. "I've got a couple of men out beating the bushes for her now."

Dereck and William returned. "Sorry, Mr. Brody," Derek said. "We found a bloodstain about twenty-five feet north of here, but no other sign of her."

"We'll send scouts out to look for her in the morning. She has nowhere to hide," Captain Holbrook put in, noting the look of fear on Martha's face. "I wouldn't worry about her showing up again. If we don't catch her the wolves or Indians will."

"Captain, there is a substantial reward, offered by my bank in Elmira, New York, for the return of the money stolen from it," Clinton interjected. He looked guiltily at Martha, wishing she were in his arms instead of Brody's.

Hunter pulled Martha closer to him. "I think all these witnesses will agree that the money should go to Martha Rockford Collins Brody for the trouble caused her and the false arrest she was forced to endure."

"That sounds most reasonable, sir," answered Captain Holbrook. He was aware that there had been something most odd about the way this whole case had been handled, and now he was beginning to understand why. He knew of the general's attempts to seduce Brody's wife, and thought this the least that could be done since Brody didn't seem to be bringing charges against the old bloodhound. "The men at the fort will be grateful that you have not sought to bring charges against the general. The sooner he is on his way back to Washington the better it will be for all of us."

"I believe Mr. Marks will be happy to accompany you to the fort and bring you up to date on everything that has happened. And he can probably fill in the missing details on the paperwork Thornton altered, can't you, Clinton?" Hunter shot the unhappy man a look of disdain.

"Of course," Marks agreed.

"Now we need only find the money the Wakefield woman stole," Thornton appended stiffly as they were preparing to leave.

Cecilia Stewart, her long braid falling gracefully over a blue cotton wrapper that matched her eyes, patted her husband's shoulder. "Why, I'm sure I know where the money is."

"Then you'd better tell them, honey," Derek advised, proud that his wife could help out.

She shyly looked at the expectant faces, then said softly, "On several occasions when I went near Miss Jannet's trunk, and once when I opened it to look inside, she nearly went into a tizzy. I'll bet the money's in there."

"I have been through that trunk," Clinton argued.

Hunter ignored the irritating banker. "Well, let's just have another look."

A hasty search proved fruitless, and they were about to give up when Hunter noticed that the bottom edge of the lining was neatly bent back. He tore off the papered sides of the old piece of luggage and money spilled out into his hands. Clinton seemed annoyed that he had not been able to find it, but Hunter counted the stash, then turned over to Captain Holbrook the twenty-five thousand dollars which had been hidden along the sides of the trunk.

"Martha and I will come in later and sign any papers you deem necessary," he said to Captain Holbrook.

"No hurry." Holbrook mounted his horse. "Oh, and, Mr. Brody, I'll see to it that that wagon of yours is promptly repaired." His lips curled in disgust as he glanced at the general who was continuing to hold his nose. "I guarantee there'll be no further delays."

"Thank you, Captain." Hunter slipped an arm around Martha.

"Please accept my apologies," Clinton said to her. He looked truly remorseful.

"Neither one of us wants anything from you, Marks," Hunter said darkly, drawing Martha closer to him.

It was all so incredible that Martha stood mute beside Hunter as they watched the two officers and Clinton ride off into the darkness toward the fort, Clinton taking one long last look over his shoulder.

"Hold that pose," Cornelius jested.

"Dammit Potter," Hunter growled, then he smiled. "All those pictures you've taken had better come out. I don't want to have hauled three hundred pounds of equipment across the country for nothing."

Cornelius returned the lopsided smile. Although he had despaired over losing Martha, he no longer doubted Brody would prove to be a good husband, and he had grown to respect and admire his strength of character. In that instant a silent bond of friendship was born between the two men.

A gray morning sky was looming on the horizon by the time the camp was again quiet. Harriet and William Belshaw and their children had returned to the tent they had taken over during Martha's absence. The Nelsons were settled in, and Cornelius had joined Happy, in the tent they were now sharing. Abe had laid down his head near his LizaBelle at the horse corral, while Cecilia and Derek Stewart, having wisely moved their bed from underneath their wagon, allowed Martha and Hunter the privacy which otherwise would have been denied them.

Hunter pulled Martha down with him onto the thick bed. He wrapped his arms around her and smoothed her hair back. "Why didn't you just tell me about Clinton?" he asked, recalling with dismay how he could have lost her.

She was reminded of what he had said at the cave. "There're going to be no more secrets." She sat up and hooked an arm around her legs, her free hand fingering the arrowhead at her throat. Then she swallowed, pressing her lips together. It wasn't going to be easy, but she would no longer keep things from him, not if they were going to build their marriage on a strong foundation.

"Clinton had asked for my hand in marriage before I left to come on this trip."

"I heard you jilted him."

Her brows shot up. "How long were you there?" Had he been listening all along, yet done nothing until Jannet was ready to drag her out for the wolves?

"Long enough to hear Jannet's confession." He noticed her troubled expression. "I wouldn't have let her harm you."

"Only frighten me half out of my mind," she mumbled.

"Between you and that camel, which seems to be so fond of you, they wouldn't have stood a chance." He chuckled. "That was pretty quick thinking, whistling for the beast."

"Yes, it was," she responded hesitantly. Truth was important, but it wouldn't hurt to let him think she had done that deliberately. She would tell him the rest. It was bound to come out later at the fort anyway. "Clinton had always worn a beard. Without it, neither Jannet nor I recognized him dressed as the aunt she hadn't seen since she was a little girl. Once I discovered Aunt Velina was actually Clinton, I was afraid to say anything. He threatened to tell you I had planned to run away with him."

"You thought I'd believe him?" Hunter decided not to tell her that he had suspected something was wrong after he'd seen Clinton, dressed as Aunt Velina, shaking her. Strange. They'd all been so wrapped up in their own daily struggles on this trip that no one had even noticed Clinton wasn't a woman.

"You seemed so preoccupied with something." She lowered her chin to her knees. "I suppose I wasn't sure how you'd react."

Hunter tensed. Luckily Martha was not looking directly at him. He quicky asked another question to draw her thoughts away from him. "Then why didn't you tell me after you read the newspaper?"

"I had to confront them and let them know that threats weren't going to work anymore."

"God woman!" He sighed. "You were innocent. Look what Jannet had already done to you with her accusations, yet you had to lay your life on the line to confront them." He shook his head. "Did you think she'd let you leave after you had it out with them?"

Martha looked daunted as he pointed out the consequences of her actions. But in the back of her mind she was glad she had faced the pair. Too many people in today's world were too quick to point an accusing finger without first taking the trouble to say what they had to say directly to the person involved.

"I wasn't hurt," she reminded him, as if that statement made her actions reasonable. "And, as it turned out, Clinton was only following Jannet to recover the money to ensure his future position as president of the bank."

"No, you weren't hurt," Hunter conceded. "But you didn't know what Marks's intentions were."

"Hunter?"

"What my little lamb?"

"Jannet won't come back, will she?"

"Most likely, if she's been wounded, the wolves will get her before she can go very far."

"I feel sorry for her."

"Don't."

"But she must have been terribly tortured to do such awful things."

Hunter reached up and drew Martha back into his embrace. Thank God she didn't hurt you, he thought. *No more secrets. No more secrets.* The words echoed hollowly in his mind. *I wouldn't have let her harm you.* No. He would do that himself, he thought miserably.

Martha was soon sleeping peacefully in his arms. But sleep was not to offer Hunter its sweet oblivion. His mind was too filled with concern over the hurt Martha would know when she found out the secret he was harboring.

Chapter Twenty-Five

Thursday, July 21, 1859—Our camp outside Fort Laramie. I am not so naïve as to believe that life holds only rainbows after a storm. But somehow I was certain that with such a nightmare behind me, my future could only be brighter. Now I fear that my darkest days are yet to come. . . .

The sky was beginning to darken from the rich blues of day into the deep hues of night when Martha awoke. She sat up feeling refreshed and ready to face the world, even though Hunter had already left her side. A happy contented feeling within her, she hugged herself. The worst was behind them now. After they filled out the paperwork at the fort they would never see Clinton or Jannet again. And she was married to Hunter. Although he hadn't yet spoken the words of love, he had risked his life for her. He had even dropped his gun when Jannet had threatened to harm her. Hunter might not care for her in the same way he'd cared for his Indian wife, but somehow she could overcome that, too. She knew Harriet Belshaw would never change, but that didn't matter. There was too much to be thankful for to let that woman bother her.

She hummed merrily to herself while washing. Hunter must have gotten her clothes from the fort while she was asleep because her trunk sat near the back of the wagon. She dressed in a loose-fitting sack of blue-checked cotton, and left the wagon to greet the others with a beaming smile. All evening she'd felt warm inside, sitting next to Hunter while he and Abe had filled the others in on all the details and then answered the vast assortment of questions which had followed.

The first part of the trip had been a nightmare. But now the worst was behind them. With Hunter by her side, there was nothing she couldn't overcome!

Tomorrow morning they would collect a tidy sum, which they would use as a nest egg. Then they would pick up the repaired wagon and be on their way. It almost seemed like a fairytale in which she'd ride off into the sunrise with her prince, Martha thought as she dreamily gazed into the fire.

That night they returned to their tent and Hunter made love to her with such urgency that had she stopped reveling in his caresses to question it, she would have wondered what was driving him. But Martha was at peace with the world, and after making love for the third time, she closed her eyes to drift off to sleep.

"Wake up, sleepy head. You're not going to get away with sleeping the whole day away." Hunter sat next to her, a cup of coffee in his hand.

Martha smiled. "Breakfast in bed. I have a lot to look forward to."

Hunter handed her the cup and turned away. He knew his expression would reveal his inner turmoil and Martha was too astute not to see it.

When he'd got himself under control, he stiffly said, "You'd best get yourself dressed. We've wasted enough time here. We have to get back on the trail."

"If I overslept, I apologize. I hadn't realized there was any need to go to the fort early since we won't be leaving until tomorrow morning."

"There's just a lot to get done." Hunter's sharp tone had softened somewhat, but the minute the words were out of his mouth, he left her staring after him.

Martha readied herself, grabbed a bite to eat, and mounted one of the horses from the spring wagon; Hunter had saddled it. He was sitting atop his big bay waiting for her, but he rode on ahead without a word. Her warm feeling of peace was tempered by his distant behavior. She tried to assure herself that he was just anxious to get going, yet a persistent feeling that something else was going on kept nagging at her.

When Hunter and Martha walked into the general's office, they were greeted by Captain Holbrook, who explained that General Thornton was indisposed.

"It seems the old bloodhound broke his nose." The captain chuckled.

"Pity," Hunter replied. "Now, what is it we have to do so we can be on our way?"

"I've taken the liberty of having your statements drawn up. And I checked the papers the general kept in his safe. They had been sent out before it was learned that Mrs. Brody had nothing to do with the robbery. That banker, Mr. Marks, said you're entitled to a thousand dollars. All you have to do is sign on the dotted line. And he cleared it with the general to give you your reward from the money recovered before he left yesterday."

Martha's mouth dropped in surprise. "Clinton didn't wait to say good-bye?"

Captain Holbrook cleared his throat. "Mr. Marks did ask me to tell you again how sorry he was, and he said if he could ever make amends, he would." He glanced nervously at Hunter. "If you change your mind, ma'am, you know where he'll be."

"Thanks, Captain. Now, where do we sign?" Annoyance prickled Hunter's voice.

Martha said nothing in front of the captain, but she had no regrets that she had chosen Hunter over Clinton. Clinton was already married—to his bank. She affixed her signature to the paper, then asked, "Did you find any trace of Jannet Wakefield?"

"We searched the area thoroughly, but my scouts didn't come on so much as a footprint. I'd say she's undoubtedly already been punished by the wolves for her crimes."

Martha stood awkwardly for a moment, thinking about Jannet; then she changed the subject. "Would you direct me as to where I might post a letter to New York and inquire about mail delivery? In all the confusion I completely forgot to check for letters from home."

The captain turned Martha over to a private, instructing him to escort her so she might see to her errands. He then watched her disappear around the corner of the buildings.

"You're a lucky man, Brody." Portland Holbrook said, turning his attention to Hunter.

"So I've been told," Hunter muttered.

"If that woman weren't already your wife, I think I'd court her myself. Marks probably would've hung around, too." Holbrook crouched in front of the safe and took out the reward money.

Hunter's head had been bowed over the document, but the captain's statement caused him to quickly scan it and scribble his name. His blacksmith friend back in Independence had commented on how he used to come up with the damnedest schemes. If Hank could only see him now . . . His plan to trick Martha into thinking she had married him was the dumbest one he'd ever thought up.

"Here you are . . . one thousand dollars. I hope I can trust you to see that your wife gets it?" The captain's attempt at levity ceased when he caught sight of Hunter's dark countenance. "I understand your wagon is waiting for you."

"Yeah, well, thanks again, Captain." Hunter put the money into his pocket, quickly said his good-byes, and left the office.

Martha was slowly strolling along the fringes of the parade ground, intently reading a missive, as Hunter caught up with her. "From home?" he asked.

"Yes. It's the strangest thing."

"What is?"

"All that trouble could have been avoided if I'd only picked up my mail when we first arrived." Hunter looked puzzled so she continued. "It's so ironic. Mother's letter describes how the bank discovered it was Jannet and her father who had stolen the money, and how I was under suspicion first because I'd left town right after the theft. Mother took care of that by showing the authorities the anonymous note I had received along with those new bills. She had tucked the note in her apron pocket and had forgotten about it until she was questioned. It seems the handwriting was finally identified as Jannet's. I suppose I was so excited to get the money I didn't recognize it. Of course, Mother didn't know Clinton had followed Jannet, though she wrote that the president of the bank had approved a personal leave for him. Won't she be surprised when she gets my letter?"

"Yeah. Surprised."

"Hunter, are you feeling all right?"

"Fine," he grumbled. "Let's get back so I can bring the Belshaws to collect their wagon."

Martha tried to keep pace with his long strides. Is this the man I married? she fretted. One who broods, who's closed and sullen? A single-minded man who will never let me really share in his life? Well, that would have to change. Something was troubling him, and she was determined to get to the bottom of it.

Hunter spoke barely two dozen words to Martha before he left with the Belshaws to pick up their wagon. She waited until he was out of sight, and then strolled over toward Abe who was beside the camel khan.

"They're the galdarnedest creatures I ever laid me eyes on." Abe leaned over the makeshift fence to get a full view of the animals settled on the ground. "Happy was tellin' me how that one over there"—he pointed to Humphrey—"has taken to you. I can sure understand why. Hunter's got himself a fine woman."

"Thank you." Martha blushed. "Abe? We never did have a chance to finish our conversation about Hunter."

"No?" His voice turned grim. "Why? Is somethin' botherin' you? He ain't beat you or nothin' like that, has he?"

"Oh, no. It's just that something seems to be troubling him and he won't talk about it. I guess I thought now we could get on with building a life together. But something's wrong. I can feel it, Abe. And I thought maybe you could help me find out what it is."

Abe looked squarely at her. Her eyes sparkled like distressed emeralds and held only concern for her man. He had always thought of Hunter as a son, which would make this young woman a daughter to him. But Hunter never had been one to speak freely of his feelings. Damn Rushes Hayes all the way to hell. And damn Hunter for his wild scheme.

Abe opened his mouth, then hesitated and patted her shoulder before he said, "Keep your chin up. If somethin' is botherin' that man, I'm sure it'll blow over."

"But I don't want to wait until it blows over. I want to share the good and bad times with him. I want a real marriage," Martha said earnestly.

"Somehow I get the feelin' he does too."

Martha thought this a strange comment, but it was evident this crustly old dear wasn't about to say anything of substance, whether he knew what was troubling Hunter or not.

She gave him a hug. "Thank you, Abe. If you hear anything, you will let me know, won't you?"

"Martha me girl, watchin' you in action I somehow figure you'll be the first to know." He gave her a good squeeze. "Don't you be worryin' that pretty head of yours no more. It's gettin' near supper time. Why don't I show you how to whip up one of your man's favorite meals?"

"Maybe that will please him," she mused.

Martha watched Abe fill the big iron kettle with water. While the fire crackled underneath it, he went to his pack and pulled out dried beef and vegetables.

"How can I help?"

"You can peel them carrots and spuds and throw them in the pot. And chop up that onion and add it, too."

"This looks like stew."

"That it is, me girl; the kind of Irish stew like no one's ma ever used to make."

Martha choked back a smile.

"We'll just let all them good things boil for 'bout one hour and then dump some flour into it and thicken it up. There's still some bread baked, ain't there?"

"Sure is."

Hunter and the Belshaws returned as Martha finished stirring the thick stew.

"I smell Abe's cooking." Hunter walked over to the fire, took the spoon out of Martha's hand, and tasted the concoction. "Just like I remember."

His mood seemed to have lightened. Eager to be a part of his lighter moments, she said, "Abe taught me how to make one of your favorite dishes, so I'll be able to make it for you from now on."

Hunter's mouth became a straight line. "Yeah, well, it isn't one of my favorites. It's practically the only thing the old sidewinder knows how to cook." He threw the spoon back in the pot and stalked off to wash up.

Martha forced herself to keep her chin up. Throughout supper she tried to keep up a cheery conversation. It was a brave front she put up. She could satisfy her physical hunger with food, but for some reason Hunter no longer seemed to be feeding the hunger in her heart.

Abe watched Hunter cut off her every attempt to draw him out, then ignore her. If he were a younger man, he'd have beaten some sense into the big oaf. But as it was, he decided that after supper he would have a few words with the grouchy sonofabitch. It was time he set him on the straight and narrow.

When Hunter had cleaned his plate, he promptly stood up. Abe got up right behind him.

"We need to have a little talk, me boy," he said, and grabbed Hunter's arm.

Hunter looked down at the gnarled fingers wrapped tightly around his arm. He slitted his eyes at Abe. The old man's voice had held a hint of reproach, and Hunter had never let any man seize him like that before without the gesture causing one hell of a fight. "This little talk had better be mighty important," he warned.

Martha watched the two men leave camp. Determined to find out what had been bothering Hunter, she got up to follow them.

"Where do you think you're going?" Harriet boomed out from behind her coffee cup. "Just because you haven't had to do your share of the chores the last two weeks doesn't mean you don't have to chip in now."

There was only one way to get away from the woman without an argument, and Martha did not have time to quibble. She

247

picked up a bucket. "I'm going to fetch some water."

"That's more like it," Harriet directed the words at Martha's back.

Once out of sight of the camp, Martha changed direction to follow Hunter and Abe. It was sneaky, and she and Hunter weren't supposed to keep secrets any longer, but if she *accidentally* happened to overhear them and that helped her understand her husband, in her mind the act was justified.

As she neared a small clearing she could hear angry, muffled voices. She crept closer until she could plainly make out every word, then settled down on the ground to listen.

"What the hell do you think you was doing treatin' a good woman like that?" Abe growled. He puffed out his chest.

"Like what?" Hunter snapped back.

"You go out of your way to save her from some general who's sniffin' after her tail. You hide her out even though she's charged with stealin'. Chrissake, man, you held up the entire train for one woman. Then when it's all over you crawl into some gloomy shell like a damned fool tortoise."

"I'd do the same for any helpless female."

"Would you now? And I'd be guessin' you'd act like some broodin' fool afterward too."

"What do you expect!"

"I expect you to treat her like a wife."

"Wife!"

"So that's what's eatin' at you. I thought so."

"Yeah. Well, it's my problem. Stay out of it."

"I damn well wish I could. Can't though. You was the one got me involved in the first place, remember? You and one of those harebrained schemes of Rushes Hayes. That woman back there's no floozy tryin' to trick you into nothin'. You must be blind as a bat if you can't see she's in love with you."

Martha was pleased inside. Old Abe wasn't wasting any words. By the time he finished with that man of hers, Hunter would probably tell her everything about himself.

"I know she's in love with me." Hunter sighed, hating himself. Not being one to try to excuse his own behavior, he now thought himself lower than the worst varmint. In an attempt to live with himself, he said, "How was I to know she really was some simple schoolteacher. If I'd realized it, I never would have come to you and asked you to play a part in that trumped-up wedding ceremony. . . ."

The heated battle raged on but Martha heard no more of it. the words *trumped-up wedding ceremony* rang in her ears. All this time she'd thought she was a married woman. She had given herself freely and willingly to him. He hadn't said he loved her, but she had been so sure she could change that. Well, he didn't love her, and it bothered him that she was in love with him. She was some "simple schoolteacher," another problem on his already burdened hands. How could she have been so stupid, so utterly naïve?

Tears began to form in her eyes. She had to get as far away from Hunter as she could. She had to run. Yet her legs had turned to wet sponges. She doubled over holding her stomach, sure she would wretch. She willed herself to be strong, but there wasn't one drop of strength left in her. Hunter had proved to be the worst kind of man, worse than Clinton ever could have been.

In her mind, Hunter had committed the most heinous crime of all. He had stolen her heart, and with a few words had ripped it out of her chest, like a wolf would have done before crushing it under his heel.

She strangled a desperate urge to cry out in her pain. She could not give him the satisfaction of knowing he had destroyed her dreams and justified her mother's warning that she would never be able to travel across country alone without the trip breaking her heart. Well, she thought, I'll prove one thing my mother said was wrong: my spirit will not be broken! Somehow I will make it impossible for Hunter Brody ever to forget what he's done to me!

Part Two

"Tribulations"

. . . we exult in tribulations . . . knowing that tribulation works out endurance; and endurance, virtue; and virtue, hope. And hope does not disappoint. . . .

—Rom. 5:3, 4, 5

Chapter Twenty-Six

Friday, July 22, 1859—Heading toward Independence Rock. I am thankful that my family is not here to view the pain of disgrace I now carry in my heart, and I marvel at how much the human body is able to endure without collapse. We are truly the most amazing of animals to be set forth on this earth. Yet I am most sadly awed at the lack of conscience He has seen fit to instill in a portion of His creation. . . .

Martha drew in long breaths of the cool evening air in an attempt to calm herself before returning to camp. She could not remain transfixed to this spot. Slowly, she willed her hands and knees to carry her a safe distance from Hunter and Abe. Her heart was filled with the intense pain and hatred provoked by betrayal. For a moment thoughts of stabbing Hunter's black heart flitted through her mind. But she returned to camp and her tent.

"Where's that water you went to fetch?" Harriet snapped.

Winnie rebuffed the irritating woman. "Leave her alone. Can't you see she don't feel so good?" Winnie took in Martha's labored steps and slumped shoulders, then scratched her head, thinking it weren't no physical ailment bothering that one. She considered going to Martha and then thought better of it. Martha had a husband to tend to her now. And by the look of her, this sure had to have something to do with that man.

"Who's going to clean up?" Harriet sucked in an indignant breath.

"Why don't you get that spoiled brat of yours off her spreadin' backside and put her to work?" Nettled, Winnie was ready to deflect any further carping.

Once Martha lowered the flap on the tent, the petty grumbling outside faded. She was too distraught for coherent thought, so she settled down on her bed and gave herself up to sleep.

Even as Martha was fending off breaking down by drifting into the void of nothingness, Hunter was receiving a stupefying shock.

Disgusted, Abe spat in the dirt. "Now that you do know she's no more than the honest schoolteacher she shows herself to be, what you gonna do 'bout it?" He was leading Hunter into making a declaration, and held his breath, in the hope that it would be the right one.

"What the hell am I expected to do about it?" Hunter glowered at the crusty old man. But his fury was really directed inward. He had been debating that very question for days. How could he just up and tell Martha that the wedding had been a premeditated hoax? Was he supposed to say, Even though I pretended to marry you since I thought you were just another woman trying to trick me, now that I've taken you to my bed out of wedlock on numerous occasions and have found out I was wrong about you, would you consider marrying me for real?

Abe watched emotions play across Hunter's face. He pushed harder. "Stop bein' a smug bastard."

Instead of Abe's words having the desired effect and forcing Hunter to admit what he felt about Martha, the attempt backfired. Hunter sat down heavily on a rock. "You're right, Abe."

"'Bout what?" The old man looked suspicious.

"I am a bastard." Convinced that Martha would never have him after what he'd done, Hunter decided to do what he thought only right. "I'll go into the fort tonight and make arrangements to get her on another train."

In his mind it had become the only palatable thing to do. He figured when she found out what he'd done she would hate the sight of him, and he couldn't stand seeing her each day, knowing he had ruined her life. Knowing he would never hold her again, knowing she would never *really* be his.

Abe's eyes nearly bulged out. "What! I thought you was a fighter? Why you're actin' like some puny snivelin' school-boy."

Hunter looked at the bowlegged man long and hard. What's wrong with me? he asked himself. He'd never shied away from a fight before. Of course, he'd never had to fight a battle like this. No. It wouldn't be right. Martha deserved better.

"I'd watch who you were calling a 'puny sniveling schoolboy.'" Hunter's left cheek twitched.

"Jesus! You're a impossible sonofabitch. All I was tryin' to do was find out if you love the girl." Abe was exasperated and almost ready to give up as he waited for Hunter's reply.

"Damn you! Of course I love her," Hunter bellowed.

"Well then, why didn't you just come right on out and say so? All your problems is solved." Abe beamed brightly. He fumbled in his shirt pocket and pulled out a crumpled piece of paper. "Here." He thrust it toward Hunter. "Horace Fishback said you was actin' a shade bit queer so he gave this to me for safekeepin'."

Hunter's face underwent a drastic change as he took the square sheet and strained to read it in the dim moonlight. "What's the meaning of this?" He waved it in Abe's face.

"It means Horace Fishback was a real preacher and that woman of yours is yours. Clear and simple."

"What?" Hunter wasn't sure he was hearing the old man correctly.

"Don't you understand plain, simple English? It means whether you like it or not you two is hitched. For real. The knot's been tied all nice and legal-like."

"You tricked me?" Hunter could not believe he had so easily been taken in by the old man.

"If you mean that I knowed from the first, when you suggested that galdarned plan, that you cared about the girl and

255

hadn't admitted it to yourself yet, yup."

Hunter's smile became exultant. It had bothered him to introduce Martha as his wife since it was a lie. Now it no longer was. She was his! Really his. And she need never know what a fool he'd been. He suddenly became serious.

"I ought to kick you in the ass for pulling such a low stunt on a friend," he declared. Then a wide grin broke out, brightening his entire countenance. "Instead, let's go have a drink to celebrate."

"I knowed it was the right thing." Abe gave Hunter a hardy slap on the back.

Much to William Belshaw's delight, Hunter broke out two jugs and passed out cigars to all the men—even to Seth and Henry, to Winnie's discomfort.

"Lord Almighty." Winnie raised a brow, shooing her young girls into the wagon. "One would think you and that wife of yours was gonna be havin' a baby."

Hunter jovially raised his cup. "We just might at that." After the words were spoken, he smiled inwardly; it was a definite possibility.

Harriet humphed and dragged Fuller and the whining Clara into their wagon to ready the newly returned prairie schooner for the morrow.

It was well past midnight by the time Hunter stripped off his clothes and joined Martha in bed. He'd had to grapple with a tied tent flap, but had attributed it to Martha's being alone and concerned about wild animals. He gazed down at his wife. *His wife.* The thought warmed him to his marrow. Marriage was the last thing he'd planned to get himself into again, yet with Martha it felt right.

Winnie's words about a baby came to his mind, and he put his palm gently on Martha's belly. He had watched her with the children on the train, and remembered what she had told him after they'd left Independence about wanting a house full of them. She would make the perfect mother for his babies—their babies. And her hips were built for childbirth. He ached to awaken her, take her in his arms, and make love to *his wife.* Longed to caress her tender flesh and let every inch of her know she belonged to him. But they would be back on the trail early and even in sleep she looked exhausted, so instead he quietly cradled her to him.

"Good night, Mrs. Brody." He kissed her lightly on the cheek and closed his eyes.

Martha awoke before dawn and stiffened. She was lying in Hunter's arms. It crossed her mind that she should shake him out of his peaceful sleep and confront him with her knowledge of his deception. She wanted to scream at him, demand to know how he could do such a terrible thing. But he'd probably laugh in her face and throw her off the wagon train. Well, he had trampled on one of her dreams, but he wasn't going to keep her from going West.

She lay there for half an hour, mulling everything over until she reached a conclusion. She would let him think she was ignorant of his deceit. Only she would leave him before he had a chance to smugly inform her it had all been a sorry joke at her expense.

"Oh, yes," she whispered softly, "I will remain Mrs. Hunter Brody for the time being. But if you think you will have yourself a pliant, dutiful *wife* for the duration of the trip or until you decide to cast me off, you're going to be quite sorely mistaken."

Yet lying next to his warm body caused her to unwillingly yearn for his touch in spite of what he'd done. That was going to be her major problem—continuing to pretend to be his wife without letting him touch her again. Somehow she had to keep him at arm's length. Hunter had already proved his virility, and he had a healthy appetite for her, which she was certain he expected to satisfy regularly.

In spite of Martha's determination to put the heat of Hunter's body out of her mind, visions of the soft candlelight in the cave where they had made love—a warm, amber glow—carried her back to the passion they had shared. She touched trembling fingers to her lips, remembering the ways he had enflamed her. Did love always have to hurt so much?

She slowly turned her head to look at him. Even in his disheveled state, he was a handsome male animal, his blond hair falling over his forehead, his bronzed arms holding her possessively. Their nights together would prove to be a problem, for even now she tingled inside at thinking of how he awakened such raw desire in her. She reminded herself that that was exactly what it was, that he had proved himself to be—an animal.

When she tried to squirm out of his arms, he stirred and his lips drew up into a warm smile. "Hello, Mrs. Brody."

He pulled her to him to kiss her, but she managed to jump to her feet.

"Come back here, I want to give my wife a kiss."

Martha bit her lip. You'll have to marry someone first, she longed to retort. She forced a half hearted smile. "I'm afraid it's my morning to get breakfast started. You wouldn't want Harriet Belshaw complaining that you give you wife"—the word nearly stuck in her throat—"preferential treatment, now would you?" As she was speaking, she hurriedly slipped into her most worn muslin dress.

"Well, no. But—"

"No buts. I have to set an example now that I'm wife to the wagon-train captain."

Hunter looked disgruntled, but he conceded with a hint of anoyance. "All right. You win. Go get breakfast started. We wouldn't want to give Harriet Belshaw something else to complain about. We'll turn in early tonight." He wolfishly eyed her.

It was not to be Hunter's only disappointment that morning. After they had finished the morning meal, he told Cornelius to ride with the Stewarts or mount the big bay. Hunter intended to drive the spring wagon so he might be near his wife. But that plan went awry. When he went to fetch Martha. She had already donned that infernal outfit she'd gotten from Happy, and was waiting for him atop Humphrey.

Hunter took one look at her and rolled his eyes. His wife should not be riding a camel. "What are you doing up there?"

"I'm waiting to get started," Martha answered glibly.

"I put an extra blanket on the wagon seat to make it more comfortable for you. I want you to ride next to me today."

She pouted. "But I thought I would spend some time with

Humphrey. After all, he did save my life."

Hunter scowled. Surely she didn't really believe that damned camel had saved her life.

"Don't you think you should at least get down long enough to say good-bye to Abe?" he grumbled in defeat.

She made a sweeping gesture to cover her heart with her hand. "Of course. How thoughtless of me."

Blithely, Martha commanded Humphrey to lower himself, then she slid from the saddle and headed toward Abe, who was over by the Nelsons' wagon, packing his supplies on LizaBelle.

Abe took one look at Martha all wound up in strange white pants and a turban, like a mummy, and he muttered under his breath to Hunter, "Jesus! If I didn't know better I'd think your scheme's come back to haunt you."

Hunter's lips tightened, but he remained silent.

Martha made a lavish display of saying good-bye to the old man, although she burned to ask him why he'd gone along with Hunter's deception. He had seemed so nice, she had almost come to associate him with the father she'd lost. For a moment she wished her father were still alive and she could climb up into his lap and be held and have her pain kissed away, as she had when she was a little girl.

"Don't you let that man get away with nothin'," Abe counseled.

Her resolve became more firm. Old memories couldn't help her now. "Don't worry, Abe. I've no intention of letting Hunter put anything over on me."

The old man gave her a weird look. Aware of the knowing tone in her voice, he hugged her.

He bid farewell to the rest of the company and then stepped over to Hunter and pumped his hand. "You sure done gone and got yourself a live one." Abe chuckled his approval, then mounted LizaBelle. After one last wave, he turned his faithful mount east.

Once Abe was out of sight, Martha linked her arm through Hunter's. "Will you escort me back to Humphrey? You know, I've missed not spending more time with him and I fully intend to remedy that. I plan to be the kind of wife who takes an interest in her husband's work. I want to be involved in all aspects of your life. And I want you always to look back on this trip and find it most memorable. So starting right now I'm going to begin learning everything I can about the camel business. And what better way is there to do that than to ride one?"

She was so enthusiastic, how could he argue with her? She could have her way today. Tonight would be a different story.

Chapter Twenty-Seven

They had been traveling uphill on the bluffs since they'd left Fort Laramie. The days were hot, and dusty due to the gusting winds, and although it was difficult to hold on to at times, Martha used the umbrella Cornelius had loaned her weeks before. It added a piquant note to her unusual, almost sculptured appearance atop Humphrey. Harriet often raised her brows, while Winnie merely shook her head; but Cecilia had been thoroughly counseled by her husband not to become further involved in anything which did not personally concern her. She silently sat next to Derek, feeling superior in her pink-ruffled garb.

Cornelius continued to wear his fancy Eastern clothes despite the heat, and took photographs whenever he had a few moments to get plates into the camera and expose them, hoping at least a few would come out. His equipment had been set up in the back of the Stewarts' wagon.

"Tilt the umbrella a little to the left, out of the way of your camel suit. I want a clear shot of it. Good," Cornelius hollered when Martha paused for a moment as he'd requested. "Hold that pose."

Hunter had shown Seth how to drive the spring wagon and had mounted his horse, intending to ride with Martha. But the disparate heights of their mounts did not encourage idle conversation, and he'd soon given up and returned to riding herd on the train.

During the day Martha tried to focus her attention on the passing scenery, staying as far away from Hunter as she possibly could. She took in the wild roses, the currants, and the seas of blue flowering larkspur interspersed with thick fields of sage. Instead of taking her mind off her troubles, however, the lovely blooms merely served to remind her of her wedding.

For two nights she had managed to elude Hunter's amorous approaches. Coming up with excuses hadn't been easy, and she had half expected him to haul her into the tent and rip her clothes off. But he had not. He had seemed to take in stride her keeping to herself. The first night had required the least effort since they had had to travel much farther than usual to find grass for the animals and everyone had fallen into bed, exhausted. By the time Hunter had wearily turned in, it had been simply a matter of keeping her eyes shut and feigning sleep. The next night he was kept busy until one o'clock in the morning, helping Derek Stewart repair a cracked wheel on his wagon.

By Sunday she watched the sun dip low on the reddening horizon with heightened apprehension. Hunter had scouted ahead a short while before, and had announced they would make camp early since he had located a nice patch of grass near a large creek.

Martha lagged behind as long as she dared—she didn't want to arouse suspicion—then she rode to the camel khan Happy had swiftly erected and left Humphrey with the wiry little man. By the time she got to the camp Hunter had already set up their tent, a job which, in the past, had been reserved for her.

She felt a tug on her heart at noting this small act of kindness, then reminded herself of his deceit. Keeping that in mind, she raised her chin and swished into the tent, only to see muscles flexing on the wide expanse of his naked back.

She blinked to drive the seductive sight of him half-nude out of her mind.

"Oh, you're too kind to set the tent up for me." She assumed a haughty pose, although her heart wasn't in it.

Hunter pivoted, his eyes hungrily taking in the softly curved body wrapped in that infernal outfit. He envisioned her writhing beneath him on a thick feather mattress.

"Why don't we lay down for a while before supper?" he asked, taking a step toward her, his arms akimbo.

Dear God! She had to think of something—fast. She summoned up her most wide-eyed look. "I'd really love to, but I fear I don't smell as fresh as I should after riding Humphrey all day." With her hand, she fanned her smelly shirt, wrinkling her nose. "I'm sure you'd much prefer a sweetly fragrant wife to one who reeks of camel."

"Any way you are is fine with me." He grinned. She did have a point though, his nose confirmed it.

"I insist. I'd never be able to give you the attention you deserve the way I am."

She leaned over and picked up a towel and that much-patched, patterned muslin dress.

"As you desire," he said blandly. He reached for a towel and soap, then held open the flap.

"Wh-what do you think you're doing?" Martha was so startled she stuttered.

"I'm going with you. I also need to wash up." She still looked astonished, so he added, "You needn't worry. I'm not going to force you into anything down by the water . . . not anything you don't want."

Had he seen through her excuses already? Surely not. It must be her imagination.

She sucked in a breath as he followed her along the narrow path toward the stream. To her relief, he found a secluded spot and left her to bathe alone.

She quickly stripped and ducked into the clear, cool creek. She had been tense but the water was soothing. Only two days of this act and she already wondered if she could continue. How actresses managed to perform under stress she could not fathom.

The snapping of a branch startled her. She clasped her arms over her breasts and swung around.

Hunter was casually leaning against a boulder, letting his appreciative gaze run over her smooth white skin. "You forgot the soap." He tossed her the sweet-scented bar and left without another word.

His seemingly simple act of thoughtfulness made Martha lather her hair with a vengeance. If he was trying to weasel his way past her guard so he could bed her, he was mistaken. Her hair rinsed and her bath complete, she toweled off and shimmied into her worn dress. It had to have at least thirty patches on it, but she'd be damned before she'd let him catch her in anything more becoming. She rinsed out what had become known as her "camel suit."

"Are you ready to return?" Hunter stood in the path, blocking the trail leading back to camp.

"Why?" she asked skeptically.

"I merely thought I would wait and walk back with you, if you're ready."

All evening she tried in vain to pick a fight, but nothing she said provoked rancor in him. He shrugged or ignored her. And when she invited Cornelius to accompany her on a stroll from camp, Hunter only looked up and said, "Enjoy your walk."

"Martha, have you been feeling ill?" Cornelius said as soon as they'd gotten a bit away from the campfire.

"Of course not. Why do you ask?"

"You have not seemed to be yourself these last two days."

So he had noticed she was behaving differently. Surely then, Hunter had. But why hadn't he confronted her? It would be so much easier to act this way if he returned to being the arrogant wagon-train captain.

But Hunter was no longer the arrogant man who had left Independence last May. Martha had changed that. He hadn't wanted her along, and she'd been a thorn in his side from the beginning. Though he had been harder on her than the others, she'd overcome all his attempts to convince her she should join a train returning to the states. And, slowly, he had come to realize she had more strength than any of the women he'd known—including Dancing Wind. Martha had turned his world around and given it meaning. He had discovered that he hadn't merely bedded another woman, he had found a mate.

264

With shuttered eyes, Hunter had watched Cornelius and Martha stroll from camp. He'd wanted to knock the photographer down and cart Martha off to the tent right then, but he'd forced himself to remember she had just been through a devastating experience, which had to be the cause of her unusual behavior. Any other woman would probably have expired on the spot had Jannet held a knife to her throat. Not Martha. She had kept her head. He could afford to be patient. They would have a whole lifetime together. If only his body would listen to his head . . .

Martha hadn't returned by the time Hunter stood up to face questioning stares. If he hadn't talked himself into being patient, he would have stormed out and collected his wife. "I suggest you all turn in now. Tomorrow's going to be a long day."

Hunter lay awake, waiting for her. Tonight he would take her in his arms and show her how much he loved her.

But Martha was harboring her own plan.

Ignoring Cornelius's attempts to reassure her with high appraisals of Hunter, she came up with a way to put the man parading as her husband off for yet another night.

She entered the tent and promptly slipped into an old, white cotton nightgown, then eased herself carefully onto the far side of the bed. If he was asleep, she could save her tale for another time.

No such luck.

"I'm glad you're back." His arms slipped around her, and he kissed her before she could resist.

His deft lips—pressing, grinding, and tasting—left her breathless, and she knew she had to regain her wits if she was going to pull off what she'd planned. When he began caressing her throat with his blazing fingertips, she pushed against his chest.

"No, Hunter." She forced herself to say it, although her body was already burning under his caressing touch.

"Martha, I know the last two weeks have been difficult and you've been under a lot of strain. Let me take your mind off all that for a while."

Why the unmitigated braggart! He had no idea how much stress she was under. What he had in mind would only add to it. She had allowed him entry to her heart as well as her body, but he had just been using her. And he had soiled her for any man who would expect a virgin bride on his wedding night, yet he wanted to continue to sate his lust with her until he chose to cast her off without a backward glance.

"We can't on Sundays," she said quickly, hoping she sounded sincere.

"We can't what on Sundays?"

"You know . . . make love."

"And just why can't we?" He thought he'd heard every excuse women used from his married friends, but she seemed to be about to come up with an original one.

"My mother taught me it's sinful." Martha lowered her eyes, feigning embarrassment.

"Sinful to make love on Sundays?" He almost had to laugh. She seemed so serious, yet so apologetic, about such an outrageously ridiculous idea.

"Yes. God created the world in six days. On the seventh he rested. I was taught that the Sabbath was a day to rest the body in every way."

Hunter tried to remember whether they had ever made love on a Sunday. He hadn't kept track. Now he wished he had. Somehow that story wasn't beyond believable, not coming from a woman like Martha.

"But we've been traveling on Sundays," he countered, mildly amused.

"Yes. And someday I will pay dearly for my sins. Please, let's not compound them with something we can control." Although she was referring to their present situation, on this night, her meaning ran much deeper.

"Maybe you can, but I won't guarantee how much longer I will be able to."

Hunter took Martha's face between his hands and placed a chaste peck on each eyelid. "I won't force you, my little lamb. Keep in mind, though, I have no inclination toward celibacy."

Nervously, she said, "You're most patient. I want you to know I do appreciate it, for, as you said, the last two weeks have been quite difficult for me." Not nearly as difficult as the last two days, she wanted to cry out.

They both lay awake for a long time afterward.

Martha wishing that what she had overheard was all a bad dream.

Hunter wondering if it were.

Chapter Twenty-Eight

Friday, July 29, 1859—Entering the Black Hills. Lately I find myself delving into my past beliefs in an effort to remember who I am. I have discovered a side of me most foreign to that which I have always held to be of value, and now fear that I may not possess the strength to return to those former principles. . . .

For five days Martha kept up her performance. She was flamboyant. She was petulant. She was childlike. She was moody. She had let her sprightly imagination create the most bewildering characters. If her relations with the others on the wagon train had been strained before, now they were stretched to the snapping point. And Martha's nerves were equally frayed, though she had always prided herself on her inner strength and her determination.

"Hunter Brody." She expelled a weary sigh. "What have you done to me to make me act this way?"

She had to fight back tears as she wistfully gazed across the river at the Rocky Mountains. They rose up, wild and jagged and barren, like the empty ache in her heart.

The road was mostly sand, and Martha was at least grateful that she was atop the sure-footed Humphrey, for the wagons sank into the fine grains and those riding on them were forced to get out and walk up the steep hill in the heat.

Hunter came up alongside Martha at the edge of the road, which dropped off sharply, allowing an extensive view of hills and green valleys, mountains and rivers.

"Oh, to have been with John Fremont or Kit Carson on one of their expeditions." She shrugged wistfully. "They're such rugged, fascinating men, and no doubt they know how to treat a lady, unlike so many of the backwoods rogues out here."

"They're more than twice your age," he ground out, smarting because of her barely concealed attack on him. She might as well have slapped his face. This last jab of hers had pushed him within a hair's breath of losing the control he'd fought to achieve. How much more he could take in stride was now debatable.

He made one last effort to initiate a pleasant conversation while they were out of sight of the others. "Isn't the view magnificent?"

Martha felt small and insignificant before this vast wilderness and she dropped her latest role, that of a simpering, yet sharp-tongued, wife. "It's breathtaking. Will we be climbing any higher?"

The serenity in her voice, lacking as of late, turned Hunter's head and heightened his sense of the inner turmoil she must be undergoing.

"No. Why don't we take a short break. The wagons won't be along for a bit and I want to talk to you," he said bluntly.

Martha grimaced as she dismounted. She knew this had been coming. Hunter had not returned her jabs, but had met her whims and moods with calm endurance. Yet he had been arrogant and single-minded for too long to maintain the pretense of the doting husband for any length of time. In his eyes she now could see his resolve weakening..

"Let me see." She whimsically placed her index finger against her lips. "What shall we discuss?" She twirled around. "Oh yes, I have it—life on a wagon train."

Hunter caught her arms and held them in a viselike grip. His blond visage darkened, and yellow fires flamed in his hazel eyes.

Martha's jaunty expression clouded. She instantly became taut.

"Let go of me!" she hissed, and tried to free her arms.

But Hunter's fingers dug into her flesh. "Oh, no you

don't . . . my little lamb." There was an intensity in his flaring eyes, a cold determination in the deadly calm of his voice. "You'll stand here and tell me exactly what's going on before you move another muscle."

She tried to bluff it out. "I don't know what you mean."

"Don't even think of trying to play more games with me."

"Why not? Aren't you *playing a game* with me?" The words exploded from her. "Didn't you *marry*"—she accented what had become an ugly word to her—"me so you could have a handy toy to warm your bed on the trail?"

Hunter gave a harsh laugh. Because of their rising tempers and his unawareness that she had overheard a portion of his conversation with Abe, he totally missed the cue she so contemptuously threw at him by stressing the word *marry*. "So that's what you think that wedding ceremony was all about?"

"I know it!" That circus of a wedding—on camels, no less— Flashed before her eyes. And the words *phony preacher* ricocheted in her mind until she felt herself begin to shake.

"Do you now?" He regarded her sardonically. She thought he had married her only to bed her. His expression lightened. Maybe that was partly true; it was that and revenge. But hadn't she bothered to note his actions at the fort and over the last week? Obviously not. He had busted his backside to demonstrate that he cared; he hadn't even touched her—in accordance with her wishees. If this was how his efforts were going to be rewarded, there would damn well be a few changes made, whether she'd come to her senses or not. "If that's what you *know,* then you also must *know* there's not much you can do about it out here, is there?" He spoke tersely and dropped his hands to his sides.

Martha believed he was fully aware that she knew about the fake wedding ceremony. Why else would he tell her that, since they were out in the middle of nowhere, there was nothing she could do about it. With the swiftness of a cat, she slapped his cheek, leaving it blotched with red.

Then she stumbled backward four steps, stricken because of what she'd just done as well as what he'd said. Hunter took a step toward her, and she ran for Humphrey and crouched at the side of the animal's neck.

"If you dare to come any closer, I warn you, you'll regret it." She put an arm about Humphrey, who was quietly chewing on a sprig of sage.

"Will I now?" Hunter cocked a calculating brow. "And just how are you going to manage to make me regret it?"

"Humphrey will bite you to shreds." She had been working with the beast, training it, under Happy's jovial supervision, for a week. Martha straightened her shoulders defiantly and ordered the camel to rise.

Hunter moved closer, his eyes mocking her.

"I mean it!" Rivulets of perspiration trickled down the sides of her face. Her lower lip trembled. He was going to force her to protect herself.

"No doubt you do." He looked dangerous in his buckskins as he took another step forward.

Shaking now, Martha clapped her hands and pointed at Hunter. "Attack!" she called out forcefully.

"Down Pasha!" he commanded, and as the camel dropped obediently to the ground, faster than a flash of light Hunter grabbed her and yanked her to him.

"Pasha? Why you—"

"You didn't think I'd put you atop one of the untrained camels, did you? This one was a gift from its namesake Mohammed Pasha, the bey of Tunis," he declared triumphantly.

"How could you and Happy be so cruel as to lead me to believe I had trained it? You deceitful, lying bast—"

"Careful, my little lamb, or I'll wash that desirable mouth out with one of your fragrant bars of soap."

"I'll never let you touch me again." She struggled against his grip.

"No? You've always proved a more than willing participant." A grim light flickered in his eyes. "This is only a taste of what you may expect."

His lips crushed hers in a swift, feral display of dominance, his probing tongue offering no mercy. He meant to punish; he also was telegraphing his urgent desire to give and take, a longing to share and join.

A thrill went through Martha as she was swept into his

271

crushing embrace and her body responded to his message. Her lips pulsed as their kiss deepened, and a warmth spread through her thighs, though she fought surrendering to his unmerciful attack on her senses.

Almost as quickly as he had yanked her to him, Hunter broke off the kiss.

Panting, she savagely wiped her lips. "I'll not *play* your wife."

He was furious, and stunned. He'd never believed she could think of marriage as some kind of game. "I'm afraid while we're on the trail you're stuck with me as your husband, whether you like it or not. Now get on that camel's back so you'll be ready to go down that grade when the wagons get here."

He swung up onto his horse and rode back toward the others, not giving Martha a chance to react.

There was a growing strangeness about her that Hunter did not understand, and after their confrontation, he had the uneasy feeling that there was more to it than she'd revealed. She had sounded as if she hated him, yet she continued to wear his arrowhead. What was going on in that head of hers?

By the time the wagons reached the top of the hill and were ready to start down the steep grade, Martha had regained her composure. She'd had time to think, and she'd decided it had been foolish to invent excuses and to make feeble attempts to discourage his advances by acting ridiculous. And she was rapidly undermining the fragile line of truce between her and the other members of the company.

Harriet Belshaw heaved her big frame down from her wagon and peered at the road, her eyes round as silver dollars. "Heaven receive us all," she wailed. "The wagons will never make it down there safely."

Was there no peace from that woman? Hunter looked skyward. The old sharpness honed his voice when he said, "Mrs. Belshaw, at this moment the only thing that may not finish the trip safely is your damned tongue."

"God will repay you for your sins," she huffed, as Hunter showed her his back and began instructing everyone to continue to walk.

Harriet's comment caused Martha's heart to lurch. She had

no doubt they were already traveling on the road to damnation. She, too, was concerned about the wagons, and rode Humphrey, as she planned to continue calling the animal, over to Hunter.

"Is there a way to be sure it's safe?" she asked, her voice a bit shaky.

If Hunter had been sitting a horse, he would have fallen out of the saddle at Martha's sudden shift in behavior. "It's a rule of thumb that if you come to a hill and can see the lowest point over the top of your horse's ear, you don't have to be worried," he said.

She nodded, not completely convinced, and moved away to gaze one last time on the Platte River before leaving it behind.

Hunter took out thick cords of rope and wrapped them around the wheel rims of the wagons to help keep the heavy Conestogas from slipping down the grade. Slowly and methodically, he then worked the oxen and the horses, holding back and then loosening the reins, forcing the animals to ease the heavy schooners over the road.

Concern for him rippled through Martha, and she had to bite back a scream when the last wagon started to slide sideways, tilting dangerously toward the drop. She took a deep breath after he regained control.

"Brody is fortunate to have someone like you who cares so much about him," Cornelius observed after taking a picture of Martha's horrified expression during the near mishap. He hoped the exposure time had been sufficient for it to register properly on the plate.

"I care that everyone makes it down that grade safely." Martha shot the tall scholarly photographer a confused look.

She had been trying to convince herself that she detested Hunter Brody. But the way she had responded to him when he'd kissed her and the distress she'd felt when harm might have come to him, these confirmed a nagging fear. While she'd thought she was married to Hunter Brody, she'd known the happiest moments of her life despite all the trouble.

Was it penance for her sins that she must go through life loving a man who had lied to her and decieved her? Would she forevermore be forced to secretly long for arms always out of reach? She shook her head. She had always had too much confidence in her ability to determine her future to allow herself to sink into a mire of self-pity. Yet her heart was burdened with the secret sorrow of unrequited love.

It seemed like an eternity before everyone made it down the hill safely. After such an ordeal they traveled scarcely five miles farther before stopping for the night.

Unable to find firewood, the children collected dried sage, which filled the camp with a spicy aroma as it burned.

After they'd all eaten, Hunter poured the last of the coffee and sat down across from Martha near the fire. She had been intently staring at the dancing flames since the last member of the company had gone to bed.

"We seem to have gotten off to a pretty rocky start."

Martha couldn't swear to it, but his voice seemed to contain a hint of regret. "Much like the mountains," she said softly.

"Yeah, well, they would be mighty difficult to scale."

"Next to impossible," she agreed wistfully, thinking of their farce of a marriage.

"What would you say about agreeing to a truce?" He noticed a fear of him tensing through her, and added, "I told you once that I'd never force you to do anything you didn't want to do as much as I did. I give you my word that won't change." He took a last sip of coffee, watching the firelight play on her face.

"What about this afternoon?"

"We were both angry." He sighed tiredly. "People often say and do things they don't mean when tempers explode. I suppose we wouldn't be human if we didn't."

He was such an arrogant, strong-willed man. Yet in spite of what he had done, there was a boy inside him who had not forgotten how to be humble. A line from Shakespeare came to her mind: "Humility is the most difficult of all virtues to achieve. . . ."

In his own way, he had admitted he had been wrong. It was a minor concession at best. Her head warned her to flee, but her heart pinned her to her seat. She told herself he was right about one thing: there wasn't much she could do about her situation out here.

"All right, truce."

They sat across the fire from each other, mutely staring. It was an awkward truce which neither one fully comprehended. Martha knew she should hate him for what he had done to her, but she'd come to accept what was done. She would finish the trip and then never see him again.

Hunter could not understand what was happening to this warm, passionate woman with the inner strength of a lionness—the woman he had come to love. At times glimpses of that woman returned to haunt him.

He escorted her to the tent and, only partially aware of Martha's mounting fear that he would insist on sleeping with her, bent to place a gentle kiss on her forehead before turning away to bed down under the spring wagon.

A stab of pain assaulted Martha as she watched him walk away. She put her fingers against her lips. What mad turn would her life take tomorrow?

Chapter Twenty-Nine

"I can't understand it." Winnie pushed an errant sleeve back up her arm and whirled the dish rag around the kettle. She set the pot aside and turned a reproving gaze on Martha, who was stacking the clean dishes. After wiping her hands on her apron, she said, "I ain't never seen two people more in love. So why has that man of yours been sleepin' under the wagon?" Winnie didn't think twice about asking a question when she wanted to know the answer.

Martha set the big, heavy pot in the crate, but reddened under Winnie's scrutiny. She had hoped no one would mention her sleeping arrangements with Hunter, although she had no doubt there had been talk behind her back. While she had no ear for gossip, this was one time she wished Winnie had kept silent.

"If you don't mind, I'd rather not discuss it. I have to get this crate to the wagon. You know how Hunter can be if we're not ready to leave when he is." Martha picked up the box.

Winnie gently put her hand on Martha's forearm. "I don't mean to be buttin' into your personal business."

"I know." Martha smiled bravely.

"Remember, if you need a good listenin' ear, I'm here."

"Thank you, Winnie. I will." A faint glow penetrated the dark loneliness in Martha's heart. She knew the crusty older woman was trying to help, but her problems with Hunter were too humiliating to share with anyone.

The crate loaded and ready, Martha quickly slipped into her

camel suit, not taking the time she usually did to adjust the fit. She had wrapped it too snugly, but she didn't want to anger Hunter by holding up the train so she hurriedly packed up the tent.

"It's not necessary for you to ride that beast any longer," he muttered as he strolled over to her. "You've already shown you have more guts than all the others on this train put together."

"Thank you for the compliment. But I enjoy riding Humphrey, and upon him, I have the best view of anyone, except for Happy."

"Yeah, well, if you change your mind let me know."

"I'll do that."

Hunter tipped his hat and was gone.

As Martha walked to the waiting camels she felt strange. In their exchange they'd behaved like polite strangers. Or had it been just an awkward respite? Hunter Brody was a difficult man to figure out. He never seemed to do the obvious thing like the men back in New York.

She was still pondering the questions barraging her when a smiling Happy stepped up and handed Humphrey over. She almost asked the little man why he had helped her train the animal when it had already been trained, but she shrugged instead. Hunter had surely put him up to it.

Three hours after sunrise, they were trudging across a great flat prairie surrounded by white-shouldered mountains. Ahead of them a solid granite rock towered like a solitary giant.

Hunter rode past the snuggling Stewarts and the dour Belshaws. Harriet was shaking her finger at a meekly cowering little Fuller because the lad had been playing with one of Clara's dolls. As Hunter passed the Nelsons' wagon, a rumpled bonnet poked out and Winnie waved him over.

"Mr. Brody, I don't usually make a habit out of intrudin' in other folk's personal lives—"

"Then maybe you shouldn't start now," Hunter clipped out. He then muttered a blasphemous string of curses. The last thing he needed was advice.

Winnie went right on talking, ignoring his foul language. "This time I'm goin' to make an exception. I don't know what's

277

goin' on between you two, and it ain't my place to pry, but that woman of yours ain't no frozen cake of ice. She ought not to be sleepin' alone longin' for her man."

Hunter grunted. "How do you know she's 'longing for her man'?"

"Landsakes, anyone who's got eyes can see that gal is pinin' away."

"Yeah, well—" He broke off. He had learned the hard way that Winnie only meant well, and he knew his suspicion that the old woman had schemed with Martha was what had gotten him into this rotten mess in the first place, not to mention his jealousy of Cornelius. "We'll be heading off the road about another mile ahead. Just point your wagon toward that big rock."

As Hunter gave the big bay his boot, Winnie hollered at his back, "Don't you go forgettin' my words."

They stopped beneath Independence Rock for the noonday meal, and Cornelius immediately hauled out his equipment and set it up.

Martha's eyes filled with tears and she shivered. The monument to the westward movement was overwhelming. As if she were touching a priceless treasure, she ran her fingers lightly over the names carved into or painted with axle grease on the five-acre rock. Then her gaze traveled upward, over the miltitudinous scribblings left by past emigrants. Suddenly her breath caught.

In big bold letters, which she was sure had been chiseled with a loving hand, she read:

HUNTER BRODY
LOVES
HIS
DANCING WIND
"FOREVER"
1847

She stood like a piece of marble, staring up at the carefully sculpted indentations, her eyes fastened on the word *forever*. "Forever," she whispered, shakily fingering the leather thong around her neck.

Hunter came up behind her, following her line of vision. "That was a long time ago."

"Yes, forever is a long time." Martha turned to the tall man now standing at her side. She would only be near him until the train reached its destination. Although his Dancing Wind had had him but a short time, they had been man and wife, and she had had his love. Abe was right; the love they'd shared was different. It had been whole, not one-sided like her own feeling for Hunter.

Tears glistened in Martha's eyes. Maybe Dancing Wind was the more fortunate one. She had suffered a quick death, not died inside a little each day over a lifetime.

Hunter noticed her tears, and he would have given anything to be free to take her in his arms and kiss the briny drops away. But she had made it understood that she was sorry she'd married him. Why she felt that way wasn't clear to him. But he respected her wishes; he made no attempt to reach out to her.

"If it's Dancing Wind that bothers you—"

She bristled and wiped tears from her eyes. "Don't overvalue yourself! I'm crying because of this magnificent memorial to all pioneers, and for those who died on the trail. It's overwhelming . . . that's all." She stalked off, afraid what was left of her composure would crumble.

Hunter took in her nicely rounded bottom as she strode off. In that damn camel suit she was a particularly seductive-looking woman, especially with those funny pants wrapped so sinfully tight about her, it was almost more than any normal man could bear. Did she think he was made of stone? She was his wife; she belonged to him. She was no longer constantly hostile—the truce had settled that—but an invisible wall still separated them. It grated on him.

All afternoon as he'd watched Martha pat and stroke, and even croon to, that damn camel, treating it the way she should treat her husband, his gut had twisted until he felt like a heated powder keg.

At the ferry that crossed the Sweetwater River, Hunter

279

peeled off three dollars apiece to have the wagons hauled across, while Martha sat quietly atop Humphrey some distance from the water, taking in the enormity of the scenery. The river cascaded wildly through high-rising, roughly carved rocks. The strength and cut of the stone, and the untamed water reminded her of Hunter. She let out a long breath. Hunter Brody. Hunter Brody. Everything she did and saw brought him to mind. Burgeoning tension flooded into every niche of her body.

"Happy, get that wife of mine off that beast and into the Nelsons' wagon while I scout for a place to get the animals across," Hunter bellowed.

"Yes, boss. Yes, boss." Happy's head bobbed up and down, and after Hunter rode off, the little man called out, waving his arms. "Missus. Missus. You come. You come."

Martha directed Humphrey toward the agitated Happy and his charges, who were waiting some distance away from the ferry.

"Boss say you cross river in Nelson wagon. I take camel for you. I take."

"Thank you, Happy." His grin was all teeth and though Martha wanted to cross with Humphrey, she got down and flashed him a sparkling smile.

Idly whacking a crop against her leg, she walked toward the others milling at the edge of the river, so absorbed in her own thoughts that she didn't notice the three rowdy men leaning against the decaying shell of what had been some emigrant's carriage.

"Is that the one we're supposed t' take care of?" whispered the biggest of the lot. He rubbed his hands on his dirty overall. "Almost seems a shame t' get paid fer it. Shit, if I'd a knowed, I'd a done it fer nothin'."

"Think she's as purty as that squaw and the mahogany-haired one? They's a strange couple a bitches," the paunchy one said, remembering their meeting with the Indian woman and child and the white woman. Then he shrugged. "Money's money."

"Hell, let's get t' it," the big man said.

"Hey, Chucker." The paunchy one with the jug jabbed the

bearlike man. "Looky, looky. What do we got us here?"

"Looks like some prairie dove, Deke, all wrapped up like a present just waitin' fer Christmas mornin'." The third man leered.

"Merry Christmas." Deke cackled and his paunch quivered. "Let's go get us our present, Horace," he said.

But Chucker, the bear of a man, scooped Martha off her feet before she knew what had happened, and plastered a wet kiss on her lips. Though she kicked and screamed and slashed at him with her whip, she struggled in vain. A booming laugh blasted from the huge man, and he easily ripped the crop from her hand and flung it in the dirt.

Horace gulped down a swig, the rotgut spilling from his mouth as he laughed. "Chucker, lookes like our present is fightin' t' be unwrapped. Bring that little ol' gift over t' Deke's wagon so we can get us a look-see if what's underneath the wrappin' is as good as those danglin' legs is."

Cornelius, who had just slid another plate into his camera so he could try to capture the dramatic landscape, dropped his equipment and ran to Martha's rescue. She was tucked under Chucker's arm, her arms and legs flailing, when he planted himself in front of the grizzled bear of a man.

"I demand that you release the lady at once!" Cornelius puffed out his chest.

"Did you hear that fellas? This here city slicker demands." Chucker's lips curled back and he roared. Then, with his free hand, he shoved Cornelius down onto a pile of cow droppings.

Clara had been watching Cornelius set up his camera, and she figured this was her chance to get even with him for taking her picture when she'd been napping instead of doing her chores. Her mother had scolded her. She ran to the camera and shrewishly mimicked Cornelius. "Hold that pose," she called out, and pressed the shutter, giggling with pleasure at the filthy would-be rescuer.

"Clara!" Harriet shrieked, horrified by what was happening. "Get back here, right now!"

"But, Mama, he's been doing it to everybody else," the girl whined, secretly gratified that she'd managed to take such an embarrassing picture of the man.

281

The others looked on, mortified, as all three interlopers walked over to Cornelius. Even the unshaven ferrymen stood by. They had learned six months before not to mess with the crazy Lucas brothers who had terrorized settlers clear across the prairies.

Her old heart fluttering wildly, Winnie gave Henry a shove. "Run like the devil's comin' for supper and tell Mr. Brody there's bad trouble at the crossin'. Now run, boy!"

Henry, his eyes stark, lit out up the riverbank hooting like a wounded sow. "They got her. They got her!" he screamed at Hunter and ran smack-dab into the big bay.

Hunter was alarmed by the young boy's hysterics. "Slow down. You're not making sense. Who's got who?"

"It's your missus—Miss Martha. You gotta help her."

The second Hunter heard Martha's name on the witless lad's lips, he raced his horse back toward the ferry. He sounded like an Indian attacking a wagon train as he descended on the three men forcing Martha into their wagon.

"Ah, shit." Horace spat the curse out as he caught sight of Hunter. "Looks like we got us a mite a sweepin' up t' do before we get us our Christmas package."

Chucker threw Martha inside, expecting her to cower there until he and his brothers had finished with the man fool enough to try to stop them. One against three hardly seemed odds to get excited about, so the burly giants waited for Hunter, bored smirks twisting their lips.

When he leaped from his horse with the fury of a prairie thunderstorm, their smug expressions disappeared. In an instant there was a massive ball rolling on the ground, legs and arms sticking out of it.

Martha, never one to sit by meekly, scooted out of the wagon. She spotted her whip a short distance away and reached it in record time, then ran back to the fray and began striking viciously at the three big men. Horace looked up just long enough for Hunter to knee him in the groin. Immobilized, he curled into a knot of pain. Martha then lashed the crop across the back of Deke's neck, causing him to yelp. Leaving Hunter to Chucker, Deke turned on her.

"You bitch," he snarled and lumbered after her.

But Martha was swift and light of foot, and manged to dance out of his way. She led him away from Hunter to ensure a more fair fight, and Deke tracked after her, lewdly describing what he was going to do when he caught her. Martha was lucky it was Deke who went after her, for he was the slowest of the Lucases due to his girth. She rounded the spring wagon, putting it between her and Deke and bringing them to a standoff.

"Ain't none of you *big brave men* even gonna lift a finger to help that little gal?" Winnie barked out. When not one man moved, she stormed over to the wagon. "What's the matter you fat lard-bucket, can't you fight nobody but a woman?"

Deke turned. "Shut your puss, old woman or you're—"

For him, day instantly became night.

Winnie had distracted him just long enough for Martha to grab the heavy kettle she'd packed that morning and bring it down on his head. Martha looked back over her shoulder at the fight. Horace was just regaining his feet. Kettle in hand, she flew at the huge man and smashed him on the head.

Without his brothers' aid, Chucker was laboring for breath, unable to best this stranger who would soon overpower him if he didn't do something—and quick.

When Martha caught sight ot Hunter's bloodied face, she screamed in horror, distracting him. It was the moment Chucker needed. He bent down and pulled a gun from his boot.

Cold, penetrating terror shot through Martha when she saw the pistol. She froze. He was going to kill Hunter, and there was nothing anyone could do to stop him.

Chapter Thirty

In less time than it takes for a man to die after being pierced through the heart, Hunter reacted. A gun suddenly seemed to appear in his hand, and he fired before Chucker had a chance to straighten up. An ugly look of surprise distorted Chucker's face. Then the gun fell from his hand and he crumpled to the ground.

Martha let out a sharp cry and threw herself into Hunter's arms. Sobs of relief racked her. She knew she was going to lose him at the end of the trip, but she couldn't have endured losing him to a stranger's bullet.

If she had expected Hunter to comfort her, she was sorely mistaken. He shoved her away from him, his eyes cold hard slits.

"Hunter?" She looked bewildered.

"Get in the wagon!" The tension that had been building in him exploded. Any consideration he might have shown her had been blown away by his temper.

Martha indignantly stood her ground. "Don't yell at me. If I hadn't given you a hand they would have beaten the life out of you."

"If you hadn't started this hullabaloo by wearing that indecent rag, they never would've tried anything. But no. You had to prove a point, didn't you?"

Horrified by the venom in his words, Martha attempted to defend herself. "I . . . I wasn't trying to prove anyth—"

"You proved how you could wiggle that tail of yours. No

man could be blamed for wanting a piece of it."

"I was doing no such thing. Furthermore, you have no right to speak to me like that," Martha hissed. She lifted her chin and then turned her back on him, not wanting him to see the tumult of emotions barraging her.

But he caught her arm and swung her around, splitting the sleeve on her shirt. "I have every right. I just killed a man because of you."

A shiver wormed its way through Martha. Had she been responsible for the bloody mass of skin and bone on the ground before her? It had once been a man. She shook her head in disbelief and, with a sob, fled.

"And take that goddamned camel suit off before I rip it off you!" he thundered at her back.

Winnie caught Martha up in her arms. "It wasn't your fault, gal. He's just mad as a bloated lizard. You get yourself inside my wagon and rest. He'll cool down after he's had time to put the brain God gave him to use."

After Winnie settled Martha in, she stomped over to Hunter, who was talking to the older ferry man. "You had no right talkin' to her like that. She weren't the cause of nothin'. Scum like those three don't need no reason to do what they done."

"If you've had your say, I've got business to tend to." Hunter said curtly. He should have dumped the camels in Independence, should have let his ranch go and walked away before agreeing to take on such a group of prying greenhorns.

"Look, mister," the ferryman said, "them Lucas brothers ain't no good, clear through. Too bad you didn't do us all a favor and kill all three. I sure wouldn't want to be standin' in your boots when Deke and Horace get freed up from them ropes you trussed 'em up with. After they see the vulture bait you made out of Chucker—not to mention your takin' their duds—they're goin' to be mad as a goose with a burr up its tail."

"I'm not going to lose any sleep over them. By the time they wake up and come up with pants to wear and find their animals and fix their wagon, the train will be far away from here."

"Don't count on them forgettin'. And with them strange

animals, you stick out like goat's milk in a saloon."

"Yeah, well." Hunter shrugged off the warning. "How much more do I owe you to cross the camels, too?"

A short distance away, from behind a tangled mat of sage, three pairs of eyes watched silently.

"I knew when you arranged to meet with those three fools they'd fail to kill Martha Collins. But you said it would work. At least now we don't have to worry about paying those idiots," Jannet hissed to the beautiful Indian woman with coppery skin and piercing eyes as black as her long straight hair.

"I have spared your tongue," the stately Indian woman said with deadly calm, "you would be wise to hold it. Have I not given my word the Collins woman will die?"

Jannet's russet eyes rounded. She remembered she'd thought she was going to be scalped when these two savages caught her and threw her to ground as she ran from the wagon train.

"Yes, but—"

"You will do best to learn patience. Before much longer you will be rid of the troublesome white woman."

"And you will have your Hunter Brody back," Jannet snapped, rubbing the stiffness out of the wound Martha had inflicted on her arm when she'd shot her.

"Yes. Daughter of the Wind and I have waited many long moons." She turned to her daughter, who knelt silently at her side, and placed a hand on the girl's arm.

"If he had been my man I would never have let anyone separate us." Jannet smirked, hating, yet fearing the pair who had been hiding in the brush the night Clinton Marks and Hunter Brody had stopped her from killing Martha Collins. "I still don't understand why you didn't show yourself before he married Martha if you'd been following the train since it left Independence."

"The way of the Sioux is not for you to understand." Dancing Wind's fingers pulsed against her knife. If the white woman could not prove useful, she would have cut her heart out when she'd stumbled onto her outside Fort Laramie—after

286

she had tried to kill the other white woman.

The remainder of the day poked along for Martha and Hunter. Martha huddled in the back of Winnie's wagon, numbly fighting to put Hunter's accusing words out of her mind. Seth had broken a wheel on the spring wagon, and Hunter had sent the others on ahead with orders to keep going until nightfall. He cursed the wretched wheel all the time he was repairing it, and his irritation sparked all over again when he saw the little distance made by the train as he and Seth finally drove into camp long after sunset.

"Two of the beasts got lame treadin' over the rocks. That's what's kept us from goin' on," Jed apologetically explained.

"Damned greenhorns," Hunter muttered and immediately went to the camel khan. "Happy!" he barked. "Make sure the camels are wearing those booty things tomorrow when we pull out. You can make them out of strips from the bottom of our tent."

"Yes, boss. I make. I make now." The little man had already started preparing the cloth shoes.

Hunter wearily ran his fingers through his blond waves, then he headed toward the campfire, rubbing his back as he shucked off his worn buckskin shirt. When he rounded the corner of the Stewarts' wagon, what was left of his patience deserted him. Five stomping strides took him over to Martha, who had been sitting quietly, finishing her supper.

Startled, she looked up and almost dropped her plate. One of his eyes blazed; the other was swollen shut, and purple from the fight earlier in the day. "Can I get you something to put on that eye?" Her worried expression belied the calm tone of her voice.

"No!" he almost shouted. Without warning, he flipped the plate from Martha's hand and tossed her over his shoulder. Totally ignoring her pleas, he headed toward the Nelsons' wagon, which had stopped some distance from the others.

Seth started to rise, but Winnie put a hand on his knee. "Sit yourself back down. That's none of our business; it's between a man and his wife. They don't need no interference from the

287

likes of us. We'll set their tent up and sleep in it tonight."
Maybe those two would finally clear the air, she thought. She
smiled smugly to herself and looked around her. "What you all
gawkin' at? You'd think you ain't never seen a man take his
wife off to bed before. Now let's get supper over with."

"Put me down!" Martha pounded her fists against Hunter's
back. "Where do you think you're taking me? Stop it!" When
he didn't answer, she hissed, "What about our truce?"

Hunter dumped her inside the wagon. Then he lit the
lantern hanging outside and climbed in. Martha glared at him,
but scooted to the far end of the Conestoga, like some cornered
animal.

"You beast! What do you think you're doing?"

"I told you to take off that goddamned camel suit," he said
with the methodical deliberation of one about to pass sentence.

Martha, believing him to be making a statement, jutted out
her chin in defiance. "You have nothing to say about what I
wear or don't wear."

"I have everything to say about what you don't wear, and
you're not going to wear that hideous rag anymore. Now take it
off."

"I will not."

"I'm warning you, take if off right now or I'll do it for you."
Despite his quiet tone of voice he was losing control. First
she'd taunted him with that tight camel suit; then she'd gotten
him into a fight with three men. On top of that, she'd
interfered, and he'd been forced to kill one of them. Now she
was sitting in front of him and telling him he had no say about
what she wore. Well, he'd settle that.

Martha bolstered her wilting confidence and stood up. "I
have nothing further to say to you," she declared, and she tried
to shoulder past him.

"Let no one say you weren't warned." He grabbed her and
tossed her onto a thick bed of blankets. She struck out and
kicked at him, but he straddled her and furiously shredded the
white cotton off her body.

"Stop! Stop! I hate you!" she screamed, knowing in her
heart she didn't really mean it. Frantically she tried to cover
her breasts when only her lacy undergarments were left on her.

Nearby, Cecilia complacently leaned over and whispered to Derek, "Aren't you lucky you married me? I dare say you are, just listen to her screaming at him. Why, I never had to be forced into your bed."

Patronizing his naïve wife, Derek smiled and reassuringly patted her hand as sharp, angry voices continued to come from the Nelsons' wagon. . . .

"Once before you were showing off those fancy drawers," Hunter said accusingly. "What were you hoping for?"

"Nothing!" Martha still didn't quite believe he was doing this to her.

"Well, they would have been a bonus to that poor sonofabitch I killed over you waving your tail at him."

"I didn't," she snapped, fighting him in earnest now.

"Oh, yes you did. But it'll be the last time you flaunt yourself in that camel suit or those drawers. From now on you'll only wiggle that luscious tail of yours in private—for me."

"You have no right to threaten me!"

"Our wedding ceremony gives me the right." He furiously ripped the underwear down her legs and tossed it onto the heap of rags that had been her camel outfit.

Martha lay naked underneath him, trembling with rage. By the look in his eyes, she thought he was going to rape her. But he pushed himself up, grabbed what remained of her clothing and stormed out. Her breasts were heaving, her heart was doing a drum roll, and quivering tingles shot through her. She couldn't leave the wagon without clothes on, and she couldn't risk putting on something that belonged to Winnie; he might strip that off her too. What would she do if he decided to come back? She wasn't merely going to lie on this bed, nude, and hope he wouldn't try to touch her. Recalling how she had bested two men earlier, Martha had an idea. She would not wait idly by until he returned.

As many hands stifled amused smirks, Hunter stomped out to the fire and flung the fragments of Martha's clothing into the flames. Then he stalked back toward the wagon.

Martha was waiting for him.

She had quickly fastened a blanket around her, and had

dragged a box to the back of the wagon. "You're not going to go back on your offer of a truce and think you can get away with it," she muttered to herself, dumping out the contents of the box and turning it over. A metal-handled bowl resembling a chamber pot caught her eye.

As she climbed onto her perch, a smile whispered across her lips. She was sorry Hunter had had to kill that man. But she had not been flaunting herself in front of him or anyone else, and if he thought he was going to come back into this wagon, he was going to be sorry.

At the sound of approaching footfalls, she raised the bowl high over her head, her every muscle taut, adrenaline surging through her with the force of rapids.

The flap snapped back and Martha struck.

In her haste, she swung too soon. The bowl completely missed him, throwing her off balance, and Hunter caught her as she fell.

"You little spitfire." He held her fast, thoughtfully gauging her.

"Get your hands off me or I'll . . . I'll . . ."

"You'll what?"

"I'll blacken your other eye," she said tremulously.

His anger drained and a laugh colored with self-mockery escaped him. "You probably would, wouldn't you?"

Laugh at her, would he? The beast! Martha balled her fist and jabbed him in the eye. But when she raised her arm the blanket slid down over her curves and onto the floorboards, and a disabling punch became little more than a light tap.

She saw raw hunger invade his eyes as he pulled her back against his bare chest. Her nipples tweaked against the wiry curling blond mat covering it, and their dark tips hardened and radiated hot, flashing streaks down to her loins.

God! How could he do this to her after deceiving her? She had vowed she would never let him touch her again, and she fought her swelling need for him as he bent over and nibbled on her ear.

"Do not deny me. Let me make love to you," he murmured softly against her ear lobe, his breath ragged, moist, and warm.

She craved him. She could not deny it, nor could she any

longer deny the bittersweet urge. She leaned into him, blinking in the misted haze of the swaying light.

Hunter swiftly lifted her into his arms and kissed her lips as he set her on the bed. His clothing seemed to melt off him. His thighs rippled with corded muscles, and his member sprang out free and hard, when he joined her. Her gaze traveled up his body until she looked deeply into the eye that was still open.

"You're a sorry sight with that black eye." Her trembling fingers hovered over the swollen, purpled lid.

"But you're the most beautiful sight I've ever seen, even out of only one eye." He groaned, and sensual fingers of fire mesmerized him.

Slowly, he mapped the curves and valleys of her body, his hands massaging and titillating her quivering flesh while he feasted on the sight before him. When a tiny cry of pleasure escaped her, he dropped his head to her breasts and caressed those yielding mounds. His tongue swirled and dipped, not neglecting an inch of rich milky skin. When he began to suckle at one peaked breast, while he fondled the other, she slipped her hands down his sides and then back up over his shoulders to toy with his ears while she kissed the top of his head.

Nerve endings never awakened in her before screamed for his touch, and her thighs opened naturally for him. As if his body were listening to her innermost desires, he responded by moving lower, kissing her stomach and the curling rise at the top of her thighs, and immersing his tongue in her. He savored the slippery feel and womanly taste of her, driving her to writhing madness beneath his mouth and fingers. Three times Martha shuddered and stiffened.

He was taking the time to make love to her, not merely satisfying his own lust. Her heart swelled despite her earlier resolve. She wanted to offer him what he was giving.

He knelt between her legs, and she sat up and stroked his stiff maleness, cupping him gently.

"My God, woman, what you're doing to me. If only I could bear to wait to enter you"—he growled deep in his throat as her fingers squeezed—"but I will explode if I don't have you now."

She nodded her understanding and guided him into her. He

felt like a white hot rod inside her, searing her with his brand. They moved as one, sensations building and building until an overwhelming, frenzied pleasure engulfed them and vibrating oscillations pulsed wildly through their enlaced bodies.

In those moments there was no right, no wrong. Tomorrow might bring cold reality, but that night he possessed more than her body; he possessed her heart and soul, her very being.

And Martha refused to allow another thought to besiege her mind.

Chapter Thirty-One

Monday, August 8, 1859—South Pass. We have now crossed over the divide to the Pacific side of the mountains. At the outset I looked upon this trip as a most glorious adventure. An adventure it has been. Now I find myself longing for its end. I must constantly seek that ever-elusive peace of mind, and there is no doubt in my troubled heart that it will continue to elude me until I can separate myself from the man whose presence haunts my every hour. Although a mixture of feelings have plagued me, I now have come to realize my only hope lies in a new beginning far from the source of the ache which drains my heart. . . .

Once they crossed Fremont's Pass the days brought cooler temperatures, and with them cold, clear nights. Martha had, indeed, found that cold hard reality had set in. When she had slipped on the patterned muslin dress, Hunter had laughed, and said, "At least now you will be riding in one of the wagons like a lady."

The look of triumph on his face had been short-lived. His comment had only made her more determined than ever. "You may have destroyed my camel suit, but you evidently forgot that I rode Humphrey before I started wearing it."

Hunter had worn a dark-slitted frown when she had defiantly mounted Humphrey, but he'd remained mute. And for a week he'd said no more than necessary to anyone in the company, stiffly bedding down under the spring wagon at night.

His lovemaking still had seemed to reveal more than physical desire. But his continued silence over the way he'd tricked her was final proof to Martha that she had been a fool for secretly allowing herself to hope, if only for a second, that anything more would come of her predicament than warming the bed of a hardened trail boss until they reached journey's end.

The days were at least tolerable. She rode the camel and imbibed the vastness of the landscape, using a botanical book given her by Cornelius to identify many new and wondrous plants. She had noticed the graves alongside the trail before. But since the death of that horrible man, she had become more attuned to the struggles which faced so many who had gone before her. The nights, however, robbed her of solace by bringing time to think, and had, therefore, become a cold enemy, stealing from her the comfort of dreams.

As the company sat around the campfire finishing the last of a jar of pickles, dried buffalo strips they had traded two shirts for, and bread, children's loud arguing voices broke the stillness of the cold night.

"You give it back, it's mine!" Clara bawled.

"You got lots," Fuller whined. "I only want one. Why can't you share with me?"

Harriet's lips became a tight line, and she left the group to settle yet another dispute between her children over the ownership of Clara's assortment of dolls, which had been spared at the disastrous river crossing.

"Poor little Fuller." Martha sighed, knowing full well Harriet would spank him and send him to bed.

"Boys don't play with dolls," Hunter commented dryly. He had had little to do with young children and the way Martha had been acting he began to doubt he ever would.

"Fuller's only six years old." Martha sniffed. She was getting colder by the minute and decided to retire early to her tent. There she could bundle up and maybe sew a cloth doll out of some old fabric. Stuffed and with button eyes, it should please a little boy who had been forced to go without.

Hunter watched Martha walk toward the tent. It was cold,

and he raised his collar around his neck. He thought he had shown Martha how much he loved her that night near the ferry, but the next morning she had again acted frosty toward him. She had even defied another command not to ride the camel—after he had been forced to kill a man due to her foolishness. Jesus! He loved her, but if she expected some dandy she could bend to her every whim, she was mistaken. The most difficult part of the trip, going through the Nevada desert, was ahead of them, and he didn't have the time or the inclination to cater to her moods any longer.

As Hunter rose, Winnie's words caught him in the gut.

"Jed"—Winnie snuggled closer to her husband, "I'm sure glad I got my man to keep me warm on a chilly night like this. It ain't no night for a married soul to be doin' without. Especially when nothin' but stubborn pride is the separatin' cause."

Winnie may have been speaking to her husband, but Hunter knew those subtly chastising words were meant for his ears. He shot the older woman a look of disgust, then settled in under the wagon. As he watched the others retire he noticed that Martha's light continued to burn, and the advice Winnie had handed out so freely some time ago surfaced in his mind:

That woman of yours ain't no frozen cake of ice. She ought not to be sleepin' alone longin' for her man. Anyone who's got eyes can see that gal is pinin' away.

At first he scoffed at the thought. But the more the wind howled down off the snow-sleeved mountains, the better everything the old woman had said sounded. Hell, Martha was his wife, after all. Why should he continue to freeze his butt off under the wagon just because she had some infernal point to prove? Another icy gust settled the issue of where he would be sleeping.

Hunter gathered up his blankets and entered the tent.

"What are you doing in here this time, or are you planning to seduce me again?" Martha snapped, as she looked up, wide-eyed, from under a pile of quilts.

"To answer your first question, we went through a wedding ceremony which gives me every right to be here. And second, I don't seem to recall having to do much seducing."

With a sharp retort Martha tossed aside the doll she had

been working on and turned her back to him. "Some wedding ceremony!"

Hunter took her to mean she'd been disappointed by the simple ceremony on the trail; he felt she had expected something more grand.

"Well, if you expected better of me, you picked the wrong man."

"Yes, it seems I did."

To Martha's chagrin, Hunter's face grew dark. He spread his blankets on top of hers, shucked his boots, and climbed under the hill of wool. Then he turned out the lantern, and, with his back to her, laid his head on his arm.

The added heat from his body radiated through Martha in warming waves, but she bit into her lip and forced herself to remember Abe's revelation which had shattered her dreams.

At dawn she hurriedly threw on her cream-quilted skirt and high-necked blouse.

"Why didn't you put on that same old dress you've been wearing?" Hunter asked sardonically. He spied the old garment in a heap in the corner and reached out to wave it at her. But when he did, the partially completed doll tumbled from the remains of the old gown. He picked it up and surveyed it. His expression softened before he spoke words that seemed to mock her. "I see the dress is finally going to be put to a good use."

Martha snatched it out of his hand. "What I do with my clothing is none of your business."

"So you said before." He slid into his boots and then left to get the company started.

"I can hardly wait until this trip is over and I can be rid of you so I don't ever have to look at that face of yours again!" she said to his back.

Hunter was already out of the tent, but he'd heard what she'd said. So that was what her behavior was leading up to, he thought bitterly. Had she merely been looking for an adventure and ended up with more than she'd bargained for when she'd married him? Hadn't she hedged at first when he had suggested the ceremony? He hadn't wanted it then any more than she did now. Yet when he'd found out he had actually married her, he had tried to do right by her. Still, if her intention was to be rid of him, so be it!

That day they made close to thirty miles; it was the farthest they had traveled in one day since they'd left Independence. Hunter had pushed them hard; allowing everybody only a fifteen-minute rest for the noonday meal.

Harriet was so frazzled by this latest pace that she ordered Clara and Fuller out that afternoon to walk while she took a nap beside little Gertrude.

Clara had had instructions to watch her brother, but rather than be bothered by the little pest, she'd enticed Henry Nelson to invite her into his family's wagon by offering to share a chunk of hard rock candy she had salvaged long before from the stock in her father's store. But Barsina climed out the back of the slow-moving wagon and joined Fuller, playing and exploring as the train moved steadily westward.

As night fell, Hunter finally gave the word to stop. There was little grass for the animals and the only water available was so strongly alkaline they had to depend on the water left in the kegs they carried. Much to everyone's frustration, with the exception of the children, the lack of water meant no baths.

With supper consisting of leftover bread and dried apples, Martha fixed a plate and set up the tent so she could finish the doll she had been sewing.

Hunter entered soon after she had settled down to sew. "I'm sure the little Belshaw boy will appreciate your efforts, but I'm tired and I'm going to go to bed. You'll have to work on that thing tomorrow."

"Go to bed if you must," Martha flung out as he stripped off his shirt and settled in next to her, "but I am going to finish this tonight."

"Woman!" He flipped the blanket over his head.

Martha's anger receded, and she couldn't help but smile at the big grumpy lump beside her.

"How can you stand to remain hidden in the brush and watch him go into her tent at night?" Jannet asked, thinking Dancing Wind a fool.

"My people do not share the white man's views of life," the Indian woman answered. "Yellow Fire does not know his woman lives." Underneath her calm exterior she was seething.

"Daughter"—Dancing Wind turned to the young girl—"have you seen that the two men know where to follow? Do they know to leave Yellow Fire alone this time?"

"Yes, Mother," Daughter of the Wind replied. Jannet studied the strongly built girl who looked more like a young warrior than a budding, half-breed Indian maiden.

"Yellow Fire?" Jannet questioned.

"The man known as Hunter Brody." Dancing Wind flashed a look of contempt toward Jannet. She had no desire to have the white woman learn any more than necessary. "Why do you not rest now? We will keep watch until the wagons move again at dawn."

Jannet moved a short distance from the two Indians, but she did not sleep. She did not trust her companions. Once Martha was dead, she knew she had to figure out a way to extricate herself from these savages who dressed in animal-skin skirts.

Just as they were preparing for another day Martha strolled to the Belshaws' wagon to give the little child the doll she had been making.

"Fuller?" she called.

Clara stuck her pudgy face out of the flap and snapped, "He's still asleep. What do you want?"

"I'll see him later in the day." Martha smiled at the urchin-like girl, though she itched to take her over her knee.

"If you want to give that dumb-looking doll to stupid little Fuller, he doesn't need one anymore," Clara squawked in her typical parrot voice.

"Then you finally decided to share?" Martha turned to ask.

"I wouldn't let him touch any of my dolls. He chews on them." When Martha looked puzzled, Clara added, "He has his own dirty old doll now and he's sucking on it."

Martha recalled that the youngster had been walking yesterday afternoon and hadn't had a toy of his own at the time. Her curiosity piqued, she walked back to the wagon. "Let me have a look at him." She ignored Clara's protests and peeked in.

Fuller lay huddled in the far corner, quietly nursing on the arm of the filthiest doll she had ever seen. Perspiration dotted his dirty, pale, little face. Martha was putting her foot up on the wagon to climb inside and have a closer look at him when Harriet's booming voice halted her.

"What do you think you're doing?" she demanded, tiredly wiping stray hairs from her smudged forehead.

"I'm going in to check on Fuller. He doesn't look at all well," Martha answered.

"I don't know what you're talking about. Clara has been taking good care of him."

"If you don't go in there right now and see to him, then I will," Martha insisted.

"Oh, very well, move over." The big woman groaned, lifted her soiled skirts, and climbed into the wagon.

Martha stood silently by until she came out.

Harriet laboriously got down from the wagon. "He has a slight fever, that's all. Now, does that satisfy you?"

"But what about that dirty doll he's suckling? Where could he have gotten it?"

"Oh, for heaven's sake, what does it matter? You'd best be tending after your own business so we don't keep that *precious* husband of yours waiting," Harriet snickered and gave Martha an icy stare before wiping the back of her aching neck as she whirled around to climb up onto the wagon box.

They had traveled about ten miles when the Belshaws' wagon began to fall behind the rest.

"What in the living hell do they think they're doing now?" Hunter heaved a disgruntled groan, and reined in his horse to set the laggards straight.

Martha, too, noticed the wagon come to a stop and spurred Humphrey in its direction.

Hunter snatched her arm as she dismounted. "Get the hell out of here," he viciously ground out, attempting to mask the worried expression on his face.

"No. I'm not leaving until I find out what's going on." She raised her chin, prepared to force him to make her go. She sensed something was deeply wrong by the harshness of his voice. This wasn't the typical impatience which had lately fired him when someone on the train had done something to displease or anger him. It was something else this time. And Martha was determined to find out what.

She pulled out of his grasp and took two steps toward the back of the wagon before Hunter caught her again. No childish voices came to her, and William Belshaw was missing from the seat. Her expression a questioning one, she looked straight into Hunter's face.

"There's a problem with one of the children, isn't there?" She knew Harriet had grown lax about watching the young ones lately, and feared one of them might have fallen out of the back of the wagon and been hurt, as often happened when families were traveling across the country and children went unattended. She suddenly recalled the sickly pallor of little Fuller's face when she'd looked in on him.

"Oh, dear God, it's Fuller isn't it! He's taken ill. I have to help."

Hunter pressed his eyes shut, feeling pain for Martha, and held her fast. "I tell you, you can't go in there," he said softly this time.

She struggled in earnest. "Why? Tell me why?"

"Fuller has all the signs of cholera."

Chapter Thirty-Two

Despite Hunter's violent protests, Martha won out. She stayed to help the Belshaws while Hunter directed the others to go a short distance farther; to where a tiny gurgling stream, not more than a crack in the ground, provided fresh cool water. It took him twenty-four hours to settle the train and still everyone's fears.

The minute he returned to the Belshaw's wagon, he pulled Martha aside. Her hair was already scraggly and her skirt was splattered. She looked a mess, but worry for her safety pricked at him as he confronted her. "Have you ever seen what happens with this sickness?"

She straightened her shoulders and prepared herself for a fight. Cholera was a grim disease, she knew. Its victims vomited profusely, and were weakened from dehydration caused by diarrhea. They withered and they died. Little Fuller was now near death, Gertrude was showing symptoms of the illness, William didn't look at all well, and Harriet had already lost nearly ten pounds from her large frame in trying to tend her family on the trek. Only Clara seemed all right, so she had been settled in a crude lean-to a safe distance from the sick, since they were afraid to return her to the rest of the company for fear she might infect someone else.

"No, not personally. A few years ago I did read a paper on it drawn up by the First International Sanitary Conference in Paris in 1851. It was reprinted in the local paper."

"So you've learned more than how to set a table. What'd

you learn, that the sick puke, spill their guts out, and then die?"

"You don't need to be so crude." She glared, but inside she knew he was only trying to make an impression on her.

"If you expect an apology, don't. I want you out of here," he said fiercely. The painful memory of Dancing Wind's death rose up in his mind. He had lost his Indian love to this disease, and he could not bear the thought of losing Martha to it.

"As long as I take precautions, I'll be all right."

"Then how did the Belshaws get it?" Hunter looked unconvinced.

"Most likely from that filthy doll Fuller found." Her face saddened as she thought of the doll she had sewn for the little boy but hadn't finished in time. "Seems it was half-buried. Probably belonged to some poor child who'd died from the disease."

"I don't understand you." He lifted his hat and ran his fingers through his hair. "That family has given you nothing but trouble, and still you insist on staying with them."

"It's simple: they need help. Personal feelings have no place during times like these. Besides, the trip has been terribly hard on them. It's not as if they really wanted to leave their home."

"I wonder if those folks would be so generous?"

"Now isn't the time for speculation. Please hurry back to the others and collect any fresh water that can be spared. Oh . . . and blankets, too."

"Sure," he grumbled, knowing it was no use to argue further with the stubborn woman. He swung up into the saddle.

"Hunter?" She stopped him before he had gone very far. "Why aren't you afraid of being here, like the others?"

"Who says I'm not."

Martha's weight dropped, and her eyes began to resemble the sunken hollows of craters. Her dress hung loosely where it had once been filled out by nicely rounded curves, but she fought on to save the little Belshaw boy, who lay inside a makeshift tent fashioned from lengths of canvas cut from the cover on the wagon. Only when Barsina was transferred from the Nelsons' camp to the area set aside for cholera-stricken patients did Martha desperately long to break down and weep. But she didn't. She knew she had to be strong.

"Barsina was playing with Fuller when he found that filthy doll. Lack of water kept her from being washed up properly," Hunter said quietly, laying the bluish-tinged little six-year-old down near Fuller. "Winnie wanted to come along, but she's got others to consider. I assured her you'd do your best by the child."

Barsina was wretching violently by the time Martha knelt beside her. Looking around for help, Martha saw that Harriet had given up hope of saving Fuller and sat blankly staring at the ground near Clara, who was hugging a blanket to her.

Exhausted, Martha laboriously got to her feet and stalked past Hunter, who was seeing to his horse.. She stopped beside the gaunt woman. "Your family needs your help. Stop feeling sorry for yourself and get back over there," she commanded.

"They're all going to die," Harriet muttered, shaking her head. "No matter what I do, they're all going to die."

Martha lost her patience with the sniveling woman, and a surge of anger overtook her. Without giving a thought to what she was doing, she drew her hand back and slapped Harriet's face, leaving it shades of red, white, and gray. Harriet only looked up at Martha with dull eyes, then dropped her head into her hands and sobbed.

"Your mother won't be any help." Martha looked desperately at Clara, and before the usually smug little girl could say a word, she grabbed her arm and began tugging her toward the sick. "Come on, I need you."

"I can't do it." Clara turned green and pinched her nose as they neared the stench of vomit and defecation.

"Just try to get some liquid down Barsina."

After Clara, hesitantly at first and then more eagerly, took charge of the child, Martha began to clean up the others.

"What can I do besides carry water?" Hunter stood over Martha. He wanted to wrap his arms around her and tell her everything would be all right, even though from past experience he knew it wouldn't.

Relief having another pair of helping hands helping caused Martha to break down and sob. Hunter drew her up into his arms and held her. "It'll be all right. They wouldn't dare die with you nursing them," he said in an effort to cheer her.

Two days later little Fuller gave one last gasp and died while Martha was trying to force fluids into him. Hunter wrapped the boy's frail body in a blanket and set it beside a gravesite he'd selected. As he started to dig, Harriet came over to him.

"Go back and help the living. I brought the child into this world. It's only fitting I be the one to bury him," she said solemnly. "When I'm through, will you and your wife join me while I read over him? And maybe build a fence so the wolves don't get him?"

Hunter obliged the pathetic shadow of a woman. "Yeah. Just let us know; we'll come."

Despite Martha's continued efforts, Gertrude followed Fuller to the grave, and Barsina hovered between life and death. With Clara's help, William Belshaw gradually seemed to be growing stronger, although years of drinking narrowed the hope that this skeleton of a man would survive.

"Go get cleaned up and rest awhile. I'll watch over Barsina," Hunter told Martha.

Too exhausted to argue, she nodded and dragged herself to the washtub they had set up close by.

Hunter watched her labored movements, saw her stop and then collapse.

"Clara, see to Barsina while I help Martha," he shouted. Almost immediately he was at Martha's side, lifting her limp body and carrying it to the blanket under the lean-to that had been her unused bed for nearly five days. He wrung out a rag and tenderly mopped her brow, afraid she had contracted the dreaded disease. "Don't get sick and leave me now that I've found you," he murmured, tears threatening to slip from his eyes. "You're quite a woman, Martha Brody," he murmured, and tenderly kissed her closed eyelids.

Hunter wasn't the only one who watched Martha collapse. On a nearby hill, behind an outcroping of boulders, two hefty men waited, poised like vultures over carrion.

"Why don't we go in there and finish 'em off now? Don't look like they're in much shape t' put up a fight." Deke rubbed the grimy stubble on his chin.

"Why you think those Injuns ain't nearby? You want t' go rushin' down there and end up gettin' whatever them sodbusters got?" Disgusted, Horace looked at his brother.

"Nope, Guess we'll wait it out. All I know's that I want that sonofabitch killed slowly fer what he done t' Chucker, no matter what that Injun says. Then I want me a taste of that woman."

Horace laughed. "If you want t' do it right, we'll both take us a turn at that bastard's woman while he's still alive and has t' watch. Then we'll kill him a chunk at a time. After he's dead, we'll get us a couple of Injun squaws and that mighty fine woman with 'em."

Deke's smile displayed a mouth full of decayed teeth. Then he turned his hungry attention back to Martha, anticipation of probing beneath her skirts swelling his crotch.

William died heaving his guts out shortly after midnight on the fifth day. Hunter dug a grave beside Fuller's and Gertrude's. He was forced to hold Harriet to keep her from jumping into the pit with her husband while Martha and a tear-stained Clara shoveled dirt over William's emaciated body. Belshaw knew his wife well, Hunter thought, recalling how the man had told him that she was not a strong woman.

"Get a hold of yourself!" Hunter furiously shook Harriet. "You still have a child who needs you. You're the only one left for her. Do you understand me?" He looked into the empty eyes which stared back at him.

Harriet swabbed at her forehead. "Yes. Yes, I do. God has punished Clara and me for our sins by leaving us alive," she said, displaying a stoicism that seemed out of character.

"Now you know that's not true. You have to pull yourself together. You've got to get everything out of your wagon and burn it. Then you must wash down the wagon with strong soapy water." Martha thought giving the woman something to do would take her mind off the calamity and would help ease her burden.

"Yes, of course," Harriet woodenly replied. "I'll take care of the wagon so no one else will get sick."

"I'll go give Barsina some of that salt water you fixed up for

305

her," a subdued Clara practically whispered, untold pain evident on her pudgy face. She cast her mother a sorrowful glance and then returned to Barsina, who needed her clothing and blankets changed again.

"Clara may need help." Martha started to pull away from Hunter's supporting arm.

"No. Leave it to her. I think that may be the only thing that'll save that little girl. She's carrying a pretty heavy load of guilt around for not watching her brother more closely. If Barsina makes it, Clara might be all right, too."

"Sometimes you show such amazing insight." Surprised by Hunter's perceptiveness, Martha was at the same time saddened that they wouldn't have the chance to build a life together and have their own children. But she had determined that it was necessary to start a new life—without him.

"It didn't take much insight. While you were sleeping, Clara told me how she felt. I guess with her mother in such a sorry state, she had to talk to someone and I just happened to be available."

Her voice shaking with emotion, Martha said, "You should have children of your own."

"I might some day." His eyes delved intently, hopefully, into hers.

"Yes." Martha lowered her gaze as the sharp pain went throught her and she turned away from Hunter before she saw the love for her on his face.

A short while later, Martha bent down over the cold and clammy little girl. "How is she?"

"I got her cleaned up, and so far she hasn't throwed up the water I gave her." Clara looked hopeful.

"Looks like Barsina might be getting better. She wouldn't be if it wasn't for your help." Martha reassuringly patted Clara's hand and the child brightened.

"You really think so?"

"I know so."

What with burying the dead and tending to the sick, Martha and Hunter let Harriet slip from their minds after she'd been instructed to disinfect her wagon. In an unnerved and desperate state, the woman climbed into the germriddled

306

schooner and slowly fingered what remained of her worldly possessions. There were few tangibles left after the incident at the river, and she had neglected her children so now they were gone. Only Clara was left. In her crazed mind Harriet Belshaw viewed Clara's lapse, not her own torment, as the cause of her suffering.

She opened one of the two remaining crates. Inside it was an extra lantern. She lit it and looked around at the few articles in the wagon. There was nothing left for her. No home. No family. Why should she struggle on for the one who had caused all this grief? An echoing voice in her mind agreed. Yes, that was what she had to do; she'd leave Clara alone to pay for her sins all the days of her life. Her eyes wild, Harriet danced around the inside of the wagon. High-pitched cackles such as hers could be heard inside the walls of asylums. She threw her head back, chanting to her dead family, and then, with one quick stroke, slammed the lantern down onto the wooden floorboards.

The fuel in the lantern made flames erupt into voracious demons that devoured the wagon.

"Oh, merciful God!" Martha cried, suddenly noticing the fire.

Hunter ran toward the blazing wagon. By the time he got to it, it was engulfed in flames. He couldn't get any closer due to the heat. Harriet's silhouette of a woman tearing at her hair lent the burning wagon a grisly aura.

"Mama!" Clara screamed, and rushed forward.

Martha caught the little girl in her arms and drew her face to her breast so she would not view her mother's morbidly chosen fate.

But Clara was almost hysterical as they stood motionless a safe distance from what had become a blazing inferno. "Hunter, please ride to camp and get the medicine box. This child needs something to calm her nerves."

"I'm on my way." Hunter hated to leave them alone, but he knew they'd be safe from wild animals, since none would venture near such a holocaust and the fire was likely to burn well into the night. At least Barsina seemed to have rallied and, with luck, might pull through. "Stay away from the brush until I get back," he called out, and then disappeared into the darkness.

"Come on, Clara, there's nothing we can do here. Let's go see how Barsina is." Martha hugged the distraught little girl to her.

Clara had undergone a drastic change. The selfish whiner had become the humble little orphan now tucked in the crook of Martha's arm. A horrifying catastrophe had struck her. She'd lost her entire family, and right before her eyes at such a young age. Martha's heart went out to the little girl. While she hadn't suffered in the same way, she nevertheless felt a deep emptiness because of Hunter's deception, and could sincerely sympathize with the shattered Clara.

After Martha checked on Barsina, who was sleeping peacefully, she cradled Clara in her arms.

"I know it's hard to believe now, but in time you'll feel better," she murmured soothingly, hoping it would be true.

She held Clara until the child cried herself into an exhausted slumber, and once Clara was tucked in, she rubbed her arms to ward off the chill and got to her feet. She massaged the small of her back, then wrapped a shawl around her shoulders and paced about the rocky terrain, ignoring Hunter's advice.

Clara and Barsina were fast asleep, and she needed a few quiet moments. She had been surrounded by death. Now that the ordeal was almost over, the terrible letdown that often sets in when superhuman strength is no longer required overwhelmed her. If she got off by herself for a few moments, she felt she could grieve in private and be strong again by the time Hunter returned. Her mind made up, Martha climbed a short distance up a hill and sat down. In the silvery moonlight she could still keep an eye on the children.

She curled up into a ball, put her head down on her knees, and allowed long pent-up tears to flow freely.

Wracking sobs so absorbed her that she didn't hear the crunching of dried branches and rock as booted feet approached.

Chapter Thirty-Three

"You sure she ain't got it?" Deke whispered as they neared Martha. "We ain't gonna catch nothin', you think?"

"We been watchin' her. She's done all the doctorin'. She ain't got nothin'. After we grab her, she can do a little doctorin' fer us too." Horace grinned.

"Yessiree. Let's get her. I can already feel myself sucklin' at her breast like that little brat was a little while ago, only she ain't gonna have no dress on when I do it."

"You got that ridin' whip that little gal was hittin' Chucker with?" Horace evilly narrowed his eyes.

"'Course, I got it. I picked it up just like you told me."

"Then before we get us a travelin' companion, take that little ol' strip of cowhide and put it next t' those two brats. That should guarantee us that man of hers knows what happened t' his woman, and follows us right inta the nice little trap we'll have waitin' fer him."

Moving like a stealthy cat, Deke slunk from their roost to head toward the two slumbering little girls. He set the whip down near Barsina and then crept back to join his brother.

Horace had moved to within three yards of Martha, and he could almost taste the flavor of her sweet flesh. Deke crouched next to him and quietly they billowed out the ample canvas sack Horace was toting. Securely holding it by the corners, they raised it overhead, carrying it toward Martha who was oblivious of the ominous cloth cloud floating toward her.

At the drumfire of horse's hooves, Deke and Horace

crumpled the sack and dropped to the ground.

"Shit!" Deke mumbled. "It should've taken him longer."

"What're we goin t' do now?" Horace croaked. He lay plastered against the sandy earth.

"Get the hell out of here and wait on another chance at her."

"What about that whip? What if he finds it?"

"They ain't gonna be lookin' around tonight. We'll get it back as soon as they're sleepin'." On his belly, Deke slithered back behind some brush.

Hunter bounded off his big bay, and spying Martha's prone form, he immediately strode the short distance up the hill to where she had fallen asleep. He knelt down and gently ran the back of his hand along her cheek. She did not stir.

Hunter's heart tossed in his chest. She looked so small, so vulnerable, lying alone in the harsh wilderness, but even if she didn't want to be his wife, he would never again deny the courage and spirit she possessed. He felt deep remorse over the way he had tricked her. He should have courted and wooed her. But he had lived on the rough frontier a long time, and wondered if he would have remembered how. That thought set his mind to work.

He took her up in his arms and headed toward the lean-to not far from the children. After he bundled Martha warmly in a woolen blanket, he checked on the girls. They slept soundly. He tucked the quilts up around their necks, and returned to Martha. It was a cold night, and he lay down beside her, cuddling her against the curve of his body.

He'd had an uneasy feeling leaving her that night, as if an ill wind were forecasting danger and the need to be alert.

In the morning, if Barsina continued to show improvement, they'd finally be able to move on. He'd never lost so many people from one family before, and that, too, was unsettling. He kissed Martha's lips lightly, then got up to pace about the camp. The nearby embers, which were all that remained of the Belshaws' wagon, cast off a smoldering red glow, lending an eerie light to the graying sky.

Martha stirred and looked around her, realizing she must

310

have fallen asleep last night up on the hill. But how had she gotten here? Hunter had returned and had found her, she told herself.

"Oh, dear—the children!" She scrambled to her feet and rushed toward the makeshift tent, running right into Hunter.

He put his arms around her, but she quickly pulled from him. "They're fine." He was answering the silent question in her eyes. "Barsina is much better."

"How soon before she will be able to travel?" Martha asked, glancing at the now-cold pile of cinders, the remains of that horrible bonfire.

"Barsina's terribly weak, but I see no reason why she can't be returned to her family this morning."

"What a horrible way to die," Martha mumbled absently, her gaze still on the cinders.

"People reap what they sow."

"No one deserves to die that way." She shivered, Harriet Belshaw's last moments still gruesomely fresh in her mind.

Hunter shook his head. He had witnessed much out here, and had become hardened. He wondered if Martha's soft heart would harden, too, in time. "Only someone like you could believe that. Come on over to the fire, I made some suckeyes and bacon for breakfast."

Martha followed him to the campfire, but kept her distance as she ate the pancakes and strips of crisp bacon. How could he be so kind and caring and thoughtful, yet do such a cruel thing to her? She wanted to confront him, to scream at him and ask why he could make love to her the way he had and still be so deceitful.

She swallowed the lump of pride in her throat—it had been blocking her burgeoning need for answers—and got to her feet. Eying him closely, she inched over to where he sat finishing his breakfast.

She forced his name off the edge of her tongue. "Hunter?"

He expectantly rose. "Yeah?"

"There's something I must know."

He took a step toward her. "What?"

"Ah . . . it's about . . . it's about—"

As Cornelius drove up in the spring wagon, Martha stopped

311

in midsentence. He jumped down and strode over to them, ending Martha's attempt to force herself to find out why Hunter could be so cruel as to pretend to wed her.

"I do hope I have not interrupted anything," Cornelius said, noting Martha's vaguely disappointed expression.

"No. Nothing." She forced a stiff smile.

Cornelius looked toward a somewhat befuddled Hunter. "I hitched up the horses at the first light of dawn as you instructed and came as quicky as I could."

"Yeah, well, you're right on time. Let's get Barsina into the wagon and take her back to her folks." There was a note of irritation in Hunter's voice due to Cornelius's timing.

The men followed Martha to the sleeping children and, without waking the two girls, carefully placed them in the back of the wagon.

"While you finish breakfast would you mind if I set up and got a picture or two?" Cornelius hesitantly asked, noting the remains of the Belshaws' wagon.

"Is it really necessary?" Martha was still sickened by the gruesome sight.

"I know it's a grim reminder, but many die on the trail."

"Just don't waste time." Hunter gave Cornelius the go-ahead despite Martha's protestations. "We're leaving as soon as we're picked up."

The moment for truth was lost so Martha silently gathered up the few items not to be left behind while Hunter collected the germ-ridden articles and buried them.

Hunter seemed unusually quiet and contemplative as Barsina was reunited with her family in a tear-provoking scene during which all the details of those nightmarish days were related. Then he hung back near the rear of the train while Happy spurred the camels to the fore and the wagons moved out, their wheels deep in sand.

Martha had washed and changed into a blue gingham dress before they'd returned to the trail and she now rode in the back of the Stewarts' wagon, so she might get some much-needed rest. She had purposely tied back the flap so she could watch

Hunter. He was behaving more strangely than he had since they'd left Independence, and she wanted to know why.

After two hours of lagging behind the train and riding in a zigzag pattern from hill to hill, Hunter finally came close enough to the wagon for Martha to wave him over.

"Are you all right?" Concern was in her voice.

"Fine," he answered, the reply accompanied by a twitch of his left cheek.

"Then would it be all right if I ride one of the horses from the spring wagon after the noonday rest? The ground is much firmer again and it shouldn't be too much of a burden for the other horses if I ride only a short while." Asking his permission galled her. He had been acting much too remote even for him today.

"Under no circumstances are you to leave that wagon today, not even to walk. Do you understand?" As Hunter's brows drew together in a warning line, Martha felt gooseflesh rise on her arms.

"Yes, I quite understand," she said quickly, having noted his intensity.

"I doubt that you do. But I want your pledge that for once you'll listen to me."

His glare could have vanquished a cougar; Martha flinched under it and nodded her acceptance of his demands.

All day they forced the failing oxen onward, allowing them no respite. Martha was certain Hunter was pushing them to make up for lost time, and suspected that he was anxious to rid himself of her. When they finally stopped for the night and he commanded that the wagons be drawn into a tight circle, speculation arose among the members of the train as to the possibility of an Indian attack. They feared what they'd dreaded was about to happen.

Although Hunter hadn't said a word about Indians, emigrants invariably thought they would be murdered by bronze-skinned savages. To heighten the party's fears, there had been a storm over the mountains and black clouds had been surging their way all afternoon. Tonight would be a perfect time for an attack, since the moon was shielded and would provide little light for the guards Hunter had posted to warn of any movement in the brush.

Heightening the uneasiness of everyone was the position of the animals. The beasts had been corralled at their usual distance from the train and were chewing on sickly patches of grass. Happy remained at the camels' side, away from the security of the wagons, tending to his duties as camel driver.

Martha joined Winnie, who was setting the gathered sagebrush ablaze so she could get supper started.

"The Belshaws' deaths were a terrible tragedy," Martha declared. She wanted to discuss what had happened in order to lay her haunting visions to rest.

"It was an awful thing, that sickness." Winnie, like the other members of the company, appeared to fidget uneasily at the mention of the Belshaws. Life went forward; any emigrant could understand that. You didn't look back, you looked to the future and kept going if you were going to survive.

After observing Winnie's discomfort, Martha decided against further discussion of the events of the preceding days, and asked, "How are Barsina and Clara getting along?"

"My Barsina looks like she'll make it. Pity the Belshaw youngun's kinfolks are all gone, but me and Jed been talkin' and it makes sense to us that we take in Clara. She'd be another pair of hands to help out once we get settled. And she seems changed since losin' her kin."

"Are you sure you want another mouth to feed?" Martha questioned, thinking of their age and of the children they already had to support.

"Who else would take her? The Stewarts are just startin' out. They don't want the responsibility. And you and that man of yours will be startin' a family of your own right soon. What with all you two got to settle, you don't need—"

As if she had quicksilver in her tongue, Martha declared, "Everything has been settled between us."

Winnie looked askance at Martha's belly, but replied, "Well, I'm glad of that. Now, why do you suppose that man of yours has us all bunched together like this?"

Martha tensed at the words *that man of yours,* but recovered without any apparent display of churning emotions. "I don't know, but I don't think I like it."

314

By the time the men joined the women around the campfire, tension crackled in the cold night air. The smell of rain was in the breeze, and none of the usual chatter was exchanged while they nibbled at the slab of fried ham, beans, and leftover bread.

Once supper was over Hunter ordered them all to their wagons and doused the fire. Martha had not been allowed to set up the tent, so she huddled next to Cornelius in the Stewarts' wagon.

"You men all had your heads together earlier. What's going on?" she asked the tall photographer.

He slipped a protective arm around her shoulders; in the other, he cradled a rifle. "I hope nothing."

"Don't be so evasive with me. I think we all have a right to know what is happening. What are you doing sitting here so close, as if you're protecting me from something—or someone?"

Cornelius squirmed uneasily under Martha's much too perceptive scrutiny, but Hunter had given orders that none of the women were to know what he suspected might happen. "I am afraid you will have to ask Mr. Brody for the answers to your questions. It is almost time for me to exchange positions with him and go on guard duty, so he should be here shortly."

Before Martha could voice an objection to Cornelius's response, a loud cymbaling of thunder caused her to jump. At the other end of the wagon Cecilia whimpered and burrowed deeper into Derek's embrace. Then lightning streaked across the sky like a flashing steel spear, lighting the camp and lending an eerie iridescent color to the brush surrounding the train.

As a downpour threatened a blustery whir ripped through the night and monstrous bonfires suddenly streamed toward the dark heavens around the small circle of wagons. Gunshots seemed to explode from all directions.

"I declare, there must be thousands of Indians out there!" Cecilia screeched hysterically as blazes flared and blasts ricocheted around them. "We'll all be massacred!"

Chapter Thirty-Four

In spite of Cornelius's efforts to stop her, Martha bolted from the wagon in search of Hunter. Another flash of lightning exposed two skulking forms moving toward her. She screamed, turned around, and scrambled back toward the others as more blasts of gunfire filled the camp, coming from every direction. Martha dropped down and lay flat on her stomach in the dirt as a bullet whizzed past her ear. Frightened to the core, she ventured to look up in time to see two male figures jump another, which by the size of the man could only be Hunter. Her heart was spinning wildly in her chest; she had to get someone to help him before they killed him. She clambered to her feet and dashed to the rear of the wagon.

"Quick! Hunter needs help," she screamed, panting.

Cornelius sat as still as a rock, his hands gripping the butt of a rifle as if he would strangle it.

When he did not respond, Martha tried to wrench the gun from his hands, which were frozen fast.

"My God, where's Derek?" she frantically called to Cecilia, desperate for someone to aid Hunter.

"Why, he's gone to help move the spring wagon away from the burning brush." Cecilia cowered in the corner, sniffling.

Martha turned back to Cornelius. In the glitter of lightning she could see the pallor of his face and hands. From the look of him, he wasn't going to be of any help. Knowing what she had to do, she grabbed for the rifle.

"If you aren't going to use the gun, let go of it!"

Cornelius stared at her, numb with fright. Slowly, he said, "The only thing I ever shot was a photograph."

"It's all right. You don't have to fire the rifle. Just let go of it," Martha said as calmly as she could.

Cornelius looked down at the weapon and opened his fingers. He had barely released it, before Martha heaved it out of his lap. She swung around as another bolt of lightning electrified the sky. One of the men was holding Hunter's arms behind him and the other was standing in front of him, his big fist drawn back.

Martha suppressed a scream and said a silent prayer as she raised the rifle and squeezed the trigger. The discharge kicked the gun out of her hands, and in the mortifying seconds that followed the blast she watched, horrified, while Hunter crumpled to the ground.

"Oh, no!" She slapped the back of her hand against her mouth. Without thinking of the other two men, she lifted her muddy skirt and frantically ran to Hunter's side. "My darling, what have I done to you?" she cried, cradling his limp body to her breast.

"Well, shit. Will you look at that? The little lady seems t' of done our job fer us." Deke's laugh was ugly.

Through her tears, Martha glared up at the two hulking men, realizing who they were as Hunter's warm blood slowly oozed over her arm.

"I'd be guessin' that she just couldn't wait t' finish what she started back at the ferry. Don't you think so, Deke?" Horace sneered.

Deke clamped a hurtful hand around Martha's arm and yanked her to her feet. "It was right nice of you t'shoot that bastard fer us." Using his free hand, he puckered her lips. "How about a little kiss before the three of us find some nice dry place and you show us what Chucker got killed fer?" He dug bruising fingers into her shoulders and pulled her against his heavy chest.

Martha spit in his face. "You filthy pig! The others will be here in a second to blow your heads off."

Deke wiped spittle off his chin with the back of his sleeve, and his lips curled over his teeth in a vicious snarl. "Maybe we

317

should give you a gun and let you take care of them fer us."

"No!" she screamed as he bent his head and fastened his crushing mouth to hers. His breath was foul and his thick tongue lay siege to her tightly compressed lips. Martha fought with all her strength, but he held fast. In desperation she opened her mouth, and when his tongue assaulted her, she bit into the nasty appendage.

"Goddamned bitch!" Deke howled, pushing Martha away from him and drawing back his fist.

She barely managed to maintain her balance, but she took a deep breath and tried to prepare herself for the worst.

"I wouldn't do that if I were you—that is, if you plan to go on breathing." Hunter cocked the hammer on the pistol he was pointing directly at Deke's heart.

Martha's eyes shot to him. He wasn't dead. Thank God. He was still on the ground propped up on his elbow, the gun in his right hand, his left hand pressed against the wound in his shoulder.

Horace's fingers slyly slid down his side toward his gunbelt. "Consider yourself as getting the same warning," Hunter said and waved Horace over toward Deke. "Throw your gun down—real slow."

Horace snarled but complied. The gun landed a few feet away from Martha, who stood to the left of Deke.

"Martha," Hunter ordered, "go over and pick up the gun and hold it on them until Jed and the others get here."

Martha nodded her understanding. In her haste she stepped in front of Deke, placing herself directly in the line of fire.

"Dammit Martha, get out of the way!" Hunter commanded.

Her steps faltered when she became aware of what she had done.

"Horace, get the gun," Deke shouted. He shoved her aside and made a leap for Hunter.

The gun. She had to get to the gun before Horace. Martha dove forward and grasped the pistol butt. Horace was not as nimble, but he seized her leg, tugging her toward him. She had never learned to shoot a firearm, but she was fighting for her life. As Horace made his way up her leg in an effort to wrest the gun from her, Martha managed to lurch around and face him.

Her fingers trembled and her breathing was ragged, but she held the gun with both hands and pointed it squarely at him.

"You ain't goin' t' pull that trigger," he jeered derisively. "Not a fine lady like you." He stretched out his hand, and his fingers cautiously began to close around the barrel of the pistol.

Almost simultaneously two bursts of yellow fire exploded, and deadly smoke patterns drifted like ghosts on the frosty, damp air.

As if the gun had suddenly turned into a poisonous viper, Martha thrust it out of her hands. Then shaking uncontrollably, she watched Horace grab his gut and fall into a heap, saw Deke collapse. Falling raindrops diverted her attention from her part in the life-and-death struggle which had resulted in two lifeless bodies lying facedown in the dirt.

With knees too weak to support her, she crawled over to Hunter, threw her arms around his neck, and wept. "I was so afraid they were going to kill you."

"Ouch!" He pushed her hands away from his wound. "Were you scared because they were going to kill me or because, since you only wounded me the first time, you might not get a second chance to put another slug in me?" he grumbled, rubbing his head. He'd gotten the bump on it after she had shot him, when he'd fallen against a rock.

"Oh, no. You can't believe I did it on purpose?" Martha looked devastated.

Hunter wearily shook his throbbing head, then let out an exasperated sigh. "No. I've come to realize you have only the best intentions every time you get yourself in over your head."

"If I hadn't intervened, they might have beaten you to death before anyone else came to your aid," she snapped, stung by his remark.

"Yeah, well, at least I wouldn't have died with a hole in my shoulder." He flinched at the pain he felt as he got to his feet.

Martha linked her arm through Hunter's good arm and tried to help him back to the wagons, but he swatted her hand away. "I think you've helped me enough for one night."

She stepped back, then, with determined steps, walked toward the Nelsons' wagon. He might not want her near him right now or after the end of the trip, and he might be a deceitful liar, but he wasn't going to stop her from seeing that his wound was cleansed once he reached Winnie's wagon. Indeed, she was so intent on seeing to Hunter's aid that she blanked out on the fact that she had just killed a man.

Jed reached Hunter. "Chrissake, all this ruckus was caused by only those two men?" He scratched his head at the grisly sight before him as Derek hurried over, followed by Seth.

"Where are the rest of them?" Derek asked.

"There were only two; the ones I didn't finish at the ferry— the Lucas brothers," Hunter answered.

"Well, I'll be. But we was pinned down by gunfire." Jed looked perplexed.

With a painful effort, Hunter bent over and picked up the much-coveted Sharp's rifle. "The cartridges that fit into this gun are what was keeping you busy."

Seth gawked at the rifle. "I don't think I understand."

"It was a trick. They doused the brush with kerosene, threw a handful of bullets here and there in it, and set it afire. As the shells heated up they exploded, making us think we were being attacked by a whole army."

"But how'd you know?" Seth was evidently awed by the big wagon-train captain.

"I didn't until I saw for sure it was those two and made out the rifle they were carrying. As I told you earlier, I found the whip Martha lost at the ferry between the two girls, and the old man had warned me they wouldn't forget their brother's killing. When I saw those two, all the pieces just sort of fell together." Hunter winced as a sharp pang in his shoulder sent waves of pain radiating through him.

"Come on, let's get you back to the wagon so Winnie can take a look at that hole in you," Jed advised. "Some of us can come back and bury those two later."

Dancing Wind nearly left her vantage point when Hunter fell, but she settled back when she saw him move. Beside her, Jannet watched eagerly as the Lucas brothers grabbed Martha.

"It shouldn't be long now," she declared, the fires of

madness in her eyes.

When Hunter gained the upper hand, Jannet rose. "No!" she screamed, but her cry was drowned out by the exploding shells. "They've got to kill her!" She lunged forward.

Dancing Wind grabbed her. "You will wait with us. In my vision I have seen the white woman perish. My visions do not lie."

The two gun blasts seemed to please rather than daunt the Indian.

"Why aren't you upset?" Jannet asked as the Lucas brothers fell.

"Do you not see the yellow fires? It is a good sign." She turned to her daughter. "You see the yellow fires. Did I not tell you about the man called Yellow Fire?" A self-satisfied smile filled her. "We shall come together very soon when he brings the buffalo spirits near our people's camp."

"You mean the camels?" Jannet thought the woman stupid for mistaking a camel for a buffalo.

"Silly woman," Dancing Wind snapped. "The animals are spirits of the buffalo, which Yellow Fire will bring as a gift to reunite us and to appease my brother's restless spirit."

"Are you certain, Mother, the gift will cleanse the blood from our hands?" the girl questioned. Jannet noticed that for the first time the young girl seemed a bit shaken, and she wondered what that meant.

"Have I not told you I have seen it so? We wait."

"But what of Yellow Fire? Is he not in danger?" The girl's yellow-brown eyes seemed to glow with an unusual concern.

"He will not perish. We are too close not to know if his life were truly in danger. Come," she motioned to them. "The time grows near."

The sky dawned blue after a night of drizzling rain and brilliant sky-rocketing displays of lightning. Martha sat in the back of the Stewarts' wagon since the Nelsons' continued to serve as a convalescent center for Barsina. She looked down at Hunter, who was still out cold from the whiskey he'd drunk in order to endure Winnie's crude surgical methods. Gooseflesh

321

rose on Martha's arms when a strange wind swept into the wagon, and she envisaged the hunting knife in Winnie's hand, probing and twisting in order to dig out the bullet lodged deep in Hunter's shoulder. The terrors of the night before rose up to haunt her. It had been a nightmare, and she would forever suffer from it for some time, although the others tried to lend their support.

"Martha," Hunter mumbled, then he lapsed into incoherent ramblings.

She laid her palm on his forehead in a soothing gesture. It was hot and dry, and she noticed that his eyes remained shut. Hurriedly she fetched a bucket of cool water from the keg which hung outside the wagon.

She had just swung around, sloshing water to the ground in her haste to return to Hunter's side, when Winnie halted her. "How's that man of yours this mornin'?"

"Oh, Winnie, he's burning up with fever." Concern pierced Martha's voice.

"I had to do a mighty bit of diggin' to get that bullet out. Just keep his wound clean. With you nursin' him, he'll be up and hollerin' orders in no time."

"Thank you, Winnie." Martha smiled bravely, wishing she were as certain of that as the older woman. Then Winnie's words about nursing caused deep worry lines to dart across her forehead. Hadn't Hunter made a similar comment about her nursing skills before the Belshaws died?

"Don't go frettin'. He's too ornery not to get us back on the trail right soon." Winnie gave Martha a reassuring pat.

By the time Martha knelt beside Hunter, beads of perspiration had sprung up on his flushed face and some of them clung to the stubble on his chin. He started to thrash about, causing the wound to turn the bandage encircling his shoulder a bright crimson. Unable to hold him down any other way, Martha straddled his waist, using her body weight to keep him in place.

"Martha . . . Martha," he muttered, tossing his head. "Tried to trick . . . wife . . . All trick . . . Abe . . ."

The rest of his words were slurred beyond distinction. But she had heard enough. In his delirium he had admitted the deception once again, and Abe's part in it. Her heart twisted into a tight knot, threatening to squeeze the breath from her. It was as painful as hearing the cruel truth about their sham of a marriage for the first time. She turned away from the sight of his flushed face to wipe glistening tears from her eyes. She knew that no matter how hard she fought against him, how determined she was to continue to fight, she could not deny her love for him. They were not wed in the eyes of God or legally, but there were moments when she could not help but believe an eternal thread bound her to him.

The cold compresses she had placed over Hunter's face had a calming effect. He ceased tossing and lay composed in sleep. Martha slid off him. Her lower lip quivered as she wondered if she'd have been considered a grieving widow or a murderess had he died by her hand. She squeezed her eyes shut, forcing such unbidden thoughts from her mind. How could she allow herself to acknowledge, even for a second, that he might die?

Then, like a desperate person filled with recriminations, Martha relived their journey. Many disasters had befallen the small train, but she felt a burdensome responsibility for the delay at Fort Laramie. While she was wondering what else could possibly happen to them, Jed's and Derek's voices drifted into the wagon with the dreaded answer.

Chapter Thirty-Five

Monday, August 22, 1859—Heading toward Sublette's Cutoff. While I have never been one to believe that a person could ever truly be considered a carrier of bad luck, I am beginning to wonder whether there could possibly be the slightest shred of truth to that superstition. I pray these feelings that I am the cause of much misfortune are mine alone and I shall soon discover the folly of my dread . . .

For two days, while Hunter convalesced and regained his strength, Jed, Derek, and Seth scoured the surrounding countryside for the team of oxen from the Belshaws' wagon and the four horses that had pulled the spring wagon. The animals had disappeared in all the commotion on the night the train had been attacked. Whether they had been frightened by the lightning and thunder or the fires, or had been run off by the Lucas brothers to further cripple the plagued train, no one seemed able to deduce. Happy had had a time of it with the camels, and hadn't noticed the other animals were gone until hours later. A search had been conducted then, in vain. There'd been no trace of the beasts, the drizzling rain had seen to that.

Derek slid from Hunter's big bay after returning from another fruitless search. "If nothing else, at least the rest of the animals have had a chance to gain back their strength." Disgruntled, he let out a groan, and rubbed the back of his aching neck.

"Yeah, well, I suppose we'll just have to make do." Hunter walked over to his horse and patted the lathered animal on the head.

Martha looked up from her chores and saw that Hunter was not using the white cloth she had fashioned to support his arm. "You're not going to try to hitch your horse to the wagon, are you?" she asked, her eyes widening. "And where is your sling?"

Hunter frowned. "In answer to your first question, no. And as to your second, if I thought I needed it, I'd have it on." He turned his back to her, effectively cutting her out of the conversation.

Damn! His actions certainly didn't fit in with his plan to begin courting her. Why did she still manage to bring out his worst side by intruding on his efforts to get the train through without any more disasters befalling it? He rubbed his arm. It remained stiff and sore, but he had to get the train back on the trail. They had gotten a late start as it was, and had had too many delays already, for him to allow her the luxury of coddling him for a mere shoulder wound.

"Start unloading the wagon," Hunter ordered gruffly. "We'll dump anything that isn't absolutely necessary. I'm afraid that includes your equipment, Potter," he called out to Cornelius, who was fiddling with one of his cameras.

Cornelius's tall frame instantly straightened. "But you cannot do that," he pleaded. "This equipment is essential to my livelihood. I have already spent a goodly portion of the money I received as an advance for the book I'm compiling, and if I'm unable to finish it I will be ruined."

"Sorry. There's more at stake here than money."

Cornelius looked devastated, and Martha felt his frustration and pain as if it were her own. If it would have helped, she'd have tossed out her trunk and let him have her space, but he had much more equipment than could be stored in the area her belongings took up. Still, there had to be another way!

She was silently searching for one when the answer came to her. "Of course!" she said. Gathering her skirts, she walked from camp with the determined stride of someone who knew

325

exactly where she was headed.

Happy jumped to his feet when he caught sight of Martha. "Missus. Missus." The turban-on his head bobbed. "You pretty in green. Very pretty. Very pretty."

"Thank you, Happy," she responded brightly. "I need to ask you an important question. . . ."

"What the hell?" Hunter snapped, as a weird sight came toward him. When he saw Martha walking behind the camels he rolled his eyes. "How I ever thought traveling in these parts was exciting before I met that woman, I'll never be able to figure."

It had not been more than two hours since Martha had left Hunter. Now she proudly accompanied Happy into the middle of the camp, behind the five camels sporting the altered harnesses of the team of missing horses, the team that had pulled the spring wagon.

"What do you think you're doing now?" Hunter scowled as he held his sore arm.

"I've brought the solution to the problem with the spring wagon," Martha said firmly, certain any other approach would be ignored.

"And you"—Hunter turned to Happy, whose grin faded under Hunter's scorching look—"allowed yourself to be a party to her scheme?"

"Missus got good idea. You listen. You listen," Happy urged, though seeming to shrink three inches in height under Hunter's scrutiny.

"From the look of those beasts I take it you mean to hitch them to the wagon. Is that a fair assessment?" Hunter said flatly.

"I thought they might prove useful until we reach the next fort and can secure horses. That way Cornelius can keep his equipment."

Hunter stood still for a moment, seeming to ponder the idea, which gave Martha hope that he was at least considering her plan. She watched expressions play cross his face, thinking how incredibly good-looking he was. The proud, straight nose, the determined chin, and the strength in those hazel eyes was nearly more than she could endure. She found herself wishing that time could be turned back yet she could still know what she knew now. Then, she wondered, would she do anything differently? It might be morally wrong, and she would surely pay for it the rest of her life, but she could not deny the ecstasy she'd known lying in his arms, making love with him.

Finally Hunter rubbed a hand over the whiskers on his chin, and asked, "And just who did you have in mind to drive such a team of camels?"

Martha glanced around her. Happy already had responsibility for the other camels, and Hunter's wound would not yet allow him to hold the reins of an unruly team. For one reason or another, Martha ruled out every man on the wagon train. It was a good idea, but there didn't appear to be anyone available who could handle the animals.

"Well, I'm waiting for your answer? Who's going to handle those camels?" Hunter seemed to be gloating.

As if a flame had suddenly sparked in her mind, Martha straightened her spine. "I am."

"You?" Hunter laughed, and the members of the train within earshot chuckled. "You can't be serious."

The sun was rising in the east when Hunter climbed up next to Martha and eased himself down beside her on the spring wagon's seat, his arm again in a sling. Though his lips were pressed into a determined line, he handed her the fragrant bunch of wildflowers he had picked.

"What are these for?" Hunter's offering surprised Martha, but she thought it a sweet, albeit a somewhat awkward and schoolboyish gesture. As tears threatened over the hopelessness of her entanglement with this big blond man, she called to mind Hunter and Abe discussing the fake wedding ceremony in that clearing outside Fort Laramie so she might bolster her weakening reserve.

"I thought you might need something to give you added courage today," he offered.

She took a whiff of the aromatic bouquet, and her ex-

pression softened. "It was thoughtful of you. Thank you."
Was he trying to court her? What's wrong with you, Martha?
she chided herself. You're not a child anymore; wishes don't
come true. And even if they did, you're smarter than to be
taken in by such an obvious ploy.

She set the flowers by her side, and took a deep breath to
force all thoughts of Hunter from her while she watched the
other wagons pull out ahead of them. But she held the reins so
tightly that if she hadn't had on the leather gloves Hunter had
given her, she was certain everyone could have seen her veins
protrude between her knuckles. To frazzle her nerves further,
one of the more cantankerous camels craned its neck back and
hissed at her.

Hunter not could help but grin. His plan to court her seemed
to be having a positive effect, judging by the look on her face
when he'd handed her the bouquet. But she had let herself in
for what was going to be anything but a boring day. He had
been tempted to ride his bay and let her fend for herself; worry
that she might get hurt had stopped him. At least if he were
sitting next to her, he could resolve any problem before it got
out of control. And the flowers had proved a good beginning
for his plan to woo back his wife.

He nudged her. "Move 'em out."

Martha barely rustled the reins, setting Humphrey into
motion. She was relieved to see the other camels meekly follow
his lead as the wagon easily fell in behind the others. It had
been a good idea to use Humphrey as the fifth camel; no doubt
she would have had nothing but trouble without him.

Shortly after they started out, four men on horseback passed
their train.

"Hey, Davey, will ya git a load of that?" The one on the gray
roared. The others immediately joined in. "I've got to git me
another look-see. I never seen nothin' like them afore."

"And there's a woman drivin'." The man rumbled with
laughter.

"What kind of folk you fellas think would hitch themselves
up with somethin' that strange?" The question was followed by
ribald remarks.

Martha knew a wagon pulled by camels was a most unusual

sight, but that was no reason for the riders to deliberately circle back and make them the brunt of ill-conceived humor. At least Hunter had managed to keep his temper; two months ago he never would have held back. And it worked out well. The intruders ended up being caught by their own curiosity. They had come much too close to the camels, which caused their horses to spook and nearly toss them all to the ground. By the time the daunted men had gained control of their animals, they were a subdued lot and rode silently on past the train as Hunter and Martha had the last chuckle.

It was nearing noon when Hunter began to pivot around in his seat.

"What are you doing?" Martha protested, thinking he might be about to leave her alone in the wagon.

"Those are our horses out there on that hill, I'm sure of it." He pointed off to the right. "I'm going after them." He took the reins from her hands and halted the wagon.

"You can't possibly try to recapture those horses, not with your arm in a sling," she quickly said.

"Yeah, well, in that case I'll just have to take my arm out of this infernal contraption." With one swift motion, he whipped the folded cotton towel over his head.

"But your shoulder—" Martha watched, apprehension wrinkling her brow as he scooted over the back of the seat and mounted his big bay, which had been tied to the wagon.

"Just keep up with the others until I get back," he shouted over his shoulder before galloping off in a swirl of dust.

Almost immediately after Hunter left, the camels began to act up. Martha was nervous over taking sole control of them, and the bad-tempered dromedaries sensed her discomfort. The camel on the left in the first pair stretched out its neck and bit Humphrey's backside. Martha snapped the whip over the offending creature, but that only caused the rest of the beasts to balk.

The team went from unruly to out of control in a matter of minutes as she fought frantically to hang onto the reins. Then the wagon lurched forward and they were off, traveling at breakneck speed. When the reins were ripped out of Martha's hands, she had no choice but to grab the wagon seat and try to keep from being bounced to the ground.

At a clip, the runaway team passed the covered wagons, Martha's bonnet blowing off and her brown hair streaming wildly behind her. Her heart raced as fast as the wagon as she fought to keep from crying out, knowing camels quickly became winded and couldn't keep up the pace too much longer. But when a wheel hit a rock, tipping the wagon, she screamed.

"Missus. Missus," Happy screeched from up ahead, the whites of his eyes as stark as his turban.

The wagon was heading straight for the rest of the camels. Martha bit into her lip, praying the beasts would stop when they reached their kind. Then she saw Happy climb up onto one of the great creatures and start for her. Nearing her, he got into a crouching position atop his camel.

"Oh, no! Don't, Happy!" Martha cried. Fear for the little man's safety brought bile to her throat, strangling any further attempts to warn him.

Happy brought his camel parallel with the harnessed team. He shouted a string of foreign commands. And, when he was ignored, sprang from his mount and grabbed at the neck of the right rear camel.

Martha held her breath. For a moment it looked as if he was going to be successful. But the creature stumbled, throwing Happy to the dust. In horror Martha felt a wagon wheel thump over him—twice.

Leading the errant horses he'd retrieved back toward the wagon train, Hunter noticed the runaway team. He immediately left the horses and raced toward Martha, fear for her safety spurring him on.

The drumming of the wagon drowned out his approach as he overtook the camels and, ignoring his throbbing shoulder deftly leaned over and grasped Humphrey's dangling reins. "Pasha! Stop!" he commanded.

Immediately, the lead camel slowed, forcing the others to ease their pace; then he halted.

Martha did not wait for Hunter to approach her. She scrambled down off the wagon and ran back toward Happy.

Hunter jumped down and quickly tied the camel team to a jagged boulder at the side of the road. Despite the increasing pain in his shoulder, he flew into the saddle, wheeled his horse around, and galloped back to Happy.

Martha was cradling the small man's head in her lap when Hunter slid from the big bay. She looked at him as he knelt down, holding his arm. "He doesn't seem to be bleeding." She muffled a sob. "But his foot looks as if it's been crushed."

"Get out of the way," Hunter ordered.

"I want to help."

Happy groaned.

"I said get out of the way!" Hunter snapped, thinking only of the wounded man. "You've caused enough trouble on this trip."

The anguish his cruel words caused was evident from Martha's expression. The others had arrived and were quietly standing over them, shaking their heads. Responsibility for the accident weighed Martha down, but she managed to get to her feet. Unable to endure accusing looks or to ascertain the damage to Cornelius's equipment, she ran from the scene.

"Let me get a look at him." Winnie shoved her way to the injured man. Her frown deepened as she turned toward Hunter. "You'd best look after your wife. You was mighty hard on that poor gal just now. I'll see to him."

"Winnie, you missed your calling. You should've been a trail boss," Hunter quipped. "Jed, take my horse and go pick up the horses I located. They're back about a mile, on the ridge."

Jed nodded. "Sure 'nuff."

A red stain seeped across Hunter's shoulder as he strode over to Martha. By the time he caught up with her, his shoulder was a sticky circle of blood.

"I'm sorry," he declared quietly. "I didn't mean what I said. I guess I wasn't thinking."

With a shaking hand, Martha smoothed back her tangled hair. Then she turned to face him. Her cheeks were streaked with the tracks left by tears. "You were thinking. I have caused a lot of problems for everyone." She hesitated, took a deep breath, then continued. "Is Happy going to be all right?"

"Winnie is looking after him. Come on. Let's get back and see if there's anything we can do."

As Hunter took her hand in a silent gesture of reassurance, Martha noticed his bloody shoulder. "Your wound, it's bleeding again."

"I'll be all right." He grunted at her touch.

Martha felt desolated as she returned to the others. She kept reminding herself to keep her chin up, not to give in to self-defeating thoughts. She tried to tell herself that the feeling she was experiencing was only momentary self-pity; it would pass. But as she watched Derek Stewart and Seth lift Happy up into the Stewarts' wagon, she seriously questioned her presence on this train, and, shoulders slumping, she returned to the solace of her tent. Nestling into a quiet corner, she picked up her journal and began to write. Tears mingled with the ink on the page as she wrote of the pain which filled her.

Jannet watched from her viewpoint on the ridge. "That woman has more lives than a cat," she ground out. "She didn't die from whatever killed those Belshaws, the Lucas brothers didn't get her, and she just got off a runaway wagon without so much as a scratch." She turned to Dancing Wind. "I'm getting tired of waiting out here in the hot sun. I'm filthy and tired and hungry," she whined. Then, as if she realized she would receive no sympathy from her companions, she stood straighter and smoothed her torn lavender dress. "Wouldn't it have been smarter to keep those horses? It would've slowed the train down instead of making it easier for them."

"Do not bother us with your stupidity. Yellow Fire was in need of the horses." Dancing Wind shot arrows of hatred at Jannet. "We grow tired of your tongue," she warned. "The time to act comes soon."

Chapter Thirty-Six

Tuesday, August 23, 1859—Nearing Sublette's Cutoff. Our bedraggled company has suffered dearly on my account, and now I feel it my obligation to perform whatever tasks may be required of me in order to avoid further delays. I truly find myself wishing my motives were above reproach, but truth is seldom measured without first separating it from intent. . . .

Martha paced back and forth behind the Stewarts' wagon, anxiously waiting to learn whether Happy was badly hurt and fearing the worst had befallen the little brown man.

Cornelius joined her. Realizing her anguish, he had first put away his equipment.

"Using the camels to pull the spring wagon seemed like a good idea at the time. How could I have been so stupid as to think I could handle them?"

"It was a most generous idea. A heroic effort on your part to save my equipment. What happened to Happy was an accident. Remember that," he said consolingly. "And don't let those other tragedies—the deaths of the Belshaws or of those crazy Lucas brothers weigh on your mind."

Martha folded her arms in front of her and let her sorrowful gaze roam over the vast wilderness. "How can this untamed land be so beautiful, such an opportunity for so many, and yet so cruel it strikes down those who would seek it out?" she asked in a halting voice.

Her lips drooping gloomily, Winnie split the flap and lumbered down out of the wagon. As she wiped her hands on her rumpled apron, Hunter reached her. Martha was right behind him.

"How is he? Is he going to be all right? Is he hurt badly?" Martha anxiously spilled forth a skein of questions before Hunter could say a word.

Winnie raised her hand to quell any further queries. "He's sleepin' like a babe, and probably'll be out for some time, what with the dose of laudanum and whiskey I gave him."

"But how is he?" Martha pressed.

"We're in luck. Happy's as tough as a plated toad. Looks like his foot's broke up real bad though. He ain't goin' to be drivin' no camels in his condition."

"Dammit." Hunter groaned and walked away from Martha and Winnie. If it weren't for his shoulder, which was still acting up, he'd take over the management of the camels. He rubbed the back of his neck. Seth Nelson was a strong boy and always eager to help out. Maybe with a day or two of instruction the lad could handle the beasts.

Martha watched Hunter retreat from her, recriminations over the accident plaguing her again. Then she directed her attention back to Winnie, fear for the little camel driver's future gripping her. "Do you think Happy will be crippled?"

"I bound his foot best I could. Might venture he'll have a limp though. But don't you fret none. A little limp won't keep him from nothin'. And don't go blamin' yourself," Winnie said sagely. "That man of yours don't mean nothin' by his grumblin'. He's just been carryin' a pretty heavy load lately so he's edgy as a cornered possum—that's all, gal."

Martha dropped a grateful hand on the old woman's arm. "Thank you." If what Winnie said were only true, she thought sadly.

At hearing Hunter gruffly directing the company to set up camp, Martha went to his side. "We won't be traveling anymore today?"

"Or tomorrow," he answered, without looking at her. He knew he faced the impossible task of training Seth to do a job Happy had spent half his life doing. One look at Martha could

334

drain him of resolve. He had intended to spend time wooing her. He grimaced. Why did something always seem to stand between them?

"Is there anything I can do to help? Perhaps I can drive the camels until your shoulder heals." She had only meant to offer assistance in a general way, but the idea of taking Happy's place had come to mind. Who, other than Hunter, was more familiar with the beasts than she? Although she knew, now more clearly than ever, that she had to leave Hunter and the train soon, he'd saved her life and offering to help was the least she could do. He had deceived her, but she did not want him to lose his ranch due to any further delays.

"Absolutely not!"

"Why not?" she retorted and placed her hands on her hips.

"I don't want you getting hurt too," he shot back. "Look what just happened with you driving the wagon."

Martha remained silent, stung by what he had said. But their exchange had brought new life to her.

The mischievous green twinkle in her eyes warned Hunter she would have to be kept busy. He'd best not waste another minute before locating the Nelson boy and teaching him to fill in for Happy.

Seth was bent over, clearing the dried weeds away from the place he had selected for the campfire, when Hunter spotted him. "Seth," he called out, "leave the fire and your other tasks to Martha. I want to see you over by the camels—right now."

Martha blinked back the disgruntled frown he deserved for having such a closed mind. She would take over Seth's duties without one word of protest. But once she'd done them, she'd watch Hunter train Seth, and there could be no cause for complaint.

The tasks which Hunter had hurriedly handed over to her took three hours, and all the while Martha carried water for the animals, gathered brush for the cooking fire, washed Hunter's shirts, and set up the tent, she continued to glance over in the direction of the camels. Under Hunter's direction, Seth had erected the makeshift khan, and now appeared to be forcing himself to approach the beasts, which looked equally wary of him.

Determined to end the constant agony being near Hunter yet knowing the truth about their marriage caused her, Martha finally stood within ten feet of the khan. Quietly she watched the scene before her.

"That's right, Seth. Hold out your hand. Steady. Don't let them see you're nervous and you'll be fine," Hunter instructed.

"You sure them hump-backed creatures ain't going to gang up on me?" Seth swallowed, cold fear threatening to set him to flight. "They don't look none too friendly."

The young man's face faded from ash gray to stark white when two of the camels curled their lips back and unfolded their legs. "I surely hope them two big ones that just got up are smiling." He stopped, weakly trying to force himself to cease quivering.

"Don't let them think you don't have the upper hand," Hunter advised. He moved closer to the lad, expecting problems. Seth was so afraid, Hunter knew he had to get him out of there before the boy got himself into trouble. In a calm voice, he said, "Slowly, one step at a time, back out of the corral. Whatever you do, don't turn your back on them."

Hunter knew the animals well enough to be certain Seth was going to have a hard time learning how to control the disagreeable creatures in just one day.

Huge drops of perspiration sprang out on Seth's face. He kept repeating to himself that he had to keep calm. But when those two tan demons lowered their heads and snorted, he could have sworn he saw smoke puff out of their nostrils.

Martha moved closer to the khan. The two camels seemed poised, ready to charge at any second. She couldn't allow anything to happen to the lanky Nelson boy. After all, Happy had been hurt trying to help her, and she already carried a heavy enough burden of remorse because of that.

Before Martha could figure out what to do, dust scattered under the feet of the two animals and they rushed toward Seth. Hunter leaped between the railing and shoved the lad out of the way.

"Humphrey! Come!" Martha screamed, visions of Hunter trampled and mauled coming to her.

Her high-pitched scream caused the two hump-backed creatures to hesitate just long enough for her to grab Happy's whip, which had been sitting nearly on top of the meager pile of his belongings.

"Hunter! Catch!" she shouted and tossed the leather piece to him.

As Hunter's big hand closed around the quirt, Humphrey charged into the backsides of the two rebellious beasts. They squealed but seemed to accept Humphrey's dominance, for they turned and skulked meekly into a far corner of the khan like trained dogs.

Martha stepped up to the rail, and Humphrey trotted over to nuzzle her outstretched palm. "Good boy," she crooned. "Good boy."

Hunter gave a sarcastic grunt. "Chrissake, how I ever managed to stay alive out here before you came along, I'll never know."

Seth had been terror-struck when the camels had charged. "I ain't cut out to be a camel driver," he spewed out. His heart still pounding, he picked himself up and started to trudge back toward camp, dusting off his pants.

"Seth, get back here," Hunter hollered. "Show these beasts you're the boss."

"I'm sorry, Mr. Brody, I don't want no part of it," the lanky lad tossed back over his shoulder as he kept walking.

"Damn!" Hunter flinched at the sharp pain circling his shoulder. Ignoring Martha's presence, he flung the whip into the dirt and stalked off in the direction of the Stewarts' wagon, muttering a long string of expletives.

She sighed at seeing his exasperation. Yet she could not fault him. What the train had already been through would try the patience of a saint. She had been watching Hunter's efforts to teach the Nelson boy, and picked up the whip. Why couldn't she learn how to drive the animals? Surely driving them had to be easier than forcing them to pull the spring wagon. If she stepped into the khan, what was the worst that could happen? She could be charged and have to scramble under the posts to safety. That would mean getting her dress dirty or torn. She looked down at the worn green calico. It wouldn't be much of a loss.

Her resolve firm, Martha cautiously entered the khan. Humphrey immediately stepped over to her. She had often spent time with Happy and she tried to recall his manuevers as a small custer of camels steadily advanced on her. But fear overtook her and she scrambled out of the khan.

"This is ridiculous," she said to herself, then brushed patches of dirt from her dress. "All right, you camels." She tied her skirt up between her legs to form a baggy-looking bloomer dress. "You are not going to get the best of me."

The sky was rapidly blackening when Hunter strode back to the khan. He'd intended to tie the beasts into a tighter column and attempt to direct them himself. But when his gaze fell on Martha his breath snagged and his brows shot into a disbelieving frown. His patience was taxed to the edge of endurance by the sight before him.

"What do you think you're doing? And what the devil is that thing you've got on now?"

"It's the same dress I had on earlier, with a few modifications. I've been practicing with the camels since you left." She straightened, proud of the strides she had made with the dromedaries but disappointed that he had not remembered what she was wearing. "I can handle them nearly as well as Happy." He took another step toward her. "Before you say anything, just watch for a minute and I'll show you."

Begrudgingly Hunter nodded his consent. Doubt in his eyes, he leaned against the post and silently waited while Martha demonstrated her abilities. His first inclination had been to drag her out of there and turn her over his knee. But she had the animals under control. The longer he stood watching, the more amazed he became. She was working the beasts like a professional.

"What do you think?" she asked, after guiding them around the khan.

"I think you're doing fine within a fenced area. But what happens if one of the camels gets it into its head to act up along the trail?"

338

"I'll take the whip to it. I doubt that there will be any problems. They're used to traveling roped together. They got rambunctious with the wagon because being separated from the others and hitched to it was foreign to them. Hunter, I know I can do it. And we can't afford to lose any more time."

His face did not soften, so Martha dropped the ropes and climbed out of the khan to face him directly. She took a deep breath, then said in a quiet, determined voice, "Please, don't refuse to let me do this."

Her eyes beseeched him. Damn! He wasn't a monster. He was simply worried about her. He didn't want his wife taking such a risk and even if she had not been his wife, she was a woman. A very strong woman, he had to concede. He studied the determined set of her lips. If he said no, she'd probably pull some ill-conceived stunt. If he agreed, at least he could keep an eye on her. He had to admit there was no one else on the train besides Happy or himself who could get that close to the beasts. And she was right. They had to move on. Grudgingly, he was forced to recognize he had no other options.

"I'll probably be sorry, but you're hired."

"Thank you." She forgot herself and threw her arms around his neck, hugging him. "You won't be sorry."

Hunter flinched at the pain her overexuberant gesture caused in his wounded shoulder, but the searing heat of her softly curving body soon pushed that into the back of his mind and replaced it with a throbbing ache of a different sort. He wrapped his good arm around her and crushed her lips to his.

"My sweet Mat," he murmured against her mouth. "Come back to the tent and let me show you how much you mean to me." He knew he was taking a chance. Athough she was capable of driving him beyond rational thought at times, he regretted trying to trick her, and was secretly glad about the way it had turned out. She was his wife. And as soon as they reached Nevada, he would spend the rest of his life showing her how much he loved her. She deserved better than he'd given her and he'd planned to court her properly; but her touch was more than he could ignore.

Martha's senses began to roll, clouding the ugly reality of her relationship with him. She fought against a disintegrating

339

resolve. Again and again, she had made up her mind to keep her distance from him until she could leave the train. Yet she had allowed herself to go willingly—eagerly—to his bed, knowing they were not truly married.

His lips wandered hungrily over her face. It was such sweet torture. His fingers roved over her, igniting her flesh. His touch was exquisite torment. How could she deny the feelings raging inside her? If she did not stop him now, there would be no denying those urges. She would never be able to redeem herself. She would be lost.

"Hunter"—she moaned, then pushed herself out of his embrace—"we have to talk—please, now."

Hunter looked down at the serious light in Martha's green eyes, and reached out to take her hand. She stepped back.

If she let him continue to touch her, she knew she wouldn't be able to say what must be said. "No. Please."

Martha seemed distant, and Hunter immediately became aware of a strange icy edge to her voice, which had not been there before, even during some of their fiercest battles. It was almost as if his touch had suddenly caused a glacial rift to come between them. He could not fathom this shift in her behavior. He had just agreed to abide by her wishes and she'd seemed delighted. Why had she turned so cold? Although he tried to swallow his frustration, it stuck in his throat.

Hoping his assessment was no more than imagination, he caught her and wrapped an arm around her waist. "What's so important that it won't wait?" he murmured.

She turned her head just as he was about to kiss her. "Hunter, I'm serious. We have to talk."

"All right." He let out an exasperated sigh and dropped his arm. "So talk."

"Can we sit down first?"

"Is it something that can't be said standing here?"

"I'd rather not," she said, forcing the words past the dry lump in her throat.

"Suit yourself." He strode over to a knee-high boulder, sat down, and crossed his arms over his chest.

With halting steps, Martha followed and perched a safe distance from him. She watched a shield drop over his face.

Should she proceed or avoid the pain confrontation would bring, for he now seemed to have shut her out. For a fleeting instant, she thought it would be wisest to leave her feelings undeclared. But she decided she could not depart from the train without finishing the conversation she had begun.

He looked her directly in the eyes, his lips a strained line. "We're seated; now spit it out."

Martha studied the ground for a minute. She had intended to let him know she was aware of his deceit, but the need to salvage what was left of her pride, as well as her fear he would find the situation amusing, held her back. Or was it that she was hoping he had come to love her?

"I have been giving a lot of thought to everything that has happened since we left Independence." She stopped and took a deep breath to give herself the courage to proceed. Nervously, she fingered the leather thong around her neck. Before she spoke again, she weighed her words carefully so as not to sound like some poor, self-pitying woman. "When I decided to go West I never dreamed I would be so foolish as to agree to marry someone I knew so little about. . . ."

He wasn't sure whether it was the circumstances of Martha's calm delivery of what she was saying, but the word *foolish* stabbed him. He knew he had made a mistake in trying to trick her, but in his own fashion he felt he had made amends. Once before, he had made up his mind to let her go and then had weakened. Had it been a mistake to open his heart? After he'd lost Dancing Wind he'd sworn he would never love again. Had he been the *foolish* one?

His eyes hardened into steely hazel strips. He was sure she was about to reject the efforts he'd made to win her back, which caused him to lose patience. "I don't have any more time to waste. I've a lot to do before morning. Whatever it is you're trying to say, say it. This wagon train has already had enough delays."

Martha's feeble candle of hope, which had steadfastly refused to relinquish its flickering flame, suddenly ceased its glow. She felt a chill inside her chest, and shivered. She wrapped her arms about her and dug her fingernails into her soft flesh. She was not sure whether she was trying to discover whether his lack of concern had numbed her senses or praying that it had. Then, as if her inner strength took over, she stiffened.

And the words tore from her, sealing her fate. "I've decided not to go all the way to Oregon with this train."

"It was never going to Oregon," he roughly retorted, becoming more intolerant of the conversation with each phrase he interpreted as a rejection. "You knew that when you got me to take you on. God knows, you've talked enough about it to the others who are going to California."

"I know, but I thought . . . Oh, I don't know what I thought," Martha burst out, confused. Quickly, she regained her composure. "You mean you took my money never intending to fulfill your part of the bargain?" Although the subject had somehow become blurred, Martha was drawing a parallel between their deceit-filled wedding ceremony and the way he had taken her money without having the slightest intention of taking her to Oregon. In her present state, she did not stop to consider whether or not she had asked the train's destination, but she did recall that the others had talked about California. How foolishly ignorant she had been. Somehow she had assumed Hunter had planned to see them through to both destinations.

"A bargain made with *Mat* Collins," he threw back at her. "But to show you I'd not forget to give you what you have coming to you for services rendered"—he ripped a fat wad of bills out of his pocket and tossed it onto her lap—"here's your money."

Martha looked down in horror at the bills. He was giving her money for *services rendered?* In addition to bringing up that nightmare with Jannet, those horrible words meant he was paying her like men did whores. Well, wasn't that what she had become? She had continued to go to his bed, knowing they were not man and wife. She had not been strong enough to resist her desire for him. Yet how could he be so cruel?

She fingered the bills, started to hand the money back, and then stuffed it into her skirt pocket. She would not keep it; she would donate it to a church once she was settled. She raised her chin. "I have no desire to cause any of the others further

342

hardship. But I will *render my services*"—she hissed the ugly words—"only by driving the camels until other arrangements can be made." She glared at him. "That way there can be no disputing that I will have honestly earned this money."

"You needn't worry. Any man who learns how you came by it would never begrudge such a woman as you her hard-earned cash," Hunter said without the slightest hint of emotion.

That Martha thought he was paying her off, like a woman who offered only her charms, only served to make her more determined than ever not to let him see how much she was hurting. She would not allow him to destroy what was left of her sense of worth.

"You're loathsome!" she snapped, and with a swish of her skirt, she hopped from the rock and left him glowering after her.

Hunter had never pretended to understand women, but he found Martha a total mystery. Why she had continued to act so strangely after he'd given her the money was beyond him. He sat there atop the rock for some time, seething, before some semblance of an answer came to him. If she believed he'd planned to keep the reward money entrusted to him at Fort Laramie for the return of the money stolen from the bank, she could not think much of him. And such were the case, maybe he'd be better off without her. The thought seared his heart.

Chapter Thirty-Seven

For two days the train had poked along behind the slow-moving camels. Martha fought to keep them going, never once looking to Hunter for help. By the time they made camp for the night at Sublette's Cutoff it was evident they had returned to being stiffly polite strangers. Martha referred to Hunter as Mr. Brody. He made it a practice to keep his distance from her, but barked commands at anyone unfortunate enough to come within earshot.

Martha was in her tent packing when Winnie quietly entered and lowered herself onto the buffalo robe she had acquired during the trip. The old woman's brows wrinkled abruptly at the sight before her.

"We missed you at supper. Thought you might be ailin' so I came to see if there was anything I could do for you."

"Thank you, Winnie. I'm fine," Martha said soberly, and continued sorting through her bag.

"You don't look so good with those dark bags hangin' low enough to curl up in your lap," Winnie observed.

"I'm just a little tired. Handling those camels took a lot out of me," Martha lied, finding herself unable to confide in the big-hearted woman.

"That ain't all that took a lot out of you, gal." Martha shot Winnie a quelling glance, but the older woman ignored her. "For two married folks as much in love as you and that man of yours, I just can't cotton to the way you two are carryin' on. Now it looks like you're gettin' ready to hightail it out of here."

She swung out her hand to point to Martha's belongings. "What in tarnation for?"

"Happy is feeling much better since you put those splints around his foot. With Seth's help, he should be able to drive the camels again."

Winnie frowned. "What does that have to do with the price of oats in Ohio?"

From past experience with the crusty older woman, Martha was only too aware that Winnie would not be easily swayed from learning the truth. Frantically Martha grasped at excuses until her mind came to rest on the most plausible one.

"When I joined the train I thought it was going directly to Oregon. I just recently found out that I had made a dreadful mistake." Martha was thinking about Hunter when she said that, although that was not the impression she wanted Winnie to gather from her explanation. "So you see, since we are at the cutoff and my *services* are no longer required, I should join a train traveling directly to my original destination."

In spite of the churning in Martha's stomach, her eyes did not waver. She did not want Winnie to see the sadness she felt so acutely at having to lie to the one woman on the train who had been kind to her.

Winnie sat perfectly still, a thoughtful expression on her lined face, studying Martha but offering no immediate response to her tale. She knew the story about Oregon was so much hogwash; they had talked about their plans before. After more long-stretching minutes, Winnie finally said, "What I see is hurt enough to feed a herd of cows for a year, and it's between you and that man of yours. What I know is nothin' is goin' to be solved by runnin' away from your man—"

Martha clipped off any further words. "He's not my husband!" she blurted out before she could stop herself.

"What?" Winnie's eyes widened in disbelief. "Why we all watched you two get hitched," she reminded her, thinking that Martha must be suffering some confusion from the hardships of the trail. "I'll just go get that man of yours and we'll get everything all cleared up before this gets out of hand."

Winnie got to her feet and had her hand on the tent flap before Martha halted her.

Their conversation had gone too far. Martha could not endure the thought of another confrontation with Hunter. She had no option left other than to tell Winnie the truth and to swear her to secrecy.

"Winnie, wait. Please. There's nothing wrong with me. Hunter Brody and I do not have a problem that can be *cleared up*," Martha said gravely.

Winnie pivoted around to see the utter anguish on Martha's face. "Gal, there ain't nothin' that can't be worked out with enough hard work," she stated soothingly and placed a hand on Martha's shoulder.

"Oh, Winnie, Hunter and I weren't really married in that ceremony." Tears were forming in Martha's eyes, and she fought to keep them at bay.

"What?" Winnie could not really understand what she was hearing.

"It was all a cruel trick."

"Now, how do you know that?" Winnie looked deep into Martha's eyes to see the silent suffering there.

"I overheard Hunter and his friend, the man who joined us at Fort Laramie, Abe Baker, discussing the phony preacher Hunter arranged to have marry us." She stifled a sob and tried to regain control of herself.

"Why that no-good, no-account horse's behind," Winnie huffed. She enfolded Martha in her arms. "You can't leave now and let him get away with what he done to you, gal. What if you're in a motherly way?"

Having babies was not a subject readily discussed in polite society, and Martha fidgeted at Winnie's bold question. She had not considered the possibility of a child. Her monthlies had never been regular, and until now there hadn't been a reason to track the dates. She scoured her memory. It must have been the end of June, or was it July? It had to be July, she finally surmised.

"I'm not in a motherly way," she said shyly, praying Winnie would not continue to press her.

Winnie stared at Martha's belly, rubbing her chin. "I hope you know what you're sayin'." She scratched her head. "I still don't understand how he could go on as your husband after you found out what he done."

Martha stepped back and pleaded, "Please, Winnie, after I told him I would not play his wife he told me that while we were on the trail I was stuck with him as a husband. Then . . ." Martha's voice faded into silence, and she lowered her head. She could not confide in Winnie, could not tell her she had been a willing participant in their lovemaking, that she had hoped Hunter would come to love her as much as she loved him.

Winnie said knowingly, "No need to go on. Women ain't so different than men, and when one's in love some things just come natural. Now, why don't you go on out there and let that man know he ain't foolin' around with you no longer. Tell him how you feel about him, and find out what he's goin' to do to right what he done."

Martha blushed at Winnie's candidness, then sobered. "I think the best thing for me to do is leave and start a new life in Oregon as I originally planned." She saw the doubt in Winnie's eyes. "You have to promise me you won't say anything to anyone about this . . . please."

"You ain't got nothin' to be ashamed of, gal."

"Please, Winnie," Martha said quietly.

Winnie mulled over Martha's entreaty. The poor gal did have a point. Even if she did accuse the captain in front of the others and he fessed up, everyone would know she was soiled goods, though through no fault of her own. What if he dug in his heels and refused to do right by her? She'd be forced to carry the shame of it, and no proper man would consider her wife material. Winnie wanted to see Hunter Brody marry Martha proper, but she had to admit that out here in the wild the man might just as likely reap no more than a few envious smirks if the truth came out. There was something wrong about the different ways men and women were treated.

Winnie let out an exasperated sight. "I won't say that I like it much, but you got my word."

"Thank you, Winnie," Martha said softly, her voice filled with soul-piercing misery.

"You get those eyes dried and show them what you're made of. I know you can do it."

"I'll join you in a little while. But first I need a few moments alone."

"You just come out when you're ready, gal. I'll be there to help you if you need it."

Martha watched Winnie leave, a band of panic squeezing her. She had to get away by herself for a little while. Someplace where she could think without being interrupted. Her mind whirring, she fled from the camp into the black night. Stumbling over rocks, she ran until her side ached and she collapsed on the ground, too exhausted to move another foot.

"What have I done?" Martha sobbed, and she curled up into a ball.

When she awoke at daybreak and looked around, nothing seemed familiar. She had been so upset she hadn't paid any attention to the direction she had taken. Unclear as to what to do, she crossed her legs and rested her chin on her knuckles. Letting tears of frustration and pain flow freely and drop to the ground, with her finger, she traced a heart in the rough grains of sand. Inside the heart she wrote Hunter's name. Then her trembling hand barely touched the scribbled letters while intensely painful memories battered her.

The heart seemed empty, like her own, with only one name inscribed inside it. For some reason she began to add her own name next to Hunter's, to fill the empty space. She had just drawn an *M* when a moccasined foot came down on her hand. Startled, Martha looked up.

"There is no need to finish your task." Dancing Wind stood tall and proud in a fringed rawhide skirt, her hair hanging free. "You will not see Yellow Fire again."

"Yellow Fire?" Martha was frightened by the hard expression on the beautiful Indian woman's face.

"Yes, Yellow Fire. Better known to you, perhaps, as Hunter Brody," Jannet said mockingly as she joined Dancing Wind and her daughter.

"Jannet, I thought you had died." Martha stared in disbelief at the ragged young woman who had always prided herself on her appearance.

"Sorry to disappoint you. You're going to be the one to die," Jannet snarled. "I was fortunate enough to be found by these two"—she waved at the two Indians—"after you shot me. They have been following the wagon ever since it left Independence."

A shudder went through Martha. She had been right from the start when she'd mentioned the Indians to Hunter as they were waiting to cross the Missouri. And these were probably the ones who'd been watching her that afternoon at the Platte River when she'd thought she'd caught a glimpse of an Indian and had called out, feeling someone's eyes on her.

Jannet went on. "They helped me. Together we have followed you. We almost managed to get those three men to kill you. They failed, but I won't." She yanked Martha to her feet and was about to strangle her when the young girl interceded.

"You are not to harm her yet." Daughter of the Wind struck Jannet's hands away from Martha, and she then took a threatening stance between the two white women.

Martha's eyes shot to the girl, and recognition sparked in them. "Aren't you the one who stole my wedding ring?"

"It should not have been given to you. It should belong to my mother," the Indian girl with the hazel eyes so like Hunter's said evenly. "To my people the life of man is a circle. That circle belongs to Yellow Fire. From it my mother will draw his power to her and they will be united once again."

"Your mother?" Martha turned to the Indian woman, who held out a coppery hand displaying the simple gold band, and her heart plummeted. She should have guessed the moment she'd seen her and the half-breed girl, who was about the right age to be Hunter's child. The incredible thought barraged Martha's mind, but she denied it.

"I see in your eyes that you possess knowledge of me," Dancing Wind coldly observed, her black eyes fastening on the arrowhead Martha wore around her neck. An ironic smile twisted her lips. "In many ways we are as sisters. We share a common bond. My people allow a brave to take more than one wife. I was Yellow Fire's first. You, I see by his gift, are the second."

Martha lifted trembling fingers to the leather thong around her neck and ran her hand over the smooth, pointed arrowhead. She could barely force herself to believe what she

349

was hearing. Dancing Wind was dead, wasn't she? Could this be the woman Hunter had loved so deeply? Was he married to both of them? And the young girl with the fine features and tall, strong body, could she be Hunter's child? Martha's pulse beat so wildly as she acknowledged that possibility, she could barely manage to force her attention back to what the beautiful woman was saying.

"You must understand"—Dancing Wind crossed her arms over her chest—"I cannot allow another woman to share my man." She reached out and snatched the arrowhead from Martha's neck, leaving a red welt where the thong had been.

And before Martha could react to or question her startling statement, Dancing Wind motioned her to be silent. "Bring her along, my daughter," she then said. "We will return to camp."

"Why not kill her now!" Jannet screamed.

"Speak no more or you will not live to see another sunrise. I grow tired of your whimpering." At Dancing Wind's warning, Jannet prudently held back her sharp reply.

For hours Hunter sat glumly near the campfire saying nothing. He could not force himself to join in the senseless chatter, for he felt cursed. He never should have listened to Abe back at Fort Laramie. When he'd discovered the truth about his marriage to Martha he should have told her the whole story and got her on a train, right then and there. The pain would have been bearable then in comparison to what he felt now.

Winnie stared at the glow of light coming from Martha's tent. The gal had said she'd join them after she got herself together. Surely she'd had plenty of time to do that by now, the kindly woman thought. She gave Lucy's braid a tug. "Lucy, put that lamb down and run and fetch Martha."

"Can I go too?" Clara ventured.

"'Course you can. Now get, you two." Winnie beamed. "At least some good's come out of this trip," she said aloud. "Those two girls has done a lot of changin'." She watched them run, hand in hand, toward Martha's tent.

In minutes they were back. Lucy's lips trembled, and Clara's face held the fear of discovery. "She's not there."

"Search the camp," shouted Hunter.

After a search that proved fruitless, Winnie stepped forward. "She was upset when I talked to her, said she needed some time to think. You don't suppose she went off to find a quiet spot, do you?"

"What was she upset about?" Hunter demanded, although he pretty much knew the answer already.

"That you got to ask her yourself," Winnie replied in a censuring tone.

Hunter sent her a dark frown; then he called to Happy. "Saddle the bay."

When Happy appeared leading a camel, Hunter growled, "I said to saddle the bay."

Happy's chin receded. "I thought you say 'saddle Humppray.' I go get horse. I go."

"Never mind. There's no time. Who knows what kind of trouble she could have gotten herself into this time." Hunter quickly mounted the camel and rode off into the darkness.

He had not gone far when he realized he would have to wait until morning. He slid from Humphrey and quietly waited for dawn, unable to sleep for all the disturbing emotions roiling in him.

At first light, he circled the camp until he picked up Martha's tracks. "So you were running, my sweet Mat," he said to himself, still resolved to find her only to let her go.

On a patchy sand mound, Martha had stopped. The indentations left where she had sunk to the ground were plain. But the grooves outlining a heart with his name inside and the footprint below it, made by an Indian moccasin, wrenched him from the camel's back. With a sickening ache in his gut, Hunter carefully ran his hand over the recessed sand. It could have been splintered glass slicing the tips of his fingers for the agony it evoked in him.

"Martha, what pain I have caused you," he muttered, hating himself for the deception he had planned.

His keen hazel eyes surveyed the area. The footprints showed that four people had been there: two wearing Indian moccasins and two others. One of the other sets of prints was Martha's, but who had worn the hard-soled shoes that clearly belonged to a woman? He looked closer. The tracks were still fresh. They couldn't have been made more than two hours ago.

"At least they're on foot," he said, reassuring himself as fear crept up his spine.

Without further hesitation, he remounted Humphrey and followed the tracks until the ground became rocky and the trail difficult to follow. "Down Pasha!" he ordered.

Hunter took to his feet leading the camel behind him as he tracked the trail left by the four people. For three hours he dogged after them, not stopping once to rest until he sighted Martha, trussed and quietly sitting alone in a clearing.

The sight of her so affected Hunter that he rushed to her side before first scouting the area.

"My sweet Mat, are you all right? They haven't hurt you, have they?" He released her bound wrists and tenderly rubbed skin made raw by ropes.

"Oh, Hunter, Jannet is alive and so is—"

"I believe you were about to say Dancing Wind, were you not?" The shapely Indian woman stepped from the brush. In her hands she held a bow and the arrowhead taken from Martha, which she had fastened onto a shaft.

Hunter swung around, his gun drawn. Astounded, he returned Dancing Wind's gaze, and the gun dropped from his hand. He did not believe his eyes. "Dancing Wind?" Was this really his lost Dancing Wind?

"Yellow Fire." Dancing Wind lowered the bow. "It has been many moons."

Hunter slowly rose.

Martha felt a stabbing pain in her heart, as if she had been shot with the arrow. She had just suffered the ultimate blow. She had lost Hunter to a living ghost.

"Mother, the white woman grows restless," Daughter of the Wind said, coming on to the scene. She stopped to gape at the man she resembled.

"My child?" Hunter let out a disbelieving breath. The girl was about the right age, he figured. He closely studied her. There was no mistaking the familiarity of her features, yet

352

there was something about her that brought undefinable questions to his mind.

"Does she possess the eyes of the Indian? Look at her. Have not at least eleven Moons when the Grain Comes Up gone by since her birth? Can there be doubt, Yellow Fire?"

The girl was born in March, the month the Indians called Moons when the Grain Comes Up. Was she his daughter? Although Dancing Wind had adeptly sidestepped his question, she had set off more thoughts.

Martha silently watched the reunion. Why was she forced to endure this? She had already made up her mind to leave Hunter. Was she to pay for her sins by being forced to watch him reach out to the love of his life? The woman whose name he had chiseled in rock, the one that he would love *forever*. Well, she was here, in the flesh, and now he had his wife, his true love. Martha felt irretrievably lost. The fear which had dogged her since she'd first seen Dancing Wind now encapsulated her.

Hunter pulled Martha to her feet. "You must let her go," he demanded.

"She must die so we may return to my people. There you will offer my father the buffalo spirit"—Dancing Wind pointed to Humphrey—"in payment for War Arrow's life."

"You killed War Arrow?" Hunter mused, a tinge of disdain clouding his voice.

"It was his just payment for falsely telling you of my death and sending you away from our camp before you could remain with my people and prove to them you could provide for a wife with your skills as a hunter. I know I will be forgiven when you offer my father the buffalo spirit. It will show him that you bring the future to my people, it will prove that I spoke the truth about War Arrow's lies, and it will redeem me in my father's eyes. I have seen it in my vision quest."

"Isn't that only for warriors?" Hunter momentarily looked confounded. Dancing Wind had always been wild, so nothing she did should have surprised him; but he never would have suspected she'd go to such lengths.

"It does not make sense that the Sun Dance should be for men only," Dancing Wind said sharply. "I needed its power to help me solve my problem with my brother. And as you can see, it has shown me the way to you, Yellow Fire."

Hunter could hardly believe his ears. He had thought he loved Dancing Wind, but before him stood a stranger who had not only defied scared tribal customs, she had murdered as well. Before words of disbelief could leave his lips, Jannet broke in on them.

"Why, Dancing Wind," she snapped derisively, feeling more confident with Hunter present, "don't tell me that you, too, are a murderer? And, Hunter dear, I do believe you find yourself with two wives." She laughed viciously. "Whatever are you going to do now?"

"I do not murder!" Dancing Wind shrilled at her. "I only kill those who do not deserve to draw breath." In the blink of an eye she raised the bow, took careful aim, and shot Jannet in the chest.

Martha screamed and rushed to Jannet's side. She supported Jannet's head as blood tricked out of the side of her mouth. Hatred and shock filled Jannet's eyes. "I . . . I sh-should've killed you y-years ago," she gasped and then went limp.

Dancing Wind did not wait for further discussion, she advanced on Jannet and yanked the bloody arrow out of her breast. "Look, Yellow Fire," she beseeched Hunter, "it is the same arrowhead that was my gift to you. It has kept you safe from harm all these moons. It has freed you from the threat of the crazed one." She motioned to Jannet's lifeless body. "Now it will free you from the white woman who would take you from me, it will reunite you with your daughter, and we shall be as one again."

Martha remained on the ground, certain she would be next to die. She gingerly touched the raw welt on her neck, made when Dancing Wind had grabbed the arrowhead from her. Hunter had said it would bring her luck while she wore it. Had her luck just run out? She doubted that he would risk his life to save hers. He had deceived her, used her; and now he had the one real love of his life back at his side. She stared at him. Clad as the Indian woman and girl were in fringed animal skins, Hunter looked as savage and dangerous as his wife and daughter. His features were just as set and determined and deadly.

Hunter put himself between Dancing Wind and Martha, while Daughter of the Wind watched with keen eyes.

"Why did you wait all these years?" Hunter asked, needing answers to the questions which plagued him.

"I, too, was told of the death of my beloved. War Arrow led me to believe you had died. It was not until the trapper, Hayes, came to our camp last year that I learned of the truth."

"Rushes Hayes?" A spark of irony lit Hunter's mind. Those undefinable questions circling in his thoughts when he'd first seen the girl suddenly rose up in ugly, precise definition, and the conversation he'd had not long ago with Abe Baker came back to him.

Perspiration beaded Dancing Wind's upper lip as Hunter studied Daughter of the Wind. "You must remember the man. He was your friend," she offered nervously.

"Yes, I'm afraid I do remember him—all too clearly. Before we talk, have your daughter guide Martha back to the train."

"No! The white woman must die." Dancing Wind lunged at Martha, but Hunter grabbed the arrow out of her hand and dashed it to the ground near where the girl stood. Martha backed away until she came up against a boulder, afraid to flee, afraid not to.

"What happened to Rushes Hayes?" Hunter's hazel eyes narrowed.

"I sent him to meet his ancestors," the girl answered, "for trying to claim my mother."

Hunter turned on Dancing Wind. "You put a child up to killing her own father?" The words poured from his lips before he realized the girl should not have heard what he had to say.

"You are her father!" Dancing Wind shrieked.

"Am I? Look at her." He roughly grabbed Dancing Wind's face and turned her toward the girl. "She bears his mark—the same birthmark he had on his right cheek. The mark old Abe Baker called a fruit mark." Hunter was hardly able to control his rage. "You told me you were going to have my child, when all along you were carrying Rushes Hayes's child, weren't you?" Hunter shook Dancing Wind with such force that Martha feared he was about to kill her with his bare hands.

"Yes! Yes! Is that what you must hear? It does not matter. It was you I wanted. I have always wanted you. War Arrow came between us. He told my father what I had done so the old man would let him send you away. But nothing stands between us now save the white woman. Do you not see? We can be together."

"This man is not my father?" Daughter of the Wind asked, her hands clenching. "You"—she turned cold eyes on Dancing Wind and put her hand to the birthmark on her cheek—"tricked me into killing my own father? You are the mad dog, not the white woman. You!" The girl gave a cry like the sound of an attacking wolf. Then she grabbed the arrow and embedded it in Dancing Wind's throat.

Dancing Wind fell to her knees, grasping at Hunter's pantleg. "Yellow Fire is all I ever cared about," she rasped. She shot her daughter a look of contempt just before she collapsed, red blood flowing freely from her jugular vein to mix with the brown earth.

With one swift motion, the girl removed the arrow and severed the head from the shaft. The bloody buffalo bone still in her hand, she stood straight, facing Hunter. "Take your woman and leave me to bury my mother. At last her tortured spirit may find rest."

"Will you be all right?" Martha asked hesitantly as she shakily came to stand over the dead woman. Shock and disbelief still overwhelmed her, but she fought to keep control over herself.

"I am Sioux. My path already has been written." The girl bent over and pulled the ring from Dancing Wind's finger. "This belongs to you." She thrust it into Martha's hand.

"I will go and explain to your people," Hunter offered.

"No! I want no more to do with the white man. Now go before more blood is spilled."

"Spoken more like a warrior than a maiden." Hunter nodded to the rigid Indian girl. He took Martha by the elbow and led her toward Humphrey. "Get up on the camel's back."

"But shouldn't we at least bury Jannet?" Martha asked in a vain attempt to resolve the emotions bombarding her.

"Just do what I say." His tone left no room for discussion.

swallowed the urge to reach out to him, and then straightened. In an unwavering voice that hid her intense suffering, she announced, "Mr. Brody, I'd like to join that train going to Oregon. Would you be kind enough to make the necessary arrangements?"

The chattering around the fire suddenly ceased, and as Hunter's expression grew darker than the night sky, a foreboding tension filled the camp. All eyes turned expectantly toward the big man to observe his reaction to his wife's declaration that she intended to leave him.

Cecilia tucked her arm through Derek's and smugly waited for Hunter's temper to erupt. She had been reared to believe marriage was for life. Of course, not everyone could be so fortunate as Derek to be blessed with such a devoted wife, she thought.

Winnie tensed and leaned forward, expecting to witness a real humdinger of a fight, but her heart ached for Hunter and Martha. Even if they were too stubborn to admit it, she knew they loved each other. It was a shame they couldn't recognize their own stupidity. But she had already had her say, and since she'd had her ears burned red by Hunter Brody's ill temper of late, she sagely decided to spare the children such language. She promptly stood up and wrung her hands on the limp white apron hanging over her rumpled gray skirt.

"I think it's time I got you younguns off to bed," Winnie announced, and waved the children to follow her lead, waiting, as usual, for the wide-eyed Lucy to gather up her lamb. She frowned down at the others, who sat like spectators at an arena waiting for the kill. "Don't the rest of you got nothin' that needs tendin' before mornin'?"

"There's no need for you to hurry them off," Hunter said coldly. He then swiveled around on the stool to face Martha and, though his face was like hardened stone, said tepidly, "As soon as you're packed, I'll take you over to the other train and see that they take you on."

The blow which would forever seal the end of her relationship with Hunter had just been delivered with such indifference that Martha wasn't quite sure what to do. He had not made the slightest effort to discourage her as deep in her

359

inner heart she had prayed he would. She had been prepared, had secretly even hoped, for an argument so she could cover any hint of remorse by laughing in his handsome face when he gloated over how he had tricked her. Instead, he was merely going to cast her off without bothering to mention what he had done. Well, she would not bring on more misery by broaching the subject now. She would leave with her pride still intact, although unnerving questions raced through her mind.

"Mr. Brody!" Winnie almost choked on her words. She was totally unprepared for the way Hunter was calmly sitting there. "You can't take—"

In a soft-spoken voice shaded by sober determination, Martha interrupted the older woman before she could say what was on her mind. "Yes, Winnie, he can." She got to her feet and, in a brittle tone, said, "I'll be ready within the hour," then scanned the stunned faces. "I wish all of you a safe end to your journey. Now, if you'll excuse me, I must pack."

Tears of disappointment threatened to mar Martha's departure as she watched Hunter get up and calmly walk off. She quickly lifted her skirts to leave before she was no longer able to make a dignified exit.

"M-Ma-Mar-Martha," Lucy whimpered and stretched out her arms.

Martha turned, tears of pain and shock and joy at hearing her name on the little girl's lips flowing freely down her cheeks. "Lucy?" She rushed back and lifted the child, who stood by the lamb, into her arms. "You spoke," she sobbed. "You spoke!"

"Jed!" Winnie cried, "Did you hear that? Lucy talked. She talked!" Jed joined them in a flash, and they all hugged and kissed Lucy and Martha, bawling and laughing, simpering and hooting. Almost instantly Seth, Henry, Barsina, and Clara surrounded them, and the scene seemed a melee of happiness and sorrow.

How she managed to free herself without being noticed, Martha wasn't sure. But in the commotion of the reunion of a family that had been torn asunder by the pain poverty had caused, she escaped to her tent, where she could weep privately and collect herself before Hunter drove her to the other train.

Cornelius, who had been silently watching the drama, had risen before Lucy had uttered her first sounds in years. He caught up with Hunter, who had also left the campfire. "Of all the things I may have thought you, a fool was not one of them."

"I'd watch real close what I said if I were you, Potter," Hunter growled darkly, anger knitting his brows together. "Particularly if you aim to finish the trip in one piece."

Cornelius rubbed his chin as he considered the absurd way Hunter and Martha, two normally level-headed adults, were acting. "Let it not be said there were three fools on this train. How much will you take to sell the spring wagon and the horses?"

"So you can go running off after my wife?" Hunter took a menacing step toward Cornelius, who stood his ground in spite of the burgeoning tension between them.

"Perhaps I wish it were true. But, since Martha has become the primary subject of my picture book on American frontier life, it just makes sense to accompany her to the end of her journey."

"I ought to knock a chunk out of your hide."

"I would venture to say your hide should be the more likely candidate for a tanning."

Hunter disliked the idea of Cornelius accompanying Martha almost as much as he disliked the idea of her leaving. But he forced himself to ignore the photographer's last remark.

"If Martha wants to get away from me so bad as to bring it up in front of the whole company, I'm not going to try and stop her. At least if you go with her she won't be alone." As he spoke, he admitted to himself that the thought branded him to the bone.

Cornelius sighed. "Such consideration."

"Don't push me any further, Potter," Hunter warned. "I'll make you a deal on the wagon if you'll promise to write and let me know where she settles."

Cornelius looked a little bewildered. He couldn't understand why Hunter was so willing to let Martha go if he wanted to know where she would be. It was a pity pride was standing between them, unbreachable as a walled in fort. After a moment's hesitation, he nodded his acceptance of the terms.

Hunter searched through his pockets and came up with a crumpled slip of paper. He studied it for a minute, then thrust it into Cornelius's hand. "This is where I'll be." Noting the befuddled expression on the tall photographer's face, Hunter added grudgingly, "I only want to know her whereabouts so I can send the divorce papers to her."

"Of course, Brody," Cornelius said skeptically.

"Get your gear together," Hunter muttered, ignoring the comment, and strode toward his horse.

Although Cornelius had decided not to interfere further in their personal affairs, his mouth dropped open and the words tumbled out. "Martha has been through a lot with everything that has happened to her since we left Independence. She probably would stay if you would just ask her." He stuffed the paper into his coat pocket.

Hunter stopped in his tracks at Cornelius's telling remark. What did the fool think he had, in his own way, been doing? Yet Martha had made it obvious to him and everyone else that she was sorry she had married him. He couldn't force her to love him! He was not going to get down on his knees and beg her to stay, nor would he stand in her way. He'd get his camels to Nevada and start his business as he'd planned to do before he'd set eyes on Martha Rockford Collins. A moment later, without looking back at Cornelius, he wearily shook his head and continued on his way.

"Did you hear?" Derek asked Hunter excitedly, upon meeting him on the way to the corral. "Little Lucy said Martha's name. She actually spoke."

"Yeah, well, that's great . . . great." Hunter forced a weak smile. He tried to be happy for the Nelsons, but at that moment nothing could ease his burdened mind.

Cornelius was a few feet behind Hunter, and he joined them when he heard the news. "Lucy spoke?" His dark blue eyes filled with joy. "I must go congratulate the Nelsons. They certainly were fortunate to have traveled on the same train with Martha. If it had not been for her thoughtfulness in giving the child that lamb, Lucy might never have uttered another word for the rest of her life." He looked directly at Derek, although his words were for Hunter. "We must go and celebrate with the others."

Two hours later Hunter stood clenching his fists as he watched Martha climb into the wagon of the middle-aged couple who had agreed to take her on. He felt like a stick of dynamite was about ready to blast his heart out of his chest, and his left cheek twitched furiously when she got back out of the wagon and walked toward him. Had she changed her mind? He said a silent prayer, the first in years.

"This belongs to you," Martha said in a shaking voice. She pulled the simple gold band from her finger and placed it in Hunter's palm before she returned to the wagon.

After long, painfully silent minutes during which he held the ring so tightly he could have crushed it, Hunter forced his attention away from Martha's haunting silhouette and stiffly shook hands with Cornelius. Unable to remain near Martha any longer because he was losing her, he turned down the invitation of the train's captain to stay and swig a jug, then mounted his big bay and galloped off into the cold, lonely night.

Chapter Thirty-Eight

"You are getting soaked. Are you certain you will not change your mind and take the umbrella?" Cornelius called out from the back of the canoe.

Martha looked over her shoulder and forced a weak smile. Although she'd had little to smile about lately, she had to admit Cornelius was a comical sight, huddled in front of their Indian guide, who was expertly working the oar. The photographer's coat collar hugged his neck, and his wide-brimmed hat flopped over his brows as he hung on to the unruly umbrella despite the downpour and the wind. "I'm sure," she said.

The sky had been a bleak gray for a week, and a constant drizzle had fallen. Martha shivered against the cold and bundled her heaviest cloak up around her throat. She looked at the mountains thick with timber, then fastened her attention on the dark, turbulent river. The tempestuous waters brought to mind her own turbulent life since she'd left New York.

After she'd left Hunter's wagon train at Sublette's Cutoff and joined this large train heading toward Oregon, she'd forced herself to keep busy. Determined to share little of her life with the other women, she walked during the day and watched the children, who kept her occupied, or she drove the spring wagon Cornelius had purchased from Hunter to carry his equipment. At night she volunteered to do much of the cooking and to help the harried women with their chores. She fell into bed too exhausted to think. Now, in the canoe, spending hours with nothing more to do than hang on to the sides, she was tormented by memories of Hunter. She kept recalling the expression on his face when she'd told him, in front of the others, that she was going to leave him and his wagon train.

A loud crack of thunder jarred Martha back to the present just before the canoe slipped into a calm slick of water. She cradled her stomach. She had not thought it likely, when Winnie Nelson had asked her to consider the possibility, that she could be carrying Hunter's child. But the older woman's suspicions had been confirmed a few short weeks ago by a doctor traveling with the train. A sudden swirl of water splashed against their frail bark, and Martha protectively drew her cloak over the tiny life growing inside her.

"Don't you worry, I'll never let anything happen to you," she whispered softly to her unborn child.

Memories of those who'd lost their lives during the trip, and of Hunter's frown of dismissal might haunt her all the days of her life, and she might have to live without him, but at least she would have her child, Hunter's child—their child—to love and watch grow up. Martha found some small measure of solace in that thought, and although she knew her life would be less complicated without a child, she swore to guard the infant with her last breath.

A tiny grin curved her lips. Cornelius had been so terribly concerned when he'd learned she was going to become a mother, many of the women on the train had at first assumed he was the father and that they were married. Cornelius had tried to protect her by remaining silent despite the probing questions directed at him. But Martha had not let him shoulder her burden. She'd told the others she and Cornelius had been members of the same wagon train, and he was continuing on to Oregon on business. She had no intention of telling any more lies. Although she had the child's future to think about, she swore to herself she would never again live a lie. Once the truth was out, the other women shunned her, but Martha ignored them and held her head high.

After joyfully leaving the canoes behind, the train transferred to a steamboat and then a flat boat. Upon disembarking from that, Martha and Cornelius bid farewell to the others. They were held up for five days, waiting for the spring wagon to be shipped down to them, and because their tempers were frayed due to the delay, they quarreled more times than she could count over Cornelius's incessant nagging that she write and inform Hunter he was going to become a father. Hunter had not wanted her, and why Cornelius kept insisting he would want to know about the child was beyond her. Once the wagon arrived, Martha was spared further discussion of the topic, for they traveled over a miserable slippery road to the village of Salem.

When Martha had started out from New York she'd been uncertain of her exact destination, she'd had only a desire to go to Oregon—until the moment when a half-dozen giggling children ran in front of the wagon, chasing a black and white dog.

"Stop Cornelius! Stop the wagon!" she excitedly called out and sprang to her feet.

Cornelius frantically looked about, at first fearing he was going to run over one of the swarm of youngsters buzzing around them. He reined in the horses and grabbed Martha's forearm to steady her. His eyes as big as china serving bowls, he barked, "What's the matter? We did not run over anyone, did we? You are not ill, are you? Shall I go for a doctor?"

"I'm fine," Martha assured him. And for the first time since they'd left Brody's train, he saw her face light up. "I think I've just found a home. Look around you at all the children. If there isn't a teacher here already, I'm sure they'll need one. Besides, this looks like such a pretty little village—a perfect place to raise a child, don't you think?"

Without waiting for Cornelius's assessment of her decision, Martha hopped down from the seat and disappeared inside the mercantile. A half-hour later she emerged from the white plank building, a broad smile bringing life and hope to her face.

While Martha had been inside, Cornelius had surveyed the surroundings. It was a pleasant enough little place, with a handful of wooden buildings, but it would not support a man in his trade for long. He let out a remorseful sigh. He knew he'd have to continue on to San Francisco, his original destination, once he'd taken the last pictures for his book. If only Martha had fallen in love with him. If only . . .

Cornelius jumped out of the wagon as she approached and launched herself into his arms. Determined not to let him see the pain she still felt at Hunter's dismissal of her, Martha proudly raised her chin and announced, "Mr. Pendleton—he's the proprietor—and his wife loved the idea of having a teacher. They want me to start as soon as possible." She took a breath, then continued at a rapid speed. "Of course, they have to get the town's approval, but they're sure there won't be a problem since there's a dire need to get the children educated. They can't afford to pay much, but they said they could practically guarantee me a little house to live in. It won't be fancy, but it'll be a start. I won't have to spend the money I have. I can save it for my baby. And they want to build a schoolhouse. Probably in the spring."

Cornelius held Martha from him. "Slow down. You're talking so fast I can hardly keep up with you." He chuckled at her excitement and swallowed the urge to get his equipment out so he could capture the sparkle in her eyes. Then he grew serious. "I hate to throw cold water on your plans, but did you tell them about the baby?"

Her smile did not waver, and was enhanced by the gleam of honesty in her green eyes.

"I told them the truth," she announced firmly. "Mrs. Pendleton was most sympathetic, and said if I was half as good a teacher as she suspected, she didn't think the townspeople would care if I were expecting twins. Seems not everyone is too narrowminded to accept the truth. Oh, Cornelius, I know everything is going to be fine." By his expression, Martha was certain he did not detect the emptiness in her excitement.

The weather was cold enough for Cornelius to see her breath as she spoke. He stuffed his hands into his pockets to warm them. Absently he fingered the contents within while Martha finished filling him in on all the details. Finally, he removed a crumpled slip of paper and thoughtfully stared at it.

Chapter Thirty-Nine

A warm summer rain beat rythmically against the roof of the one-room cottage Martha shared with her three-month-old baby. For a moment she stood leaning against the window frame staring blankly out at the gray day and at the newly constructed schoolhouse. It was one of the few days since she'd arrived in Salem that she hadn't planned to keep herself busy. "How fitting"—she forced back a sob—"that it should be raining on what should have been my first wedding anniversary."

A whimper came from the crude cradle given her by one of her pupil's parents, tearing her thoughts away from the man who continued to haunt her. She stepped over to the crib and picked up a tiny blue bundle.

"It's all right my precious little one," she said, then cuddled the baby to her breast and settled into the rocking chair. Cornelius had bought it for her just before he'd reluctantly left for San Francisco, having promised to send her a copy of his picture book as soon as it was published.

It had been difficult to say good-bye to such a dear friend, but Martha had come to accept life's bittersweet lessons. She knew Cornelius had had a deadline to meet, and his presence had continually brought to mind heart-wrenching memories of Hunter.

She rocked back and forth until the baby stopped fussing. The journal of her trip across the continent, which she'd had bound in red leather, lay on the doily atop the table next to the rocker; a corner of a letter from Cornelius sticking out from between the pages. With the baby now sleeping soundly, Martha reached over and picked up the journal. After rereading Cornelius's letter she flipped to the last entry she had written in the book.

Saturday, November 12, 1859—Salem, Oregon. Sometimes I think I should pinch myself in order to believe I have actually reached my original goal. I have, indeed, been fortunate to secure a teaching position and a home in which to live and rear the child I carry, which is due in the spring. I am grateful for the generosity I have been shown. Yet there is a most persistent emptiness inside me, that I fear time will never fill. Nevertheless, I shall not let the misfortunes of Fate destroy my life or the happiness of my child. . . .

She set the journal aside and hugged her baby. The infant was the very image of his father. She would forever have a living memory of her love for Hunter Brody. But was that enough? Sensual dreams of the rugged wagon-train captain, intruded on her sleep each night, but they did not ward off her loneliness. She had Hunter's child. Their child. She now enjoyed a respectable position in the community, and two of the town's most eligible bachelors had begun calling on her.

She held the baby boy away from her and smiled through the threat of tears. "My little Logan," she crooned, glad she'd had a son to name after her father, "you look so much like your daddy, with those big eyes and fuzzy tufts of blond hair, you're going to be a heartbreaker someday."

The word *heartbreaker* struck her with particular force. What was wrong with her? She had always known her own mind, had always been independent and confident. Yet there was no denying that she still loved her child's father. She frowned. She had her pride; she couldn't just pick up and go running off after someone who didn't want her or love her, despite the constant urgings in her mother's letters, for she had written and told her mother the unhappy truth.

Martha placed Logan in his cradle and then paced the floor.

School would not be in session again until the fall, since the children were needed to work the land. She had too much time on her hands now. She had saved most of her wages and still had the money Hunter had given her. The money. Thinking of it brought more bittersweet memories. It wasn't until Cornelius had reminded her that it was her reward for the return of the funds stolen from the bank that she realized how utterly wrong she had been to think Hunter had tried to pay her for *services rendered*. She forced that recollection from her mind. There was no use dwelling on foolish mistakes. Maybe if she used the money for a trip to San Francisco to visit Cornelius it would help ease the burden of loneliness she was plagued with.

She went over to the jelly jar she'd salvaged from the basket of food her mother had sent along when she'd left New York. She now used it as a bank. As Martha spilled its contents onto the table near the wood stove in the corner of the room, two of the new, shiny twenty-dollar gold pieces she'd received from Barton Wakefield to help pay for her trip tumbled to the edge of the table. It was ironic that the very coins she meant to use for a joyous trip had caused such immeasurable pain and suffering. She sat down heavily.

The glint and feel of the gold pieces sparked long-forgotten memories. With a trembling hand Martha fingered the coins, remembering Barton Wakefield's words: *There are times in one's life when pride dictates that one struggle on alone, but there are those times when letting pride get in the way is self-defeating.*

Was that what she had been doing? Had she been struggling alone because she had been too proud to allow Cornelius to write to Hunter and let him know he was going to become a father? That small flicker of hope that Hunter would someday come to her resisted all attempts to extinguish it. Because of it, she had refused Cornelius's suggestions that she divorce the man so she could get on with her life, since Hunter hadn't bothered to try to locate her or to dissolve their union, or that she try to find him.

Was she fooling herself by trying to ignore her feelings for Hunter Brody even though he'd made no effort to find her and must have found it easy to forget her? After all, he was her child's father. Little Logan had a right to grow up with him. And hadn't Hunter married her? She bitterly laughed at that thought, and then grew pensive. Even if it had been meant to be a farce, there were times when he'd seemed to care for her. And hadn't she been determined enough to overcome every other obstacle put in her way on the trail?

She had managed to cope with the ostracism of the women on Hunter's wagon train, and had learned to ride a camel. She'd been cleared of the charge of theft, had faced illness and death. Yet she hadn't been deterred from realizing her dream of traveling to Oregon. Thoughts of everything she had managed to overcome renewed Martha's will to fight for the man she loved. Yes, loved, despite how easily he'd let her go. During her pregnancy she had forgotten what a fighter she was, but she could no longer ignore all feelings she harbored for Hunter Brody. It was time to do something about them. As if a candle had been relit to guide her path, Martha knew what she was going to do; she would journey to Nevada. She loved Hunter Brody and he was going to have to bodily remove her and their child if he didn't want them in his life!

Her mind set, she bundled up Logan, threw on a cloak, grabbed the umbrella Cornelius had left her, and rushed out the door.

The full moon cast a muted light across Hunter's face, illuminating the deep stress lines around his eyes. He walked back into the sparsely furnished bedroom in the tiny, hastily constructed ranch house he occupied along the Carson River not far outside Carson City. The wooden, three-room house sorely lacked a woman's touch, but met the need of a roof over his head.

He had slaved to build his business, and his camel train had proved highly successful at hauling firewood from the river into town. Now, with the silver strike in Virginia City, he was negotiating to carry salt from the Rhodes Salt Marsh to the silver reduction mills. With salt selling at one hundred twenty dollars per ton he stood to make a tidy profit on each ten-day trip.

An invitation, reeking with perfume, lay on the bed. He had to laugh. He was rapidly becoming the area's most sought-after guest, although he had displayed indifference to the women paraded before him.

He shrugged off his shirt and washed off the day's dirt. Earlier, that cantankerous Humphrey had tossed him to the ground, triggering those cursed memories of the first day after Martha had left the train at Sublettes Cutoff. They stabbed at him like Indian tomahawks. Hunter dried his face with a towel, then sank heavily onto the bed, taking a long swig from the whiskey bottle which had been sitting nearby on a stool. He wanted to drown out his recollections of the ugly scene he'd had with Winnie Nelson that morning in August nearly one year ago. . . .

The night was fading into dawn when Hunter, unable to sleep, strode over to a nearby knoll to watch the train Martha had joined pull out. Twisted knots tightened around his heart and threatened to cut off his breath as each wagon fell in behind the next. He felt a vital part of him was dying and there was nothing he could do about it.

So engrossed Hunter was in this final chapter of his life with Martha, he did not hear Winnie approach from behind. "I wondered whether that conscience of yours would let you sleep after what you done."

Hunter swung around to scowl furiously at the rumpled, gray-haired woman standing with feet apart and fists on hips, her eyes glaring at him.

"You can direct your wrath toward someone else. It was what she wanted," he answered knowingly. Then, maybe out of guilt or the need for absolution, he added, "You heard her say so in front of the entire company. Chrissake, what was I supposed to do, hog-tie her and keep her a prisoner for the rest of the trip?"

Winnie's frown deepened. "You might of done the proper thing and married her."

"What the hell do you think I did back on the trail? In front of all of you, I might add."

Winnie's voice rumbled like the thunder of a disapproving god. "Before Martha left she told me all about that phony preacher."

"Oh, so she did, did she? And just where did she learn about his so-called phony preacher?" Hunter's hazel eyes became mere slivers of ice.

"She overheard you and Abe talkin'." Winnie raised her chin, defying Hunter to deny it.

Hunter grew strangely pensive for one who'd been known to express himself colorfully. "So that's what caused my *loving* wife to change so drastically?" he muttered. "Just for your information, the trick was on me. Abe was supposed to play the preacher, but instead the old reprobate sent a real preacher." He rubbed the stubble on his chin for a long moment.

Winnie's eyes grew as large as boulders. "If that's true, what you standin' here for?"

"If she didn't think enough about us and our future together to bother to come right out and face me with it instead of turning tail and running after telling you, she can just go to Oregon with that photographer," he spat out, leaving Winnie befuddled.

"Well, landsakes." She shook her head and called out after his retreating back. "For someone smart enough to stay alive out here for so long, you got to be one of the dumbest, most stubborn creatures God ever set to walkin' the face of the earth."

Hunter tensed, and his fists balled at his sides. As angry as the Nelson woman could make him, he couldn't help but admit there was truth to what she said. But no matter. It was already settled. He did not respond to Winnie. He'd had enough of this group of ignorant greenhorns. The sooner he reached his destination and unloaded them, the better!

For the rest of the trip, they were going to have to keep up with the pace he set or find themselves stranded in the desert to wait for the next train or to have their bones bleached by the hot sun.

True to his word, Hunter's train made record time, reaching his ranch the first week in October. There, he made arrangements for the thoroughly exhausted members of the company to

373

travel on to California with another outfit.

After they left he set out with driving vengeance to save hi
ranch, make his camel train a success, and to forget the woman
who continued to have a hold on his heart.

Now he set the invitation aside and laid his head down on the
pillow and closed his eyes. But he could still picture Martha
smiling, laughing, her arms open to him, ready to enfold him in
her loving embrace.

"Damn!" He bolted into an upright position and, with the
back of his hand, wiped the sweat from his brow. Was she going
to haunt him for the rest of his days? God knows, he'd tried to
forget her. But every time he'd escorted one of the respectable
women to some social event, he'd seen Martha in the woman's
eyes. Even making use of the whores in Virginia City had
turned into a fiasco, for he had been unable to get Martha's
touch out of his mind.

He leaned over and lit the lamp on the table near his bed.
Propped up against the base of the lamp sat an unopened letter
addressed in Cornelius Potter's handwriting. For the longest
time Hunter stared at the missive, the Oregon return address
boldly challenging him to open it.

Unsure of whether he did it out of fear that Martha had
chosen Cornelius or someone else, Hunter let the letter remain
where it lay, and leaned back against his pillow and crossed his
arms behind his head. But sleep eluded him.

Without knowing when it had happened, he suddenly
realized that Martha had destroyed all the protective barriers
he'd erected years ago. She'd done it with her strength of
character, and her kindness and quiet determination. Another
thought hit Hunter like a club: He had been fooling himself.
Martha was his wife and he no longer wanted to live without
her.

He jumped out of bed, rushed to the window, threw it open,
and hollered toward the barn, "Happy! Happy! Get over here—
now!"

The rain had let up by the time Martha returned to her
cottage after explaining to the Pendletons that since her

teaching services were not needed until fall, she and Logan were going to visit a relative living in Nevada. The kindly couple had been concerned about her traveling such a long distance with a baby, but they had wished her a safe and speedy return.

She dragged a tattered bag from under the bed and was about to pack when piercing screams whistled through the air and mingled with the thudding of hooves as horses wildly careened down the muddy streets.

Unaware of what was causing all the commotion, and fearing for her baby's life, Martha grabbed Logan and rushed outside to see the strangest, most wonderful sight heading directly toward her. Tears of immeasurable joy escaped her as she stood on the tiny, covered porch hugging Logan to her chest.

The town's residents were scurrying for cover as Hunter rode a camel past them down the center of the street, holding the lead rope for another following behind. Atop the single-humped creature Hunter looked larger than life in a drenched buckskin jacket and denim pants, blond hair peeking out around the edges of his wide-brimmed hat.

He rode directly up before Martha and stopped. Long, endless moments stretched between them until Logan broke the silence with a healthy wail. Hunter's gaze shot to the tiny bundle in Martha's arms, and a million questions scurried across his face.

Unable to endure the suspense any longer, he asked, "Whose child is it?"

Martha's face changed from pink to livid red; then an amused flush settled over her features. "And just whose child do you think he might be?" she said much too calmly, which should have warned Hunter. But he suddenly felt the happy reunion he had been anticipating since he'd left the ranch was about to be spoiled.

He stared at the little tyke. He should have opened Potter's letter. Perhaps, still thinking they weren't really married, Martha had married someone else. Could it have been that damned photographer?

"If I knew, I wouldn't have asked," he answered shortly, his temper and his fear that he might have lost her threatening to get the better of him. "Did you marry the man?" Hunter asked darkly.

Martha glared at him. he didn't even realize Logan was his own child. Well, she was not going to make it easy for him after what he'd put her through! "Would it matter to you?"

"Of course it would matter."

"I thought the father of my child didn't want me."

Hunter's face grew murderous at the thought that some sonofabitch had taken advantage of a sweet, innocent young woman like Martha. His heart ached, and he determined to see that she was taken care of before he returned to his ranch. Why he'd kill the bastard if the man refused to do right by her! "Where is he? I'll fetch the rotten so-and-so back here and see to it that he owns up to his responsibility."

You're a fine one to talk about responsibility, she thought, thinking his was a typical male reaction which ignored his own part in the situation.

But the more Martha considered what he'd said, the more difficult she found it to maintain a sober expression. Hunter's presence in Salem had caused her doubts about his love to desert her. Winnie Nelson had been right all along, as had Cornelius. Hunter's determination to force the baby's father to marry her only proved that he did love her. Would he want her when he found out Logan was his child, and she hadn't told him?

"Would you really force the baby's father to make an honest woman out of me?"

"If I had to blow the sonofabitch's head off."

"What if he insists he doesn't want me?"

"He'd have to be a complete fool not to want you."

"But what if I didn't want him?" she prodded.

"A child needs a name."

"My baby already has a name," she said stoutly. *No one* was going to imply that her child was a bastard. "He's called Logan, after my father."

"Oh?" Hunter's left brow shot up, and his cheek twitched furiously. "And, exactly who is Logan's father?"

"Hunter Brody," Martha said, straight-faced.

"We'll just see how long the sonofabitch gets away—"

Hunter broke off as realization hit him hard. He slid from the camel and stood mute in front of Martha, gaping at the tiny blue bundle.

"Aren't you going to force the baby's father to marry me?" Martha quietly asked, a hesitant grin tugging at the corners of her lips.

"My sweet Mat, we're already married," he said hoarsely, mesmerized by his own flesh and blood.

"I know," she said quietly.

"You do?"

"Yes. I received a letter from Cornelius in San Francisco. It seems he ran into a very exhausted Winnie Nelson and she told him what happened."

"Then why didn't you tell me I'm a father?" he asked, not sure whether to be angry with her for keeping it from him or to be the happiest man in the world.

"I was afraid you wouldn't want us."

"Wouldn't want you?" Hunter choked back a display of emotion. "You're the only woman I'll ever love," he forced himself to admit. "That is my child and you're my wife."

"How did you know where to find me?"

"Potter sent me a letter."

"Then you knew all along about Logan?"

"I didn't open it. I was afraid you might have divorced me and remarried," he said openly.

"Never." Her eyes filled with tears.

"At least I don't have to shoot the sonofabitch who got you with child." He smiled and wiped a salty tear from her cheek.

"I wouldn't want you to do that." Her fingers closed over his hand, feeling the warmth of his love.

Then a movement caught her eye, and she noticed a crowd had begun to gather around the two camels. "Why don't we go inside?"

He kissed her open palm. "First I have something to return to you."

"You do?"

"Yes." He took the simple gold ring out of his pocket. "The symbol of our love. I gave you this on our wedding day, so I reckon our first anniversary is a good day to try again." While tears of joy edged off Martha's lashes, Hunter slipped the band on her finger.

"It's a wonderful day." She sniffled, seeing him through a blurry mist of happiness.

"Martha, about Dancing Wind. I want to explain—"

She looked into clear, open hazel eyes. There would be no more secrets. Not in those eyes.

"Only if you're certain you really want to."

Martha listened quietly as he described meeting the beautiful young Indian girl while he was out trapping, and how they'd fallen in love. He told of his difficulties with her family, which had led to his being told she and his unborn child had died of cholera while he'd been away selling furs. He depicted the lonely years that followed, and let her know how they had hardened him until she'd come along. He even related how he'd felt when he'd discovered the truth about Dancing Wind and the child, and when he'd seen how she'd changed.

Martha reached out. "Thank you for sharing what I'm sure was a very painful time in your life." She smiled. "But now what is important is the future. Our future. Not the past. Please, come inside," she begged, knowing her blush of emotion was visible to the onlookers.

"If you let me hold my son . . ."

Early that evening, the Pendletons delivered a package to Martha on their way home. Though somewhat befuddled by the turn of events, they were introduced to Hunter and drank a toast with the couple before they left. As soon as they had gone, Martha tore the brown wrapper from the package to find a gold-lettered book. She opened it and saw a photograph of herself atop Humphrey. It was the most delightful picture book she'd ever seen, and it was Cornelius Potter's.

For hours, Martha and Hunter pored through the photographs, reminiscing, and laughing and sharing memories of the trip that had brought them together.

And, after Logan had been put to bed, Hunter and Martha lay on the buffalo robe in front of the crackling fireplace, entwined in each other's arms. Their naked bodies glistened from their lovemaking, and they reveled in the feel, fragrance, and taste of each other while the flames faded to a muted glow.

Finally, Martha kissed Hunter, then rose to stoke the fire into blazing warmth, like the love they had for each and their son—a love which would carry them through a lifetime. When she returned to his side, he took her in his arms and made love to her again, as if it were the first time. With tender loving care, he knelt between her open thighs and lowered himself deep inside her, in a union of their bodies and souls.

Long after they were spent, they remained joined, planning the wonderful future they would have together and deciding that the next day they would set off for their home. At long last they had shared all their secrets—except one. Martha's eyes trailed to the journal which lay on the table nearby. A cryptic smile hovered about her lips. Someday she would let him read her treasured book.

HEART-THROBBING ROMANCES BY
KAY MCMAHON AND ROCHELLE WAYNE
FROM ZEBRA BOOKS!

DEFIANT SPITFIRE   (2326, $3.95)
by Kay McMahon
The notorious privateer Dane Remington demanded Brittany Lockwood's virtue as payment for rescuing her brother. But once he tasted her honey-sweet lips, he knew he wanted her passionate and willing rather than angry and vengeful. . . . Only then would he free her from his bed!

THE PIRATE'S LADY   (2114, $3.95)
by Kay McMahon
Shipwrecked on Chad LaShelle's outlaw island, lovely Jennifer Gray knew what her fate would be at the hands of the arrogant pirate. She fled through the jungle forest, terrified of the outlaw's embrace—and even more terrified of her own primitive response to his touch!

FRONTIER FLAME   (1965-3, $3.95)
by Rochelle Wayne
Suzanne Donovan was searching for her brother, but once she confronted towering Major Blade Landon, she wished she'd never left her lavish Mississippi home. The lean, muscled officer made her think only of the rapture his touch could bring, igniting the fires of unquenchable passion!

SAVAGE CARESS   (2137, $3.95)
by Rochelle Wayne
Beautiful Alisha Stevens had thanked the powerful Indian warrior Black Wolf for rescuing her as only a woman can. Now she was furious to discover his deceit. He would return her to her people only when he was ready—until then she was at his beck and call, forced to submit to his SAVAGE CARESS.

UNTAMED HEART   (2306-5, $3.95)
by Rochelle Wayne
Fort Laramie's handsome scout David Hunter seemed determined to keep auburn-haired Julianne Ross from doing her job as a reporter. And when he trapped her in his powerful embrace, the curvaceous young journalist found herself at a loss for the words to tell him to stop the delicious torment of his touch!

Available wherever paperbacks are sold, or order direct from the Publisher. Send cover price plus 50¢ per copy for mailing and handling to Zebra Books, Dept. 2640, 475 Park Avenue South, New York, N.Y. 10016. Residents of New York, New Jersey and Pennsylvania must include sales tax. DO NOT SEND CASH.

SURRENDER YOUR HEART
TO CONSTANCE O'BANYON!

MOONTIDE EMBRACE (2182, $3.95)
When Liberty Boudreaux's sister framed Judah Slaughter for murder, the notorious privateer swore revenge. But when he abducted the unsuspecting Liberty from a New Orleans masquerade ball, the brazen pirate had no idea he'd kidnapped the wrong Boudreaux—unaware who it really was writhing beneath him, first in protest, then in ecstasy.

GOLDEN PARADISE (2007, $3.95)
Beautiful Valentina Barrett knew she could never trust wealthy Marquis Vincente as a husband. But in the guise of "Jordanna", a veiled dancer at San Francisco's notorious Crystal Palace, Valentina couldn't resist making the handsome Marquis her lover!

SAVAGE SUMMER (1922, $3.95)
When Morgan Prescott saw Sky Dancer standing out on a balcony, his first thought was to climb up and carry the sultry vixen to his bed. But even as her violet eyes flashed defiance, repulsing his every advance, Morgan knew that nothing would stop him from branding the high-spirited beauty as his own!

SEPTEMBER MOON (1838;, $3.95)
Petite Cameron Madrid would never consent to allow arrogant Hunter Kingston to share her ranch's water supply. But the handsome landowner had decided to get his way through Cameron's weakness for romance—winning her with searing kisses and slow caresses, until she willingly gave in to anything Hunter wanted.

SAVAGE SPRING (1715, $3.95)
Being pursued for a murder she did not commit, Alexandria disguised herself as a boy, convincing handsome Taggert James to help her escape to Philadelphia. But even with danger dogging their every step, the young woman could not ignore the raging desire that her virile Indian protector ignited in her blood!

Available wherever paperbacks are sold, or order direct from the Publisher. Send cover price plus 50¢ per copy for mailing and handling to Zebra Books, Dept. 2640, 475 Park Avenue South, New York, N.Y. 10016. Residents of New York, New Jersey and Pennsylvania must include sales tax. DO NOT SEND CASH.

TURN TO CATHERINE CREEL—THE REAL THING—FOR THE FINEST IN HEART-SOARING ROMANCE!

CAPTIVE FLAME   (2401, $3.95)
Meghan Kearney was grateful to American Devlin Montague for rescuing her from the gang of Bahamian cutthroats. But soon the handsome yet arrogant island planter insisted she serve his baser needs—and Meghan wondered if she'd merely traded one kind of imprisonment for another!

TEXAS SPITFIRE   (2225, $3.95)
If fiery Dallas Brown failed to marry overbearing Ross Kincaid, she would lose her family inheritance. But though Dallas saw Kincaid as a low-down, shifty opportunist, the strong-willed beauty could not deny that he made her pulse race with an inexplicable flaming desire!

SCOUNDREL'S BRIDE   (2062, $3.95)
Though filled with disgust for the seamen overrunning her island home, innocent Hillary Reynolds was overwhelmed by the tanned, masculine physique of dashing Ryan Gallagher. Until, in a moment of wild abandon, she offered herself like a purring tiger to his passionate, insistent caress!

Available wherever paperbacks are sold, or order direct from the Publisher. Send cover price plus 50¢ per copy for mailing and handling to Zebra Books, Dept. 2640, 475 Park Avenue South, New York, N.Y. 10016. Residents of New York, New Jersey and Pennsylvania must include sales tax. DO NOT SEND CASH.